MURDER ON A GOD'S GRAVE

DANIEL JAMES MOORE

Murder On A God's Grave

Edited by Dylan Garity and Claire Ashgrove

Cover art by MiblArt

Published by OtherWorldly, LLC

ISBN 979-8-9867398-1-6

This book is for those that believed in me

PROLOGUE
THE WAR

A furious maelstrom of heated vapor erupted from the geyser; warm water condensed and trickled from the treetops, seeping into the soil beneath. The setting sun cast a reddish glow across the forested mountainside, refracting through the mist and illuminating the waiting soldiers within. A pair of worn leather boots crunched the still-dry pine needles as a young captain shifted his crouch near a rotting log. The heavy metal of his breastplate scraped lightly against his pauldrons, the friction wearing away the polish where the two met. Steam flooded the sloped forest, just as it always did during a geyser eruption. The captain breathed in the momentary peace and steadied his mind for the slaughter to come.

"Captain! This is it! After four hundred and ninety days, three thousand seven hundred and twenty-one dead citizens, we can finally end this war right here, right now!" Commander Legast shouted, his voice eager. He looked to the sky, droplets pattering across his deep black skin. A few moments went by, yet the twenty-two-year-old captain still crouched behind the log. "Captain? Roykur! We only have a few precious minutes before the geyser fall ends. If we let this opportunity slip by, it could be months before the monsters let their guard down. Get your men out there now!"

Roykur's eyes shot open, and he rose from his meditation, towering above his commander. The young captain was a brute of a man, several heads taller than any normal man and twice the bulk. He pushed his cheek-length blond hair from his lightly tanned face, showing a look of calm resolve, but a raging fire shone in his bright blue eyes. Roykur tightened his gauntleted grip on the polished wooden handle of his large, single-headed axe. The blade of the axe jutted out from the handle in a wavy crescent shape, with the bottom edge descending nearly halfway down the handle. It rang softly with the sound of the warm, falling mineral water.

"Don't worry, Legs. We shall get this bloody work started," Roykur said, cracking a smile. Then he raised his axe high above his head in a silent signal, and his company of soldiers emerged from their cover within the dense cluster of pine trees.

Commander Legast, only two years older than his captain, rolled his brown eyes at the display. "It's like you practice being over-dramatic."

"Get some more kills under your belt, then you can critique my style. Keep up this time and you might get a few." With that, Roykur and his men started a steady trot toward the enemy position. The downward slope of the mountainside propelled them forward, and before long, they were in a full sprint. Commander Legast signaled the last company of soldiers to their positions, then followed Roykur.

The wall of steam flooded past Roykur from behind, making it hard for him to see more than just a few feet. In a moment, he picked out hundreds of shapes materializing through the fog and trees. Bellowing a cry of built-up anticipation and excitement, he slammed his plated shoulder into the first figure, smashing it into the closest tree. The naked man crumpled to the ground, gasping for air. Roykur did not pause for the mind-flayed, once-Human creature that lay there, ribs certainly broken. The Kolkrabba's Husks were nothing more than meat puppets—minds stolen, humanity lost.

The axe he carried finally tasted flesh as he spun, holding the edge of the handle, swinging with maximized momentum to cleave a Husk at the neck. The force of his blow pushed the axe through collarbone and ribs, straight to the hip in a single blow. Blood splashed across his face, but Roykur paid it no mind, the warm falling water quickly washing his face clean. The blade was embedded deep in the Husk's pelvis, and the captain had to wrench hard to dislodge it.

The loud snap of a branch alerted Roykur, and he pivoted deftly to the side as a female Husk flailed two wild swords at him. He glanced at her eyes, and in that second, he thought they were rather pretty despite their empty lack of focus. They twitched back and forth in constant motion, never settling on one thing. The loud clang of metal on metal sounded as Roykur parried the swords, which swung at him with impassionate savagery.

A man screamed nearby but was promptly silenced—a Husk had bested one of his own. This distracted Roykur for only a moment. He spun the hook of his axe, catching the two blades together, locking them in place so neither he nor his opponent could move their weapons. Focused on maintaining the friction on the blades, he let go of his handle with one hand and reached out to grab one of the sword handles. The Husk reacted inhumanly fast for such a clumsy creature, biting his gauntleted hand. A few pieces of chipped teeth plinked quietly against the blades before falling to the ground. Shocked, Roykur froze, trying to figure out what exactly was going on, why he had been stupid enough to let this happen.

"Titless draugker!" Roykur cursed. He took a second to look over the Husk, as if he needed to remind himself that he was twice the size of this creature. Instead of pulling his hand free, he gripped the thing's lower jaw and jerked down and outward, tearing the muscle and sinew from the rest of the head. Blood sprayed, and the tongue wiggled like a fish pulled fresh from the water. The Husk's pretty eyes showed neither pleading nor pain, no emotion at all, and she continued to struggle for a few moments longer before the blood loss drained her of strength. Her arms lowered, and she took a few steps, choking on blood, then fell slowly to the ground. Roykur stared at the corpse, panting, not just from the exertion, but also from sheer primal thrill. He had killed hundreds of Husks during this war, and it always felt this way. *Should I feel guilty? They aren't Human, not anymore. Right?*

A dagger whipped through the air, slicing into his thoughts, and Roykur turned to see another Husk fall to the ground a single pace away, the blade planted in its chest.

"You okay? What the fuck are you doing just standing there? You must be injured if I'm having to save your ass," Legast said, pulling the dagger out.

"Lost my focus for a moment there. Thanks for the backup."

"Don't worry, I'll hold this over your head forever. Oh, and that's one for me." The commander gave him a fierce grin.

Remembering the battle, Roykur turned from the fresh kills, and they both jogged through the forest to the edge of the tree line, heading toward the sounds of fighting and the trail of Husk corpses. In a small clearing just ahead, Roykur's company of soldiers had gathered, with no further signs of Husks in the area. They were good. He had trained them, but they had been killing Husks for a long while now, and nothing was a better teacher than experience.

In the clearing, the steam had finally dissipated a bit, and he saw them. The Kolkrabba.

It always made Roykur pause for just a moment, every time they located a group, and this was no exception. The Kolkrabba were massive, slimy creatures with long, thick tentacles. Their outsized, egg-shaped heads faced up toward the falling water, transfixed by it. A series of four eyes ran along the length of each side of their oblong heads. The semi-translucent blobs narrowed at the front, forming a mass of small tentacles that could only be a mouth. Each flailed in excitement at the falling water.

Their bodies were made of eight thick tentacles as well, each connected to its neighbor through thin webbing, ultimately giving the Kolkrabba a height of approximately fifteen feet. Each tentacle that supported the hulking mass of the creature divided near the ground into eight smaller ones, though still larger than those around the mouth.

Despite their horrifying visage, they were far more terrifying in battle. The Kolkrabba moved quickly for their size, possessed incredible strength, and were intelligent enough to wield various weaponry. Usually, they used whatever they could steal from Human villages, which tended to be wood axes, pitchforks, and the like. You had to throw entire companies of men at them until they sustained enough damage—or you caught them just after a geyser burst. The latter was preferable.

The seven Kolkrabba were slowly changing color, from dark green to light orange, as they soaked in the warm water. The soldiers had not discovered this strange ritual until a year and a half into the campaign against the Kolkrabba. The reason for it remained a mystery. Regardless, it had given the Humans hope they could win this fight and drive the Kolkrabba away, or preferably wipe them out entirely.

Roykur and Legast caught up with the other men, and the captain spoke in a hushed tone. "Spread out. I want to hit them all at once. We're running short on time."

He still wasn't sure if noise could interrupt their trance, but better not to find out. The forty soldiers followed his instructions, spacing out to match the spread of the Kolkrabba, and then, as quietly as they could, they charged the last bit of distance to the undulating mass of deadly tentacles.

Despite their bulk and ferocity, the Kolkrabba were easy to slice through. Roykur's axe cleaved one of the supporting tentacle trunks with a clean stroke, causing the creature to stumble and begin oozing black goo. The Kolkrabba didn't make any noises at being dismembered, emitting only a steady, low hum. Legast swung a quick short sword at another limb, and Roykur at another, until the creature could no longer support itself and toppled to the ground.

Still in a deep trance, it didn't even put up a defense. Roykur held his axe high and chopped downward, slicing deep into the front of the Kolkrabba's head. Stepping around the severed twitching limbs, he dragged the axe through the massive scalp, making a full circle. When he arrived back at the front, half of the creature's head slid off with a gelatinous plop.

Looking around, Roykur could see his company taking only a bit longer to finish off the other Kolkrabba. Not a minute later, the water ceased to fall.

"Nice work, soldiers. Looks like we managed to pull this off!" Roykur shouted as they drifted over. "Alright, time to take a look around. Sergeant Dunvick, take a squad to collect our dead. Sergeants Twilt and Zaven, you have the list—start harvesting what those damn Witches wanted. The rest of you begin a sweep of the area. We have to report any . . ."

Roykur trailed off as he noticed something out of the corner of his eye. He whipped around in time to see a Kolkrabba propel itself from the tree line into the clearing, moving with monstrous speed, heading straight for a group of soldiers farthest from Roykur's position.

"Look out!" the captain screamed, but before anyone could react to his warning, the Kolkrabba fell upon the men. The pure chaos boiled down to a series of sounds—the crunch of metal compacting in on itself, the cracking of bones, the squelch and pop of blood and organs breaking free from their flesh casing. And screams of terror.

Roykur ran forward, axe gripped tightly in both hands. He couldn't believe they'd missed one. He wasn't sure what he'd be able to do, but he had to try something.

"Bows out! Fire as soon as you have a shot," Legast called to the fifteen men on the far side of the fight, then took off running to catch up to Roykur. "Don't get close to that thing. Are you absolutely brain dead?"

The flailing mass of fury and tentacles obliterated three more soldiers. Arrows loosed, flying past Roykur and Legast, but only a few hit their mark. The Kolkrabba moved too erratically, dipping and diving from one soldier to the next.

"Fine!" Roykur cried out, his voice spiking as his fury reached a pitch. "Go back to the motherless hole you crawled out of!"

He skidded to a halt, using his momentum to pitch his axe in a powerful overhead throw toward the Kolkrabba. Despite the creature's constant movement, the blade clipped the mouth tentacles in half, causing it to stagger in a silent wail of pain. The Kolkrabba did not have vocal cords as far as Roykur knew.

This one recovered quickly and turned to him—he had gotten its attention.

The Kolkrabba dive-rolled to the side, avoiding another volley of arrows, then lunged toward Roykur. The captain started juking to the side to avoid the beast, but it was too fast. It closed the gap, and he braced himself. "Oh shit, shit, shit—"

A thick, slimy stalk swept him off his feet, practically knocking the air from his lungs. It wrapped around his body, pinning his arms to his sides. The smaller, fingerlike tentacles squeezed, attempting to press into his eyes and mouth.

Just as suddenly as it had grabbed him, three arrows pierced the creature's back, and Legast, who had not foolishly thrown his weapon, sliced away the tentacle that held Roykur. The Kolkrabba reeled, flailing, and tossed the captain aside like a hot coal. Fortunately, he landed near where he had thrown his axe, in a sloped patch of dirt. The impact left him dazed, his vision blurred for a moment, and he felt under his breastplate, where he was sure there were some fractures if not outright breaks. Somewhere between his close encounter and landing, something had ripped his pauldrons free.

Looking toward his feet, Roykur saw his blade lying a few paces away, buried in the torn-up land. Legast rushed to his side, out of breath. "Get up—it's sufficiently wounded now, it will bleed itself out soon enough. Let's go finish this."

Roykur struggled to get to his feet again, wincing from the pain.

Before he could stand fully, the soft dirt eroded as if being poured into a small funnel. Roykur and Legast leaped forward as the unstable ground collapsed beneath them. The commander caught the edge of the opening, but Roykur caught only Legast, and the rapid flow of soil dragged them down.

The hole was not deep, maybe ten feet. Roykur and Legast rolled down the sloped, earthen wall. Spitting dirt from his mouth, Roykur sat up and glanced about him. The cavern was expansive and dark, but the opening from their entry provided just enough light for him to see ten paces to the wall on the other side. He tried to climb the slope he had come from, only to pull greater amounts of dirt on top of them both.

"Hey, could you not dump the entire mountain on me, please?" Legast asked, shaking his head. "I just got the last pile off."

But from the falling dirt emerged his axe, tumbling to the cavern floor with a clatter of metal on stone. Grabbing the weapon, Roykur used it to stand uncertainly. To his left, the cavern sloped downward, and he could swear he saw a faint light coming from somewhere below. In the other direction it moved up, possibly toward the surface, but an instinctual curiosity washed over him. He had to see what was down there. Grimacing, Roykur forced himself to stride forward, holding his side.

"Where in the world are you going? We want to go up and out, not down and extremely lost," said Legast.

Roykur ignored him and continued forward.

"Here, at least drink this," said the commander, and reached into a pouch attached to his belt to remove a small vial. Roykur took it and pulled out the cork, downing the elixir in one gulp. It tasted like old onions and vinegar. Now he had another reason for the sour look on his face. Any effect would take more than a few minutes, but he knew his injuries would soon go numb, and he would gain an alertness. Roykur strode forward, wincing occasionally at the pain. As he descended into the cavern, his pace normalized, and he ceased holding his side, eventually carrying his axe instead of using it for support.

The descent continued for several minutes, and Roykur started to reconsider his decision. He glanced at Legast, who had a worried look on his face. The commander was usually a jovial man, even in the worst of circumstances, but now he was quiet.

The path turned sharply into an archway, and beyond lay the source of the dim blue light. Roykur signaled Legast to one side and pressed himself to the opposite wall. From behind the archway, they both peeked carefully around. Roykur froze, mouth slightly agape, as he saw what lay there.

Through the arch was a large, perfectly cylindrical chamber that rose at least thirty feet high, though the darkness concealed the ceiling from his view. The ground depressed gradually toward the center of the chamber, focusing the area on the opening of a small pool, raised slightly above the ground. The pool itself was the source of the blue light. It emitted a faint glow, illuminating only the lower portion of the chamber. There were eight tall, irregularly shaped stone pillars set around the circle, seemingly at random.

As impressive as this chamber was, it was not what drew Roykur's attention.

"By the eight gods . . . what is happening here?" he whispered.

Legast motioned frantically for the captain to keep quiet.

Two smaller Kolkrabba circled the pool, their limbs moving in rhythm. *Are they throwing something in?*

Roykur slipped through the archway to the nearest pillar to get a closer look. He moved with care, holding down loose bits of his armor to avoid making noise.

Crouching from behind the pillar, he could see the pool area better. For the first time, he noticed the line of Husks extending from the pool to a different entrance on the opposite side of the chamber. One of the Kolkrabba grabbed the first Husk in the line as they came around the circle. Without missing a beat, they ripped the Husk in half. The body sprayed an excessive volume of blood; a string of intestines fell from the Husk and dragged along the ground, leaving behind chunks of viscera. The fresh blood joined the soaked floor, like an artist adding a layer of paint to a canvas. Before the Kolkrabba made a full lap around the pool, they dropped the body into the water, smoothly scooped up another, and continued their silent ritual. The Husks just stood in a neat, obedient line, waiting for their turn to be sacrificed.

Roykur's heart was throbbing. He knew Kolkrabba were somewhat intelligent, but knowledge about them was slim outside their propensity for skirmishes and raids. They were clearly more sentient than he had assumed. *Silaine will have a field day when she hears of this.*

They both knew, based on their ability to turn people into Husks, that Kolkrabba were not simply wild animals, but this went far beyond what Silaine could ever have dreamed. What could those creatures possibly be doing with those Husks? Were they eating them? But that didn't explain why they were wiping the blood on the floor. *Maybe . . .*

Before Roykur could theorize more, the ground trembled, causing the waters in the pool to bubble and spill over the sides. The luminescent liquid swirled with the blood covering the basin floor, glowing blue and dark red, forming a striking contrast. Thick lines of the mixed fluid creeped outward along grooves in the floor, traveling up the incline. When the lines reached the stone pillars, several smaller lines branched off, filling in carved corrugations in the stone face and forming symbols. Roykur rotated and watched a flow of liquid move past him and up the walls of the chamber. The lines spread across thousands of cracks in the walls, fully illuminating the chamber. Now, with full visibility, Roykur could see small alcoves pocketing the walls every few feet, filled with translucent spheres. The spheres ungulated, coated with a wet, thick film of mucus.

A sudden realization washed over him. Eggs. Those were Kolkrabba eggs. This had to be how they reproduced. Elaborate for a reproductive process—

He shook his head. Focus! He couldn't let these hatch. If they did, this war would go on forever.

Roykur looked back at Legast and pointed up at the walls. The commander squinted for a moment. Then his eyes grew wide with surprise. He tore his gaze away and gave Roykur a look of determination. They both nodded in agreement.

Turning back, the captain watched the two Kolkrabba circling the room, spiraling outward as they moved. There was no sign of the long line of Husks extending from the opposite end. They had vanished in the few moments he had his back turned. As the creatures moved toward the edges of the chamber, Roykur noticed how they took almost graceful steps over every line of fluid running along the floor.

At the far end of the chamber, the Kolkrabba reached a stone pillar and touched the glowing symbol embedded on the surface. An immediate pulse of energy flowed back along the lines of liquid and into the pool. A similar pulse repeated for the next two that were touched. Then the bubbling stopped, and a black object floated to the water's surface. The object drew in the light, disorienting the surrounding space. It was hard to look at, but he could not look away.

It was small, and the substance ebbed back and forth from solid to smoke and then to liquid, all the while forming designs and patterns within itself. Tendrils whipped out and receded, making the thing seem almost living. However, the repetitive geometric shapes gave it the appearance of something mechanical. At the stone pillar along the far wall, the Kolkrabba moved back to the pool to retrieve its prize.

Taking a deep breath, Roykur slid his hands down along the smooth wood of his axe and tightened his grip around the leather straps at the base of the weapon. He waited patiently for the closer Kolkrabba to come activate the final stone, the one he hid behind.

As it neared, he leapt from his crouch, screaming with all the nervous adrenaline he could muster. In a wide, upward-arcing swing, he sliced a full trunk from the monster. It flailed backward in surprise, tripped, and splashed into the lines of water and blood, its own sanguineous liquids mingling. The other Kolkrabba froze, then broke from its apparent shock and moved away toward the far side of the chamber.

Odd. Why wasn't it attacking?

Roykur needed no more time to consider his luck. Legast responded quickly to his lead and was soon right beside him, swinging his short sword with wild abandon. They struck quickly at the wounded Kolkrabba, giving it no chance to recover. Roykur's axe hacked away at the base of the head where the limbs protruded, and with several swings, he severed all of them. The second Kolkrabba still hadn't left the chamber. It had stopped to gather eggs from the wall on its way out. That just gave Roykur enough time to leave his first foe still squirming and chase it down.

Uncharacteristically, the second Kolkrabba was very slow, fumbling with the large number of eggs it tried to hold amongst its tentacles. Determined not to let this monster escape, he hurried to block its path but tripped on the uneven ground. Roykur caught himself on his hands and knees, splashing the water and blood. This only added to the mess of blood and dirt already caked on his armor and face. The elixir might have numbed his pain, but his strength still waned from his injuries.

Legast took the lead and ran to block the other doorway to the chamber.

The Kolkrabba, if possible, appeared panicked, and it started moving faster as it saw the two of them closing in. Then it stopped —it must have realized it could not avoid a confrontation. The creature began shifting, shuffling eggs between its various tentacles. In a sudden burst of movement, it lashed out with two limbs as they stepped into its reach. One tentacle whipped Legast back against the chamber wall. He impacted with a heavy crack. The other cut past Roykur's guard and latched itself to his chest. Roykur dropped his axe due to the force of the blow. The thin finger tentacles punctured into his exposed armpits on either side of his breastplate.

Roykur winced at the pain and reached for his axe, but the tentacles held him firmly in place. Panicking, he slipped a belt knife out and stabbed the one that still clung to his chest and began to saw. Twitching violently, the Kolkrabba maintained its grip on him and tried to set the eggs down gently. The tentacle released its grip as Roykur's knife went all the way through the limb. The severed appendage writhed at the captain's feet as he picked up the axe.

Still breathing hard, he closed the distance and began swinging his axe at the Kolkrabba before it could strike again. Roykur chopped at the tentacles as each one moved to stop him. His blows became more frantic, and he started screaming in a frenzy, moving faster and faster despite the fatigue in his shoulders.

Finally, he stopped. The Kolkrabba was in dozens of little pieces, all glistening with a black sheen. He forced his breathing to slow and looked around the chamber. Legast lay on the ground where he had fallen. The commander was not moving.

Roykur knelt beside him. Legast's peaceful expression was marred by the blood and dirt caked across his smooth ebony features. The captain released a sigh of relief when he felt the unconscious man's breath. Twisting around, he sat down next to Legast, taking in the chamber fully as he wiped the grime from his own face. The incongruous black object still floated in the small pool. The Kolkrabba had not grabbed it.

Roykur stood slowly and approached the pool. He looked down at the strange thing as it undulated its hypnotic sequences. An urgent desire came over him—a desire to touch it. He squashed that quickly. This was no time to be poking things, several levels underground, in an unknown Kolkrabba breeding chamber, completely cut off from his company.

Then he felt a cold sensation on his fingertips. Looking down, Roykur found that his hand was already on it. In an instant, the object squeezed between his fingers, nearly too fast to see, and smashed into his face. The cold substance forced itself into his eyes, nose, and mouth. It took less than a second for the object to disappear entirely into Roykur.

Inhuman screams echoed in his head. Horrific scenes flashed through his mind, overwhelming it. All manner of nightmares outside the capacity of Human comprehension flared in Roykur's brain. He could not think, move, or even breathe. Only seconds had gone by, but it felt like an eternity. His brain and nerves were freezing and melting at the same time. His body went rigid from the shock.

Then the sounds and images stopped all at once, and Roykur sucked in air like he had been drowning.

Besides the lack of air, none of the blinding pain he'd felt lingered. The images were already fading, and the sheer terror was distant, as if it had all happened in a dream long ago.

Hundreds of eggs still lined the walls, with an assortment scattered around his feet. Roykur had work left to do. The stern expression on his face broke ever so slightly, and a little smile crept onto it. *I won. I beat you slimy djavuls.*

In an icy voice, he whispered, "You've taken my friends, my soldiers, my fear, and now you shall take my malice."

He hefted his axe and with his foot, then rolled an egg directly in front of him. Heaving, he swung the blade around and brought it down hard.

CHAPTER 1

THE GREATEST MYTH

The axe hit the side of the large birch tree; small chips splintered away, and Roykur loosened and pulled the blade free. The wood cracked, groaned, then slowly toppled over, crashing to the ground.

Roykur winced, rubbing at his back. It ached from the day's work, meager as it had been. He was very active for his age, but at seventy-eight, his body was like a rusted axle. It moved, but with great effort, and was always on the verge of collapse. It had taken him nearly the whole afternoon to fell a single tree, but truth be told, he had never been good at tree cutting. It was more about technique than brute force, but he always seemed to have enough of the latter to refuse to learn the former. Now he had neither, and he leaned on the axe for support, wiping sweat and bits of wood from his forehead. Roykur's considerable bulk had faded, but a thin vestige of muscle remained hidden beneath his loose, sun-spotted skin.

The man set the woodcutter's axe on the ground—not nearly as elaborate as his battle-axe—and wiped his shaking hands on his brown wool shirt. Taking a long drink from the canteen, he tried to

15

ignore the dull throb of his bones. He once again remembered why he wasn't supposed to come out with his workers anymore. The reverberations from every swing rattled him fiercely. Grabbing block and tackle from his pack, he began tying a few knots around branches at one end of the tree and then fed the rope through the pulleys attached to a sled. He began ratcheting the lever, but the repetitive motion and the strain from the day seemed to conspire against him, and his elbow locked up. Cursing, he tried to prod his arm back into compliance, but Sauget and Brour, his carpenters, rushed over to finish.

"Don't worry, Lord Roykur, you did the hard part. We can take it from here," said Brour.

Clearing his throat, Roykur moved out of their way with a curt nod. They were fine workers, always quick to step in and help, usually when it was unwanted, but this time he accepted. *This is it, Roykur, your last time out here. You could barely fell a tree, and you certainly can't haul it.*

Carefully, lest his back also go out, he picked up his axe and followed behind the carpenters, who dragged the sled to the wagon with twenty logs. He let out a heavy sigh. That wagon had been empty hours ago. Roykur climbed into the driver's seat of the wagon and waited patiently for the last tree to be loaded on. Sauget and Brour settled next to him, Brour coaxing the two draugkers onward. The draugkers responded slowly, the wooly animals lumbering forward, pulling the heavy load of trees through the brown, grassy field back to Manor Heimvelt.

Draugkers, though not a fast pack animal, were very large and strong. Both beasts retracted their protruding claws from the ground as soon as they had enough momentum. Their shaggy, hulking bodies provided the kingdom all the wool necessary for basic clothing, and on their enormous heads sat two massive, twisted horns, which made for an impressive visage. The genuine treasure that these magnificent creatures produced was their cheese, which had become a true staple of the kingdom and city of Ver'a'saile. Draugkers, just like all the resources the noble houses were responsible for, were vital to Ver'a'saile's economy and survival.

Manor Heimvelt was very modest as far as manors went. Nothing compared to the other outer city manors, such as Manor Relaine or Manor Chesture. Legast, long since ascended to the throne, had given Roykur his title and land as a gift for his many impressive years of service in the Sentinels as a soldier and then as a Conservator. Even after a few years, Roykur had not yet come to terms with being one of the few people in the kingdom to have a second name. Like the other fifteen noble houses, in exchange for this lavish living, he oversaw a part of the crown's property and income. He had poured himself into his new job as caretaker of the king's property and improved the manor from the previous owners, all killed in some terrible tragedy, restoring it to a well-run estate.

While some noble houses ran the king's orchards and plantations, or the aquifer, Roykur kept the king's many herds of draugkers. The trees in the wagon were destined for the new cheese-aging storeroom and represented probably the last improvements he could have a hand in, physically, on the estate. He mostly supervised construction these days, but he knew that this project, judging from the sheer size, would most likely be his last.

They rolled by a few dozen draugkers grazing in the fields, and a head poked out, followed by vigorous waving from the herder, Cybal. The carpenters in the wagon next to him were just two out of the fifty people he employed. The secret to his successful revitalization of this noble house was that he paid all of them very well. He had a very large stipend after the wool and cheese sold, a large majority of which went into paying his workers extra. They lived on the manor grounds, and it made him more comfortable knowing his workers were well taken care of. In return, Roykur received hardworking, invested employees. It was a simple concept, yet one the other noble houses seemed baffled by. Besides, the manor itself needed very little of those funds to be maintained.

Coming around the bend of a hill, Roykur admired the majesty of his home as the manor came into view. Its foundations had been cut from large, black stone blocks, polished to a reflective shine and used in the columns and chimney as well. Larger logs created the frame of the first and second stories, much like in some of the other manors. A combination of many original woods formed intricate patterns in the walls of the structure. The lighter woods stood in stark contrast to the black stone. The mastery of the carpenters and stonemasons was plain in their exquisite showcasing of the materials' natural beauty.

Brour pulled the draugkers to a stop, and the carpenters jumped out and started to unload the trees. Roykur, exhausted from the day's work, left the care and storage of the wood in their charge and started walking to the manor. Despite his exhaustion, he spotted a blur from the corner of his eye and had just enough time to brace himself as a young woman of seventeen years slammed her arms around him in a tight embrace.

"Adalia!" Roykur exclaimed. "Not so tight. You're going to give me a heart attack, sneaking up on me like that."

She was tall, nearly as tall as Roykur, and strongly built. She adopted a mischievous grin, and with a powerful set of legs, she hoisted him up easily. "Ah! Down please! Alright, congratulations, you can pick up a frail old man. Put me down."

Adalia set him down, and he turned to hug his granddaughter properly for the first time in months. She moved around, posing dramatically to show off her Sentinel uniform, a newer version than when he had worn one. Her polished armguards reflected the sunlight and trailed up to her shoulder to meet the crisply pressed brown jacket that buttoned at the sternum. It tapered down at the back, passing her midthigh. A shiny badge was pinned to her jacket, showing her status as a Sentinel, and underneath was the standard-issue white linen shirt. Her brown leather trousers ended at knee-high boots, which were adorned with polished metal plating to match her arms. She wore her golden hair in a neat bun, accentuating her angular face. Roykur noticed that her lightly tanned skin had gotten darker since he last saw her.

"I'm sorry, Grandpa, I was just so excited. I missed you so much! I have some fantastic news to share with you!" Adalia beamed at him. Despite being rather tall herself, she still had to look up slightly to meet Roykur's eyes. They both continued toward the manor.

"Well, I should say so. It's been the full seven months. I assume you passed your training?"

"I did! You are looking at the newest initiate to the Ver'a'saile Sentinels!" Adalia practically squealed in excitement.

"Wonderful! I am so proud of you, my little Dralm. Let's see your Conservator badge." Roykur squinted at the badge pinned to her jacket, trying to make out the eye flanked with wings that would be above the normal insignia.

Adalia hesitated for a moment. "They assigned me to the patrols division."

Roykur stumbled over his own feet, his eyes wide. "The *patrols* division? You can't be serious, that's—"

"They do things differently now. Everyone goes through patrols, and then, after a few years, if you do well, they can select you for the Conservators," said Adalia, sounding sheepish.

"That's ridiculous! How are they supposed to get the best and brightest if they waste away their talents in patrols?" He stopped as he glimpsed his own disappointment reflected in Adalia's expression. "I'm sorry, you will be the best Sentinel in the division and get selected in no time." Roykur cleared his throat. "Have you told your mother?"

"Not yet. I only just arrived. I saw you as I pulled up . . ." She trailed off, looking down at his sweat-soaked shirt. "Don't you have guests to greet? They should be here within the hour."

"Guests? Guests! Olacka! The party is tonight?" Roykur said, the weariness of the day creeping back to his face.

"Uh, yeah. You planned it so I would be back in time, remember?" Adalia rolled her eyes impatiently before giving him a wry smile.

"Alright, smartass, it appears we will need your help. Go on and let your mother know you're here before we're all in trouble."

"I left all my bags on the carriage," said Adalia.

"Don't worry, I'll have Xandar bring them to your room. Let your mother know I'll be getting ready."

Adalia gave him a peck on the cheek and hurried ahead, leaving Roykur alone on the back porch of the manor. Turning around, he postponed his urgency, taking a moment to admire the countryside. The brown autumn grass sloped downward in the direction they had come, the tree line poking out above. Beyond, endless forests stretched across the mountainside and onto the next. The red, gold, brown, and orange of the maples, aspens, and birches flowed seamlessly in between the evergreen pines, spruces, and firs, a testament to nature's bountiful splendor. In the distance, water from a geyser crested the leaves, splitting the waning sunlight into sparkling prisms. From this view, it was possible to make out Mount Vulpan, to the south, on which resided Saft'don, the closest kingdom to Ver'a'saile.

Sighing with contentment, Roykur stepped inside. He walked down a long hallway and into his chamber's washroom to wipe away some of his grime before the night's festivities. He toweled off the dirt and wood chips from his face and upper body, then combed back his short, ear-length white hair. He picked up a razor and touched the blade to his face, but the shaking of his hand made him rethink that decision.

He looked around for his usual finely made beige shirt to go with a gray woolen vest and black jacket. It was a reserved outfit, but it suited him. However, hanging in the room's corner was what Visari had left for him: the newest fashion. Despite the cold mountain weather, the kingdom's fashion had taken to shocking other party-goers with extremes, either hiding an elaborate outfit that somehow fit beneath your travel clothes or wearing as little as possible once indoors.

The silk or satin red vest and short jacket would befit a man of his stature to wear, but he preferred wool. Wool was what most people could afford to wear, and he had grown up wearing it.

Besides, they dyed most silks ridiculous colors for fashion's sake. The browns and grays of draugker wool were all anyone needed. Apparently, he was not afforded the luxury of choice this evening. Thankfully, Visari had also left him a black silk shirt to wear underneath. He was long past his years of showing off skin.

Roykur did up the buttons, and his trembling hands fumbled repeatedly. He finished the shirt after a frustratingly long time, and he still had the vest and jacket to go. A huff of exasperation blew out at his predicament when he heard the thrum of voices through the walls—the guests arriving, most likely. Quickening his pace, he only decreased his already low dexterity, and he had to force himself to slow down before he made any progress. Finally, fully dressed, he smoothed the front of his outfit and strode out from the washroom.

Adjusting his sleeves, Roykur took a deep breath, affixed a smile, and stepped through the door into the banquet hall. The low thrum of conversation leaped to a dull roar, but just above the din was the chorus of several cellists playing an upbeat tune. The largest room in the manor was warm from the crackling fire in the hearth. The redwood interior reflected the fire's warmth, giving the hall an open and inviting atmosphere. On either side of the hearth were two long tables, each with draugker heads intricately carved into the center. The furniture was fashioned from draugker horns, each piece uniquely employing the various horn shapes into the design. Opposite the hearth, wide, ornate doors stood propped open. The chilly evening air pierced the comforting shell of the hall.

A large group of guests had already arrived—other lords and ladies, prominent merchants, doctors, factory owners, engineers, magisters, and more. Thankfully, Visari and Adalia were already at the door greeting people as they came in. Roykur's daughter-in-law and granddaughter both wore sleek, form-fitting dresses, one turquoise, the other purple. Much to his dismay, Adalia's dress had a long slit running up the side almost to her hip, and her neckline was far too low. *I guess she really has gone and grown up on me.*

The two women had somehow found time to put up their hair in matching thick braids placed delicately on the left shoulder. Roykur moved toward them, servants bustling around him, carrying trays of food and bottles of ale.

Standing proudly next to the two women in his life, he joined them in welcoming the newcomers. "Magister Didris, how are the children? Myrmilla, I have a proposal you must hear later this evening. Doctor Arakul, pleasure seeing you again."

Small talk was his specialty. Roykur could always remember the little details that others dismissed. It was what had made him such a great Conservator. However, it was much more exhausting to do it with a smile.

"Ah! The guest of honor! Commander Volmirk, get in here and have an ale. I'm buying." Roykur glanced mischievously at Adalia and Visari and received his customary groans and eye rolls.

The guests mingled amongst themselves in the hall, and the ale flowed. For his own part, Roykur's eyes wandered to the large tables in the back, now filled with food, and he finally felt the pangs of hunger he had not known were there. The meal itself was a delicious-looking fowl, its brown, crispy skin still dripping broth. The rest of the dishes were an array of cheese pies, fruit pies, and fruit salads. Roykur grasped a plate from the server, and he even took a few bites before Lord Wisiel and Lady Ingrail of House Becoven spotted him by the food table and made their way over.

"Great, the only two people I cannot stand talking to," Roykur complained under his breath. All nobles were difficult to converse with while hiding his obvious derision, but these two were the worst. He quickly put on a cheery expression as the couple neared and he feigned noticing them for the first time. "Wisiel, Ingrail, wonderful of you to come. I hope you find my home accommodating?"

Lady Ingrail inclined her head slightly. "Your quaint little home definitely has . . . charm, Lord Roykur, though I don't know how you manage with so few servants. I cannot imagine how anything would get done, but you seem to get by."

Roykur could not have described Ingrail as an attractive woman, the pompous attitude aside. With one hand, she fussed at her large, hooked nose, and the other held a heaping plate. A steady drip of gravy ran down her bright green dress, cutting across the yellow and red stripes that spiraled from her waist down. Roykur understood stripes should give a person the appearance of being slimmer. They did not have that effect on her.

Lord Wisiel stood beside his wife and straightened his brocade of matching colors, which only amplified their differences. Wisiel winced visibly as his wife spoke. His fragile frame and demeanor alluded to a life without a single day of manual labor. Where his wife was shrill and irritating, his temperament leaned toward slimy and hateful.

"We are stewards for His Majesty, are we not? I wouldn't want the crown's coin wasted on my comfort when the king's herds and cheese stores need tending," Roykur said, smiling.

Wisiel narrowed his sunken eyes and lifted his pointed chin with an air of superiority. "Lord Roykur, you have been a lord for just over a decade and already accomplished more than other noble houses have in generations. I guess no one should underestimate your savvy maneuverings, considering you managed to acquire the first lordship granted in over two hundred years. At this rate, I dare say you'll have more influence than House Tremane one day."

The mention of House Tremane was a slight jab directed at Roykur. Everyone knew the powerful house because of their connection to the Treemolkvar people, or Witches, as they were sometimes called. The elixirs that the Witches brewed were too valuable to society for the kingdom to ignore, and House Tremane had been the only noble house to become intertwined with them through marriage. However, elixirs had caused the death of Roykur's wife, Silaine, and indirectly that of Oskur, his son. Roykur dug a fingernail into the side of his thumb, the pain distracting him from his blossoming anger, and all the while he kept the fake smile on his face.

"Oh no, I can assure you I only want what's best for the kingdom.

Ensuring the continued prosperity of our city is paramount. Besides, at my age, ambition is hardly a factor." Roykur laughed with forced joviality.

"Oh please, your modesty is commendable, but we understand your desire for a legacy. This organization you formed will last the ages, with your name as its founder. Your house will enjoy political sway and deference for generations." Lady Ingrail punctuated each of her sentences with overly delicate sips from her glass of ale.

"Your assessment is flattering, and no doubt the reason you joined, but my granddaughter is now part of the Sentinels. I want to make sure she has all the resources possible at her disposal. This organization will ensure she has an easier time at the job than I did."

As if sensing his discomfort, Adalia appeared at his side.

"A noble as a Sentinel? Why, that's absurd—" Ingrail cut off at a rough throat clearing from her husband. "Forgive me, I forgot you do not share our well-established noble traditions."

"You realize you are standing in the home of a man who *earned* a title by being the best Sentinel who ever lived? No other House can say they've earned their title in, what was it, two hundred years?" said Adalia. She was one of the tallest people in the room and had the fire of youth on her side. Roykur's smile became genuine.

Ingrail's sneer had devolved into a snarl. "You mean doing his job? I believe I know of thousands who fit that particular criterion, my dear. Besides, he never caught the most prolific killer of all time. So, Lord Roykur, if you could not catch the worst of them, can you really be considered the best?"

All pretense of veiled insults was gone entirely.

"He's long dead," Roykur said flatly, and reached down, touching Adalia's arm, stopping her from taking a step forward. Smile gone, he maintained his eye contact with Ingrail.

It was her turn for a genuine grin. "Well, it certainly appears that he is not, unless someone has taken up his mantle. An admirer perhaps?"

"After nearly twenty years? Where did you hear that? Where are you getting your information?" Roykur tried to remain skeptical, but curiosity creeped into his voice.

"How could you not have heard? Oh, that's right, you are retired. If you do not attend your own organization's meetings regularly, how can you expect to stay informed? You cannot have it both ways, Lord Roykur." She let the tension build for a moment while he processed the news. "To your credit, the Conservators seem utterly bewildered. It's been weeks, and not a single suspect. Or perhaps your instruction to new Conservators has bred a similar incompetence?"

Roykur's face was flush. "How dare—"

"Attention everyone! Attention!" Sentinel Commander Volmirk shouted above the din of party guests. The room fell silent, and everyone turned to the commander. "You all know why we are gathered here today, to celebrate the great culmination of hard work and intelligent minds. We have all benefited immensely from the creation of the Initiative. Conviction rates have gone up, and crime rates have plummeted. In the ten years since its founding, this group of individuals has come together like never before and made this kingdom a better place. Or well, it has definitely made my job easier."

A small chuckle rolled through the crowd. "So, without further ado, please allow me to introduce our host, and the mastermind behind this whole Initiative, Lord Roykur of House Heimvelt."

The party guests applauded politely as Roykur made his way to the front of the crowd. Roykur addressed the gathering in his deep baritone voice. "Some of you know me well, and it appears we have some new members. Well, for those of you who are new here, let me tell you a bit about my past and how I founded the Initiative. I am a bit old, so this might be a history lesson for all you younger folks. After the eradication of the Kolkrabba, there was no longer a need for a military, so the Sentinels were reformed as a law enforcement organization. The kingdom could only afford to keep a limited number of soldiers in the Sentinels. As a result, a great many came home without work. I was lucky enough to become a Conservator, a newly created section within the Sentinels. I spent the next forty-five years catching the worst our city has to offer: killers, rapists, and gang leaders. I didn't catch all of them, and some of the ones I did catch were released because I didn't have enough to prove their guilt."

He paused for a moment to let the implication settle in.

"Now, I have seen that with the help of this Initiative, we can prevent killers from eluding the law. I have seen the people here pool their resources for the betterment of this society. This Initiative has become more than just a benefit to our ability to fight crime. It has provided advancements in the fields of medicine, industry, science, and much more. I thank you all for your commitment to this endeavor." Roykur raised his glass. "To a new world, and a better kingdom."

The guests all raised their glasses and intoned the toast almost reverently. Roykur moved away from the front of the gathering and sat himself decidedly away from the Becovens. After his speech, a few other individuals got up to speak, each presenting something to the group. The first was Myrmilla, the always nervous engineer, who was now calm and poised for her speech.

Roykur shook his head. *She must have taken an elixir for her nerves. Nobody can do anything without having at least one elixir pumping through them these days.* He had a flash of memory to the elixirs he had used to stay awake during the long nights of solving murders, but it sickened him to think of grabbing one of those again.

Myrmilla presented her design for a metal rail that would propel an object along it through the cranking of a lever. The schematics she showed were of a circular design, but she indicated the possible adaptions around the city for transportation.

The genius these people have! Although it looks like that handle would get painful to operate after a few hours. Roykur nursed his elbow as he thought about it.

Next, Doctor Arakul presented his research into the psyche of a multikiller. He described scientifically what Roykur had seen first-hand. Another speaker was Wahrlich, a Witch, who presented ways elixirs could be combined to increase truthfulness out of suspects. Roykur despised having a Witch in his organization, but he was outvoted with logic and reason on her account. Wahrlich's contributions to the cause could not be discounted, and the backing of the Treemolkvar people eased investigations that ventured into their portion of the kingdom.

Wahrlich, like many of the Treemolkvar, had bark. Hers was thick and reddish-brown, covering everywhere bone met hazel skin, and she was showing a lot of skin. Her honey-colored silk dress hung loose and left little to the imagination. Treemolkvar had extremely vibrant hair; her light blue and green strands were done up to frame her features without taking away from bark that ran along collar and cheekbones.

It was near the fourth speaker when Roykur felt his eyelids droop. He had been much more physical today than he should have and was having trouble finding the energy for this party.

In the middle of the presentation, he spotted Sentinel Commander Volmirk at a spot near the back of the banquet hall and made his way toward him.

"Can we speak somewhere privately?" Roykur whispered.

"Of course," Volmirk replied. "Lead the way."

The two men stepped through a side door in the hall and entered a small room. At the end was a solid wood desk with various papers scattered across its surface. Roykur lit a lamp that stood on the desk. The walls were lined with bookshelves, and next to the door stood a tall clock that clicked rhythmically. On the wall above the leather-bound desk chair was a large battle axe, the polished metal glistening in all its famed barbarity. He had not used the weapon in a very long time, but it still reminded people who came into this office of what he had once done for the kingdom. Regardless of its threatening visage, he was retired, and at his age, he was not sure he could fight in any capacity, much less with that monstrosity of a weapon.

Sitting on the makeshift throne, Roykur gave Commander Volmirk an appraising look. "I come to the Sentinel barracks once a week to give instruction—we talk practically every time I am there. Were you ever going to tell me about this new imitator, or did you fancy waiting until I died of old age?"

"You mean like in the next few days?" Volmirk said, smiling.

"By the eight gods, you're infuriating," Roykur scolded. A smile creeped onto his face, but it faded quickly. "From what I hear, there has been a string of murders, and your Conservators are practically useless. There hasn't been anything like this in your time as commander, and you don't have the expertise or experience to deal with this. The worst part is I had to hear of this from Lady Ingrail."

Volmirk grew solemn. "We don't need you, Roykur. Do you know what retired means? You are far too old to be running around solving cases."

"Retirement is the greatest myth. I created the Initiative, I sit on the king's council, I run my estate, and I even felled a tree today." Roykur sat straighter in his chair after tallying his current endeavors.

"All I see is that you have a great deal of trouble just sitting back and relaxing. You really are pushing your limits, my friend." Volmirk eyed him sympathetically, and then the smile returned to his face. "Can you even get out of that chair?"

Roykur closed his eyes for a moment, feeling the day's exhaustion seep into his bones. He pushed on the chair, his arms shaking with fatigue and age.

Volmirk just gave him a blank stare. "You're not even using your legs. I swear your humor has not aged nearly as well as you."

Roykur gave the commander a sly smile and jumped up, admittedly not as smoothly as he would have liked. "Nothing gets by you. I see I taught you well."

A shattering of glass and a scream came from the banquet hall, and the two men rushed from the study. A circle formed around a single party guest. A woman, Myrmilla by the look of it, was convulsing violently on the ground. The cellists had stopped their playing, staring on in horror.

"Quickly, grab her head and turn her on her side!" Doctor Arakul shouted while rushing to her side to check her vitals.

The engineering woman's eyes snapped open and rolled up into her head, her jaw locked open, her arms and legs bent at awkward angles. She screamed with a sound Roykur had heard only once before, something of pure terror and pain. It faded into gurgles as the convulsions intensified. The veins along her arms and legs elevated through her skin and bubbled as if her blood had begun to boil. Before anyone could react, an axe came down swiftly on her neck, cleaving the head from her body. The doctor jumped back in surprise, a spray of blood sullying his fine clothes.

The axe was Roykur's, the blade that had not tasted blood in years. He hadn't even seen Volmirk grab it on the way out of the study. He placed a hand over his heart as if he could slow its beating —it had been a long time since he had witnessed firsthand such a violent death. This particular version he had not seen since his wife had died.

"Calm down, everyone! Calm down, it's over," Volmirk commanded.

The guests quieted their hysteria, but an indistinct murmur of exchanges continued.

A man fell to his knees in front of the body, crying, and picked up the body in his hands.

"No! Myrmilla!" The man's words were muddled between his cries of despair. "You killed my wife, my wife!"

"Her death was certain; I merely spared her hours of pain," Volmirk said.

Roykur stepped back from the ring of people, feeling his heart racing. He leaned against a table for support, his chest tight.

Adalia let go of her mother, who sat frozen in a chair near the hearth, and put a hand on Roykur's shoulder. "Grandpa, are you alright?"

"I'm fine, just in a bit of shock."

Roykur turned and looked at his granddaughter. Her eyes were locked on the body. Her usual tanned face seemed drained of color, and her expression was the essence of a child's innocence shattering. The look shattered Roykur as well.

Volmirk stepped up to the man. "Sir, what is your name? Did your wife have an incompatibility? Did she have any enemies? Did she consume any elixirs recently?"

The sobbing husband just held the headless body close, ignoring the questions.

"Alright, we are not going to get these answers here. Sir, you will accompany us to Sentinel Headquarters. You can answer our questions there. Sentinels, bring a tarp and remove the body."

To Roykur's surprise, there were six patrol Sentinels, garbed like Adalia had been earlier, standing in the banquet hall. He was usually very aware of his surroundings, but the commander's escort had come in during the commotion without him noticing. Getting over his initial shock, Roykur stepped up to inspect the body as the Sentinels placed it on the tarp.

He looked at Volmirk. "Definitely an incompatibility." Something occurred to him. "Is there anyone else in this house who has an incompatibility?" Roykur inquired of the room.

There was a brief pause, during which the crowd of people shook their heads uncomfortably. Roykur scanned the room with a disappointed look at the lack of positive responses. Well, incompatibilities were rare.

A youthful man Roykur did not recognize in the corner piped up. "I do. An incompatibility to enhanced . . . stimulation."

The entire room turned to face the young man, and silence lingered for a long while. The redness of his face continued to deepen the longer everyone stared, and his efforts to shrink back were in vain.

Likely not the same incompatibility as Myrmilla. Turning back to the body, Roykur opened the dead woman's handbag and removed an empty bottle of elixir. He ran a finger along the rim and tasted it, then handed it to Volmirk.

Volmirk sighed. "Roykur—Lord Roykur, we will have a Conservator here in a few hours to examine the scene."

"Nonsense, I am already here." The commander's distress was evident, but Roykur ignored it for the more pressing matters at hand.

He picked up Myrmilla's cracked pewter mug from the floor and, with a finger, sampled the contents. The subtle hint of burnt wood and rusted metal flashed across his tongue, the taste barely perceptible in the beer's bitterness. He moved to the tables of food at the far side of the hall, where he picked up a large serving fork and began examining pieces of food and eventually tasting each dish.

Volmirk eyed Roykur curiously. He held up the bottle the lord had given him. "What are you doing? If someone swapped her elixir, we will have one of the Witch—I mean, one of the Treemolkvar examine the contents and make a determination."

"I believe you will find nothing amiss with the contents of that elixir, Commander. You should take samples of the food and drink for testing. Someone spiked the meal rather than swapping the elixir. The taste of elixir is present in the food, but different from the one in the bottle. They might have lacked access to Myrmilla's supply of elixir, or they were hoping to catch a wider array of victims tonight. Either way, this is a murder at the very least, and an attempt at mass murder at worst," Roykur said firmly. The thrill of a mystery rose within him, expelling some of his previous revulsion at the decapitation of one of his guests.

Volmirk waved for a Sentinel, who retrieved a few glass jars from their carriage. Then the commander moved quickly to Roykur's side, whispering so the other guests would not hear. "Please, say no more of this in front of your guests. This is now part of a bigger investigation."

"Of course, of course. Everyone here is a suspect. I shall give my full statement and have my staff turn themselves over to you as well," Roykur said absently, deep in thought. "There have been several more incidents of incompatibility murders recently, haven't there?"

After a moment, Volmirk sighed again. "I had a feeling you would come to that conclusion. Three so far. There were empty elixir bottles at each of the scenes as well, although my Conservators never bothered checking the food."

"Why would you? Elixirs don't survive any sort of cooking. It must have been poured on the food sometime after it was cooked. That means it was done recently. I don't recall feeling any differently. It must have diffused enough that the effects weren't potent." Roykur scanned the faces around the hall, narrowing when he spotted Wahrlich. *Godsdamn elixirs.*

"Just one out of the forty-odd guests or your eleven staff members." A Sentinel handed Volmirk a small journal with a fountain pen, and he began scratching down names.

"Don't forget, someone could have snuck in a side entrance with all the commotion of the party preparations and dosed the fowl before it was served, then snuck back out."

"Great. Just great." Volmirk just wrote in large letters *or anyone* at the bottom of his notes.

"This started happening near the end last time our *friend* was out and about; the spiked food is a new adaptation, though. Regardless, no one would accept the connection back then. I know you're not stupid enough to disregard the connection now."

"Two killers working together, or a killer with alternating or evolving kill patterns," said Volmirk.

"Exactly. You need me."

Volmirk rocked back on his heels and glanced around the room again. "Look, I appreciate your insight here, but it will not happen. My own Conservators will handle this investigation, and you will stay out of it, do you understand?"

The serving fork Roykur was holding slipped from his fingers and clanged to the floor. Roykur grabbed his chest, and he found himself unable to support his own weight. Volmirk caught him as he collapsed, slowly lowering him to the floor. His vision blurred, but he could make out various bodies moving around him.

"Grandpa! Someone please help . . ." Roykur heard the voice dwindle as everything faded to blackness around him.

CHAPTER 2

NO ONE LIVES FOREVER

Roykur awoke the next morning in his bed. Adalia and Visari rose from their seats as they noticed him stirring. Both were still in their evening gowns from the previous night. It was obvious they'd spent the night worrying about his health. In another chair to the right sat Wahrlich, flipping casually through a book. She briefly glanced up from her studious reading. An exquisite woman, or Witch, with a slim and a narrow face, she appeared to be in her thirties, though age with Treemolkvar was difficult to discern. The bark and leaves that adorned her cheekbones creaked as she yawned. She removed the spectacles that had rested on the bridge of her nose, then leaned forward on the arm of the chair, still wearing her dress as well.

"Grandfather, how are you feeling?" Adalia asked. "Here, drink this."

"I feel like I had the worst dream," Roykur said through a grunt as he sat up to accept the cup from Adalia. "Did someone die in our house? Please tell me that was a dream."

"Afraid not, Da—also, you apparently had a heart attack as well. Wahrlich here stepped up and took good care of you. Without her help, you surely would have died," said Vasari while pressing a warm washcloth to his head and gesturing at the third woman in the room.

"Nonsense, I did nothing to help you survive. The elixir I had on hand was merely to dull the pain you might experience and relax the muscles. You recovered all on your own somehow. Honestly, you should be dead considering your age and lifestyle. You really shouldn't be so active," Wahrlich said with matronly calm. "I can brew you a more potent elixir once I get back to the enclave and I have some proper ingredients. Until then, you should stay in bed."

Roykur tensed at the first mention of elixirs, and his grip tightened around the cup. With as much calm as he could muster, he said, "No. No thank you, Wahrlich, but that won't be necessary. I have a strict no-elixir policy that I have followed rigorously for years—or until last night, it seems. I'm sure your efforts were purely noble ones, but you have violated my person. Now, please leave."

Visari winced visibly at her father-in-law's terse words. "Da! That was completely rude. She just saved your life!"

"By her own admission, she did not. Now I thank you, Wahrlich, good day," Roykur said with irritation as he got out of bed.

"You have nothing to fear from me, Lord Roykur. I assure you that my elixirs are not in the least bit dangerous," Wahrlich said in her smooth, smoky voice.

Adalia chimed in, "Grandpa, she just said to stay in bed. It's not like she's forcing you to take more—"

"Get out!" Roykur snapped in a flash of pure rage.

Visari and Adalia jumped at the outburst. Standing straight at the side of his bed, he blocked the light, casting a shadow across their faces. Roykur directed his stern gaze at their guest, but Visari edged back regardless. Wahrlich, however, seemed unfazed, still leaning calmly in the chair. She closed the book a couple of seconds later, as though finished on her own time, and stood without the slightest hint of hurry.

"No need to fuss any longer. I understand Lord Roykur's reservations. I shall see myself out. However, if you ever reconsider, you can find me in the enclave. Just ask around and you will be pointed in the right direction. Good day." Wahrlich inclined her head and glided from the room.

"I swear, someday you will have to learn some manners. She stayed awake all night in the room here making sure you didn't die, and that's how you repay her selflessness?" said Visari. Despite being his daughter-in-law, she often took up the role of his disappointed mother, scolding him whenever she felt it was necessary.

"How could you let her put that poison in me? You know how I feel." Roykur let the accusation fill his voice.

"We were more concerned with saving your life than the possibility of your wrath if you survived. Shocking, I know," Adalia piped in.

"What are you doing? Get back to bed. You need your rest after such a traumatic night," said Visari.

"Visari, I've fought a war against monsters, chased murderers and rapists. I think I can handle a little . . . heart issue. Besides, I have a council appointment which I cannot miss. The king apparently has a big announcement for the kingdom. As councilmembers, we have the privilege of hearing it first and providing suggestions." Roykur grabbed an outfit from the dresser and turned to Visari, who stared at him, her fists on her hips. With a heavy sigh, he said, "Do I have your permission to rescue the king from a dull meeting with bickering idiots, or shall I inform him that my nursemaid daughter has insisted I waste away in bed?"

"Oh, I'm sure Legs would be more than happy to hear that his friend is taking care of himself for once," Visari said, scowling. "He did always insist you enjoy your retirement more."

"Legs? You dare disrespect King Legast of House Morfar in such a way?" Roykur said in feigned shock. "Where are those famed manners that I've heard so much about?"

He mimicked Visari's stern expression. She continued staring daggers at her father-in-law while her foot began tapping. A mischievous smile crept onto Roykur's face.

"Oh come on now, not even a chuckle? Oh well, I guessed humor skipped a generation." Roykur said, and winked at Adalia as she turned away from her mother, trying to force down a smile.

Visari threw up her hands in exasperation and stomped away. "I guess I'm just the crazy one in this house. I'll go check on the staff to see if they started breakfast."

Roykur and Adalia exchanged goofy faces and silent impressions of Visari before Adalia followed her mother out. Roykur dressed himself in his sturdy work attire, less formal than the silk vestments, yet still a quality he would have been hard pressed to afford in his youth. The outfit was a thin beige linen shirt with a brown wool vest and lined trousers, topped with a long coat to keep the frigid mountain air away. Should a geyser erupt, the trousers and coat had an outer shell of dark brown, treated leather to keep the water off. The coat had a large collar of wool that lay across his shoulders. The weather had not quite turned so cold yet for a coat like this, but he didn't care for having a coat for every season, especially one as fine as this. With some stiffness, he pulled on midcalf, dark brown leather boots and slipped some gloves into the pocket of his coat; he would need those later.

Roykur traipsed through the banquet hall, where the blood stain still marred the beautiful wood floor. He knelt to examine it. Adalia, having changed herself, lowered herself beside him, gnawing on a hunk of cheese.

Glancing over to her, Roykur said, "I know you only have a few days before you have to return to the barracks for your assignments, and Visari wants you to spend some time with her, but how would you feel about coming with me to the council meeting?"

Adalia nodded absently. "Sure, sure, that sounds great. Here, I have . . . Wait, what?"

Roykur smiled. "Come with me to the council meeting. I'd like you to see what they are like. After all, you may have to attend them one day."

"Aren't only councilmembers allowed at the council meeting?" asked Adalia.

"Members bring secretaries all the time. It will be fine. Plus, you get to see Uncle Legs, and watch me get put on this murder investigation."

"I knew it! I knew you were going to try to work your way into this case," Adalia said with hushed excitement.

Roykur chuckled. "Try? No, I will get on it. Legs can't say no to me. He knows how personal this one is."

"Speaking of this investigation, here—I took some notes for you. I thought you would have examined the area more thoroughly while it was still fresh, so I took down what you always mentioned were important observations."

She handed Roykur a small sheaf of papers. He leaned over and gave her a peck on the top of her head.

"Also, please let me know if I missed something, or if my notes are too sloppy, or—"

"I am sure they are well organized and extremely detailed, just like I taught you," said Roykur, sticking them into his coat pocket. "We can look them over on the way to the palace, and I'll let you know my thoughts."

"Okay. I mean, thanks. I just want to be a good Conservator like you were," Adalia said, anxiety bleeding through her tone. "There aren't a lot of women in the Sentinels, and most of them end up as clerks. I just want to make sure I don't fall into that hole."

"Good? Were? Adalia, you wound me," Roykur said with a dramatic flair, clutching his chest.

"Amazing and fabulous. Better?"

"Eh, a little late, but I'll take it," he said with a shrug. "Listen, everyone has to earn their positions in the Sentinels. You know this. Even if they make you go through patrols first, you have to show your strength to be accepted. You are just as physically strong as any recruit, but you have to remember, there are many kinds of strength, and you cannot just rely on a single source. I was a very physically powerful person. But if I hadn't shown strength in my ability to solve mysteries, and of course not taking no for an answer, we wouldn't have become nobility. You showed remarkable initiative and ambition with these notes. You will do great. You learned a thing or two from the best."

Adalia gave him a tight hug, then left to find Visari. Roykur turned to one of the manor's maids, who was passing by. "If you could please inform the stable master, I shall visit the palace immediately."

The maid bobbed a curtsy and went off to do as she was told. Roykur snuck through the kitchens and grabbed a piece of cheese from a wheel, a few pieces of dried meat, and a couple slices of bread, and shoved them into a small satchel. He didn't have time to eat a proper breakfast, but he would have plenty on the carriage ride to the palace.

Roykur stepped outside just as the driver brought around a simple but sturdy carriage pulled by a single draugker. This beast was of a slimmer variety, although still six and a half feet at the large hump on its back. The horns corkscrewed a good three feet, straight back from the head. A young man sat in the driver's seat, well dressed in finer clothes, the kind Roykur would never choose to wear. However, Visari ran the household day-to-day, and she made sure the house, new as it was, presented a respectable air, even if Roykur had little care for it.

Adalia jumped into the carriage, setting down an armful of baubles, and started shoving them into her satchel. "Didn't want you leaving without me, plus Mother is not happy."

Roykur let out a light chuckle while pulling Adalia's notes from his pocket. The carriage slowly pulled away from the manor.

The manor houses of the nobility were not far removed from the city proper, and the road twisted through a thick swath of trees designed to obscure the manors from the city and vice versa. The carriage broke the line of trees, and the clattering of wooden wheels on cobblestone began.

The carriage entered the city of Ver'a'saile at the surface level of this engineering wonder, carved straight into the mountain itself. The vibrant hustle of the city engulfed them. Countless shops and carts were crammed together along the road, while performers and craftsman occupied every alley and street corner.

Roykur watched a wagon of goods descend a ramp down the labyrinth of tunnels and caves that ran beneath the surface, teeming with as much life as the towers soaring into the sky. He tried to play a little game every time he came into the city, counting as many of the mingled shops, houses, taverns, factories, hospitals, and workshops scattered and stacked along the height of each tower. He tried to make sense of the chaos, create a pattern of the buildings across every level of the city. The only one he could come up with had been that people enjoyed living close to their work.

On the northern ridge, the city existed mostly underground, the towers delving deep below the surface level, while those on the southern slopes were primarily aboveground. The carriage passed into the Old Town district but quickly veered off the surface level onto a ramp leading up and northeast to the palace. The draugker's claws dug into the ramp, pulling the carriage up without breaking stride, showing off the true strength of the majestic creatures.

They went up and down along platforms, bridges, and ramps that connected each tower to the other. They passed by thousands of people moving on the complex network of pathways, going about their lives through the vast heights and depths of the city.

In contrast to the manor estates, the buildings in the city relied more heavily on metal. The large, multistoried buildings varied in style and architecture throughout the city, a mix of old and new construction. Other buildings stood out for different reasons. Roykur could immediately locate a population of Vogels in some sections of the district because of their entirely unique designs. Roykur spotted a grouping of Vogel houses on the third upper level. Their blockish, uniform homes stacked neatly together, twelve fitting in a space that would have only held three Human dwellings.

The small, intelligent species handled most of the mining operations, plumbing, and new tunnel excavation, and held an affinity for jewelry making. The Vogels had helped construct the city, and despite being integral to its history, the small, furry folk isolated themselves from Humans and Treemolkvar. Unburdened with emotion, they found the other citizens of the city frivolous in their endeavors. They preferred to communicate in their native language, an indiscernible series of clicks made with their mandibles.

Roykur's carriage traveled along Crescent Road, inclining through the heart of the city. The carriage gradually gained elevation as it moved toward the palace. A heavy deluge smacked down on the roof. Adalia and Roykur broke away from their notes to watch the city absorb the brief geyser fall, a frequent occurrence. A few street vendors and food stands secured cover under a higher-level bridge while the rest huddled beneath their fixed umbrellas.

Looking out the window, Roykur glimpsed the massive aquifer built into the mountain, far above the city to the west. Constructed near a series of consistently high-volume geysers, it provided the only source of water to the city. The water ran through the ground and into piping, which went to the city plumbing. Without the ingenious design of the aquifer, a city on this scale would not have been possible. Small villages outside the city always formed around smaller geysers, creating miniature systems of their own to have some sort of access to water.

The only exception was the city of Saft'don, which sat on the top of a massive inert geyser, miles wide.

The citizens of Saft'don claimed their geyser to be bottomless, that it connected to the watery core of the Erden. Saft'don's people seemed strange to Roykur, living on the edge of an endless pit of water. He took baths, of course, but the thought of being surrounded by *that* much made his skin crawl.

Roykur shivered and turned back to the notes he was holding. There was a reason the rest of the sane world waited for the water to come back down.

The palace came into sight. It was built on the far eastside of the city, carved directly out of the mountain, where it overlooked the rest of the sprawling metropolis. The tall towers and bridges ended abruptly near the palace, leaving it isolated from the network of public access, save for the Crescent Road.

The carriage pulled closer to the only entrance, the main gate, which stood open. A courtyard lay beyond, where a small contingent of the Royal Guard and a palace steward met the carriage. The steward eyed Roykur's driver disapprovingly as Roykur exited the carriage without assistance. However, Xandar had learned the hard way that Roykur enjoyed being treated like he was helpless even less than he enjoyed his workers adhering to needless ceremony.

The Royal Guard wore the traditional armor that Roykur had worn during the war with the Kolkrabba. Their heavy plate was polished to a metallic sheen, with gold inlaid in the etched designs on the breastplate, helm, and small buckler. They all held broad-bladed halberds that seemed extremely unwieldy, yet Roykur had zero doubts the guards could be highly effective with them.

The steward turned a forced smile on Roykur. "Welcome, Lord Roykur of House Heimvelt. You honor us with your presence today."

"Uh huh." Roykur ran his hand through the draugker's wool as he walked by. It pressed its thick neck against him and grumbled. He scratched up near the horns, and a hind leg thumped heavily. "Thank you for pulling us all that way, buddy."

The steward cleared his throat, and Roykur rolled his eyes, taking his time pulling a few small coins out of a leather fold. He handed it to Xandar, and the carriage pulled away to a sheltered stable.

The protected courtyard was decorated with potted fir trees, and the ground kept the natural granite, which was polished into a slick surface that reflected the morning light. The front of the palace itself rose several stories, with the tail end of its architecture fading into the mountain it was carved from. The effect was quite mesmerizing —the building appeared to be almost sinking into the rock face.

Roykur and Adalia were led into the palace by the steward and two of the guards. The long hallway floor and walls were made of pure white marble, with deep red tapestries hung evenly spaced throughout. Every hallway they passed seemed similarly designed, and the sheer brilliance of it still amazed Roykur, always making him feel as if he had entered another realm.

After a few twists and turns, he was brought to a small room, at least as far as rooms in the palace went—it was nearly the size of Roykur's banquet hall. Inside was a heavy curved wooden table stained completely black, a stark contrast to the pure white surrounding it. An array of elegant, cushioned chairs bordered the outer edge table, all facing toward a smaller round table just on the other side. A single glass flask rested there, filled with a luminescent yellow liquid.

A good many of the council's other members were already seated, waiting impatiently for the meeting to begin. A low din rolled around the room, heavy with impactful bargains, sloshing ale glasses, and pompous boasting. The council comprised all representatives from the noble houses, and influential individuals from various city functions such as the hospital and miners—and, of course, the Witches. Lord Wisiel was here without his wife, in hushed discussions with Lady Poppit of House Chesture.

"Roykur! How're ya now, ya ol' djavul?" A portly, middle-aged man greeted him jovially, getting up from his seat and grasping Roykur's arm. His clean, fashionable outfit made an odd contrast to his scruffy face, which looked like it was perpetually dirty.

"Bode, I thought that smell was you—or a wild boar rutting so hard its hair caught fire." Roykur smiled, returning an equally firm grip.

Adalia's eyes grew wide with shock, but Bode barked out a gravelly laugh and said, "Eight gods! That's a new one."

A few of the other members turned in their seats and waved a polite acknowledgement. He waved back.

"How's the family?" said Roykur.

"Oh, whiny as ever. Son-in-law lost his job and now he's just been lying around the house. Won't be taking any job offerings from me though, mind you, too proud or some such nonsense. He thinks 'cause he married to me daughter, he gets a free pass. Only free pass is me boot, I'll tell ya that."

Roykur tried to squeeze in a word. "Well, that sounds—"

Bode continued right over him. "Then, the other day, one of me decent truffle birds got lost out on a trail, and I'd be certain it was snatched by one of 'em terloqs. Nasty fuckin' creatures, don't know why Witches like 'em so much."

Desperate to hold back the tide, Roykur gestured like he had remembered something important. "Bode, I'd like you to meet my granddaughter, Adalia."

"Pleasure to meet you," she said, taking his hand.

"Why, ain't you a pretty thing?" Bode pulled her in with his handshake, eyeing her up and down. "She sure got those tree legs of yers, Roykur."

A muscle twitched in Adalia's jaw. "Legs aren't the only thing I got from him."

Bode's impish grin faded, and he tried in vain to pull his hand out of Adalia's viselike grip. Roykur heard a pop before she released the man's purple hand.

"Strong as a draugker and feisty as a terloq. I can respect that," said Bode with a chuckle, though he rubbed at his palm.

"Lord Roykur! By Tabiat's grace, so glad to see you are alright. You gave us all quite the scare last night. It really is not my place, but should you be even attending this meeting in your condition?" said Commander Volmirk, striding into the room.

Bode hesitated a moment before shaking the commander's hand. He turned to Roykur. "Yer condition? What happened now?"

Volmirk shook his head. "He sustained a heart attack from overexerting himself. At least, that is what the Witch said."

"Damn Witch blurting out my business. I am perfectly fine, I assure you," Roykur said, straightening his posture and looking down at the Sentinel commander.

Adalia put a comforting hand on Roykur's shoulder. "Yes, but we will take it easy anyway, right Grandpa?"

"Don't ye be listening to that Witchy nonsense. Ye got two toes in the grave already, friend, might as well do what ye want while ye can. Just like me aunt Susla. The other day she walked out in the cold in naught but her skin and . . ."

Before the stout man could continue his incessant storytelling, the doors on the other side opened, and the king walked in. Roykur glanced at his old friend and nearly had another heart attack. Legast was young. Well, not exactly young, but he should have looked like he was nearly into his eighties, like Roykur. Instead he looked just like he had when he was in his late fifties, maybe early sixties. The deep violet doublet with gold stitching drooped significantly less on his healthier frame. This was impossible. Roykur had just seen him a week ago, and he'd had to be carted around in a wheelchair. Now he had somehow lost nearly thirty years.

From the gasps around the room, Roykur was not the only one who noticed. At least he wasn't going mad.

"Raum guide me, Yer Majesty, what sorcery is this!" Bode blurted out, ignoring any etiquette required of the meeting. However, everyone in the room was too stunned to care.

"No sorcery, Master Bode," said Legast.

"Well then, how much is it for one of those royal makeovers? I could use a few years taken off myself." Bode chuckled at his own joke and looked around the room. No one else seemed to find the comment amusing.

Legast smiled through his impatience. "Master Bode, if you would allow me more than a moment, I could address this, and we can proceed through the rest of today's discussions. In truth, this is the big announcement many of you were told to expect."

Adalia must have worried at Roykur's shock, as she guided him to his seat. Noticing his aches more acutely, he was grateful to take her assistance, and lowered himself gently. Adalia stood behind the high-backed chair, mimicking the other scribes or attendants.

However, she still shifted and glanced around, clearly nervous. Each of the members took their turn in astonishment as the last of them arrived.

The king sat down at the small round table, facing the councilmembers. The servants, having deposited the last of the spiced ales, left and closed the meeting hall doors behind them. Legast gave Roykur a very long stare. Roykur nodded to his old friend, and the king flashed a brief grin, then cleared his throat. It was almost like he had needed that small bit of solidarity before beginning.

"I am not younger. Let us get that out of the way to start. I am merely regenerating, as my chemists have put it. They have developed, through tireless research and experimentation, an elixir that returns the body to its prime state. It should only be a few more weeks until I reach my prime state. I am told that once there, I will not die of age."

Legast lifted the flask of glowing liquid from his table, and a wave of murmurs burst furiously through the councilmembers. "Please quiet down. I know you will have many questions, so let me point out some aspects of this new revelation."

He set the flask down and opened a lacquered wooden binder containing several documents. After straightening them out, he pulled some reading spectacles from a pocket. "First, a person consuming this elixir must consume another elixir every thirty days to remain in their prime state. If someone does not drink the follow-up elixir, their body will return quickly to the state their age usually reflects. For example, if I stop drinking these elixirs a few years from now, I will most likely die based on the state my body had been in.

"Second, just like every elixir, there could be the usual side effects —rejection, addiction, or alternative reactions. Luckily, I do not seem to have had any adverse effects so far. Third, because of our limited supply, we have not tested drinking the elixir too often. So, anyone with prior elixir addictions should abstain until further testing has been done. Lastly, the method for creating these elixirs is strenuous and resource heavy, so production will be slow, and stock limited.

This issue has been brought before the council to discuss how the crown should handle distribution of the elixir, whether it should be sold, and what impacts to the city we can expect. Now, to hear your thoughts, let's begin with—"

An elderly male Witch shot up from the far end of the table. "This is outrageous! You dare claim to know the secrets of making elixirs. And not just any elixir, but Leyflendi, the elixir of life, one that only exists in Treemolkvar myth. You have stolen our culture, our way of life!"

"Pipe down, Witch. You will have your turn to speak, and in a civil tone," Roykur spat across the table.

"All of you, enough. Yundlich of the Treemolkvar, you may speak. However, I ask you to refrain from further outbursts," said Legast, continuing his cool, even tone.

Yundlich took a deep breath, but he was visibly shaking. The dark midnight bark along the ridges of his ashy white face had small branches with amber leaves on the ends. They quivered with his angry tremors. "Your Majesty, the secrets of elixir making are sacred. Not to mention the treaty that was signed many centuries ago."

"That treaty stated Humans would not steal the secrets of elixirs from your people. It said nothing of discovering a method all our own," said Legast.

Yundlich scoffed. "It is not possible to make this discovery on your own."

"And yet we did."

Ripiq, a thin, stately woman and a representative of the merchants' guild, spoke up. "Sir, if I may. Like Yundlich, I have my concerns. If people start living forever, there is no telling what this will do to the economy of Ver'a'saile. We could be looking at a total collapse."

"And what about the population?" said Halot, a balding man from the association of agriculture. "There just isn't enough food. We would have to stop having children to keep everyone from starving."

"Ye just told me I can look young and live forever. This is the best damn news I've ever heard!" Bode chimed in. A small cheer in agreement came from a few representatives of the factory unions, the engineering assembly, and the platform crews.

"What does the representative of the Vogels think about this, Rongeur?" Legast said, turning to the smallest member in the room.

Roykur eyed the Vogel representative, who sat in a specially carved seat, tall enough for the small creature to see above the table. The tallest of his people stood no more than three feet, and Rongeur was no exception. However, the large, pointed ears atop his head accounted for another foot of height. His saucer eyes were vaguely Human but seemed to take up most of his horizontally elongated face. Two long, furry prehensile tails protruded from between his shoulder blades and through a finely tailored suit. Like all other Vogels, Rongeur's mouth contained two sets of long, insect-like mandibles that were more familiar with clicks than Human speech.

He clicked his mandibles several times before switching to the common tongue. The voice was void of emotion and mechanically precise. "The Vogels do not drink elixirs, they have no effect on us, and we will continue to work with Humans and the Treemolkvar, regardless of how long you live. The Vogels do not have an opinion on this."

At barely shoulder height with the rest of the elderly members, Rongeur sat back in his chair, tails resting over the back. A moment went by before Yundlich jumped in again.

"We had an understanding! Regardless of this elixir's implications, you had no right to create one without the consent of the Treemolkvar. The treaty stopped the endless violence. This will start the bloodshed anew!" Yundlich punctuated his last point with a fist planted firmly on the table.

Legast narrowed his eyes at that fist, and his jaw clenched. Then he relaxed and smiled. "My dear man, we have done no such thing. Our treaty is still unbroken. We had several Treemolkvar involved with testing of this elixir, and they agreed it to be wholly different from the kind the Treemolkvar craft. Though they were just as disturbed as you, they confirmed that it in no way was a theft of your secret methods."

A low muttering started at that news.

"Impossible!" cried Yundlich.

"Are you calling me a liar?" The room went silent. Legast's smile was fixed—a practiced politician.

Yundlich's anger was undercut by a few quick, nervous glances around the quiet room. "No, but give me their names. I would know the traitors to my kind."

The king shook his head. "Unfortunately, a stipulation to their help was their anonymity, I assume for this very reason. If you'd like, you can be the first to have a sample for you and your people to examine once further production is underway."

"We do not want this abomination." Yundlich's voice rose, and his fist trembled on the table. "I will not sit here and have my culture disgraced and my people mocked! I shall hear no more of these insults." He raised the fist above his shoulder. "I motion for this 'elixir' to be destroyed immediately."

"I *motion* for you to show our king due respect. The king makes the decisions for this city, not this council," said Roykur, his own hands now curled into fists on the table.

"Not yet, but soon, and we should have increased weight in these decisions if the transition is going to be smooth," Lord Wisiel said, then cleared his throat. "Assuming the transition is still happening? Your decision hasn't changed along with your sudden youthfulness?"

"You are correct, Lord Wisiel. This council will rule without a king, regardless of my physical disposition. Well, I am looking forward to discussing the details further. We shall go into all your expected impacts and recommendations for the elixir based on your positions and experience after a brief respite. If you will excuse me for a moment, Lord Roykur, Commander Volmirk." Legast stood gracefully and walked toward the door he had entered through.

Roykur struggled to push his chair out in time to rise with the rest of the council, and he felt his frustration flair, still hot from his outburst. Adalia, caught off guard, fumbled about, trying in vain to pull out the chair like the valets were doing for the other senior members, and only succeeded in nearly knocking the thing out from underneath him. He wrestled his way to his feet and pushed the chair back harshly, as if it were at fault and not his failing limbs.

"Sorry, I didn't know I was supposed to be ready," said Adalia, looking mortified.

Roykur turned to her, and his temper flickered out. "No, not at all. I just got my leg stuck."

He knew he had a short temper; it had served him well for many years, but he did his best to not unleash it on his granddaughter. In hindsight, he wished he had taken that approach with Oskur.

Adalia, Roykur, and Volmirk followed the king out into a massive open hall littered with ornate furniture. Wide twin curved stairs led to a balcony, open to the fresh air. Roykur took his time on the stairs, with Adalia matching his pace. She glanced around, obviously monitoring him, like she always climbed stairs at the speed of growing grass. Roykur's knees clicked loudly on the last few steps, and he had to take a moment, huffing at the top. The glass doors swung open, and a cool fresh air washed over him, a relief from the stuffy meeting room.

Legast leaned on the railing, looking out across the sprawling city. "I love this view in the morning."

Roykur rested his back on the railing next to the king. "What, by the wisdom of Raum, was that? Just casually drop immortality. Plus, you expect that room of idiots will figure how to not let it destroy the city? Normal elixirs are bad enough. I hate to say this, but I agree with the Witch. This is a bad idea."

"Stop whining, you fucking grouch. I really didn't ask for your opinion. I just wanted you to hear the announcement before it went public—and to do you a favor." Legast's poised tone had fallen away.

"Nice to see your newfound youth hasn't stopped you from yammering on endlessly. Just spit it out," said Roykur.

Commander Volmirk shifted back and forth on his feet, clearly uncomfortable with the informality. Adalia, however, had seen this exchange often growing up and was shaking her head, clearly trying to disguise her amusement at seeing her superior's superior squirm.

"Commander Volmirk here is having issues closing his current investigation. I recommended he request your help on the case, and he insisted his Conservators could handle it. Well, after a month of no results, I am officially demanding we put your retired ass back to work. I figured you could use a break from herding my draugkers."

An enormous grin spread across Roykur's face. "Ah Legs, you know me too well. This will be good for me. Put some youth back into me . . . the old-fashioned way."

Commander Volmirk sputtered. "Your Majesty, no offense to Lord Roykur, but he can barely survive one of his own parties, much less take on a murder investigation."

"I'll have you know I felled a tree on my own yesterday," said Roykur sardonically.

"Then you proceeded to have a heart attack." Commander Volmirk gave him a defiant stare.

"What? Roykur, is this true?" said Legast, looking stricken with concern.

Roykur waved it off. "Hardly. I was just overwhelmed by the day's events."

Adalia snapped to attention. "Grandpa—er, uh, Lord Roykur collapsed. His heart had stopped working correctly for several minutes before we could get him settled."

Roykur squinted over at his granddaughter, not quite believing what he heard. Still at attention, Adalia subtly inclined her head toward the commander, and Roykur rolled his eyes.

"This is why the timing of this elixir is perfect. You don't have much time. You have to drink it, and soon." Legast reached into a pouch at his belt and produced a much smaller flask than the one on the table. The yellow fluid still glowed faintly in the brightness of morning.

Roykur put his hand up to stop his friend. "No. No elixirs. Especially not this one. I have no desire to live forever, my friend. I have led a good life, and I will accept it when my time comes."

There was a glimmer of sorrow before the king nodded. "Take it with you, anyway. In case you change your mind. Do me this favor?"

With a deep sigh, Roykur took the flask and slipped it into his coat pocket.

"Roykur will not take over this investigation. He will be there to consult and advise the Conservators," Legast said with a significant look at Roykur before turning to Volmirk. "However, I expect you, Commander, to accommodate Roykur. He will have the full might of the Sentinels at his disposal. Is that clear?"

"Of course, Your Majesty." Volmirk's tone went flat, and his expression and posture snapped back to his usual professionalism.

"There is one thing, Legs—I want my granddaughter to assist me and the Conservators," said Roykur.

Volmirk's eyes bulged at the request. "She's barely even a Sentinel. She's not had her first assignment. This is not how my organization works!"

"Done," Legast said without hesitation, and strolled back into his palace, leaving Roykur, Adalia, and Volmirk standing alone on the balcony. The commander stood there, face flushed, staring at the way the king had gone.

"Shall we meet you at the garrison? Let's say early this afternoon?" Roykur asked with a fixed grin on his face. Volmirk just nodded solemnly. Roykur winked at his granddaughter, then strode back toward the stairs.

CHAPTER 3

REAL JOBS

Hundreds of kerosene lamps burned brightly in the evening hour, providing illumination for every story of the towering buildings and the bustling cobbled streets below. Activity in the city waned as night fell, yet a life of its own blossomed in the light of the moons. Crowds of wealthy, well-dressed couples traveled in tight groups or in carriages, likely headed for one party or another. Then there were those who lurked in the darkening shadows, like Teufel, ready to take advantage of the blissfully unaware individuals of high society.

Teufel stared up at the three moons, each in varying phases. They gave off far too much light tonight for his liking, especially on a night when he had to work, which was most nights.

The chilled autumn wind whipped around him in a gust, and he pulled the oversized coat tighter. All his clothes were too big for him. He was small for fifteen, very small, but in truth they did not fit because they were made for someone else, the original owner. All very fine pieces, an embroidered deep red vest and gray jacket, both hidden beneath the heavy wool overcoat, which he'd had to cut for it to end at his calves. That was the style. He only had one other change of clothes, so this outfit, despite its finery, was worn, tattered, and far from clean. Underneath, someone might think Teufel starved; skinny did not quite describe his skeletal appearance. He ate well, but it seemed no matter how much he ate, he never seemed to put on any weight.

Stepping out from behind the shadows, Teufel felt the moonlight bathe his midnight skin, and he had to shield his amber eyes while they adjusted. He took off into the street with a determined pace and direction. Focusing on his feet, he guided himself with his peripherals directly toward a group of twenty partygoers who were lost in their loud conversation. Teufel nimbly slipped into the middle of the group, making muffled apologies and pardons as he passed through. His small hands had deftly glided into as many pockets and purses as he had time for, and he quickly disappeared down a side street. He looked over his spoils, but his masterful talent had produced little more than three copper coins, a button, and a piece of paper that looked to be a receipt. He sighed and stepped out onto a different street.

Winding through alleys and down smaller streets, he contemplated leaving the surface. The upper and lower levels were less risky but far less profitable. However, the purses were light tonight, and the occasional roaming Sentinel was making him jumpy. No. He had begged for the chance to skim on the surface. He would be damned if he bailed now.

He continued his practiced maneuvers for another hour, until he noticed a small gathering of people at the base of a tower. A glint of polished metal poked out from among the crowd's midst, and he now recognized the people's angry gestures. A kid of no more than eight was staring at Teufel. He started tugging at his mother's coat, pointing directly at him. *Ah, shit.*

Teufel sprinted back down the side street he had just come from and squeezed onto a busy street. He immediately slowed to the flow of the traffic.

Minutes ticked by. Teufel listened to the regular din of the crowd and clatter of wagon wheels—no sharp whistles or charging Sentinels. He scratched his short, frizzy hair and frowned at his meager earnings for the night. Best not to not push his luck.

Splitting off from the main street, he took the twisting ramp that wrapped itself around the building and up to the first upper level of the city. He crossed several bridges to other buildings, and after just a few minutes of walking, he veered down a narrow passage that stood between several shops. The passage ended at a fitted iron door.

He knocked, and a thin slider at the top opened. Teufel had to clear his throat for the person to look down in his direction. The slider snapped closed, and the door opened, revealing another long hallway.

"Evening, Tiny," Teufel said to the guard. The man, who had to crouch to avoid touching the ceiling and looked like he would have difficulty fitting through the door he guarded, merely grunted in acknowledgement as Teufel strolled in. He pushed through the door at the end of the hallway and was greeted by the raucous jubilance of the bar's patrons.

"Look who it is—the master thief in the flesh," said a man, sitting at a table in the corner. He threw a hand of cards on the table, and the rest of his companions groaned loudly. The man scraped his earnings back with a grin.

Teufel changed his careful tiptoeing to a saunter, like he had seen all the greats do after a big job—a certain style, a confident step. Keeping his shoulders square, he let his arms hang loose, his thumbs hooked on his belt. He had grown up admiring the people in this sticky bar. They were family—well, better than family. They actually liked him.

"Evening, boss," said another man, inclining his head. Teufel nodded back as he passed by. Boss was a pet name the members of the Jaspers had given him. He had loved it when he was a little younger, but didn't much care for it now. Complaining about a nickname would only get you a worse one, though.

"Let me buy you a drink, boss," said a frightfully ugly woman with an eyepatch. She gestured to a seat next to her. Teufel hid his discomfort at the predatory, one-eyed stare and accepted the invitation. With his stature, he practically had to climb onto the bar stool, and once there, he had to sit as far forward as possible to rest his arms on the bar. The woman watched him with a grin, and when he finished, she slid a tankard of ale over to him. He stopped it, and a good amount sloshed over the rim, soaking his hand. Grimacing slightly, he shook the liquid off, unintentionally spattering the man next to him.

"Hey! Watch it there, ya little brat!" The man slurred his words. Teufel, without hesitating, swung his tankard so a good half flew out and hit the man directly in the face.

The man shook the beer out of his scraggy beard and aimed a right hook at Teufel's head. With how drunk he was, he didn't have the stability nor the balance to execute his maneuver. Teufel merely leaned back, and the punch sailed past his face, causing the man to launch himself out of the seat and onto the floor. The one-eyed woman exploded with raspy laughter, and the drunk man stayed on the floor, groaning. Teufel took his first sip, fighting hard to not make a disgusted face at that sharp, bitter taste. *How does anyone enjoy drinking this?*

"Oh boss, by the way, *the boss* said he wanted to see you when you got in," said the woman.

Teufel slid off the bar stool, careful to not step on the man on the floor, who appeared to have fallen asleep.

"Thanks for the ale, Marge. Best not to keep him waiting." Teufel walked toward a side door, his palms growing sweaty as he approached. These conversations never turned out well for him.

"Buying you a drink is worth every copper. You never finish your drink, and something hilarious is bound to happen. It's a win-win," Marge called after him with a smile, revealing far too many missing teeth. She raised his cup in a salute and pounded back the remaining contents.

Teufel stepped in and closed the door behind him, the sounds of the bar muffled within the storeroom. He passed the tall shelves that held casks of ale and wine, some with smaller bottles of spirits. In the far back of the room, a tall, muscular man with dark skin like Teufel's leaned on a table, counting stacks of gold coins. A fortune, to be sure. Beside him at the table sat a Vogel, his fur speckled with browns and whites. He was wearing large spectacles and writing in a ledger book.

"Hey Pop, you wanted to see me?" Teufel's voice broke them of their concentration, and both looked at him with some annoyance.

"Damn, do you have the last count, Sekrymour?"

The Vogel nodded and clicked its mandibles. Without looking up, Teufel's father began counting again as he spoke. "Manage to get anything this time, or do you think I won't throw you out?"

"I got two silver and thirteen coppers." Teufel pulled the wad of papers, lint, and coins from his pocket.

"Thirteen and two." Leondal said the word without expression, and stopped counting. He looked at Teufel for a long moment. Then his tone turned serious, commanding. "You're a man now. It's time you quit picking pockets like a child and take on an actual job. You are going to pay your membership dues to the Jaded Jaspers like every other member out there or take the boot."

That was the way a member got kicked out of the Jaspers. No money, naked save for a single boot, and depending on the reason, a few broken bones as well.

"That's the same deal everyone else gets," he continued, "and I won't have you thinking you get any special treatment just because you're blood or because you're so damn tiny, ya hear me?"

Teufel started to argue. "I eat less than the average—"

"Shut up." The icy stare didn't give room for disobedience, but his coiled intensity, thick with violence, dared Teufel to try.

Teufel clenched his teeth and stared down at his scuffed shoes.

Satisfied with the lack of protest, Leondal relaxed and pulled out an envelope with a broken wax seal.

"This one is simple and pays really well. Anyone out there"—he motioned toward the bar and its patrons—"would kill for this job, so don't say I don't give you chances. Get this done quick and you'll have enough to stay square for a while." He slid the envelope across the table, and Teufel picked it up and shoved it quickly into his jacket pocket. "That there is a map to a scroll worker's apartment and instructions to get inside. Some rich fancy prick wants documents from a chest. Blackmail, if you ask me. Bring all of them back for the client and you get one gold piece."

"One gold piece? That's not enough to pay my dues. I thought you said I would be square with the Jaspers for a while?" Teufel asked with some confusion. He winced as he heard the whine in his own voice. He could see the immediate annoyance from his father in response.

"Oh aye, you will be. The client is offering to pay much more than that, but the Jaspers are keeping the rest as payment for your previous and next two membership dues." Teufel gaped a bit at that. More money than he had ever owned in his life. The membership dues paid for two hot meals a day and a bed for a month, which was not cheap. Ale was extra, but he didn't care for the taste. What would he do with a whole gold piece that he didn't have to spend on food?

As if he could read his thoughts, Leondal said, "Now don't go spending that gold piece before you've even earned it. The job needs to be done tonight—you better get at it. Oh, and remember the first rule?"

"Don't get caught," Teufel recited mechanically.

"Good. Now get out of here." The man returned to his counting, murmuring figures to Sekrymour.

Teufel left the storeroom and repeated back some farewells to the bar's patrons and fellow Jasper members.

"Be back soon, Tiny," he said at the end of the hallway.

Another grunt, and Tiny pulled back the door. Teufel sauntered out, thumbs still hooked on his belt. The second he emerged from the doorway, the chill late-night breeze closed in around him, and his forced swagger vanished as he clutched desperately at his coat, trying his best to keep off the cold.

Pulling out the envelope, Teufel read through the job specifics. The apartment was on the third sub-level, and nearly three blocks northeast. At least bottom-side, he wouldn't have to deal with this cursed wind.

Teufel moved to the edge of the first upper-level platform and descended the spiraling ramp. The building the Jaspers used to house their outfit had been picked for its access to all eight upper levels and five lower levels, a very popular building, and the public traffic concealed their hideout well. They used to have a spot in the Sky Garden district, to the south, but all above ground, which made it difficult to take on lower-level jobs.

By the time Teufel stepped off the ramp on the third sub-level, the chill had faded. The underground roads were spaced just like the ones on the surface level, with enough room for two wagons to pass by each other. The building Teufel moved down on poked out of the stone walls with ramps carved out on the sides. Just like every level, the farther away it got from the surface, the less well off the neighborhoods tended to be.

Besides that, the sub-levels had a unique subculture that the surface and upper levels did not have. The underground didn't get any direct sunlight, so the locals had very little incentive to adhere to normal hours. It was also much warmer. With practically no wind, Teufel relaxed his death grip on his coat. The street bustled with activity on both sides, and even the small mom-and-pop shops kept their doors open, oblivious to the late hour. Teufel's eyes wandered over the storefronts as he passed by, curious what he might spend his first gold piece on.

After thirty minutes of walking, Teufel finally arrived at the tower building indicated on the instructions. The building had many storefronts, and stairs leading to apartments above them. He was looking for a particular set. In this part of the sub-level, the sizeable crowds had dwindled to a few individuals glancing through shop windows, shopkeepers waiting in the doorframe for potential customers, and people milling about the decks of their apartments. Teufel used a pathway to circle the tower building until he noticed the scroll worker's shop, which faced west. This was the one. There was a small apartment above, and the light in the little shop showed it was open for business.

He took a deep breath. *Let's hope whoever lives here is working and not home.*

Following the instructions he'd been given, Teufel casually climbed the stairs, then felt around the bottom edge of the doorframe. When he touched the right spot, there was a mechanical click, and a piece slid away, revealing a little carved nook hiding a key. Teufel raised his brows and glanced around before sliding the key into the lock.

Very fancy. Did not think that was going to work, if I'm being honest.

The door creaked open, and he peered in briefly before realizing how that might look to people walking by. He stepped in, closing it behind him. There were no lights in the room, and Teufel felt around blindly for something he could use to see. His hand felt a wall dial and he turned it, hearing the familiar clicks of strikers. After the third turn, three wall lamps flickered to life, illuminating the small apartment.

The space was immaculate: a bookshelf, a small desk, one plain rug across the floor, and a wood-burning stove in the corner. Searching through the common area, he noticed a fine layer of dust on books and chairs. The apartment was neat but unused. Most likely, the owner spent all his time in the shop below. That was good for Teufel, and he let out a deep sigh, knowing there was less of a chance of being interrupted during this burglary. His initial search of the area was unsuccessful, but he wasn't expecting to find a chest just lying in the common room.

There were two doors. He opened the first, which revealed another set of stairs, this one directly to the back of the shop. Closing it carefully, he went for the other.

The second door stuck. Teufel yanked it hard, and a seal of wax around the edges he had not noticed shattered, sending flakes all about him. Then it hit him—the foulest smell he had ever experienced. He quickly covered his face and gagged, barely holding back the vomit. Peeling open the door, he forced himself to look into the room.

A rotting body dangled from the ceiling.

Without taking a second longer to look at the horrific visage before him, Teufel sprinted from the apartment and down the stairs. He almost made it to the main street before he emptied his stomach on the walkway. Then he ran.

CHAPTER 4

ALWAYS ONE MORE

The table was filled with stacks upon stacks of folders, each containing detailed notes, medical reports, and explicit depictions of scenes and evidence. These were everything from the most prolific killer of all time, when he was active nearly twenty years ago. Pinned along the wall was an organized timeline of the more recent murders, with all the supporting documentation attached beneath corresponding dates.

Roykur breathed in the stale air of the large conference room and sipped his bitter black tea, then let out a nostalgic sigh. From the corner of his vision, he saw Adalia scooping another helping of honey into her tea while blinking with exaggerated effort to keep her eyes from involuntarily drooping. They had spent the entire afternoon and evening poring over recent case files. It was now nearly midnight. Adalia had been less than thrilled on the carriage ride, mumbling the entire way about special treatment, which was understandable. Normally, he would have let her work her way through, as this would make her stand out in the Sentinels, and not in a good way. However, he had seen men and women stuck in one division their entire lives, and he had spent too much time preparing his granddaughter for her to be wasted in the Patrol Division.

Despite her initial reluctance, Adalia had taken to the case files like a wildfire in a valley with no geyser. She'd finished with the recent files before dinner and had now almost gone through the entire archives of the old Husk Slayer. Roykur smiled proudly and glanced around the room. His smile curved into a sneer as he saw the other three Conservators assigned to the case yawning and looking half asleep. Each had a single file in front of them, untouched for the past hour. They were assigned to this case because they were, supposedly, the best Volmirk had. Roykur had seen these three novices in his lectures before, half interested and even less humble with the few minor cases they had managed to solve.

That wasn't going to work for an investigation like this.

When Volmirk stepped back into the room, Roykur gave him one of his best glares, then cleared his throat. "Fritch, Binjek, and Simune, summarize your findings for the commander."

They bolted upright in their chairs, completely unaware that someone had entered the room, much less their commander.

"Sir, why is this old bag of bones in here dragging along his little pet?" Simune said, running his hands through his hair. Standing up, he took a step toward the door as if he was prepared to walk out but stopped, seeing Volmirk's stern gaze. "We've spent the entire day catching them up on the recent murders. They're wasting time that could be spent catching the killer."

"How about you stop wasting *my* time and give me your damn report?" said Volmirk.

Simune fumed for a moment longer, but he moved to the time-line on the wall. "*Sir,* there have been four murders in the last three weeks. The scene has been the same in all four. The victim was cut in half and drained of blood, and the liver, heart, and kidneys were missing. This is where the similarities between the Husk Slayer and this new killer end."

Binjek stood up and chimed in. "There has been an unidentified, yellow, saltlike substance along the wounds of the victims. Victims were all located on the surface, in wealthy neighborhoods, and all women. Most importantly, they have never been Husks. In fact, they weren't even born during the war with the Kolkrabba. We believe our killer to be a male, probably a miner or laborer who works on one of the lower sub-levels. This individual is likely preying on young women and using the methods of a famous killer to mislead us. Despite Lord Roykur's theory about this new elixir, the rest of us believe that there is a new killer who is imitating the Husk Slayer's methods rather than the actual Husk Slayer."

Commander Volmirk nodded to himself slowly throughout the summary, then turned to Roykur. "You agree with their conclusion?"

"I would rather gargle my own piss for three hours straight than agree with that load of nonsense," Roykur said with exaggerated disgust. From behind the commander, he could hear Adalia snort loudly. "First off, Volmirk, there isn't a lick of information in these recent reports about the scene, regarding the surroundings. I am sitting here imagining our victim floating in an empty void."

"It's at the end, *Grandpa,* or did you forget how to read?" Simune said, his voice flaring into a pitch.

"A small room, brown walls, small bed," Roykur read out loud. He threw the report onto the table in front of Simune. "Thrilling detail. Clearly you failed to read any of my *well*-written reports, or you would know that the Husk Slayer constantly evolved his methods but always left a signature somewhere at the scene. Did you even look in these rooms at all?"

Simune's face flushed with anger, but he didn't respond. Instead, he took his seat again, waving for Roykur to continue.

"Oh, by your leave then," Roykur said with a sharp bow in Simune's direction. He regretted the unnecessary jab at the young man as pain pinched and throbbed at his lower back. He pushed himself straight with some effort and saw Simune's smug face, which only soured his mood further. He continued, "Every Husk Slayer kill has been improving, becoming more efficient. He started out just harvesting organs and blood, and he made quite the mess. Then he got more efficient at his collection, and eventually we didn't have pools of blood at every scene. He started adding his own minor flares, cutting them in half and stitching each half of the body closed, and then he added hanging them from the ceiling. Each addition was sloppy at first, but he refined it. These yellow crystals are most likely part of his next addition."

Roykur took a long sip of his tea while keeping his eyes on Simune, just to make sure he did not interrupt. "As for your victims, it is not unheard of for killers to change victim type. For the Husk Slayer, it is almost expected. It's pretty obvious. There are no more Husks."

Adalia cleared her throat, and the room turned their attention to her. Roykur had not seen Conservator Fritch move, but he now sat beside Adalia. A fresh bagel lay divided between the two of them, smattered with a cheesy spread. Adalia finished her chewing and said, "Pardon, why did the Husk Slayer target people who had been Husks? I can't seem to find the report that mentions it."

Roykur opened his mouth to explain, but Fritch spoke first. "It's not your fault. It was only mentioned in one specific report."

The conservator reached into the small crate of case files and deftly plucked a folder without breaking his eye contact with Adalia. "Here you go, though. It seems you were only a few reports away."

He smiled pleasantly at her as he handed it over. Adalia took the file and returned the smile. Roykur narrowed his eyes at the two of them, and when Adalia finally glanced at him after a period of silence, she blushed furiously.

Adalia read the report for a moment, and her face became disgusted. *"They turned against us once—they will do it again. They are the enemy."* She set the file down with a delicate reverence. "Well, I guess that was a pretty obvious message, but they didn't choose to be Husks."

"No one chose to be turned into a mindless slave, and no one knows why those people were affected in the first place," said Fritch.

Roykur chimed in, "Yes, after that first declaration, we interviewed the family and friends, and we discovered they had been Husks during the fight against the Kolkrabba, and every victim since has had that same message. Well, not every victim."

"Here we go," Simune moaned.

"Just listen, you little fucker, and you might actually learn something!" Roykur realized he was nearly screaming, and cleared his throat. His hands shook, but whether from his temper or age, he wasn't sure.

"By the gods . . ." Adalia muttered not so quietly under her breath. She gave Simune a disapproving glare.

The conservator threw his hands up and leaned back against the wall. "We're all listening, Grandpa. Go ahead."

Voice hoarse, Roykur began, "There was a murder before the Husk Slayer wrote that message, which I believe to be his actual first murder. A triggering event, a personal tragedy, that caused him to lash out before he had planned for his crusade."

"However, the murder was completely different," said Binjek, glancing down out at his notes. "A young couple was torn apart in their home. Nothing was taken, and they were never Husks."

"So, he didn't keep the blood or organs of these victims, unlike the rest?" Adalia asked with some confusion. "Then how do you know that these were his kills if they were so completely different from the rest of his murders?"

"Two things," Roykur responded. "There were letters written in blood along the floor, the same style as his signature declaration. A bit thin, I know, but then years later, a similar event occurred, with the victims torn apart. It was clear he had come intending to use his usual methods, but again, something had set him off, and he lost his characteristic control. We found bits of twine he had been using at the time, a shattered glass jar that we assumed was brought for collection, and there were letters written on the wall."

"What were the letters written on each of those scenes?" asked

Adalia, enveloped in details Roykur had always thought her too young to hear.

"E N I A L I S and R U K S O," he recited from memory. "They were terribly smudged and—"

"See, Commander? We've just been playing catch-up this whole time. We need to finish contacting witnesses and looking into this elixir killer connection," Simune interjected.

"Refreshing the facts of the case is never a waste of time, but yes, back to the matter at hand," said Volmirk. "We will not assume anything, nor will we ignore any leads, no matter how small. The entire city, including the king, is closely watching this case, so we better do the best godsdamned job we can."

Volmirk looked pointedly at his conservators and then at Roykur. "No part of this investigation will be disregarded. Conservator Fritch, you will work to figure out any pattern in the new victims—interview the families again. Conservator Simune, you will take the lead on the elixir killer angle. Find the connection, and we could find both killers.

"Fritch, Roykur and Adalia will assist you with your part. Take this opportunity to explain the finer points of being a conservator to Sentinel Adalia." Volmirk turned to Roykur. "Not to say you haven't already done a wonderful job passing down your experience. However, aspects of the job have changed since you worked here."

"It would be my pleasure," Fritch said, smiling first at Volmirk, then at Roykur. They locked eyes; the conservator's held a defiant challenge. Or was it a mischievous expression? Either way, Roykur didn't like it, and he narrowed his brow.

He was about to object when Volmirk spoke first. "Enough about that. I want all of you to start at the location of the latest murder and make your various ways from there."

A young woman, a few years older than Adalia, burst through the set of oak doors in the conference room. "Commander, you asked me to only disturb you if—"

Volmirk sighed. "If there was another murder."

There was a long silence in the room as everyone shared distant stares at nothing. Roykur finally broke the silence. "Well, at least I won't have to rely on your wretched reports for the state of our killer's disposition."

The attempt at grim humor was more out of habit, and it failed to pierce the tension.

Volmirk tightened his loose leather belt. "Disregard my previous orders, Conservators. Let's go take a look at this poor djavul."

CHAPTER 5

NO ESCAPE

Teufel did not stop running until he made it all the way back to the Jasper's hideout. His thoughts were a tumult of panic and disgust. Tiny let him through the door, and he sprinted to the back, ignoring any inquiries from the usual patrons. Bursting into the storeroom, he found his father in the same spot he had been when he had left. *How long was I gone? An hour, two?*

"Ah, so you finished the job already? I am glad to see that you're finally stepping up and—"

"I didn't get the chest," Teufel blurted out, panic and anger boiled in his voice. Leondal moved out from behind the table and frowned.

"What?" His father's voice was flat, but his posture was that of a wild terloq about to pounce on its prey.

"There was a dead body! No one said anything about dead people. It was awful, he . . . he was hanging from the ceiling," Teufel said, the last part causing his voice to crack.

"Were you paid to gawk at a body? Were you paid to give up at the slightest inconvenience? Were you paid to foul up the job in every way possible?" With every question, Leondal's voice got louder. He had taken a step closer to Teufel, and now stood towering over his son. Teufel felt a slap across his face before he even saw his father make the motion.

The blow knocked him to the ground a few paces from where he had been standing. "You useless son of a whore! Worthless draugker shit! You are the most disappointing investment I have ever made. If I knew how pointless—nay, how much it would cost me to keep you alive this long, I would have beaten you out of your mother the day we found out she was carrying you."

Leondal grabbed Teufel before he could scramble away, slapping him hard across the other side of his face. The boy's vision swam as he tried to keep his eyes open. Then another flash of pain exploded square in his stomach, and he gasped desperately for air.

His father dropped him and turned his back, the anger seething through his teeth as he spoke. "Go back and get that chest. If you come back empty-handed, you won't get the boot. I'll kill you myself. I won't let such a failure of mine exist in this world."

He moved back to the table and started scraping coins into large bags. Teufel struggled to his feet and headed to the door, pausing for a few seconds before his breath fully returned.

Teufel arrived back at the building with the scroll worker's shop. It had taken him longer this time to find his way to the correct place. He had spent most of his attention on the shops on the way there, and in his haste to escape the horrible sight, he had lost the envelope with directions and instructions.

He stopped. Something wasn't right. On this side of the building, the street was empty, yet he could hear the sounds of distant crowds.

He rounded the outside pathway, and the distinct noise grew louder. With every step, Teufel's stomach twisted in knots.

A sizeable crowd had gathered outside the scroll worker's shop, and several Sentinels were trying to keep their curious fervor at bay. Teufel paused at the scene before him. Wagons, carriages, and people pressed in from the road, gossiping and trying to push farther to the shop to get a better look. *What am I supposed to do now?*

Despite his overwhelming anxiety, no one seemed to pay any attention to him. So, with a feigned nonchalance, he nervously crept to the side of the crowd and craned his neck to see if he could glimpse any sign of the chest he was supposed to retrieve. Teufel kept to the outer edge of the crowd—he was too small to see anything if the mass of people swallowed him.

Teufel rubbed his cold, clammy hands for what seemed like an eternity. Finally, a Sentinel emerged from the apartment holding an envelope between metal pincers, but not just any envelope—Teufel's envelope. The Sentinel wore the insignia of a captain, and he motioned over a junior Sentinel carrying a wooden box. The captain placed the envelope in the box, and the junior carried it out of sight. Teufel racked his brain for any way those instructions could be linked directly to him or the Jaspers. It seemed silly. No one signed their name on those kinds of things, and yet a spike of worry wriggled at the back of his head.

The captain turned back to the apartment door, where he was handed the simple iron-banded chest. Teufel cursed under his breath. *Where on Erden was that the whole time I was in there?*

There was no sense sticking around anymore. He made a note to just keep an eye on that chest and follow the Sentinels. Teufel's only hope now would be to take it while they transported it.

He began backing away from the crowd, side stepping the way he had come, still trying to see where the chest was being placed. Then he turned, just in time to smash his face directly into the breastplate of a looming Sentinel.

"By all the gods!" Teufel cursed loudly, holding his nose. "I think it's broken."

The Sentinel leaned down to examine his face for a moment. "I am so sorry. Move your hand so I can see."

Teufel removed his hand and blinked through his blurred vision. His eyes focused on a face inches before his own. It was a woman. Her large, light brown eyes shone with concern. Teufel took a step back to see a beautifully sharp jawline accentuated against her delicate features. He stood dumbly, his own jaw hanging open, for what seemed like forever, just staring at this gorgeous woman.

"It's not broken—you'll be fine. Where are your parents, kiddo?" the Sentinel said as she stood up straight. Teufel's transfixion broke when she prodded his still-tender nose. She stood up straight, and he realized just how tall this woman was—he had smashed his face into the lower portion of her breastplate. He stammered a bit, trying to piece together a coherent thought.

"Aww, it's okay," she said. "We'll help you find them. Are they back there with all those people?"

Teufel tried to look taller, pushing his shoulders back. "Ma'am . . . I was running a job when I got distracted by the crowd. I apologize for the—"

"Job? How old are you? You look like you can't be more than eight."

"I am almost sixteen. Please, I need to be getting back."

"Fifteen? You're barely above my waist," she said, eyebrows raised.

"Well, Your Giantess, we all can't be scraping the top of the lower level. And I said sixteen."

The Sentinel eyed him suspiciously. "What job are you working right now?"

"Deliveries."

"What do you deliver? Who did you deliver to? What's your name? What is the name of your business?" She pulled out a small pad of paper and a pen.

"Well, Sentinel, I deliver, uh, potatoes. Special potatoes. I delivered them to the owner of Leathers and Buckles, just over there." He gestured to a shop across the road. "My name is Teufel, and our business is called . . ."

The Sentinel laughed and put the pad away. "Relax, I'm just giving you a hard time. My name is Adalia. Glad to have met you, Teufel, and again, sorry about your nose. You are free to go."

Teufel's body relaxed, and he smiled back once he realized what was happening. *Maybe I can get her to help me with the chest.*

Adalia was turning to walk away, and he had to speak up to grab her attention again. "Well, I am sorry for calling you a giantess, although you are the most beautiful giantess I have ever seen." Teufel fell into a practiced awkward charm routine he reserved for getting out of trouble. It helped that her attractiveness made his awkwardness very real. "I can tell what a kind person you are as well —do you mind helping me find something? Afterward, I could buy you a meal, in thanks. Do you happen to like potatoes?"

Adalia rolled her eyes. "Potatoes? Wow, you really know how to entice the ladies. I'm working right now, but I'm sure there are plenty of ladies who would jump at the chance for a good potato."

She continued to smile broadly at Teufel, and he had difficulty discerning whether it was fondness for an adorable child or if she was responding to his less-than-subtle advances.

Then a voice boomed from behind Adalia, snapping away her focus. It came from a small group of individuals a dozen paces away along the street, which Teufel had been too distracted to see.

"Adalia! Arrest that boy, now!" an extremely tall, ancient-looking man shouted. He stood in stark contrast to the elderly shopkeeper woman and the other uniformed Sentinels around him, towering over everyone there. With his dark, wool-lined overcoat, he exuded an impressive image of authority.

It took a second longer than it should have for Teufel to switch gears, his head still full of compliments, and register the word "arrest." Luckily, it triggered an ingrained instinct in his mind before he had fully acknowledged the meaning. His muscles tensed, and his feet were automatically moving to flee. However, he had been too close to the beautiful warrior woman, and her reflexes were nearly as quick as his own. Teufel had made it only two steps away before her hard, gauntleted hands snapped around his arms. To Teufel's infinite embarrassment, he was lifted off the ground and slammed forcefully into the nearby rock wall of the lower level.

Cold steel bindings clamped down on each of his wrists. The second the bindings clicked into place, they fell to the ground with a metallic clank, and Teufel couldn't help but smile to himself. He had been placed in bindings a few times before, and always with the same result. His arms were too skinny for the restrictive metal. His mirth was short-lived. The Sentinel lady, Adalia, pressed her weight against him, his front side digging into the wall. Teufel was about to complain when he felt her thigh against his hand. His face was suddenly hot. Was this the first time he had felt a woman's leg? It was certainly all he could think about now.

He barely registered the muttered curses from under her breath, but he instantly recognized the sound of a leather belt pulled quickly from her uniform trousers. A brief spike of panic tore through him before she began wrapping it around his narrow wrists. The edges of the leather pinched at his skin, but he held in any yelps to avoid appearing more like a child in front of Sentinel Adalia, and now his own gathering crowd.

With his face flattened against the rock wall, he could do nothing more than wait and try to avoid more sharp pinches. The elderly man in the dark coat spoke more softly now that he was alongside Adalia. His deep voice still seemed to boom, echoing in Teufel's ears.

"The shopkeeper back there says she saw you leaving the victim's dwelling several hours ago, young man. Care to explain yourself?"

Everything that Teufel had been planning was dashed away. He let out a ragged sigh. Then his stomach bubbled from anxiety, and he puked.

CHAPTER 6

STICKS AND STONES

The scroll worker's apartment lingered with the stench of the long-decayed dead. Roykur stepped through to the back room to examine the scene free from the bias of the Conservators. The crumbled wax on the ground crunched beneath his boots, and he slid his fingers along the door seam and over the wax that still clung to it. How long had it taken to seal this door in this way?

Poking his head through the doorway, he saw the body of the scroll worker still hanging from the ceiling. The pale, middle-aged man was in two pieces. The hands, bound by rope, held the torso upright, while the bound feet held the legs upside down. Both halves of the man hung over his bed, the only thing in the room, which was barely large enough to contain it.

Slad, age forty-six, medium build, scroll worker. Quiet, good neighbor, no strange visitors before that kid out there. Highly doubt our witness paid that close attention, nosy but occupied with her own business.

Roykur moved closer and shifted the torso slightly so he could see the cut more clearly. Just as the recent reports had described, these bodies were not stitched like the ones when Roykur had been investigating as a Conservator. Rather, there was an opaque, yellowish substance sealing the bottom of the torso, acting as a type of cauterization. Peering through the glassy material, he could see skin and specks of blood coagulated on the other side.

He turned the body to view the other side and saw no other cuts that would show an alternate entry point. Roykur retrieved several small glass jars he had tucked into his coat pocket, and with a thin metal file, he scraped some of the yellow substance off and into the jar. Almost all the yellow crystals fell, flaking away easily and revealing smooth skin where the gaping hole should have been. He poked the flesh with the file. This new flesh was less pale than the rest of the body, as if any remaining blood had pooled after it had grown over and sealed the upper torso.

He examined the lower half of the body, hanging just beside, and found the same crystals and a similarly fresh patch of skin. Scanning the rest of the tiny bedroom, he spotted something stuck between the bed and the wall that reflected a bit of the outside light. He knelt, his knees popping loudly as he did, and pulled out a long, skinny vial. This wasn't the typical shape for an elixir—they were usually sold in round vials and almost always had an etching of the Treemolkvar on the side.

He held the vial up to his nose and recoiled. Much more potent than any elixir he had previously encountered. Definitely a strong-smelling residue, although this had a sweet honey smell behind the acrid stench, likely masking the flavor.

Roykur stepped back outside the apartment and motioned for the doctors to remove the body from the scene. The lead doctor who walked up, trailed by two others, was Doctor Arakul from the dinner party the night before.

"Doctor! I am surprised to see you here—and looking rather . . . youthful. It seems that has been going around lately."

The elderly man, now appearing maybe forty or fifty, had a look of befuddlement on his face as his eyes tried to focus from behind his spectacles. *Brilliant man, but incredibly oblivious to his surroundings.*

"Oh, Roykur! Well, who do you think helped the king with his elixir, hmm? I am the leading expert on the subject. As for why I am here, the Initiative has become quite concerned with these murders, you know. This is why we joined, after all. It's important to have everyone working this case, including yours truly."

He motioned toward the man and woman in the billowy, maroon-colored smocks of the medical profession. The woman carried a tan canvas bag, and the man had a stretcher tucked under his arm. "They are the normally assigned doctors who assist the Sentinels with their cases, but the Initiative insists that they wanted someone with 'intimate experience' out here helping to solve this murder. If you remember, I had only recently been assigned to provide medical examinations just before the murders started."

Roykur snapped his fingers. "That's right. I had forgotten you've been involved with this case nearly as long as I have. I mostly spoke with that other doctor at first—Beck, was it? Regardless, I for one am glad you are lending your valuable insight."

Doctor Arakul just chuckled. "I certainly hope my insight is still valuable. I examined the bodies, true, but that was a long time ago. The asylum is where I spend most of my days now. The needs of the living have always been more pressing for me than the mysteries of the dead." He waved away Roykur's protest before Roykur had a chance to speak. "Yes, yes. I know the importance of this work. That's why I am here."

The two other doctors emerged from the apartment, the body hoisted on the stretcher between them, a sheet covering the remains. "I am looking forward to your findings, Doctor. I collected a sample of the substance from the body. Can you have someone take this to be tested and compared with the other samples?"

"It really has been a while since you were at this game, hasn't it?" Doctor Arakul said, giving Roykur an impish smile. "Follow me and you'll see fruits of your labor, my friend."

Confused, Roykur followed the doctor, noticing that the crowd had been moved back toward the main road and makeshift fences had been put in place to keep them at a distance. The wagons, which had carried the Sentinels and Roykur's group, had been pushed together with the addition of the medical wagon to form three sides of a box. Sentinels strode around the wagons with purpose, laying out tarps, lashing poles, and wiping clean a large steel table at the center. Maroon-smocked assistants laid out towels, as well as jars filled with viscous fluids and various sharp instruments.

What had sprung up in front of Roykur's eyes was a tented laboratory. He gaped at the intricate setup and how quickly these vehicles had been converted into a functioning testing site.

"I thought you might get that look." Doctor Arakul's smile broadened. "The Initiative provided several engineers a few years back to see if they could improve anything. This is the result. Among a few other fun toys, we also have our own Treemolkvar to perform the chemical analysis."

"One of the Witches works in there?" asked Roykur.

"Of course, they do their part. Like I said, the Initiative is eager to see this murderer caught. Now, if you will excuse me, I have some work to do." Arakul followed the stretcher through the tent flaps, and Roykur could see him hand off the sample to an individual behind their own separate table filled with distilling equipment.

The tent bustled with the practiced precision of the medical staff, and after he marveled a while longer at their efficiency, a thought occurred to him.

Roykur squeezed around the medical staff, heading to the back, and stood next to a fiery, red-haired Treemolkvar. The Witch had green-tinted bark along his cheekbones, and vibrant green leaves. He was in the middle of winding a crank, which kept several small vials spinning rapidly in a circle. The rest of the table was jumbled with jars, tools, and tubes.

"Witch. I have something else I would like that sample compared to."

"Excuse me? What did you call me?" The red-haired chemist looked incredulous, turning around and removing his spectacles.

"Look, I have this elixir here, and I would like it compared to the crystal sample from this scene." Roykur pulled the bright elixir from his coat pocket and held it forward. He became acutely aware of all his aches and pains as he held their cure in his hand. This was a miracle, a chance to be his best forever. But at what cost?

Silence drew his gaze from the elixir to the chemist, who had his arms crossed and was staring back at Roykur, the spinning vials still clicking.

"I don't care who you think you are, I don't work for racists," said the Witch.

"I am not racist." Roykur let out an exasperated sigh. "Look, I don't have time for a name game. Just test the sample against this elixir. Get it done or I'll make sure you get jail time for impeding this investigation."

Roykur shoved the rounded bottle into the chemist's chest and stalked from the tent. He shook his head ruefully and moved to sit on the step of a nearby wagon. It had been an extremely long day and his legs ached fiercely, as did pretty much everything else. People just needed to do their jobs. Was that so hard? There was so much he needed to catch up on. Maybe coming back into the field this quickly was a mistake.

Sitting, he let out another long sigh and rubbed at a twinge in his knees. Directly in front of him, a Sentinel stood holding a chest, clearly unsure what to do with it. Roykur waved until he caught the young man's eye, and the Sentinel came over. "Uh, yes? Can I help you?"

"That chest. What's it for?" asked Roykur.

"It is evidence. I was just waiting for the captain to let me know where I was supposed to log it in."

"Let me have a look at it." Roykur reached for the chest.

"I really need to log it first." The Sentinel clung tightly to the chest.

"Son, it will get logged. Now give me the damn box."

The man handed it over, then stood just to the side, anxiously bouncing back and forth on his toes. Ignoring the jittery Sentinel, Roykur slid his hands over the darkly stained, smooth wood and down to the iron latch. He lifted the lid and grabbed a bundle of papers, its only contents. He methodically unwound the twine, then peeled open a carefully folded sheet.

The first page was pure gibberish, a series of scribbles and symbols, alien yet somehow familiar. He stared at its bizarre design, committing the strange markings to memory before unfolding the next page. The second was a cipher to the strange symbols, as were the next thirty pages—each symbol correlated to a phrase, an idea. Page after page, the cipher continued, until the last few. It was a note fully written out in plain text. The answer, perhaps? The symbols laid bare?

Before Roykur could begin reading them, he heard the rhythmic clinking of metal on stone and looked up to see Adalia jogging up to him. Roykur noticed the concern on her face.

Adalia skidded to a halt, urgency in her tone. "Grandpa, the boy we arrested—the other Conservators are really roughing him up. They aren't even asking him any questions! They told me to leave when I objected to their treatment of the suspect. I can't find the commander, so I thought you should know."

"Those damn idiots. Where are they holding him?" Roykur stood up, wincing, then stumbled, almost falling back down. Adalia moved to help him, but he waved her off, pushing himself off the wagon.

"Over near that storage area, behind the crates." Adalia pivoted on her heel and almost grabbed his hand on instinct. She had always taken his hand to show him new and exciting things around the manor grounds.

She cleared her throat and led the way in the direction she had pointed to. As they both arrived, Roykur heard muffled whimpers, followed by a hard thud of a not-so-gentle beating underway.

They rounded the crates to see Simune and Binjek circling the young boy. One of his eyes was nearly swollen shut, and his lower lip was bleeding. At the sight of these grown men beating on such a young lad, Roykur's blood boiled, and his face grew flush with heat. He didn't even announce his presence, just grabbed a plank of wood from one of the nearby crates. Pulling, he staggered slightly as it ripped free.

Simune had his back to Roykur as he continued his circling and quickly whirled around when Roykur splintered the wood plank across Binjek's face. The man's head was whipped back, and he toppled into some of the surrounding crates, more wood splintering as he fell.

"Mauzix damn you!" Simune screeched, and tried to pull his short sword from its sheath, a mixture of confusion and fear on his face. Roykur caught his hand with a strength he did not feel he still possessed and smashed his head into Simune's. Both men staggered back, but Simune was the one to collapse to the ground with a dumbfounded look on his face. Roykur took a step forward, and the Conservator cowed backward.

Adalia grabbed Roykur's arm. He stopped but remained tensed to strike, the red in his vision slowly fading.

She stepped over to the boy and untied the belt around his wrists. He sat motionless on the wooden crate and stared wide eyed at Roykur, then at Adalia. When he spoke, his voice was shaky, less fearful than Roykur had expected. "So, those were the bad Sentinels. Are you two the good Sentinels?"

Despite himself, Roykur snorted. "That was not how Sentinels, much less Conservators, should handle themselves, son. Can you stand?"

"Yeah, they hadn't got to my legs yet, sir." The kid still tested his balance regardless of his confidence.

"Here, take this, Teufel. Try to stop the bleeding." Adalia handed him a handkerchief from one of her pockets. The boy had just started cleaning himself up when several Sentinels, along with Conservator Fritch and Commander Volmirk, rounded the crates, responding to the commotion.

"What in the deep is going on here?" Volmirk demanded. The other Sentinels had short crossbows drawn.

"That crazy old djavul attacked us! Someone check to see if Binjek is alive," Simune cried out, desperately trying to shake himself from his stupor. Binjek stirred and opened his eyes, pressing a hand to the bright red rectangle that stretched across his cheek.

Volmirk took a moment to take in the spectacle before him. "Roykur, is this true? What have you done?"

"These men were beating this boy senseless. They weren't interrogating him, it was torture." Roykur's anger flared anew as he spoke.

"Roykur . . . you can't just assault your own team. You are not part of the Sentinels anymore. What they did is not excusable either, but you should have stopped the interrogation and brought this to my attention rather than take matters into your own hands."

He blinked in stupefaction. "Are you fucking kidding me? Are you complicit in their savagery, or has bureaucracy shoved its arm so far up your ass that you can no longer think rationally? They were going to kill the only actual suspect this investigation has had in nearly two decades."

Volmirk's face went sour, and his voice rose to a near shout. "I have tolerated your draugker shit for far longer than necessary because the king asked me to let you help with this case, but I will not put up with this charade any longer. You were too involved to begin with and should never have been here. You can run back to the king and whine all you want, but he will have to fire me before I let you continue to work with my Conservators." The man was practically hoarse by now. "I cannot bar you from this investigation entirely, so from here on you will conduct a separate line of inquiry, away from the Sentinels and away from the Initiative's resources, understood?"

"Away from the Initiative's resources? Seriously? Are you upset I punished your terloq after it started biting your guest? You and your Conservators are incapable of solving this case without me."

"Shut your fucking mouth and get back to scraping up draugker shit where you belong, Grandpa," sputtered Simune.

"Conservator Simune, that's enough! You and Conservator Binjek are suspended effective immediately. I am sure the newer Conservators are dying for a chance to work this case. Conservator Fritch, you are the lead on this investigation now. I'll work on finding you some additional help."

"If I may, Commander, Adalia has proven to have excellent instincts for this work," said Fritch. "Might I have her continue to assist the Conservators?"

"Commander, I tried to report the situation." Adalia looked sheepishly at Roykur, but he gave her the slightest of nods.

Volmirk threw his hands up. "Fine—just get back to figuring out who this killer is. Sentinels, please escort Simune and Binjek away from my crime scene. Roykur, you are coming with me."

Roykur glanced over his shoulder to see Conservator Fritch leading Adalia back toward the tent.

Once they were out of earshot, Volmirk harrumphed, twisting one end of his bushy mustache. "I bet it felt good, but did you have to smack those two arrogant djavuls around? Everyone is watching this case right now, which means I need all the help I can get to accomplish anything. So when my Conservators bend the rules, I look the other way if it gets the job done. I can't stop you from working this case, but you need to stay away from my people, is that clear?"

Roykur gave a stiff nod, and Volmirk, satisfied with his response, let go of his mustache and folded his arms. "So, tell me, now that you have had a firsthand look at a fresh crime scene, what's your assessment?

The lord took some time to straighten his coat, collecting himself and his thoughts. "The states of the previous victims were described as haphazard, and the scenes themselves were messy. The body and room here were nearly pristine, not counting the smell. This could fit the imitator theory, or the killer learning to get better, but I believe the Husk Slayer got his hands on the life elixir somehow. The more he has returned to his younger self, the steadier his hands have gotten." Roykur cleared his dry throat. "I am waiting on the sample comparison, but if I am right, he has had the elixir long enough to be part of the king's test group, or he's been stealing it. That's my lead, the elixirs."

"By the gods, even if you're wrong, this is going to change everything we know about profiling murderers." Volmirk set a hand on Roykur's shoulder. "Go home and get some rest. It's been a long day, and you have many more ahead of you. I'll inform Adalia of our arrangement and have her pass along any developments. Oh, and have Visari bandage that hand for you, too."

Roykur looked down at his hand and saw the shredded skin littered with slivers of wood. As if looking at it summoned the pain, his hand began throbbing. Tender as it was, it was a welcome distraction from the constant fatigue and aches that this day, every day, wrought on his body.

He followed Volmirk back to the carriage. Sitting on an amply cushioned seat, he pulled a notebook from the inside pocket of his coat and began listing areas and people of interest. The carriage pulled away from the scene, the rhythmic trotting of the draugkers lulling Roykur to sleep before they had gone two blocks.

CHAPTER 7

HOT AND STICKY

The interrogation room was small, and built completely out of wood. It had a single chair, also wood that Teufel now sat on. The space was slightly bigger than the cell he had slept the night in, and he had already spent an hour switching from pacing to sitting and back.

The wooden box was set on the eighth lower level of the Sentinel headquarters. At least, that was how many levels Teufel had managed to count on his way down. The stairs they took spiraled on the inside of the building, and it was difficult to determine how far they had actually descended. The heat in the box had been a welcome change to the chill of the jail cell at first, but now it had grown uncomfortable. Teufel was sweating profusely, and he had stripped down to just his linen shirt—the vest, jacket, and overcoat lay across the back of the chair.

He wiped his sweaty palms on the tops of his knees, hoping to dry them off, but he knew that would only be a brief reprieve. Dirt from his trousers matted his wet hands. With a deep sigh, all he could do was stare at the gross mess he was in.

Teufel tried to find a clean area of his trousers to repeat his useless drying act on while continuing to watch the door to the room with furtive glances. After Adalia had insisted on treating his wounds personally, she had promised she would be present the next time he was interrogated to make sure there would be actual questions. *Strong and compassionate? What a woman.*

The door opened as if on cue, and Adalia strolled through. A good-looking male Sentinel followed close behind her. Teufel tried to mask his emotions, but the heat of this room was doing its work well, and he knew that any composure he hoped to present had long since melted away.

"I brought you some water." Adalia's expression was less friendly now, but he couldn't help smiling dumbly, regardless.

"Thanks." Teufel winced inwardly at how his voice croaked before he quickly downed the entire glass and handed it back.

"This is Conservator Fritch, and I am Sentinel Adalia. We just have a few questions, and if you answer them truthfully, you will be free to go. Just one second." Adalia began sifting through pages of a notebook she had tucked under her arm. Teufel was suddenly very aware that she was not wearing her breastplate and was sweating heavily. The damp brown shirt clung to her frame, outlining a robust figure that had not been visible previously. His head tilted to better see the curves that were being revealed through the dampness.

From the corner of his eye, he caught Fritch staring at him, so he tried to advert his gaze, casually of course. Fritch leaned over and whispered something to Adalia, and she quickly closed her book. She leaned over to be face-to-face with Teufel, testing the limits of his ability to maintain eye contact.

"Let's get straight to it. Did you kill Slad?" said Adalia.

"Who?" he asked, genuinely confused.

"The scroll worker."

"No! Of course not!"

"Why were you at his house?"

"I was there for a job," Teufel said.

"What was the job?"

"Potatoes." Sticking with his lie.

"Nope, try again," said Adalia flatly.

Why am I lying? I never actually stole anything.

"Fine. It was a delivery. I was hired to pick up a chest from the scroll worker and drop it off somewhere else. Strictly legal, of course. Actually, you should really be thanking me. I mean, if I hadn't been there, you know, on my job, no one would even know the old guy was dead. I provided a service." Teufel tried to flash his best "trust me" smile.

Adalia gave him a long, calculating look. "If you were providing a service, why did you run?"

"There was a dead body! Wouldn't you? No, of course *you* wouldn't. That's your job. You probably see dead bodies all the time. Well, people like me don't, and it freaked me out, alright?" This time, he was content to stare at his feet.

Adalia squatted down, drawing his eyes unbidden to hers. Her face was scrunched up, a mixture of disgust and concern. "This was my first as well. I'm not even a real Conservator yet."

"Let's get to the point. Where is this chest now?" said Fritch. He was pacing, a deep frown beneath that wavy hair.

"What do you mean?" said Teufel. "It was the chest that you Sentinels took out of the house."

Fritch pulled out a notebook of his own and flipped through a handful of its pages, then slid a finger down its face. "There was no chest listed on the items that were recovered as evidence."

"I saw them take it out of the building when I was standing in the crowd. Everyone there saw it too!" Teufel looked away back to Adalia, pleading, but her eyes had narrowed once again. Then realization dawned on Teufel, and he sank back in his chair, resigned. "He got someone else to get the chest."

Leondal had so little faith in him that he'd sent someone else to do the job. *My father assumed I would fail again. The second I left that room, he had abandoned me. He never intended for me to come back.*

Fritch and Adalia instantly perked up at Teufel's comment, both leaning in with interest. "Who? Who do you work for? Who wanted the chest stolen?"

In the silence that followed their questions, Teufel's heartbeat pounded loudly in his ears, getting faster, accompanied by the harsh grinding of his teeth. *Fuck him. I don't need him or the Jaspers.*

The tips of his ears grew hot, and his breathing was tight. He sat up straight. The sweat stung his eyes, but he stared at the two Sentinels without flinching. "I worked for Leondal of House Jasperion."

There was no look of recognition from Adalia as she scribbled the name down, but Fritch just sputtered and laughed outright. Adalia jumped slightly at the abrupt outburst of her counterpart and gave him a disapproving glance. Teufel shifted uncomfortably in the hard wooden chair. Nothing good ever came from a sudden outburst of laughter.

"You are saying your employer is the leader of *the* most infamous gang in Ver'a'saile? Do you think we are stupid, or do you think Leondal has become so desperate that he has to hire children?" mocked Fritch.

"I'm not a child. I am almost sixteen, and my father has always used every tool at his disposal, but I don't think he's ever been desperate. And yes, I think you're stupid."

Roykur had spent the morning visiting all of the recent victims' families, interviewing them to verify the reports and fill in much of the missing details. He even coaxed out a story from one witness who claimed to have seen the Husk Slayer, a colossal beast with a glowing golden claw. Unsurprisingly, the Conservators hadn't recorded that statement. More importantly, he stopped by Myrmilla's house in the Sky Garden district, on the seventh upper level. Her house revealed very little, and her widower even less. The space was neat but cold, packed with an assortment of tools and schematics, both of which were neither new nor strange for the tinkerer. Her widower was barely sane, mumbling incoherently mixed with bursts of quiet sobs. Despite Roykur's efforts, he was unable or unwilling to help.

The last visit on his list, an elderly merchant woman named Ilienie, was a remnant of his old informant network. He had heard she was bedridden, but that could never stop her from keeping an ear to the ground.

Ilienie was rich. She lay propped up in the largest and most lavish bed Roykur had ever seen. Expensive, polished furniture adorned every corner of the room, and a window against the far wall provided a splendid view of the sprawling city below. The woman set down a bowl of soup, her shriveled hand shaking with the effort. With the other hand, she wiped at some that had dribbled from the corner of her mouth. Her skin was pale and thin over her gaunt, sunken features, yet she still seemed to brighten when he walked in. *Tabiat's grace, the decades were not kind. She's younger than me, but she doesn't look it.*

"Ilienie! How have you been? It's been a few years—still ravishing as usual. After all these years of playing the mistress of secrets, it's good to know you were able to let all that go and retire in comfort." After all these years, he still remembered which buttons to push.

"Oh, I still got secrets. Those ungrateful parasites I call children work for me until the day I die. They bring me all the juicy gossip." Ilienie labored a cough, then smiled mischievously, teeth pink with blood. "You're still as handsome as ever. Just because you're so cute, I'll tell ya what I think you're probably looking for. After the usual game, am I right?"

Roykur nodded.

"Right. So, someone bought ma ol' factory 'bout a month back—

buyer wouldn't meet direct, but it was too good a price to refuse, so I kept my eye on it of course. It's always good to keep an eye out on recent sales just in case—"

Roykur interrupted her. "Let's keep this on subject, shall we? We aren't getting any younger." *At least not yet.*

Ilienie sniffed and spit red off to the side of the bed. "Before the official sale, I was paid quite nicely to store odd shipments, heavily laden wagons, large and covered in the warehouse beneath the factory. I figured I could squeeze a last bit of coin from the place before I turned it over. Actually, I met this one, real shady fellow. Liked his privacy. I didn't like him."

"You find out what was in those wagons?" asked Roykur.

"Oh yeah, sent some boys to check it out—metal beams, gears, and the like." Ilienie looked out her window, pensive, building the anticipation before the big reveal. "Also, jars containing Human organs."

Roykur's eyes widened, and he sucked in a sharp breath. Her dramatic reveals always caught him off guard, but this was something else. Ilienie licked her lips, savoring the delicious moment. "I told them to fetch one as proof, but the wagons were gone when they returned. Never did figure out where the shipments went. He moved them quick, whatever they were. Then the factory started up a week or two ago. However, my boys say they've still been seeing that shady fellow heading in and out."

"So, when the killings started up again, you didn't think to mention this 'shady fellow' to the Sentinels?" asked Roykur.

"Like I said, he paid quite nicely, and I don't do anything for free. You know that."

Roykur grunted in understanding and began backing slowly away toward the door. "You still got it, Ilienie. Always just what I need to hear."

Turning, he bumped into a broad man with tree trunk arms. A cudgel hung from his belt. "Ah, yes, your fee." He pressed a pouch of about fifty silver pieces into the large hands. The blockheaded man judged the weight and nodded to Ilienie before stepping to the side.

I bet she wouldn't hesitate to take the new elixir. Not for one second. After all, she'd ruthlessly sought power and wealth her whole life and ruined many others in the process. How many more would she be able to if she lived forever?

The morning had well and truly transitioned to late afternoon as the carriage passed by the large factory on the second sub-level, where Ilienie had indicated the deliveries had taken place. The factory here was in a warehouse, with a single guard posted to accept deliveries and keep out trespassers.

"Woah, woah. Stay back, old man—this place is off-limits." The lone guard stood up from his stoop. His face was scarred and sported a nose broken many times over.

"Hello there, I am here on official Sentinel business," said Roykur.

"Sentinel? I don't see no uniform."

"I am consulting. I was a Conservator for many years. Now if I could just take a quick look inside."

A short sword slid slowly out of the burly man's scabbard. "You deaf as well as stupid, old man? I said this place is off-limits."

Roykur took a step back, raising his hands. "Hey! Let's take a deep breath. I am with the Sentinels, and I need to look around inside. I'm sure we can work something out. This job probably doesn't pay well."

"Nuh-uh. Don't try to bribe me. A few extra coins ain't gonna help me much after I lose my job."

"I was going to offer you a job. I pay my workers very well."

"You're offering a job? I thought you were with the Sentinels?"

"I am, but—"

"I've heard enough. Keep walking. I won't be gentle just cause you're older than dirt."

"Fine! Can I at least ask who owns this factory?"

"Yeah, alright, that's no big secret. Ilienie. She owns a lot of places around here, and she pays her employees just fine." The guard relaxed a bit but still kept a loose grip on his short sword by his side.

Roykur let his hand drop. It seemed the guard had not been informed that the factory had been sold. The new owners likely wanted him to still think he worked for that old crone. He glanced around and spotted a balcony across the street with a few tables. *Fantastic. A vigilance patrol it is.*

Across the long street, which connected two towers, the loud grinding sounds of industrial machines faded slightly. There, a small bar called the Fire Moss sat above a hat shop. The bar had a patio and an unobstructed line of sight of the warehouse delivery door. Roykur tossed a copper piece to the bartender, took a seat, and soon had a watered-down pint of ale in front of him.

The bar was relatively empty. A couple of nervous-looking men talked in hushed tones in the corner. Another, nearest to him, was facedown on the sticky table. The man's snoring was interrupted by the occasional hiccup. Roykur drained the pewter mug and waved to the bartender, holding several more coins between his fingers. A much larger mug of ale soon replaced the empty one.

This was the sort of situation where he was glad to be out of the oversight of the Sentinels. He could enjoy a vigilance patrol without those self-absorbed idiots. It would have been nice if Adalia was with him, so he could be there when she experienced her very first, but it was just as well. He had gotten her in the front door—now was her time to prove herself as a Conservator.

Roykur focused his attention on the factory warehouse, considering his options. He could try to figure out who owned the factory in an official capacity. However, he would have to submit a request, which would take months to come back with information, if it ever did. It would inevitably tip off this shady man as well, and the Conservators would show up to an emptied warehouse. The other option would be to patrol the area and figure out a way inside, then inform the Conservators once he discovered and track it if they tried to move it. He weighed both options for a moment and had a flash of memory of the long nights of seemingly endless paperwork. *Option B.*

Roykur was only halfway through his third pewter mug when a letter slapped down on the table in front of him. Looking up, he saw the courier bent over slightly. The man was breathing hard. Roykur squinted, trying to place him. "Were you at the crime scene yesterday?"

The courier nodded and spoke between breaths. "Sir . . . I'm glad I recognized . . . your carriage outside. Been running around for hours." He stood upright and inhaled deeply, steadying himself. "An urgent letter for Your Lordship."

The letter was short and choppy, barely legible.

Sample analyzed is definitely elixir based. Crystal composition is likely a match to the contents of the vial you provided. No further testing can be done. The chemist Witch won't stop complaining about the elixir not being theirs. Crystals formed from an elixir, sealing wound. Unknown if sealing occurred pre or post death. Good leads on our end. Let you know more tonight. See you soon. - Adalia

"Thank you. It must have taken a while to find me. Let me buy you a pint before you go."

They sat in silence while the courier drank his ale. Roykur reread the note several times before the courier excused himself and left him to his contemplations.

The king creates an elixir of life, and the Husk Slayer starts killing again. Had his victims consumed the new elixir on their own, or was he feeding it to them before he killed them? Then a shady man with organs in jars shows up as a new factory sets up shop.

Roykur thought he might just have an idea who owned this factory, and what it made.

CHAPTER 8

SWEET AND SOUR

Agust of wind hit Teufel sideways, and he had to grip the railing of the walkway for fear of being blown off. He peered over the side of the flimsy railing and stared at the geyser steam that floated through the streets. Obscuring the ground, it gave the height the look of an endless abyss.

Tearing his eyes away from certain death, he pushed back the rising nausea. He usually tried to avoid the upper levels, and the top level most of all. Adalia and Fritch were several paces ahead, and the boy started jogging to catch up to those long-legged giants.

He wasn't sure if his telling the truth had worked and they were honestly impressed with his underworld ties, or they were just switching their interrogation tactics, but they had offered to buy him lunch. Considering he hadn't eaten breakfast, mixed with the fact that he had no money, he accepted their offer graciously. The restaurant they chose had sounded nice; he hadn't realized at the time that it was so high up.

However, his nausea receded with the first sip of hot maple cinnamon tea. Then came the freshly baked pastries. They flaked and melted in the mouth, smeared with just a touch of sweet strawberry jam. Teufel devoured each item, closing his eyes and savoring every bite. He was on his fourth plate when he noticed Adalia and Fritch staring, having barely touched their own food.

"What?" Teufel asked with half a pastry shoved to the sides of his cheeks.

"Kid, I never thought someone your size could fit that much food. Did you even take a breath that whole time?" Fritch looked downright impressed.

Instead of answering, Teufel let out a burp that echoed through the restaurant. A silence washed over several disturbed patrons, followed shortly by low grumbles of disgust.

"Great, now I won't be showing my face around here anytime soon," said Fritch. He gave Teufel one of those grins people use when they're upset but are trying to smile through it.

"That was awesome! My grandpa and I have competitions at home to see who can burp the loudest. He usually wins, and it drives my mom crazy." Adalia beamed, oblivious to the grumbling.

"Is your grandpa still around?" asked Teufel.

"Of course. You met him already."

"You mean that really tall old guy who smashed up those other Conservators? I like him. Doesn't stand for crooked Sentinels on his watch." Teufel's eyes narrowed at Fritch. "No offense, Fritch—you seem like a decent fellow."

"Oh, what would I have done without your approval?" said the Conservator, rolling his eyes.

Teufel turned his attention back to Adalia. "So, grandpa and mom, no dad in the picture?"

"No, he died when I was really young. Elixir addiction," said Adalia, a bit of her cheerfulness dimming.

"My mom had that for a while—hooked on eyesight elixirs, of all things—but she got help after a fashion."

"Really? It's so hard to break. How did she manage that?"

"Well, my dad caught her taking money from the Jaspers' funds one day to go buy another round, and he beat her up so bad she couldn't make it out of the house. Next time she tried it, he did the same thing. It only took five attempts before she stopped trying."

Fritch chuckled after taking a sip of his tea. "Now *that* sounds like Leondal."

Adalia sat back in her chair, shaking her head at her partner.

The Conservator leaned back defensively. "What? It sounds like him. The guy is a tit-less draugker."

"That's awful!" said Adalia. "At least she isn't dead, I guess. We lucked out . . . after Dad was gone along with all our money, Grandpa took us in, and we've been living with him ever since."

"I would like to meet him—you know, in a more normal setting."

"Yeah, I think he would like to meet you, too. I'm sure we could arrange something like that."

"Well, I think the great Conservator would really like to meet you if you first found out what was in the chest. Do you think you could ask a few questions for us back at the Jaspers' hideout?" Fritch was side-eyeing him while attempting to sip his tea casually.

Teufel had known this question was coming. "First things first, Fritch—you know as well as I that asking those kinds of questions is how you get killed. Second, we make it a rule to not ask about our clients' business. Thirdly, and something I am sure you've figured out by now—I didn't get the job done. I know you know what that means."

Fritch just sighed. "Sure do, means you're absolutely worthless. I just thought there might be more here, but I assumed too much. You're free to go."

"Why does your father have two names? Was he a noble?" asked Adalia.

Fritch spoke first. "Not a real one. Gave himself that second name. He fancies himself as the 'Lord of the Underworld.' Another one I heard was the 'King of Crime.' Ridiculous." Fritch chuckled and stood up. "Adalia, this morning was pretty much a waste. I'm going to head back to headquarters to see if I can salvage what's left of the day. I'll let Volmirk know you have the rest of the day off." He cleared his throat and dropped his voice an entire octet lower. "My offer for an entertaining night still stands if you're interested?"

Teufel looked away, but he caught Adalia's face redden. "Some other night, perhaps. My mom is putting on a big family affair tonight."

"Alright then, see you bright and early tomorrow." Fritch strolled out of the building, whistling the same short note over and over.

"Isn't that guy your boss or something?" Teufel asked, voice cracking slightly. "A bit old for you, if you ask me."

"Nothing like that!" Adalia said quickly. "Well, I have a have a feeling he meant to show me more than the usual Sentinel taverns . . . but he's not my boss, more like an instructor, teaching me how to be a Conservator."

He noticed her discomfort and decided to not push the subject, instead focusing on taking a long drink of his already lukewarm tea.

"If you still would like to meet my grandpa, you could always come to family dinner tonight. Unless you have somewhere else to be?"

Teufel inhaled sharply at her invitation, then began coughing furiously from the tea he had breathed in. Adalia looked briefly worried, but it quickly turned to a sly smile once she realized he wasn't in danger of choking to death. "So, is that a yes?"

"Yes, sounds great," Teufel croaked out after his fit had subsided. He used the napkin to wipe away tears that had formed from his brief asphyxiation, as well as to give himself a moment to think. She turned down tall, dark, and handsome to invite him to dinner. That had to be a good sign. *Oh gods, I'm meeting the whole family already? Well, a family dinner could mean she just sees me as a younger brother. That's probably more likely.*

"Let's get going. It's a fair distance to the edge of the city—from there, we can pay a carriage to the manor." She started walking back toward the bridge they had crossed to get to the restaurant.

Teufel frowned in confusion. "Wait, *the manor*? I thought you were a Sentinel, not a noblewoman."

"Oh, that's right. I forget that not everyone knows who my grandpa is. He's Lord of House Heimvelt, although most stories are back before he got his title when he was known as Conservator Roykur."

"*The* Roykur is your grandpa?" Teufel felt slightly sick. He had been casually flirting with a noblewoman for almost two days now. And not just any noblewoman—the granddaughter of a man he had read about in school, a war hero who was almost single-handedly responsible for exterminating the vile Kolkrabba and then reducing the murder rate in an overpopulated postwar city to nearly nothing.

Teufel's father had seduced and swindled wealthy merchant women occasionally, but even he had never been foolish enough to try nobility. Trying to avoid the aftermath of a scorned or cheated merchant could make for a few miserable weeks. A nobleperson had the resources and influence to track down and utterly destroy a man.

Despite his rising nerves, he felt at the two coppers he had left in his pocket and remembered he was not only out of a job, but a family as well. Besides, Adalia and Roykur seemed like good people, and he didn't plan on swindling them. Although, he was a thief. It would be pretty stupid if he did not at least consider taking a small item or two. Rich people had so much, they didn't even know when half of it went missing.

They walked for a while along the high tops of the city. The view of the mountainside was breathtaking the few chances he got to glimpse it, though the crowds that bustled along the bridges and across the platforms were better walls than windows. It didn't bother him very much; he was used to keeping his eyes low and alert. This environment was where he excelled. He slipped in and around groups of people passing by, never missing a beat in his stride. Adalia, on the other hand, had to pause frequently to avoid bumping into people. The end effect was that Teufel could actually keep pace with her without breaking into a jog every few steps.

A familiar movement caught his eye. With a flash, he snatched at a boy's wrist as it was gliding out of Adalia's satchel. The commotion startled Adalia, but she quickly ripped the wooden figurine out of the street urchin's hand and shoved it back into her satchel. The young kid, around eight years old, pulled free of Teufel's grasp and darted into the throng of people.

"Wow, thanks for catching that," said Adalia, giving him an appraising look. Teufel hoped it was a favorable one.

"My pleasure—that kind of thing happens more than you think." Teufel gave her a wink. *I guess I just can't help myself.*

"I suppose you would know. Delivery boy." Her look, now suspicious, was far less favorable.

CHAPTER 9

LOST DESIRES

Roykur stepped through the awning that led to the king's personal study. The steward, who had run on ahead, stood impatiently on the threshold.

"The king has a moment to spare for you, Lord Roykur. You may enter."

Roykur was sitting down in an expensive red upholstered chair before the steward had finished. He looked back at the flustered man until he finally bowed and left them alone.

"Social call or . . ." Legast set down his pen and reached for a decanter.

Just a couple days, and the king appeared to be reaching his early forties. He smiled with an arched eyebrow, and Roykur's mind raced to the days when his best friend had last looked this young. Days when the two of them would sit in these same seats, drinking and discussing the troubles of work, life, family. His eyes drifted from his friend's hand on the decanter to his own, skin thin and spotted.

"Pour the booze, Legs, don't be pedantic."

Legast smile widened, and he scooped up the decanter, filling two glasses with a flourish. The brown liquid swirled in Roykur's glass, and the fumes stung pleasantly in his nose.

He looked at the desk. "What were you writing? Anything interesting?"

"A mining dispute. Just resolving some land claims." Legast sighed and rubbed at his temples. "Nothing a council couldn't resolve. I may have regained some years, but I can't regain the wasted time of putting up with this draugker shit. I am tired, Roykur—I can't wait to be rid of the crown."

"The council! They would take the simple matter you have decisively acted on and turn it into a three-week debate. Then forget what the issue was about in the first place. I honestly don't know if that room of incompetent crackpots is going to accomplish anything when you're gone," said Roykur, nearly forgetting to breathe through his impassioned rant.

"You're on that council, too." Legast's wry smile returned.

"Exactly. I know just how ineffective we all are. Perhaps you can reconsider naming a successor to the crown?" asked Roykur.

The king rolled his eyes. "Which house shall Morfar pass the crown to? House Becoven? House Tremane? They would tear each other apart, along with the city, if they thought they had a chance to claim the crown."

"Ugh. Just look around for someone with brains and a strong stomach." Roykur took a long swig from his glass. "Or now that you're immortal, get married, have a child for gods' sake."

"If I wanted that, don't you think I would have by now? I love your unexpected visits, Roykur, truly, but we both have duties to attend to, however unpleasant. What can I help you with, my old friend?"

Roykur dug his nail into the side of his thumb. "It's about your new elixir."

"You've decided to take it at last?" The king nearly jumped from his seat.

"No, not that."

Legast slumped back in his chair. "Olacka! Why not? You don't have to live forever, just a bit longer, spend some years with your retirement at an age you can actually enjoy it. Or you could journey with me to the other cities."

"Torn apart by wind spouts? Savaged by tribes of carnids? Boiled by geysers? There's a reason no one leaves the city." Roykur just shook his head at the ridiculous notion.

"The expeditions have grown very successful, the guides more experienced. Have you seen the travelers from Maw'licor and Saft'-don? More arrive each year for trade," said Legast, excitement clear in his voice.

"It's a wonder they can transport anything without wagons. Can you really see yourself carrying nearly your weight all the way to another city while also avoiding death at every turn?" asked Roykur.

"Better than dying having seen so little of this world," said Legast with a touch of sullenness.

"I ain't dying yet, Legs. Can I ask about the elixir?" The king waved a hand, sipping from his glass with the other. Roykur leaned forward. "I found a strong lead to the Husk Slayer, tracked it to a factory. A factory on the third lower level in the Fifty Fingers district." Roykur paused, but Legast just stared back. "Is that not where you manufacture the elixir?

"Oh . . . possibly? I don't handle the logistics. I put Lord Wisiel in charge of its management. It seemed appropriate. House Becoven already had the equipment for brewing ale and spirits. Elixirs can't be that different," Legast said, then took another sip.

"I also need to know who created this elixir—and how."

"You know, I never learned that myself. A bit beyond my comprehension. The team of chemists was put directly under the purview of House Becoven, along with all their secrets." Legast straightened in his chair and spoke with a more serious tone. "A word of caution, my friend. You are nobility, and with that comes certain restrictions. House Becoven has officially been charged with this resource, and you cannot create even the slightest appearance of trying to take over that resource. That was how the last civil war started."

"Yes, I know my history," Roykur said. Then, abashed, "But I had forgotten about this issue."

"I only wish to remind you the protection of my city outweighs your investigation. I suggest not asking for a tour." He relaxed back into his seat, swirling his glass.

Roykur considered telling Legast his elixir was responsible for reviving this horror in the first place, but decided against it. There was a connection now, and he needed to keep a few things close to the chest. "Fine. I will keep the investigation to the relevant facts of the case and nothing more. I need to investigate the factory and the warehouse beneath it. I need a writ—and could a few of your Royal Guard accompany me? There was a particularly . . . uncooperative sentry."

Legast narrowed his eyes, leaning in. "Why can't you bring Sentinels along?"

"There was an incident," said Roykur under his breath.

"Already?"

"Legs, can I have the backup or not?"

The king sighed and rubbed his temples. "The Royal Guard isn't a group of thugs for hire. They have a very specific job, and they are very good at it. However, I will give you that writ. Hopefully, it helps."

Roykur beamed. "Well, it is certainly better than nothing. Thank you. I mean it."

Legast set his glass down and scooted forward in his seat, grasping Roykur's head in both of his hands, and kissed his friend's forehead. "Of course. You know you mean the world to me. So, you must stay safe out there, alright?"

The king released him and Roykur slapped his thighs, standing with some effort. "Well, I'd like to make some progress on this factory before dinner. Visari is preparing a big feast for the family and the staff. You should come if you're not too busy?"

Legast cocked his head at the invitation. "It's been a while since I've been to one of Visari's big family dinners. The gods know I could use the conversation. What's the point of being king if I can't do what I want?"

Ӂ

ONCE ADALIA and Teufel reached the platform, they turned toward the ramp, nearly to the carriages. Teufel was wrapping up one of his more amusing stories about a wig maker when they finished making their way down one level.

"Then she said, 'But sir! Your hair has fallen in your soup.'"

Adalia was laughing so hard she was nearly in tears. It wasn't even close to one of his best stories, but Teufel was happy with the reaction. Perhaps she heard very few jokes in the noble circles. A bit distracted, he missed the large group of people before they shoved their way in between the pair.

Teufel was pushed from behind, causing him to stumble. The group continued belligerently, kicking his feet out from under him as he stumbled. Teufel fell to the ground, but he was well acquainted with the extreme rudeness of people. Using the momentum of his fall, he tumbled forward and rolled right to his feet. He looked around for the group, but they had already melted into the crowd behind.

He brushed off some dirt from the street, although it did little to improve the state of his coat. "Now, if you thought the last story was funny, I have another great one about my aunt and a bin full of apples I think you'll enjoy." Teufel whipped his head around but couldn't spot Adalia. A spike of concern rising in his throat. "Adalia? Adalia!"

A small parting in the massive flow of people gave Teufel a

glimpse of two stocky individuals, nearly twenty feet away, supporting a limp figure between them. Adalia's enormous frame was difficult to misinterpret. They set her down in the back of a wagon and hastily left in different directions.

The wagon set off at a quick pace, and Teufel stood stunned for a moment. This woman, a Sentinel, had arrested him, locked him in a hot box, and inexplicably shown him kindness. He glanced about for the ones who had taken her, but they were already out of sight. The wagon continued to pull farther away, so Teufel did the one thing he knew he had to. He took off at a run, following. *Gods, I hate running.*

CHAPTER 10

FULL CIRCLE

The afternoon air was slowly cooling around the Fire Moss, a sign that the daylight on the surface was retreating. Regardless of the season, the underground always kept its warmth. Roykur continued to stare at the elegantly scripted writ in his hand. From the carriage, he had seen the warehouse across the street opened briefly to admit empty wagons for outgoing shipments. The loads were covered in a thick tarp, and it was difficult to make out anything in the warehouse from this distance. The light inside was dim, and his eyesight was not what it once had been.

Roykur had debated with himself several times how he should approach this situation. He doubted a piece of paper was going to do much with that djavul of a guard. Sneaking in had been his first instinct, asking forgiveness if he got caught, but that would likely end up with that guard stabbing him. Didn't seem the type to accept excuses. His hands squeezed, longing for his once-familiar axe. Even after all these years, those memories got his blood pumping. Pointless thought—he could barely take down a tree these days.

Roykur's back ached, so he stepped out and began his usual remedy of stretches, hearing and feeling the satisfying pops along his spine. He hadn't reacclimated to the strenuous hours that this job demanded, and he was still tired from yesterday's activities. Before he returned to his seat, a small wagon surged into view, with an underfed draugker pulling it.

He frowned at the harshness with which the driver pushed the draugker. They were gentle beasts, and it pained him every time one was mistreated. The wagon turned into the warehouse entrance, and the guard jumped up and yelled for the gate to be opened. As he waited, the back of the vehicle faced Roykur, and he could make out some kind of cargo. He squinted. Was that a leg sticking out? More bodies for the butcher's block?

Finally, no more prancing around. That person could still be alive.

Reaching into the carriage, he produced a large, sheathed dagger. He tucked down the backside of his trousers and make sure his coat covered the hilt. Roykur was about to give instructions to his driver, but the man was missing from his seat. He turned and almost smashed into a ragged-looking woman. It was difficult to tell her age with all the grime coating her face, but she appeared to be in her midforties. She looked up at him sheepishly and lifted her cupped hands.

"Please sir, can you spare a few coins? I lost my job, and I can't afford to feed my children," the woman pleaded. Roykur's first instinct was to put a hand to his nose. She reeked of piss and vomit, but an idea blossomed in his mind, and he gave the woman a sympathetic look.

"I don't believe in just handing out money. You'll have to do something for me."

The woman took a few steps back, tensing, a look of stubborn resolve on her face. "No, I'm no whore. I won't do anything like that."

Realizing how his statement sounded, he cleared his throat, his face getting hot. "Oh no, nothing like that, I apologize. I wasn't being clear. You need to cause a scene for me. I'll give you a whole gold piece if you go around to the other side of the warehouse, that door over there, and try to force your way in."

She relaxed slightly, but her face remained locked in concern. He pulled the coin from his pocket and showed it to the woman. Her eyes widened, and Roykur swore he saw a bit of drool trickle from the corner of her mouth. She reached for the gold, but Roykur pulled his hand back.

"You get the coin if you do what I asked. You don't have to wait around long, just until you see that guard." He pointed his finger discretely across his chest. She nodded with a puzzled look, clearly not quite understanding the situation. "Good. I'll meet you here when I am done, and I'll give you the coin."

The woman began her trek around the side of the warehouse to the single door that Roykur had spotted earlier. He followed her up the street a bit to get a better vantage point. A small cart with dried meats decorating its exterior was parked along the street, and a greasy man in a vest stood hawking his low prices. Roykur stood pretending to examine the meats, keeping his eye on the entrance. Then he spotted a young boy sprinting down the street.

Something looked terribly familiar. As he drew closer, Roykur recognized him from the crime scene. This was the boy who was being beaten senseless by the Conservators. Roykur moved to intercept the kid, putting up a hand to stop him. The boy spotted him and stopped abruptly, nearly collapsing. He was breathing hard, and his body was slicked in sweat. He tried to speak, but nothing intelligible came out.

"What are you doing here? I thought you were in custody?" Roykur asked, frustrated and confused.

"Were . . . those . . . your men?" the boy squeezed out between breaths.

"What men? Take a moment and explain yourself."

He took several deep breaths, and his breathing calmed. "You're saying you have no idea what is going on? Adalia gets taken away, and you just happen to be where they've taken her." The boy's demeanor was indignant, but Roykur's stomach twisted. He leaned down, grabbed the boy's arm, and pulled him close.

"Boy! You said Adalia was taken? By whom? When was this? Where did they go?" His voice pitched with rising panic.

"Look, a couple of men grabbed her and threw her in a wagon, and I've been chasing it nearly halfway across the city. I think I saw it pull off the street, but I don't see it now."

"I think I know." Roykur paused for a moment, considering the escalating situation. "Alright boy—"

"Teufel," he corrected.

"Teufel, the Sentinel barracks is just a few blocks back the way you came. I need you to go there and tell Commander Volmirk what is happening. Tell him to send a squad to lock down this entire factory."

"What are you going to do?" asked Teufel.

"I am going to make sure nothing happens to Adalia until the calvary arrives." Roykur watched him open his mouth to protest but cut him off. "Don't argue. This is the best way you can help, understand?"

Teufel gave a sullen nod.

"Go now!" Roykur commanded.

The boy turned and lethargically started his run back. His tired legs weren't moving any faster than Roykur could walk.

Roykur whipped around as he heard faint screams and yelps, accompanied by loud banging from the other side of the warehouse —his cue. The guard at the entrance flinched at the noise and moved to investigate. Roykur walked with a quick step to the door beside the large vehicle gate. The door was set ajar, and he pushed it in with a creak, then closed it behind him

The only light in the place seeped through the door seams, revealing shadowy outlines. Peering into the darkness of the large, open space, Roykur let his eyes adjust. The outlines of many stacked crates on shelves lined the walls, except for one wall, where tall stairs led to what Roykur assumed to be the factory floor.

In the center of the space was the wagon.

Taking great care, Roykur moved forward to inspect the back.

However, just like the rest of the warehouse, it was vacant. Letting out a long breath, he cursed to himself as he moved to inspect the driver's seat. Empty.

Closer to the back of the warehouse, at the far end, he spotted a writing desk.

Roykur dropped into the desk chair and shifted through the papers, looking for some kind of clue to Adalia's whereabouts or the hidden purpose of this warehouse. Everything he looked at was impossible to read clearly without better light, but they appeared to be standard shipping records. Nothing hinted at nefarious dealings. He shoved a few in his pocket, just in case.

Growing frustrated and desperate, he began opening drawers and lifting to check underneath every pen holder and paperweight on the desk. There was nothing present in any of the drawers, nor anything special about the pen holder. He pounded the table with his fists, then scolded himself immediately at the stupidity. He listened for a moment, but there was no sign anyone had heard his outburst. A wave of weariness hit Roykur, and he leaned back, preparing for the dizzy spell that usually followed.

That was when he saw it. A string dangled from underneath the desk, and tied at the end was a small key. *Must have dislodged it from its hiding place.*

Adrenaline sparked, pushing away the weariness for the moment. He pulled the key and string out. A small roll of paper was tied just above the key. Roykur slid the paper free and unrolled it. He maneuvered the tiny scroll to face a small beam of light through the vehicle gate.

It read: *Third crate up, turn the key four times. Watch your step.*

He raced to the wall behind the desk, feeling around the crates. After nearly ten minutes of scouring, his fingers brushed it—a keyhole. Roykur's heart beat loud in his chest, and his unsteady hands fumbled to insert the key. He turned it with a loud click. Then he paused, holding his breath for any sign of movement, before turning the key again.

On the fourth turn, an avalanche of clicks, whirls, and ticks ran from the crate in front of him and into the ground and walls nearby. The noise was jarring compared to the stillness of the warehouse. *Someone is definitely going to hear that.*

The clanking machinations continued, and the three crates depressed into the wall, hissing sharp gouts of steam. They stopped a foot in and started sinking slowly, sliding into the ground. Roykur did his best to watch what lay beyond this slow-moving door, as well as checking the outer door and stairs for any signs of alerted personnel. Nothing so far. Behind the descending wall piece was the beginning of another set of stairs heading steeply downward. There was an absence of light, a deep void that hung at the edge of the first step. This structure was not supposed to go down to another level, at least not far enough to be visible to the next sub-level. Illegal excavation, to be sure.

That same burning curiosity flamed bright in Roykur, just as it had in the cave all those years ago and many times in the years since. Roykur had developed a cautious side, grown from his numerous blunders. He picked up the paperweight, a small rock, from the desk and wedged it in the track the crates had rolled on. The small rock should be able to stop the mechanical door from closing all the way. Roykur stepped through the opening and turned to face the stairs, then climbed down them like a ladder. Always the safest option in a dark space.

The stairs went on for a while through the narrowly carved stone. It was a good thing that he decided to crawl down—the ceiling dropped low, and it would have made even someone of normal height smash their head. Reaching the bottom, he could stand, but the low ceiling here kept his head bowed. A faint light shone at the end of a long narrow hallway, illuminating only a single side passage on the left.

Roykur shuffled along the dirty stone floor, his boots scraping despite his efforts to step lightly. He made two lefts and then a right, and with each turn, the light got brighter. The last turn opened into a large circular room. The familiarity of the room hit him immediately. Memories flashed across his mind—the cold cave, the strange symbols, and monsters tearing people apart.

The room itself looked like a modern version of the ritual chamber, except for eight monolithic stones. They were the exact eight stone pillars that had been in the chamber fifty-six years ago. Roykur walked through the re-creation, his hands cold and clammy. They shook as he reached out to touch a pillar to see if this was all real.

In the center of the chamber was a round metal tub filled with murky water. Between the lamps scattered about the chamber and the murky water, it was difficult to make out, but he could see the delicate glow of the water's bioluminescence.

An intricate circle of metal filled the space between the tub and stones. Tubes stretched out and connected to the stones, looping through to the tub on the other side. It had gears and pistons positioned all round its exterior, with a smooth metal ball placed atop the circular rail. The mechanic device was as strange to Roykur as the ritual chamber itself, but it reminded him of something he had seen recently. He fished in his pocket and produced a clump of wadded papers. He dropped them one at a time, frantically searching for—

There. It was a schematic he had taken from Myrmilla's home, the rail system she had described the night she died.

Shock had dulled his senses briefly, but his faculties returned just in time to hear the scraping of feet behind him. Still, age had slowed his reflexes. Before he had the chance to turn, a sharp prick shot pain along his neck, followed by a hard push that sent him falling forward to his hands and knees. His vision blurred, all sound muffled, and then nothing.

CHAPTER II

SHARP ENDS

Teufel waited tensely outside the warehouse for what seemed like an eternity, although it had only been a few minutes. There were no thoughts of running away, not for one second. He had only jogged ten feet before Roykur was so focused on sneaking into the building that he had forgotten all about the boy.

He respected Roykur, but just like everyone else, the lord assumed Teufel was incapable of being useful. This time would be different. This time, he would get the job done. Besides, he had just spent an entire day explaining himself to Sentinels. He was not about to go through that all over again.

Teufel's foot started tapping rhythmically when the guard returned to his post. The raucous noise on the far side had ceased. Roykur was taking too long. Even if he found Adalia, the guard had already blocked the escape route. Teufel took the outer walkway around the warehouse and circled to where Roykur's distraction had occurred. On this side of the street, there didn't appear to be any guards. There also didn't appear to be any way to enter the warehouse from here. Walking closer to the building, he could make out the sounds of heavy machinery from the factory above. A door, barely visible from the street, blended into the walls, but the closer he got, the more apparent it became.

Teufel pulled out a lock-picking kit he had received on his seventh birthday and looked around hesitantly. No one was looking his way. From the little experience he had breaking into places, it was better to appear that you belonged there than to try to hide. The lock was rudimentary—a click, and it opened easily. Once inside, he was confronted with a tall shelf full of boxes, blocking his view of the rest of the expansive warehouse. Crouching down, he peered through the opening between two boxes and could see the cracks of light trickle through on the far side.

Teufel stopped holding his breath as soon as he confirmed that no one else was in the area. He eased around the shelf and made his way to the wagon to see if Adalia was still in the back. One step past the wall of crates, and a hollow echo sounded beneath his feet. The false floor he stepped on tipped inward like the lid of a box, not placed all the way across.

Teufel grabbed at the smooth, wooden tipping floor but found no purchase. He rolled down into the pit and continued to descend a wide stone slope. As he slid, Teufel got his feet underneath him and slowed his momentum before he reached the bottom. The palms of his hands were scratched, and his pants were torn from hip to knee on his right side. *Well, I guess I had been needing a new set of clothes anyway.*

The bottom of the ramp was pitch black, and Teufel had to wave his arms in front of him as he walked in slow circles. With a bit of surprise and growing trepidation, Teufel found no walls. The area was much bigger than he had expected. He moved onward, eventually finding a wall, which curved into what he assumed to be a doorway.

As he entered the next room, his knuckles banged into something hard, and he grunted, shoving his other hand into his mouth, trying to suppress his urgent need to howl and curse. Breathing through the pain, he felt around what he had hit. A table. Teufel continued to feel his way around but stopped when his hands skimmed hair, then skin. His hands wrapped around, and he could feel the facial features—eyes, nose, ears. The form convulsed awake and began violently straining away from his touch. A muffled scream came from the body, undoubtedly restrained and gagged.

Testing his luck, Teufel whispered, "Adalia?"

The body instantly froze at hearing his voice. A flurry of unintelligible mumbles came from Adalia.

"Shh! Stop, stop. Someone kidnapped you, and I came to rescue you. They might still be here, so you need to be quiet, okay?"

She stopped her barrage immediately.

"Good, I'm going to take the gag out, then we can get out of here." Teufel lifted her head and untied the cloth, then pulled out the small towel that had been shoved into her mouth.

"Bleh!" Adalia spat.

"Shh!"

"Sorry, I'm still tied to the table. Can you get these ropes off me?"

"Yeah, hold on a moment." Teufel felt along Adalia's shoulders to her quite impressive arms until he found the rope. He traced the rope underneath the table and came up to the other side. The knot was nestled between her breasts, and he retreated at the discovery.

"Oh, come on, this is no time to get all fussy over some anatomy. Just untie me, please."

"Yes, of course, sorry." Teufel continued the work, fumbling and awkward. Of course, that just made it take longer, which made his embarrassment grow even more. He was glad she couldn't see his face at that moment. Finally finished, he moved to the rope, which held her hands and waist. Teufel thanked the gods for the ease with which this knot came undone. From there, Adalia sat up and could untie the rest of the knots herself.

"Try to find us some light," she said.

"Right, of course." Teufel circled slowly away from the table, keeping his arms in front. His hand found a counter; sliding his fingers along it, he touched papers, chalk, inkwells, books, and matches.

He struck a match, and a flare of illumination flooded the room, blinding him for a second. The match's flickering light burned down out a few seconds later, but Teufel spotted a lantern in the room's corner. He lit another match as the first went out, and used it to ignite the lantern. Teufel breathed a sigh of relief at having a stable light source.

The room had the look of some kind of complex workshop. Along the walls were chalkboards with intricate equations; the countertop was cluttered with scientific books and piles of notes.

Teufel felt Adalia's hand on his shoulder as he was examining a large drawing on the chalkboard, a design that appeared to be a maze of circles and lines with eight unevenly spaced blocks. There was an extremely complicated equation in neat writing next to the drawing, with many iterations of it poorly erased beneath it.

"What's this part say?" Adalia asked, moving the lantern in Teufel's hands to reveal two large words slashed across the left of the board. *It Works!*

Teufel felt a chill run down his spine, and he turned to face Adalia. "What works?"

They shared concerned looks for a moment.

"Well, I say we don't find out. Let's get out of here. Which way did you come from?" she asked.

"Over here." Teufel took a few steps, and then he remembered. "Roykur! He came in here to find you. Just a few minutes ago. Maybe he went to the factory level."

Adalia sighed. "Perhaps, but I don't want to leave him here wandering around looking for me. We can meet up and get out of here together."

"Right. I think I saw a way through over here." Teufel lifted the edge of a weighty curtain hung on a doorframe and exposed a dark tunnel. The tunnel curved, and beyond, it flickered with a faint light. They strode along the tunnel, just making out the low hum of voices, the clinking of glass, and the jingling of metal. They slowed their pace, if only to mask the sound of their approach. They could not be sure who they would find down here. The closer they got, the more apparent it became that it was not voices they were hearing but *a voice,* male by the sound of it, speaking to himself in obvious excitement. Pausing near the precipice, they listened to see if they could make sense of the ravings.

"So kind, came to me, didn't need plan A, B, or C. Wants you to have it, but I want it. I will be better. I know the secrets; he does not know the secrets. Just have to do the opposite, run it backward, it comes out, then I run it forward. Oh! I can't wait to see what comes out!"

"What the fuck is this maniac going on about?" Adalia whispered to Teufel. He just shrugged and inched his way around the curve in a low crouch. He peeked around the corner just as a loud grinding sounded, along with the snap of a mechanical crank locking into position. It was followed by a pained scream that seemed to come from the ceiling of the room.

Lord Roykur hung suspended above a metal tub of water, which glowed bright. The old man was fully clenched, straining against the chains wrapped around each of his limbs. His eyes bulged open, and his scream faded to a soundless howl. The circular machine whirred steadily louder, a smooth ball rolling faster and faster counterclockwise around the rail.

Teufel was shoved aside as Adalia rushed into the room. "Wait! Adalia! Shit." He ran in behind her, continuing his curses. Once fully in the room, he could see glowing tubes flowing into the stone pillars, illuminating symbols he had seen written in the previous room. Teufel looked around but couldn't see the one who had been talking to himself. He almost ran into Adalia as she halted, staring at her grandfather.

Teufel looked, and nearly dropped his lantern as a black sludge poured from Roykur's gaping mouth and began seeping out the edges of his eyes, ears, and nose.

"Grandpa!" Adalia screeched, and reached up to release Roykur's restrains.

"Adalia, get back! Don't go near him!" Teufel grabbed her waist and pulled as hard as he could, but he only succeeded in getting dragged forward. Adalia tried to pull his hands from her waist. Then an arrow whistled through the air, inches from her head. Instinctively, Adalia dropped to the ground and shouted, "Get down!"

The warning was unnecessary—her sudden drop had pulled Teufel down as well, crushing one of his arms beneath her.

"Random variables. There will always be the variable of random chance to everything." A man stepped out from behind a pillar, and with the click of a crossbow string, sent another bolt their way before knocking another. He wore a strange mask. It was carved with lines spreading from the eye openings; there was no hole for his mouth. Instead, a bouquet of sticks protruded.

The masked man sighed and raised his weapon, pointing it at the two of them. "I have what I need. I don't need you—you should leave, but not now. You've seen too much. Oh well."

The black mass that had been coagulating in the air below Roykur finally detached and plopped into the water with a splash. Adalia took advantage of the spray of water to scramble away. Teufel lay paralyzed, staring at the bolt pointed at his face. His mind screamed to run, but his body wouldn't move. The man cursed and turned his weapon to follow the real threat, but he lost her behind a pillar. Still, he wasted no time, running immediately to his crank, which he began pulling furiously in the opposite direction, all while keeping his eyes and crossbow pointed in the direction Adalia had gone.

The ball ground to a loud halt, sparks flying around the room, then began circling in the other direction. Teufel crawled back the way they had come and picked up the lantern.

Once the ball had its momentum going, the water in the tub brightened further, and the man moved quickly around the circle, touching the symbols carved into the pillars. Teufel shined the lantern on Roykur's lifeless form, his painfully contorted expression frozen on his face. *I really did like the guy.*

A pang of sorrow hit him, but another whiz of a crossbow bolt forced it away with no more than a second thought. Teufel moved toward the mechanism, hoping he could stop this madness from the crank. He set the lantern down on a table next to the whirl of gears, pistons, and levers. Reaching down, he gripped the handle with both hands.

"Don't!" the masked man shouted, and a bolt flew through the air, hitting Teufel in the shoulder. The boy was thrown backward into the table, knocking over the lantern. It fell, its glass smashing to pieces. The bolt had much more force than Teufel had expected, and it hurt more too, the world shrinking down to that sharp pain. Teufel did not have time to consider it long, though, as the smell of burning wool and the flood of light informed him that his coat was on fire. He shook and patted the coat, his shirt sleeves almost catching in the process. No longer aflame, he searched for the man with the crossbow.

Teufel blinked in surprise. Adalia had the man in a choke hold, and it appeared he had dropped his weapon to fend her off. He ran to help Adalia, the bolt heavy and wobbling in his shoulder. It shot lances of pain and spurts of blood with every step. The masked man pulled a knife from his belt and slashed at Adalia's arms. She cried out in pain and let him go. Teufel landed a swift kick to the man's knee, and he lurched down to the side, in front of the last stone pillar.

Before Teufel or Adalia could do anything, he reached up and pressed the symbol.

A low hum filled the room, the stones pulsing. Teufel turned to see the black mass rise slowly through the glowing water to sit upon its surface. Patterns danced across its form, twisting into strange symbols and shapes. A light flickered from beyond the tub, back at the crank. The oil from the lantern had not just ignited his coat, but the table as well. The humble beginnings of an inferno blazed before the onlookers.

Teufel focused his attention back to the mad man crouched next to him, who did not seem the least bit worried about the fire destroying his lair. The man pulled himself to his feet and darted toward the black mass, hands outstretched. Adalia was already behind him, her own hands wrapping around his neck. The flames flickered in her eyes, the calm, friendly woman replaced by fierce determination and murderous intent.

Teufel stepped into the fray, throwing punches at the man's ribs. He felt a sharp pain in his chest, similar to the crossbow bolt, but somehow different. Looking down, he saw the knife blade buried to the handle in his left breast. Teufel looked up into the eyes of the man through the strange mask and saw the firelight dancing in them. He thought he heard Adalia call out, but he was uncertain. His senses dulled, and then, with a blinding agony, they were pulled back into focus as the knife was pulled out. Teufel tried taking in a breath, but the air would not come. He felt blood foaming on his lips, and he stumbled back, falling into the tub. Light from the fire flickered, the room consumed above the water's surface, and as he sank to the bottom, he still hoped that Adalia would make it out.

CHAPTER 12

GOING THROUGH CHANGES

A vast, watery abyss encompassed all things endlessly. The torrents of flowing current swirled around the formless entities battering against them, with no effect on their infinite rhythm. They all traveled to a point, connected to a slumbering void. The light from a nexus of stars and infinite universes revealed itself within a pinprick of the celestial's opening eye. The imprisoned god, the dead god, had awoken.

Bursting from the surface of the tub, Roykur tried to scream. The haunting vision had set a burning behind his eyes. Only jets of water came forth. He coughed and retched until his whole body was sore from the effort. Once his lungs were free from fluids, he took in desperate gasps. He attempted to survey his surroundings, but the darkness enveloped everything.

Within the darkness, he smelled the charred aftermath of a fire and burnt meat. The smell made him hungry. Roykur pulled himself from the tub and fell on his side, not quite able to catch himself. He was disoriented from the darkness, dizzy from hunger and fatigue, and a weakness that went deeper than fatigue. *Fear.* The vision had disturbed him in ways he could not describe to himself, and it permeated his shaking body.

Roykur crawled on his hands and knees, creeping with one hand out in front of him until he found a wall. Unsteadily, he stood, leaning against the wall and sliding along it to guide him. Time blurred, his movements monotonous, and only a vague recognition of his actions came as he climbed out from the pit and exited the warehouse. His feet moved as if on their own, his thoughts lost in those watery depths.

Clarity hit Roykur, and his world snapped to focus. He stood facing his home, Manor Heimvelt. Aches and pains crashed down on him, the cuts and blisters on his feet from the miles he had walked from town. He was shivering fiercely; the frigid wind and his still-damp clothes encouraged the cold creeping farther into his bones. It was still dark out, but the soft glow of sunrise pressed against the distant mountaintops.

He walked around to the back of the manor to the door that was usually left open. Before he even reached it, he knew something was wrong. He looked up at the door he normally had to stoop to enter; now, his chest stood even with the handle. Roykur knew he should probably be more alarmed by this sudden height disparity, but his mind was overwhelmed by hunger, pain, and exhaustion.

He pushed his way into the manor and aimed straight for the kitchen. The quiet house echoed with the sound of every cabinet he opened. Not caring about the racket, he gathered a whole cheese wheel and a loaf of bread, then wandered to his room, devouring the pieces as he went. He stopped at the tall mirror next to his dresser and stared at the small boy who stared back at him, cheeks packed full of cheese.

Feeling a flush of warmth after a bit of food had reached his stomach, he lit a candle on the dresser and moved closer to the mirror, trying to examine himself in the flickering light. The first thing he noticed was his size. He had always been the tallest man in the room, but from where he stood compared to the dresser, he guessed he was barely taller than five feet. Then he recognized the narrow face and bright amber eyes. It was that boy he'd rescued from the Conservators. *Damn, boy, did you ever eat anything?*

Roykur flexed his arms in the mirror, more bone than flesh. He removed the wet shirt and dabbed at the painful wound in his chest, and another in his shoulder. They did not bleed. He ran his hands through his springy black hair, still damp. Then he moved to the washroom and toweled off what he could.

"Alright—" He jumped, startled at the sound of his voice, a reminder of the first time he had been this age. "Alright, either I am now living in the body of a child, or I am having a horrible nightmare. Please let this be a nightmare. I don't think I could stand going through puberty again."

Roykur rolled back the sheets, and just in case, he locked the bedroom door. No need to have Visari stumble in on him if he still looked like this in the morning. He blinked only twice before he was sound asleep.

THE EYE GREW WIDER, and the expanse of endless space and blinding light surrounded Roykur. A pull, an energy drew him toward the infinite horror before him.

A loud pounding on the bedroom door freed Roykur from his dreams.

"Hello? Roykur? You in there?" Visari's voice came through the door.

"Yeah!" Roykur winced as his voice cracked in a very unpleasant, grating way. Still a child, it seemed. He cleared his throat and attempted to deepen his voice. "Yeah, late night again."

"Oh, okay. I was worried when you and Adalia didn't show for the family feast last night."

Shit! Adalia!

Thinking quickly, Roykur lied. "Sorry about that. We got caught in a bit of trouble last night. Nothing we couldn't handle, nothing serious, but it took up most of the night, and Adalia decided to go back to the barracks to rest."

"I see . . . I guess as long as you both are alright, that's what matters. If you are hungry, I can have breakfast started?"

"No, that's alright, I had a snack before bed. Which was probably a little more than an hour ago. I'll probably try to catch a few more hours."

"Oh, of course, sorry to wake you. I was just worried. Sweet dreams." Visari's footsteps faded back down the hall.

My dreams have been anything but sweet. Stirred by the realization that he didn't know what had happened to his granddaughter, he threw himself from his sheets, hurrying to slip his feet into the gross shoes he had stumbled in with. Moving quietly through the manor, he listened to the sizzle of breakfast and took in the wafting smell of cured meats cooking nearby. He was still hungry, despite his earlier snack. But he had more important things to do.

Roykur eyed the road that twisted through the trees and out of sight. He sighed and started his long trek back into the city, but was startled by his light step. Testing his movements, he transitioned into a jog. With a bit of excitement, he realized he felt great, despite the various bruises and wounds covering his body. They were different aches—none of the usual stiffness, the dull throbs or cracking joints. He really was young again. Maybe he should have taken Legast up on his offer when he had the chance. *I could have prevented this mess, I could have saved Adalia, and I would have been young in a body taller than an ale keg.*

Roykur's newfound youth didn't equate to boundless stamina, but his burning lungs and calves filled him with nostalgia for his long days of Sentinel training. The towers of the city loomed just ahead, and Roykur conserved his energy and walked the rest of the way. *Adalia. Please be okay, please be okay.*

Thoughts of his grandchild kept him anxious and dark. He tried to remember the events of the previous night, but after entering the warehouse, the only thing he remembered were the nightmares. Roykur wasn't sure how she ended up in that warehouse, but it was probably because of him. Was someone trying to tell him to back off? Or had he been lured there?

Once he reached the bustling streets of Ver'a'saile, he moved with purpose through the crowds toward the Sentinel headquarters. He figured someone there might have answers by now, and if not, the warehouse was just a few blocks in the same direction. His progress slowed, however, and his frustration grew at his new physical perspective. Before, when the throng of people grew tightly packed, they would still yield to his distinct looming figure. Now, he was jostled, other people distracted by their own hurry. Once or twice, he was knocked completely down, barely spared a glance. It took him a while to figure out, but he moved faster once he realized he had to be the one to dash out of the way.

Roykur pushed open the door to the surface level of the Sentinel headquarters. This level was dedicated to administration and was where citizens could request nonemergency help from the Sentinels. Most of the requests were trivial—noise complaints, Sentinel presence for events, and the like. Several long lines of people stood restlessly waiting their turn at the counter. Roykur didn't bother waiting in line. He pushed past a few people, who responded with some obscenities but nothing more, clearly preferring not to lose their spot. Roykur pressed straight through the door marked *Sentinels Only* and met the gazed of a confused recordkeeper.

"Hey. You're not allowed back here, can't you read?" said the overweight, spectacled man, sounding almost bored. Slightly louder, he called, "Can someone get this kid out of here?"

The room was a buzz of typewriter clicking and voices from scribes and recordkeepers, moving about and processing citizen requests. A few familiar faces glanced down at Roykur as they passed by, their expressions dismissive, the large man's request ignored. Roykur could see that this man didn't care enough to do anything about the situation himself. *Time for the old tried-and-true.*

"Look, I am here on official business. I am collecting the report on the warehouse incident for Commander Volmirk. Do you know where I can find a copy?" Roykur tried to keep his back straight in his most imposing manner—or rather, it would have been imposing before his change. The man just shrugged nonchalantly, giving up his own attempt at authority.

"I told the commander the report won't be finished anytime soon. I can't seem to get her to type any faster. Go over there and see for yourself. The little bliest just ignores me." Roykur glowered at the man for his foul words, but his heart skipped a beat when he realized who he must be referring to. He made his way in the direction the man had pointed, weaving between identically paper-strewn desks. Roykur stepped around a support beam, and there she was, sitting calmly at a desk in the far back corner of the room. He stopped just short of reaching her.

"Adalia?" asked Roykur, and he hoped she recognized the boy well enough so he could ask how she was doing. Adalia turned slowly in her chair to look at Roykur, her eyes red and puffy from, presumably, a night of tears.

"Teufel?" Her eyes widened in surprise. "Teufel!"

She leaped from her chair and scooped him up in a powerful embrace. Roykur was used to his granddaughter's overly enthusiastic hugs, but at this moment, he had to assume this was what being a doll felt like. He let out a groan from the strain and the sharp pressure on his wounds.

Adalia released him. "Oh my, your chest. I'm sorry, are you alright? How did you survive? I thought you were dead!"

Well, she remembers him at least.

Roykur's hand went to the bruised area at his chest he had felt all day. He carefully undid the top two buttons of his shirt and stared down at the knife wound, which looked like it had barely begun healing. There was a distinct lack of blood or bandage. Thinking quickly, Roykur tried to be as vague as possible.

"The knife didn't cut very deep." He quickly redid his buttons. Then he saw her bandaged arm. "What about you? Are you okay?"

"I'm fine, just some scratches." Adalia's face paled. "I left you to die in that horrible place . . . I am so sorry, Teufel. The fire spread too fast, I didn't have time to grab you or my . . ."

She trailed off, forcing back tears. "I am glad you're okay, I really am. I just can't believe Grandpa is gone."

The tears rolled down her cheeks in earnest.

A weight pressed against Roykur; he could never stand to see her cry. Even when she was a baby, Adalia had always been a happy child. He cradled her hand in his.

"I am glad you're okay too, little Dralm. I was worried sick about you." Roykur felt his own tears well up in his eyes. "It's alright to cry, no point in holding it in. You will feel bad about this for a long time, but it will get better, trust me."

Adalia sniffled back her tears, and a small smile crept onto her face. "My grandpa used to call me little Dralm. Did he tell you that?"

Shit. I can't very well tell her now. I need to stay close to her, and I can't do that if she thinks this Teufel kid is absolutely mad.

"Yeah . . . I overheard you two talking during that crime scene." Roykur patted her hand tenderly and let go. "So, what happened to the man who stabbed me?"

You're not her grandpa right now. You have to play a part for the time being.

Adalia's face darkened. "The djavul got away. Once he saw you fall in the water, he *freaked* out and went wild. Knocked me down and ran out."

"Olacka! So he's still out there then," said Roykur, and Adalia nodded grimly.

"I haven't been allowed outside the headquarters since. Fritch says that it's for my protection."

"Well, I should say so! You were abducted out on the street. Clearly you're a target."

Adalia looked abashed at his words. "I never thanked you for saving me. I would probably be dead if you hadn't come along."

Roykur raised his eyebrows. "He did? I mean, I did? I did. Uh, you're welcome."

I think I'm starting to like this kid.

Adalia leaned down and gave him a quick peck on the cheek.

"My hero," she said with a wry grin.

Okay, I like this kid less now.

To Roykur's relief, a door flipped open from the second story, and Conservator Fritch trotted down the stairs. He walked up to the pair of them, giving Roykur a confused look. "Adalia, I thought you said this kid died at the warehouse?"

"I'm hardier than you think. It's tough to kill this old man," Roykur said reflexively, then realized how that might sound. *Good gods, this is going to be harder than I thought.*

"I don't even know what that means. Weird kid." Fritch shook his head. "Adalia, they finished with the scene and have recovered the body. We—we need you to identify it."

Adalia's expression was grim. She looked like she might be on the verge of throwing up. "Your mother is being informed now," he continued. "I know you said you wanted to be the one to do this, but we can wait for her."

"No, I'll do it."

"I'll come with you," said Roykur.

Fritch stepped in front of him. "Oh, no you won't. You are going back to the holding cells until we can figure out what your role is in all this."

"Please, Fritch, I want him there," said Adalia, her voice fragile.

Fritch raised a finger to object, then paused, taking a moment to consider her request. "Alright, but he isn't leaving my sight."

Adalia nodded. "Thank you."

They followed Fritch back up the stairs to the second floor. The surrounding building seemed to flow faster, the people swarming about their work, while the three trudged somberly to a cold tile room with several long metal tables. The one at the far side of the room had a clean linen cloth draped across a large body. Roykur's body. It was certainly tall enough.

"Oh, merciful Elska . . . shield my heart," Adalia mumbled to herself, and Roykur gave her another consoling pat as they moved into the room.

The morgue custodian gave the group a nod. "Just tell me who you think it is."

He lifted the sheet, and the pungent smell of charred meat wafted to Roykur—the same smell he recognized from his dazed revival. His stomach twisted. The coppery, burnt smell had made him hungry yesterday, and now that he knew, it sickened him. Memory flooded him of the time he had been called to the aftermath of an arsonist. The scorched remains of the victims had the same acrid smell. Something was different. He wasn't sickened because the smell was repulsive. He felt sick because the body smelled . . . delicious.

Roykur still hadn't had a proper meal yet, and he was starving.

"I . . . I can't really tell. I mean, it sort of looks like him. Yes, yes, it's him. No one else is that tall, and his face is shaped right." Adalia looked extremely uncomfortable and was probably feeling a little sick. At least she was sick for the right reasons. "I'm not feeling well." She hurried from the morgue, but not before emptying her stomach across the clean tiles. She slipped in a quiet "sorry" before continuing out.

Roykur followed and found her sitting on the edge of a seat, looking stunned. His attention was diverted as Fritch grabbed his arm roughly.

"Teufel, leave her be. She needs to be alone right now. And you have to answer some questions . . . well, *more* questions." Fritch pulled him from the morgue and into the hallway.

Roykur scowled at the Conservator. He was still unaccustomed to others manhandling him this way. Even after he had grown frail, he always had intimidation or respect, and now he had neither. He attempted to jerk his arm free without success. It was a solid grip. "Let go of me, and then we can have a pleasant chat. But first I need something to eat—"

Roykur's thought vanished as Commander Volmirk came around the corner at a quick pace, heading for the morgue entrance. He was trailed by a midnight-skinned man in a finely embroidered coat. The man had a beard that was long, dark, and squarely trimmed. His face was impassive, but his eyes sat on the brink of tears.

Legast had de-aged more, now looking exactly as he had when they'd both fought against the Kolkrabba. The two men walked past Roykur without even glancing his way. A long moment passed, and a pained wailing sounded from the morgue.

Roykur had been old, and he knew that he could have died at any point, but seeing the pain firsthand tore his heart apart. He stood listening to his best friend's cries for a while before he turned to Fritch. "Alright, let's go. I can't hear this anymore."

CHAPTER 13
COINCIDENCE OVER EVIDENCE

The investigation continued. That was all Roykur was told, as two entire weeks went by sitting in the drafty cell in Sentinel Headquarters.

Food was the only thing he had to break the monotony of his day. At first, his hunger seemed voracious, especially considering how small a person he now was, and the enormous meals he consumed never made a dent in his scrawny physique. After a few days of regular meals, though, his hunger pangs had subsided. He knew the procedure for an investigation, and they were within the law to hold him during their preliminary case development and analysis. However, two weeks was the limit. He should be free to go unless they officially accused him of something, which he had yet to hear. Roykur was growing slightly weary of his situation, but he had faith in his fellow Sentinels. Truthfully, the nightmare that came to him each night worried him more. Every time it came, it was slightly different, but it always left him with the same foreboding dread.

Roykur had finished breakfast and was preparing to see if he could beat his previous record of three pushups when a fully armored Sentinel came through the hallways. Roykur cocked his head. *This Sentinel looks to be on official business, yet completely lost.*

Roykur whistled and waved. Giving directions to a lost newbie was at least something to do. "Hey Sentinel, looking for someone?"

"Uh, yeah, you." Adalia lifted the visor of her helmet and gave him a wink. The gesture held no genuine mirth.

"Adalia! Good to see you. How are you doing? How is the investigation going? Are they going to let me out soon?" The questions spilled out.

"Woah, slow down. Here's the thing—we are kind of in a rush, but we don't want to look like we're in a rush, okay? I'm just going to get you out of that cell, and then we can go somewhere, and I will answer all your questions." Adalia spoke slowly, calm and deliberate. Roykur's face dropped at that tone, the tone for keeping yourself and everyone relaxed in an intense situation. He'd taught it to her, after all.

"Ah . . . olacka." Roykur sighed. "Okay, no questions. Let's break out of here."

Adalia raised an eyebrow at his cool resolve but maintained her soothing voice. "That is good, very good. Now, no panic or rushing about. Just act like we're going for a pleasant walk."

She led Roykur by the arm through the maze of cells and out a large door. A Sentinel was sitting at a desk just to the right of the door, and Adalia gave him the briefest of nods as they walked right on by. *Very impressive.*

Despite her calm composure, Roykur could feel tremors in her grip.

Upstairs, they casually walked past the busy flow of Sentinel workers and didn't seem to attract any attention. Adalia hurried to the left at the sight of several Sentinels chatting amiably at a back door, then began climbing the stairs. She mumbled something Roykur thought sounded like "Plan B." *Great.*

The third story was far less populated, and they found the exit unguarded. The exit was unguarded because it led to a balcony that circled the building just below the second-level platform; there was no way down or up from here.

"What now?" Roykur, for all his experience, had not thought of ways to escape this place. His place. Adalia ignored him and rounded the balcony, stopping as a rope dropped from the platform above. She gave it two tugs and then began shedding her armor. She stripped to only a loose linen shirt, the stiff padded trousers, and the boots of the uniform. They appeared plain enough. The cool breeze whipped at her, and she shivered.

"Teufel, you first, up the rope." Roykur scrambled up, and his shoulders immediately began burning with the strain. *I have zero upper-body strength, it seems.*

The rope must have been somewhere around thirty feet, and by the time Roykur had made it to the top, he swore it was a hundred. *By the strength of Idrok, I hate being weak.*

He was hoisted the last foot by a brawny arm and tossed unceremoniously on the platform.

"There's a coat and stocking cap for you," Fritch said, watching the rope tighten around its anchor. Roykur picked up the smaller of the two coats, both tailored short at the sternum and tapered to midthigh in the back. It was not the warm wool overcoat, but these would do for now. Adalia made it up the rope much quicker than he had, and accepted the coat eagerly. The three of them walked in silence for a long while, and Roykur assumed they were trying to put a respectful distance between themselves and the headquarters before they would explain things to him.

The ground rumbled, an ominous omen, but they made it to their destination just as the geyser water poured down. It was a small but quaint tavern. Once they were seated and drinks were ordered, Roykur broke the silence.

"Alright, I can't say I've been more bored in my life, but can one of you please tell me why we just made ourselves targets for the entire Sentinel force? They'll have posters up before dark, and then we won't be able to hide for much longer."

"It wasn't safe there anymore. At least not for you or me," said Adalia, looking down at her mug of warm cider. "Things got bad fast."

"What do you mean?"

"Right after you were taken to the cells, my mother came to identify the body, but she claims it wasn't Roykur. She says that she spoke with him that very morning." There was a lump in Roykur's throat.

Oh no.

"There was a lot of confusion, and Sentinels were sent to search the manor. They found . . . things. They're calling them trophies."

"Trophies? What trophies?" Roykur tried to pull himself up higher at the table.

"They found a false floorboard in his office. There was a box with envelopes in it. Each envelope had a name of one of the Husk Slayer's victims . . . and a bit of their hair," said Fritch.

Shock hit Roykur like a punch to the gut. "No, that can't be. Someone is framing me—Roykur. He is not the Husk Slayer!"

His mind raced. *They tried to kill me. Tried to kill my granddaughter. Now they are set on ruining my name as well.*

"We agree with you," said Adalia, gesturing to Fritch and herself. "However, there hasn't been another murder since Grandpa died. In two weeks, not a single one."

Roykur already knew what the implication was, but Adalia continued to explain it to him, a kid who would not know. "The Husk Slayer killed sporadically, but never more than a few days apart. Two weeks without a victim means that either there is an elaborate conspiracy in which the Husk Slayer is involved, or . . ."

"Or I—Roykur was the killer." His eyes went wide in disbelief. "What about Visari? She said Roykur was still alive, wouldn't that put a hole in their theory? And what about the warehouse where you and I were?"

Adalia just shook her head. "Things got weird. Witches ran their blood test, came back as a match. Sentinels just think Mom spoke with a servant. She admitted the voice did sound different. Also, the warehouse records say it was being run by the Heimvelt house."

Roykur's heart sank a little further. A possible defense slipped from his fingers. "That's impossible. The warehouse and factory are owned by the king. It's where the new elixir is being made. House Becoven was in charge, not Heimvelt."

"I don't know where you could have possibly heard that," said Fritch, getting annoyed. "Any proof to back up your claim?"

He reached for Legast's note and remembered it was likely burnt to a crisp along with the rest of his body. "No, sorry—I just know what I heard."

"You seem to have heard a lot of things in two weeks of lock-up. Unfortunately, the paperwork says otherwise. I can't just take your word for it." Fritch leaned in, sipping his cider with some venom.

Adalia piped in, "Anyhow . . . many of the Sentinels started convincing themselves that this was the reason Roykur never caught the Husk Slayer. They think whatever Roykur was doing in that warehouse finally caught up with him. They quickly got worked up, pointing fingers at you and me as accomplices. They started demanding that the commander officially arrest both of us. He refused, with there being no evidence, but that just made things worse."

"Did they not take your statement into account?" asked Roykur.

"They did. I lost them somewhere between 'black goo' and 'psycho in a mask.'" Adalia threw her hands up.

Psycho mask? Black goo? What the fuck is she talking about? I need to hear her statement.

Fritch leaned back, setting his cup down. "That's when I decided we needed to get you two out of there. Escaping could make things worse, but if we had stayed . . . well, I have seen what happens when a group of people are whipped into a frenzy. They become so convinced that they're doing the right thing, they lose all common sense. Like that incident a couple of weeks ago, with the Mining Guild."

"You mean the miner labor dispute?" Roykur ventured, recalling the document Legast had been working on.

"Yeah, that 'labor dispute' was an attempt at mass murder. Collapsed a tunnel on a group of Vogels working in the mines, all because they won the city contract over expanding the city underground," said Fritch.

"Did they survive?" Adalia asked.

"Yeah, they weren't crushed, and Vogels can dig their way out of anywhere."

"Just a moment." It was Roykur's turn to lean on the table, the little he could lean. "If it was just Adalia and me that were in trouble, why did you come with us?"

"I didn't—I'm out working a lead right now. I figured it would be a good idea for me to stick around and hopefully steer this Husk Slayer investigation in a saner direction. Especially with Simune and Binjek back on the case."

Roykur scoffed. "Olacka, what are those two idiots doing back on it?"

"Well, they were only suspended after beating the piss out of you. Ever since they got back, they've been dead set on proving Roykur was the Husk Slayer," said Fritch.

"Of course they are." Roykur sighed, waved the server over for another cider. "So, what's the plan now? Do we just keep our heads down and wait for you to unravel this conspiracy?"

"Do you have a better plan?" asked Fritch.

Roykur slapped a hand on the table. "Yeah, I want to go back to the warehouse and figure out what on Erden was going on in there."

"I said a *better* plan. Not a 'wander in active crime scenes and get murdered by a mob' plan."

"Besides, you saw everything already," said Adalia. "Anything left has been burned away."

I really need to hear what happened. Roykur dug his nails into the side of his thumbs. "Fine. Where are we holing up?"

Fritch grew a wicked grin. "You gave me an idea. You two aren't just holing up. I contacted your extended family, and I've hired them for protection and to keep us informed of any word on the street."

"My family?" Roykur said, trying frantically to guess what Teufel's family connections were.

"Wait, I thought that was dangerous for Teufel. The plan was to go to the Witch Enclave," said Adalia, concern rising in her voice.

Great, I have a new dangerous family.

Fritch waved a hand, dismissing Adalia's argument. "It will be the backup. The Witch Enclave is too far from headquarters. If you two are close, I can check in and maybe keep you appraised of the situation. If you behave. Besides, my contact is already here."

"Boss! It really is you." A large woman in a sleeveless tunic plopped down next to Roykur and wrapped her thick arms around him, squeezing tight. His face was pressed into the hairy pocket of the woman's armpit, and the pungent body odor forced him to gag. Pulling back, he looked up at her greasy curls, one eye covered in a leather eyepatch, and the several gaps in her mischievous grin. "There was bettin' going around whether or not you kicked it. And I just won a lot of money."

She gave him a wink, or Roykur thought it was supposed to be a wink. It was hard to tell with only the one eye. He tried smiling back, and an uncomfortable time passed. There was a considerable amount of information he was supposed to know, and Roykur just hoped someone else would do the talking. Finally, Fritch broke the silence.

"Okay, this is weird. Marge, you said you could protect these two?" Fritch moved in his seat and began rummaging through his pack.

"Oh yeah, they can stay in the spare room in my apartments, top level. They can do some cleaning while they stay." Marge smiled back at Roykur. "Don't worry, Boss, I'll make sure *the boss* doesn't know yer there either. He was pretty upset when we found out you were alive; put his money on the other side of the bet, a lot of money. I told him this was just a simple protection job."

"I see . . . Thank you." Roykur was choosing his words carefully, but they must have sounded somber, because Adalia reached over and put a hand over his, a sympathetic look in her eyes.

"This is for the Jaspers." Fritch pulled out a round sack the size of a melon. "The agreed-upon amount."

Both Roykur's and Adalia's eyes widened at the sight of the money. *Jaspers . . . sounds familiar . . . oh! That was a newish criminal organization I had heard about. How on Erden did a kid like Teufel get into the Jaspers?*

"Where did you get that much coin?" asked Adalia.

Fritch just snorted. "Your mother. She insisted she help support you and this investigation. So, I suggested this idea to her, and here we are."

There goes all my money.

Marge lifted the leather sack, weighing it. She reached in and selected a handful of the tarnished coins, jiggling them in her palm before slipping them back into the sack. Letting out a nasal laugh, she wheezed, "Of course, for the Jaspers."

"Is that not enough money for Teufel to square his debt to the Jaspers and them some?" asked Adalia.

"It ain't about the money for Leondal anymore. Can't say I can relate. It's always about the money for me," she said, chuckling.

Steam rose off the damp streets as Roykur and Adalia followed Marge up to the eighth level. Roykur always loved the warm, humid air after a geyser eruption. The reprieve didn't last long, though, and before they reached the top level, he was shivering at the harsh bite of the wind through his light jacket. To Roykur's relief, Marge's apartment was only one tower over, and soon they were inside.

The apartment was practically empty, yet somehow still incredibly filthy. The entryway served as the living room and kitchen, with only a wood-burning stove and an upholstered chair, worn and stained. Roykur could see a tipped bin overflowing with refuse just behind the chair, and a pile of dirty clothes spilled out from the hallway.

"Room at the far end is yers for now, only got the one cot though." Marge plopped herself down in the chair, pulling out a thick book and a leg of meat from the side of the seat cushion. Roykur read the title of the book: *The Integral Influence of Vogel Culture on Modern Architecture and Infrastructure.*

Roykur and Adalia looked at each other, then back at Marge.

"What? I like to read," she said defensively.

The weight of the day rested on Roykur, and he felt his shoulders grow heavy. He retreated to the far room, which to his surprise was relatively clean. Though, he figured it was because no one ever went in there. *Different cell, same waiting game.*

He sat on the floor, leaning back against the wall. Adalia joined him, her back to the wall opposite. *What is going on? What is happening to me? What really happened in that warehouse?*

Roykur looked at Adalia with a determined glare. He was going to find out the truth. "What happened in that warehouse? It's a bit fuzzy for me. I remember seeing Roykur outside, and next thing I was waking up in a tub of water."

Adalia looked up from her feet with an exhausted, confused look. "What? You don't remember that night?"

Roykur rubbed at the dull throb at his temples. "I'm having trouble remembering a lot of things, actually. Please, just humor me?"

Adalia's expression turned ominous. "My grandpa always said it was better to get these things off your chest rather than let them fester. You were heroic. I woke up to a dark room, and a few minutes later you were there to untie me." She cleared her throat and looked back at her feet. "Then we found the ritual site with the man in that terrible mask. There was a contraption that had a spinning thing and tubes. Then a black thing that came out of Grandpa, or the machine put it there, or . . . I don't know. It fell into the tub of water."

Another deep breath. "There was a bit of fighting, and then you got stabbed. Soon as you fell into the water, the masked man ran. I didn't even have time to save you or Grandpa. The fire was just too hot, so I got out of there."

"I should be dead," Roykur finally said after a long silence.

"What? Absolutely not, it's just fortune that you fell in the water—"

"I died. I know I died, and yet here I am," Roykur interrupted.

"You didn't die, Teufel, you survived that evil ritual. You survived getting stabbed, and now we are being unjustly accused of a crime. It's a lot to take in, I know, but we will get through this. You are a good person, I can tell."

Roykur looked into his granddaughter's eyes, saw her pure selflessness in that moment. He had never been prouder. Here he was, wallowing in his own troubles, and the person he was supposed to look after was doing her best to be a foundation of support for a complete stranger. His shoulders felt a little lighter at that moment.

"You're a good person too, Adalia. I just want you to know how proud I am of the woman you have become." Roykur's last words were drowned out by Marge yelling from the main room in the apartment.

"Dinner is ready!" she wailed. Each word grew in volume and intensity.

Adalia just smiled at Roykur. "Let's get some food and get some shuteye early. We'll want to be well rested for whatever the next few days throw at us."

Roykur couldn't argue. As always, he was starving.

CHAPTER 14
SPARE PARTS

arge's cooking was terrible. The bird was dry, bland, and on the verge of rancid.

After that, Roykur insisted on cooking their future meals. The following day, he found an entire shelf of seasonings in a cabinet, which was odd, since Marge hadn't used any when she cooked. Adalia tried to spend her time tidying the bare landscape of the apartment, but she was done the morning of the second day. Instead of throwing the discarded bones out, they boiled and cleaned the bones and etched numbers on the sides for an impromptu game of Woldst. Normally, the numbers were carved on draugker bones, but fowl bones were a decent miniature version.

They had all finished dinner and were draining the last of the tomato-basil soup from their bowls when there was a knock at the door. Marge stuck her head out. A quick mumble of words was exchanged. Closing the door, Marge flung her coat on, grabbed a lantern, and motioned for Roykur and Adalia to do the same. Without a word, they followed Marge out of the apartment and into the cool evening air.

Marge spoke over her shoulder as they walked. "We got us a

fresh kill. Could be the Husk Slayer and the Sentinels haven't gotten to it yet. Sent word to have that handsome Conservator . . . Fritch, was that his name? Yeah, Fritch, he's gonna meet us there."

The harsh wind still stung at his numb face even after they left the eighth upper level. Roykur found himself making use of his two sizeable companions. They made excellent shields against the freezing evening air. The post-dinner crowds swelled the farther down they went. Lanterns hung in shop doors, a warm hearth visible from the street, attempting to entice potential customers in from the cold. The glow from a window illuminated the bright-eyed face of a small girl as she rode atop her father's shoulders. It was a reminder of the time when Adalia had been that young, a beacon of hope after he had lost his son. The father set the girl down, and she ran to a young couple.

"Grandma! Grandpa!" squealed the little girl. The couple scooped her up together, and there was a chorus of joyful laughter. Roykur gawked at them as he walked by. *They hardly look old enough to be adults, much less grandparents. The elixir of life has changed everything.*

The three of them made their way down to the fourth level. The loud grinding of a metal shop and the ring of a blacksmith's hammer came from the windows on a second story. The noise kept this platform clear of casual perusers and left only those few individuals with serious business. Fortunately for the group's clandestine purpose, there wasn't much business at the blacksmith at this time of day.

Underneath the shop, on the first floor of the platform, was a wide garage that held a variety of scrap, from rusted stove tops to metal support beams. A hooded figure stood just outside and made a sign with his hand to the group. Marge waved another hand signal in front of the lantern. The figure nodded and wandered off. Handing Adalia the lantern, Marge stepped to the side of the garage. "I'll keep watch from out here. I can smell something already, and I'm not getting paid enough to poke around with these kinds of things."

Roykur eyed the streets nearby. It appeared clear, so he followed

Adalia into the garage. The air was thick with the smell of rust and musty disuse. Then a faint, familiar scent of decay drifted to Roykur's senses, and the farther into the garage they went, the stronger it became. Ducking under a beam, Roykur's foot slid across a splash of blood slicked along the floor. The smell had become especially potent.

With a gasp, Adalia stepped back, bumping into him. Guiding her to the side, he looked at the mangled body before them. Roykur expected to see a horrific scene, but the Husk Slayer murders had purpose, had a progression of skill and style. This was pure rage.

He was about to say just that when Adalia spoke first. "This is the Husk Slayer's work."

"What makes you say that?"

"He lashed out like this before . . . when he got his name." The memory of that infamous scene flooded back to Roykur.

"Yes, it does bear a resemblance to that day," Roykur said as he moved methodically around body, taking in what he could in the dim light.

Adalia shook herself, turning to Roykur with a confused look. "What does that mean?"

He grunted in frustration. He was growing tired of pretending to not be himself. "The day he got his name, the papers quoted Roykur saying that this scene was a significant day for the Husk Slayer. Something happened to him, and he lashed out in anger. Well, doesn't this look angry to you?"

Roykur gestured to the display before them. A man hung from an iron rod that jutted in through his mouth and out the back of his skull. The man's back was torn open, ribs broken outward like two doors to a vacant Human cage. Every organ that had been in the man's body was on the floor underneath, smashed to a pulp with repeated blows. Both arms and legs had been removed at the hip and shoulder. Roykur moved Adalia's arm, holding the lantern closer, and he could make out the yellow crystal substance that coated and sealed those areas. Scanning the room, Roykur spotted the limbs thrown into the far end of the garage. A leg had been skewered up high on another metal rod.

"The yellow crystals definitely prove the connection to the other murders . . . but he didn't take the organs this time, just like his previous lash-out," said Adalia, putting together the pieces.

"I'm not so sure anymore. It seems this effect would happen to anyone who had consumed the elixir. Don't forget the most important part—this is recent. There is very little decay, I would say, only a couple days old, no more than a week. Once Fritch gets here, we can hand off the evidence and hopefully clear up Roykur's name and get us out of Marge's place."

"When did you become an expert on corpses?" Adalia planted her fists on her hips, narrowing her eyes at him. A high-pitched squeak was muffled as she shoved her face into her elbow.

"What? What's wrong?" asked Roykur.

Adalia lifted her head out of her elbow, but she kept her eyes down. She took slow, calming breaths, desperately trying to keep herself together. Then she raised the lantern to the body's face. It was difficult to recognize with all the bruising and the broken jaw, but it was, without a doubt, Conservator Fritch.

"Wutheril have mercy. Husk Slayer must have got him right after he left us," said Roykur. He leaned in closer to inspect the surroundings. Adalia did her best to look anywhere else.

Just below Fritch's mutilated body, a tin sheet was propped up, and Roykur spotted what appeared to be letters painted onto the side.

"You're awfully calm for your second body," said Adalia.

"Godsdamnit!" Roykur snapped, his hand going over his mouth to quiet himself.

"I take that back. What is it?"

He pointed to the painted letters, which spelled out a name: *Roykur.*

Two rhythmic drums beats sounded off the wall, the signal that someone was coming. Roykur immediately heard voices at the entrance. *Damn, she couldn't give us more warning than that?*

Roykur motioned for Adalia to follow him, and they squeezed through a cluster of large stoves, doused the lantern, and lay quietly on their bellies. Soon enough, another light source illuminated the garage, but Adalia and Roykur remained as still as possible, breathing in slow and shallow. *Please don't look over here. Do your jobs with your usual incompetence.*

Voices finally broke the silence. "What the fuck? I got guts all over my shoes. By all the gods, this is a fucking mess."

"That smell . . ." One of them dry heaved.

"I swear by the eight gods, don't you dare puke on me. You're a Conservator, for fuck's sake, get a stronger stomach," said the other voice.

"Oh, fuck you man, it was one time, and I had been out drinking the night before."

Simune and Binjek. Of course those two idiots would shove their noses into this. *Do they know the body is Fritch?*

A third voice interrupted their not-so-playful banter. "Gentlemen, I trust you are having a good evening."

"I usually have a good evening when you swing by, my lord. It usually means I am about to get a bonus."

"Dispensing with the pleasantries, as usual, I see. Very well. Half now, and half after we see results." Roykur could hear the jingle of coin exchanging hands.

"What's the job this time? Want us to make this one go away?" Simune asked.

"No, everything about this vileness can stay. We just want one detail altered on your report. This happened three weeks ago, understand?" said the stranger.

Binjek whistled. "Man, you must have really hated Roykur."

Three weeks? They have no clue that the body is Fritch, and yet they're still covering it up.

"It is not a matter of hate. The Initiative doesn't hate, it does what must be done." Roykur blinked dumbly at the back of the metal stove. Disbelief gave way slowly to boiling anger. *The Initiative is trying to frame me? I formed that lot of ungrateful djavuls!*

"His death presented us with an opportunity in this tenuous moment in history and gave him one last chance to serve a greater purpose," the stranger continued. "I am sure he would have been pleased to know the lives he is saving with the simple cost of a reputation."

What lives are being saved by hiding the identity of a killer? Why the fuck would I be happy about this?

"Yeah, well, fuck that guy. Hit me in the face with a plank of wood," Binjek whined.

"Yes. He was rather disagreeable."

The voices trailed off, the Conservators and the stranger leaving. Roykur lay there a moment, taking it all in. His own organization was trying to frame him for the murders of over three hundred innocents and, by consequence, covering for the actual killer. A monster who had evaded him most of his life, the failure that had haunted him. He saw the victims, every face, each one staring through lifeless eyes, accusing. Their condemnation was clear: *You promised us justice!*

An ice-cold shiver ran down his spine, and he felt sick—sick of his failure, sick at the Initiative's betrayal.

Roykur slid out from their hiding place, carefully avoided the gore-spattered area, and stalked to the scrap garage entrance. Sentinels had created a perimeter around the opening, Simune and Binjek stood just outside, barking orders to their armored counterparts. Simune subconsciously patted the large purse on his hip. A well-dressed figure in a tall hat slipped away from the Conservators into a small gathering of curious bystanders.

Roykur caught the eye of Marge, who lingered on the edge of the platform across from the blacksmith shop. She caught his eye, nodded, and sauntered right past the perimeter. Her jacket shrugged off her shoulders as she leaned in, propositioning the two Conservators with extreme vulgarity. She forced the top few buttons of her shirt open, revealing more hair than cleavage. Roykur couldn't hear what Marge was whispering, but based on the gestures, he was fairly certain he knew. Every Sentinel turned to watch the spectacle. and Roykur heard Adalia clear her throat uncomfortably. The two Conservators' expressions were of complete horror and revulsion. It was almost enough to break through his dark thoughts. Almost.

Roykur and Adalia slipped out of the other side of the garage easily and rounded the corner. Adalia breathed a sigh of relief.

"That was close. Marge has quite a . . . unique sense of romance," Adalia said, letting out an uncomfortable chuckle. Roykur barely heard the comment as his eyes hunted through the sparse late-night crowd. Then he saw the long, embroidered coat, the puffs of wool above the collar. Atop his head was an elegant hat curved up at the brim and adorned with the tips of draugker horns. A lord always stood out in a crowd.

"There he is. Follow me." Roykur shot through the crowd, trying to maintain visual contact with the nobleman. His shoulder and chest twinged, the healing not quite finished. Once he had closed a suitable distance, he slowed, matching his pace to the lord's.

Adalia strode alongside Roykur and leaned in. "Who are we following?"

"Shh. Hat with horns," he whispered.

"You think that gaudy man was the lord inside the garage? Isn't that outfit a little conspicuous?"

Roykur just shook his head. "You grew up in a more practical noble house, Adalia. Most nobles do their best to stick out, to be noticed, so much so it becomes second nature. I'd imagine that he thought he was being exceptionally stealthy when he picked out this outfit."

"Excuse me? The dress code for milking draugkers and curing cheese was very high class, I'll have you know," said Adalia with feigned offense.

He sputtered out a laugh. "Oh, forgive me my lady, I gave you too much credit then."

Adalia scoffed, but she kept smiling. "Rude."

She punched his arm affectionately. Then her expression grew grim once more. "What are we going to do once we find out who he is and where he's going?"

Roykur's mood turned dark once more. "We are getting answers, by any means. I have been in the dark far too long. The Initiative has bought this investigation, and this man can tell us why." He would not let the Initiative corrupt the system they were created to protect. He would not let this monster keep killing. And he would not take the blame for this evil.

They followed the lord for a while, twisting along platforms, across bridges, and up several ramps until they were almost back to the eighth level. On the seventh, the lord ducked into a gambling den, the Tantalizing Turloq. The sign was hung across the door-frame, which only let out into the side corridor, not visible from the streets. Roykur walked past the door, noting a back exit to the den. *For a lord to visit a den this high up, he must really want some discretion.*

He and Adalia paused outside the building. "Okay, what's the plan, Teufel? Are we just going to wait here while he plays some games and then hope he's in a chatty mood afterward?"

Roykur bounced on his feet, the cold eating at him. "Something like that. There's a back exit. We will go in and keep an eye on him. When he goes to the bathroom, we grab him and take him to Marge's apartment. It's just a few minutes from here."

"So, we're just going to drag a struggling lord for a pleasant stroll through the streets?" asked Adalia.

"I assume you remember your submission techniques. Knock him out, and if anyone pries, we'll say he got too drunk."

"I remember my training . . . but why am I subduing a lord?" she asked, crossing her arms.

"He will not talk to us unless he has no choice. We can't arrest him, so this is the next best thing. I would do it, but in case you haven't noticed, I'm practically the size of a Vogel. Now can we please go inside? I'm freezing my ass off here," said Roykur, continuing to rub his arms and bounce in place.

They stepped into the den, and the warmth of the room flooded into Roykur. He and Adalia sighed in unison. An upbeat tune came from a piano somewhere out of sight, and there was an indistinct murmur of conversation at each of the gambling tables. Partitions and curtains separated them, giving the players their privacy. Women, barely clothed, continually supplied the tables with drinks. Roykur spotted an unoccupied table, close to the back exit and the bathrooms.

They paid for ales, and before they finished their first drink, Adalia leaned over the table, sporting a stern look. "You could ease up, we're in this together. Tell me what you're thinking, and we'll work out a plan. Only way this works is if we're on the same page, alright? You keep trying to call all the shots, and I'll just leave you tied up back at Marge's."

Roykur was taken aback. He was about to scold her when he realized how the situation must look from her perspective. Some bratty kid shows up in her life and starts telling her how to do her job. That couldn't be a good feeling. "You're absolutely right. We're a team, and I have been overzealous lately. I know I have some control issues. I appreciate you calling me out. Please let me know if it happens again."

Adalia sagged back in her seat, her prepared rant defused. "Wow. Uh, thank you. That's very mature of you."

A familiar outfit passed the small opening in their curtain. Adalia raised a brow. "That was quick."

"Needs an elixir, for the small pisser," Roykur said in a childish melody, causing Adalia to snort.

She stood up first and waited a five count before they followed the lord to the washroom. The man stood, pant legs loose around his knees, relieving himself. A sharp kick swept his legs off the floor, and Adalia guided his descent, slamming his head into the ground. Roykur glanced back into the den and saw a few heads poke out from curtains. A very wide man with thick arms and a bushy beard strolled up to Roykur.

"Is something the matter?" the bouncer asked.

"Not at all! Our friend here just fell over, must have had a bit too much. We'll get him home straight away."

The bouncer just grunted. "See that you do."

"Can you pick him up?" Roykur gestured to the unconscious lord.

"Yeah . . . you need to pull his pants up before I do that," Adalia said with a disgusted look. Roykur sighed but obliged. Then she hoisted the lord up, and Roykur finally got a good look at his face—Wisiel. He looked different from what Roykur remembered, younger.

"Lord Wisiel of House Becoven. We are going to have a fascinating chat, you and I," whispered Roykur, almost to himself.

"No! Are you serious? Well, I'm feeling a lot less guilty about quick-dropping a lord," said Adalia, keeping her voice low as well. "Such a dick. Wait. How do you know that? How do you know the Becovens?"

Roykur rubbed his temples and sighed wearily. This was getting ridiculous. "I'll explain later. Let's just get him out of here."

Carrying the body back to the apartment was even easier than Roykur had thought. They didn't get a second glance from a single soul the entire journey. Once inside, they sat Lord Wisiel down in Marge's chair and stuffed a rag in his mouth for a makeshift gag. They bound his wrists, and then they waited for him to wake up. Fifteen minutes went by before they both were pacing.

"Should we splash some water on him?" asked Adalia, looking at the sink.

"Might as well try something."

The front door swung open, and Marge came in, shaking some water from her coat. She scanned the room, and her eyes fell on the unconscious man, restrained, a pot of water held just over his head. For a long moment everyone stared, an awkward silence prevailing.

"Oh olacka no! You ain't torturing a man in here." She stomped over to the back room where Roykur and Adalia had been staying.

"We're not going to torture him, Marge!" Adalia called to her, still holding her pot of water.

Sounds of commotion stirred Roykur's curiosity, and he moved to the other room to see what Marge was doing. The bed had been flipped on its side, and a trapdoor was open where the bed had stood. A sheet was spread across part of the floor, and on top was a chair with various leather straps bolted to it. Marge closed the trapdoor and handed Roykur a small hammer and a vegetable peeler. Roykur just stared, perplexed, at the tools he now held.

"This here is the torture room, not out there on my comfy chair. Now I got some good tips for new torturers." Marge cleared her throat and raised a hand in front of Roykur's face, listing an item per finger. "Strap him down tight, and keep the gag in until you want him to speak. Avoid damaging the head or major arteries, unless you want him dead more than you want answers. Blunt force with that hammer can cause blood clots that kill just as easily as a sliced throat. It don't take much to kill a man, so try to get creative with it and do as little permanent damage as possible."

"Oh, is that all? Sounds like you are very . . . proficient," said Roykur.

Marge just gave him an unsettling smile, raising the last finger. "And remember, you kids have fun." Without another word, she left the room and then the apartment. Roykur looked once more at the tools in his hands, and he tried his best to prevent his mind from getting creative.

Once Wisiel was strapped into the chair, Adalia sat down next to Roykur on the mattress and began fiddling with the small hammer. "Are you going to be okay with this?"

"Adalia, this man, the Initiative, they destroyed our lives. Who knows how far they will go or what other damage they have caused? I'm not sure why, but I am sure they are working with the Husk Slayer. If we don't figure out what's going on, they will continue to cover for the murderer, and he will keep killing."

"I mean, *he* could be the Husk Slayer for all we know. He could be covering for himself."

Roykur considered it for a short while, not entirely dismissing it. "It's possible. He would have to have started killing before he was eleven or so. That's awfully young."

"But still possible," said Adalia, determination burning in her eyes.

Roykur conceded, "Yes, but not likely. Regardless, we need proof, and before we can get that, we need him to talk, to give us answers."

Adalia visibly shrank back. "I am a Sentinel—I should bring him to justice, not torture him. This isn't right . . ."

"Hang on, you think you can bring Wisiel, a lord, into the Sentinel headquarters and accuse him of paying off the Conservators assigned to the Husk Slayer case in order to frame *your* family? Please explain how that would work."

"I, uh . . . well, we could take him discretely to the commander, or even to the king. My grandpa was best friends with the king. There's no way he will believe that Roykur is the Husk Slayer," said Adalia, hope rising as the thought unfolded.

"We will need one of them eventually," Roykur admitted. "But we need some kind of proof. Volmirk's first instinct is going to be to lock us up. Legs could protect us, but for how long? With the council taking over, he's king in name only at this point. Plus, our version of the story will fizzle out. Meanwhile, the Initiative will keep fabricating evidence and spinning the truth."

Adalia tilted her head, and her eyes lit up with a mischievous look. "You call the king Legs? You dare disrespect King Legast of House Morfar in such a way?"

Roykur took in Adalia's challenging stare, remembering that he had used the same line on Visari. Could she know? She was very intelligent. She'd probably figured it out by now. Maybe it was time to tell her.

Adalia exploded with laughter. Surprised, Roykur jumped. Her laughter was contagious, and he was soon smiling and then laughing with her. They reached the point of tears, and as he wiped them away, he could feel how much they needed that.

Their reprieve from the recent trials was cut short as Wisiel shifted.

Adalia gripped the hammer tight, and Roykur moved to face their prisoner. Wisiel groaned through the gag. Blinking, he studied Roykur with nervous confusion in his eyes. His gaze danced toward Adalia, and then he mumbled something incoherent into the cloth. Roykur hesitantly removed the gag to let him speak.

Wisiel started shouting, "What the fuck is this? Who the fuck are you? Do you know who I am—"

Roykur jammed the rag back in. "Here is how it's going to work. We are going to ask you some questions. You're going to answer them. If you refuse, we get to . . . explore our creative side."

Wisiel just rolled his eyes and gave a muffled chuckle. *That's right, keep laughing, you piece of shit.*

CHAPTER 15

SIMPLE TRUTHS

Roykur stood on the apartment stoop, sipping a bitter tea, his eyelids drooping low. He muttered curses under his breath, watching the sun rise on their fruitless night of interrogation. So far, Wisiel had not said a word, aside from threats and curses. Adalia had insisted on taking the lead, refusing any physical harm to Wisiel. It was clear how inexperienced she was, and they were running out of time. Two people were not equipped to care for a prisoner for any extended period. If they couldn't get answers soon, they would have to figure out how to feed him and keep his hands bound while he relieved himself, a task more daunting than the possibility of engaging in torture. Roykur had suggested using the vegetable peeler or breaking at least a finger, but Adalia was firm and looked squeamish at the sight of the tool. It would be wise to send her out for more groceries and finish what needed to be done while she was out.

Trying to restore himself, Roykur closed his eyes and drank in the sunrise's beauty before withdrawing into the apartment. Adalia stood at the stove, stirring a small pot of soup in tired circles.

Evidently, the lack of sleep was affecting her as well. She turned, hearing him approach. "Alright, let's peel his skin off."

Roykur blinked with shock. "Wait, what?"

Adalia covered a yawn. "Well, not necessarily that . . . but we need to turn this up a bit. I am exhausted, and someone is undoubtedly searching for a missing lord, so I'm making the call. Teufel, I know you might have some understanding about what to do with all this because of your *family,* but it is my responsibility to get Lord Wisiel to tell us what we want to know. This was my investigation, my grandfather who died. Got it?"

Roykur smiled at her, poured himself a bowl of soup from the pot, and gestured with the vessel. "Lead the way."

Soon, they were staring down at their prisoner. The lord glared back at them with pure hate, still gagged. "Shake your head," said Adalia. "Are you going to tell us why the Initiative is framing my grandpa?" After a moment of defiant looks, she continued, "No? Okay."

Adalia swung the hammer down hard. An unnerving crack was followed by muted screams. Wisiel's right thumb lay dangling from his hand, which remained on the chair arm. Blood spattered onto the tarp, followed by a steady trickle. Adalia wound up for another blow, but Roykur stopped her with a hand on her arm.

"What?"

"Look." Roykur pointed to the wound, as little slivers of pale yellow crystal began forming where the break had occurred. Sure enough, it staunched the bleeding and began slowly reknitting the skin back together. It hadn't dulled the pain, not that Roykur could tell. Wisiel still writhed in agony.

"I knew it. The crystal formation results from the elixir consumption. The Husk Slayer is using the elixir on his victims. But since the other half of their body isn't attached, the crystals just seal the wound. His next evolution . . . a more time efficient way to pull off his signature." The epiphany spilled out of him involuntarily, but the moment he finished speaking, he knew it was a mistake. He had said too much.

"Okay, that's it!" Adalia grabbed Roykur by the arm and dragged him into the main room, the soup sloshing out and coating the floor. "What's going on with you? How do you know all that stuff about the case? And don't give me that draugker shit about *overhearing things.*"

Roykur looked into Adalia's sleep-deprived face, the dark circles and bloodshot eyes emphasized against her unusually pale features. Her grip on the hammer was tight, and it shook with the strain. He had planned on telling her when they had a more reasonable moment, but now was not the right time. He knew her well enough to know she was not in the mood to handle such a radical truth.

I will tell her. Just not while she's breaking bones.

"Okay, fine, I was an informant for Roykur. He . . . never really stopped investigating the Husk Slayer. He paid me to help him follow clues. So, he told me everything he knew about the case. That's really why I was at that crime scene. He told me not to tell anyone. I'm sorry, I should have said something after he died." The lie flowed out —it was not an excellent story, but at the very least it would explain his intimate knowledge of the case.

Adalia's stare was stern and appraising, as if she were trying to decide whether or not to believe him. The faint screams from the adjacent room had subsided to a pitiful moan. "Whatever, let's just finish this."

Back in the room, she stood in front of the whimpering man. Tears rolled down his cheeks, and Roykur glanced at Wisiel's hand. The thumb appeared attached and functional again, the yellow crystal flaking away as he moved it.

Adalia addressed the lord. "Alright, ready to talk?"

The man nodded with fervor, and Roykur untied the string around his head and pulled the rag free.

"Adalia, let me say how nice it is to see you. Though not as nice as the party. You looked prettier in that dress." Wisiel's voice was breathy from the pain, yet it still dripped with vileness. "Roykur liked to brag about you, you know. Gush about how brilliant you were. But I always knew you would grow up to be a fucking cunt."

Blinding rage shot through Roykur, and he smacked Wisiel across the face. "Watch your mouth. We asked you a question."

Fire blazed in the lord's eyes as he regarded Roykur for the first time. The slothful demeanor that Roykur had grown accustomed to seeing in the lord was gone. Adalia kept her gaze away, focusing on the wall, but her face was bright red, with anger or embarrassment he did not know.

"*You* asked me a question? And who even are you? You are some fucking child swept up in events you cannot possibly comprehend. And you, Adalia, training your whole life to be a Sentinel. Why? So, you can wallow in the shadow of your grandfather's greatness?" He paused, looking her up and down, his tone softening as he leered. "Actually, probably the best thing you ever did. It appears to have slimmed your fat ass down a little. Though not all of you."

Adalia's face reddened further, but she blew out a calming breath and turned to their captive, her expression now stone.

"I said watch your fucking mouth." Roykur punched Wisiel in the jaw, and his knuckles burned. Wisiel barely reacted to the hit, still keeping his attention on Adalia. *Maybe I need a running start.*

"Your boyfriend is defending your honor? That's adorable," he jeered.

"Who killed Roykur?" asked Adalia, her voice a level monotone.

"You know, Visari and me had a little thing on the side a few years back."

"What is the Initiative trying to accomplish?" asked Adalia.

"She was so lonely after your dad died."

"Who is the Husk Slayer?"

"So that makes me the closest thing you have to a father right now."

"You sick monster!" Roykur screamed, and grabbed Wisiel by the throat, squeezing as hard as he could, trying to end this miserable excuse for a Human. Roykur could see Wisiel's eyes grow wide with fear, and he reveled in it. Out of the corner of his eye, he could see Adalia reacting, reaching for his arms. She stopped just before touching him and retreated, moving back to the edge of the room.

Darkness seeped out of Roykur. He could feel his skin ripple and ungulate from all over as dozens of tiny tendrils burst through his skin. It came out like a black smoke through his pores, thick and heavy, snaking out and then pulling toward Wisiel like iron drawn by a magnet. Roykur let go of the man's throat and stepped back, bumping into the bed, smoke still streaming from him.

Wisiel's body drank in the smoke. It penetrated his mouth, nose, and eyes. The lord began convulsing, his lungs desperately trying to take in anything other than that smoke. The stream stopped after what felt like an eternity, and Wisiel breathed in air again, eyes wide with primal fear. A strong and unfamiliar feeling washed over Roykur, something he had never felt before, something foreign. He shivered and did his best to shake the feeling, to push it away.

The nightmare was not over. Wisiel seized. Every muscle in his body began twitching, expanding. The straps holding him down strained, and the old leather threatened to tear.

As quickly as it began, it stopped. The lord's narrow physique now seemed larger and well defined, as if months of weight training had suddenly been bestowed upon him. Wisiel coughed furiously before regaining his composure. Awe was quickly replaced with a wide grin as he examined his body.

Roykur was drained of energy, and his knees buckled. Weak, sweaty, and feverish, he felt his stomach ache with hunger despite having just eaten. He knew he'd overdone it, much like pushing his body too hard during exercise. But the hammer lay on the floor in front of Wisiel, and the man was still restrained. Roykur lunged for the hammer and held it above his head, ready to strike. "Tell me . . . who killed . . . Roykur!"

Wisiel's grin slipped, and darkness crept along the sides of his eyes, like they were reaching out and grabbing hold of his irises. He turned his head slowly to face Roykur, his veins bulged along his neck as if straining against an opposing force. He spoke, voice tight, like he was holding his breath at the same time. "Doctor Arakul."

Roykur was stunned. He had known the doctor for such a long time—not extremely well, but he didn't seem like he would have become a crazed cultist. Then again, he was part of the Initiative, and they were becoming rather cultlike. Roykur forced himself to push past it. "Why?"

"He was trying to recreate the ritual." Wisiel intoned in his breathless voice.

"Ritual? The Kolkrabba ritual? Why was he trying to recreate it? *Why?*" Roykur had lowered his arm. Wisiel twisted in obvious discomfort, but Roykur did not care. He was finally getting answers.

Then veins pulsed all along Wisiel's body, and he released the breath he had been holding after all. Whatever had gripped him had faded, and the lord's panic was returning. "Olacka! I shouldn't have said anything! They'll figure out, you know; they'll figure out it was me that talked. *He* will know. I have an incompatibility, he knows. I'll be dead in a week."

"How will they know? Please, work with us and we can help you." Roykur's voice was almost pleading.

Wisiel strained against his bindings, his hysteria pitching. Then they snapped. Not the leather straps, the wooden joints of the chair, like kindling prepared for the fire. Splinters sprayed across Roykur's face, and he stumbled back. Wisiel stood up, the legs and arms of the chair still attached to his limbs, while the rest of the chair clung to his back like a shell. He turned and ran, or more like hobbled quickly into the main room. Adalia shook away her shock and gave chase.

Roykur could hear the commotion from the other room, but he focused on pulling at a single tiny sliver of wood that was stuck under his eyelid. It hadn't pierced anything, but his eyes had watered up, and it stung terribly. With delicacy, he plucked it out, blinked furiously, and then ran to the next room to help his granddaughter.

Adalia lay sprawled upside down across Marge's comfy chair, and the front door stood wide open, with Wisiel nowhere to be seen.

"Adalia! Are you alright?" Roykur rushed to her side and helped shift her right side up.

She groaned. "My head is throbbing, though that might be partly due to not having had a decent meal in the last few days."

"You're bigger than Wisiel. How did you end up like that?"

She scowled. "I . . . I don't know. He just pushed me, hard, and I flew back into the chair."

"We should go after him." Roykur moved toward the door, but Adalia held him back.

"Don't! He's long gone, and far too strong now. What did you do to him?" she said, recoiling from Roykur. She tried to stand, but a fit of dizziness forced her back into the chair.

"Easy, easy." He sighed. "I have no idea what happened back there. But I have a theory."

"You better have more than just a theory." Adalia leaned away, her expression filled with hurt and mistrust.

Roykur scratched his head. "I had a lot of time to think about what you said happened at the warehouse and now with what we heard from Wisiel. Remember, you said there was a black ooze that came out of Roykur and fell into the tub, right?"

"Yeah . . ." Adalia shivered at the recollection.

"And I was stabbed? However, the last thing I remember is I came out of the tub of water. So . . . what if the black ooze got inside of me?"

Or maybe it's inside Wisiel now.

"What is *it*? Why was *it* in my grandpa? Why was it in you?" asked Adalia.

Roykur shrugged. "How on Erden should I know? I'm just as new to this situation as you are."

"Are you? Or are you hiding something else you were sworn to not tell anyone?" she snapped.

"Look. Let me tell you everything I know. I won't leave anything out, okay? I know I don't remember the warehouse. There was a hole in my chest and a hole in my shoulder when I woke up. Both should have killed me, but they didn't. I know that I've had nightmares since that night. If I take more than a nap, I dream of monsters. Horrible, dark things, and I wake up terrified every time. This was the first time that black thing has done anything more than haunt me. I just want answers."

Adalia relaxed a bit, a sympathetic look creeping in. "I get it. Just . . . please tell me everything from now on, okay?"

"I will tell you everything. Except I am going to keep one thing to myself. For now." Adalia looked at him with obvious objection, but he held up a hand. "It's a personal matter, and I'd rather not share just yet. Trust me, I will tell you, but I'd rather do it when things have calmed down a bit. When the time is right."

I am your grandpa. He sighed. *One crazy thing at a time.*

Adalia shifted uncomfortably in the chair, not meeting his eye. "But what do you think was the point of what we stumbled upon in that warehouse? What would have happened if we hadn't interrupted Arakul?"

"Well, I'm only guessing, but it sounded like Arakul would have gotten the black ooze from Roykur." His mind flashed to the dark cave and the frantic ritual performed by the Kolkrabba. "Maybe it's a weapon."

"Why do you say it's a weapon?"

"Just look at what I did to Wisiel. I turned him into a monster. Well, he already was one, but now he matches physically. Who knows what else this black ooze can do?"

"So, if it can make people stronger, why are you still so . . . you know . . . petite." Adalia cleared her throat. She reached out and easily wrapped her finger and thumb around his laughably thin upper arm.

Yeah, yeah, I'm not impressed with this kid's workout routine either.

"I don't know any more about this than you. Maybe I can only make other people stronger. Maybe that was all I have, and now it's gone. Hang on . . ." Roykur turned to listen to a buzzing sound, something just to the side. No—it wasn't a sound, but the shadow of a feeling faintly outlined in his mind, a direction through the walls and floors. It was moving in a hurry, away from Roykur, the feeling slowly getting dimmer. He didn't know how he knew, he just did.

"I think . . . I think I could find Wisiel if we hurry. I can *feel* him."

"*Feel* him? That's really creepy, and we will talk about that some more later. But let's say we find him. How would we confront him, with a tiny hammer and an ooze you know nothing about? No, we should go ask the Witches about this, and let the legion of armed Sentinels take care of the somewhat-buff lord running around." Adalia winced and stood from the worn fabric chair, steadying herself with a hand on Roykur's shoulder.

He groaned. "Why the Witches? All they do is brew elixirs."

"They know all kinds of weird stuff that no one else thinks is important. If anyone knows anything about your ooze, it will be the Witches." Adalia slipped on her coat and handed Roykur his.

Gods, not them.

Roykur threw on his coat and brushed off the dust. He grimaced and wiped specks of blood from the tips of his shoes. "Alright, going after Wisiel is a bad idea. But we can go visit the Witches and ask all manner of strange questions later, after we unravel this conspiracy. I think not getting executed for working with a serial killer takes precedence over black smoke or ooze."

"You don't think it's one big thing? Your ooze, my grandpa's death, and the Husk Slayer are all connected. The more we know about the ooze, the better chance we have at understanding why they want it and why they want the Husk Slayer protected," said Adalia.

"I don't disagree with you. You have very sound logic, but you are missing a crucial point. We are on a timetable now. Someone will find Wisiel, and then this safe house is compromised. We are going to run out of places to hide, and quickly. Taking the offensive is the best move now. We have an actual lead, but we need proof to tie

Doctor Arakul to Roykur's murder . . . or to the Husk Slayer." Roykur held a hand by the side of his face to block the beams of dawn from blinding him.

"Okay fine. You win. Where will we find this proof? His house? His office? An elixir of improved proof-finding?" Adalia was clearly feeling better.

Rolling his eyes, Roykur pressed on. "His office is a good start, his house a good second. We should keep an eye out for obvious evidence like that ritual mask, or trophies of his kills. Also less obvious things, like things that showed he used the warehouse or—"

A loud throat clearing cut off Roykur's thought. He and Adalia whipped around to see a large figure standing in the open doorway. The morning sun on his back shadowed his features.

"I thought you were dead. You being alive cost me a whole heap of money, as usual. Should have stayed dead, boy." The man spoke in a deep, rich voice that seemed to thunder in Roykur's ears.

"Who the fuck are you?" said Roykur, straining to see his face through the bright light.

The man just stepped forward and slapped Roykur across the face. Hard. In his already fatigued state, he collapsed into Adalia's lap. His cheek stung, a sharp whine filled his ears, and water welled in his eyes;. The room started spinning.

"What a little shit you are. No one believed Marge when she told us what had been going on. You, alive, and working for the Sentinels. Then Sentinels showed up looking for you . . ."

The man turned and left. Several Sentinels rushed in, light glinting off their full patrol armor. They forced Roykur and Adalia to the ground, the wind knocked from their lungs as they hit the floor. Once they were bound, the Sentinels shoved a foul-tasting gag into his mouth. A cloth sack was pulled down over his head and cinched tight around his neck. Exhaustion sapped at Roykur's will to resist, and it sounded like Adalia had given up as well.

They were led from the small apartment, stumbling down the steps, and pushed onto the hard wood of a wagon.

Marge's gruff voice rang out, "It's nothing personal, Boss, but coin is coin."

"Don't worry, Leondal, your son is just sick. It's our job to make sure he gets better," a slimy voice cooed.

"I don't give one draugker shit about your false reassurances, Doctor; I am not the boy's mother or a weepy nursemaid. I give a shit about the coin you promised."

"Very well." The jingle of coins reverberated in Roykur's ears, the price of his execution.

CHAPTER 16
MIXING IT UP

The wagon ride was long and slow, but Roykur could tell they were heading north, and down to the lower portion of the Fifty Fingers district. The northern part of the city was also the oldest part, and Roykur could hear the uneasy creaks and groans of the bridges as they passed between platforms. Focusing on the street noises, he tried to remember the path they had traveled, which helped Roykur distract himself from the soft sobs coming from Adalia. Tied up and gagged, there was little he could do to comfort her. He had tried patting her leg from behind his back and shushing, but shushing didn't work with a gag. All he ended up doing was scratching at her knee like a flailing, hyperventilating maniac. So, he had given up.

Maybe I am a little crazy if I thought that would have gone any differently.

When the wagon stopped, Roykur was pulled out and onto his feet with a splash of water only an inch deep. The water seeping into holes in his shoes and soaked his socks. One reality of the lowest level, or the bottom, as most people called it, was that geyser water trickled down, and with nowhere to trickle to, it pooled on the stone roadways. The bottom was in a constant state of more than damp, but never quite flooding. It was humid and hot down this far, especially compared to the top level.

The procession splashed across the road, and Roykur lost all sense of direction as they entered an extensive structure, wound through corridors, first up ramps and then down stairs. Sounds of distressed people echoed through the hallways as they passed. The suppressed moans and howls reminded Roykur of childhood stories he had heard of souls drowning forever in the depths of bottomless geysers.

Roykur tensed as his captors stopped him and began unbinding him. A strange anxiety washed over him as the cord around his hood came loose; did he want to see where he had been brought? Then the hood and gag were stripped away, leaving Roykur to adjust his eyes to the dozen lanterns filling the room.

Despite all of the fixtures illuminating the space and the corridor behind him, there was no natural source of light, and it created a sickly, ominous atmosphere, like the light was always barely holding back an oppressive darkness. Roykur had never enjoyed staying long at the bottom for that reason.

During their journey through the building, Roykur's escort had changed from Sentinels to brown-smocked nurses. The two nurses, a man and woman, lifted Roykur effortlessly and placed him in a metal reclining chair in the center of the room. Roykur tried to struggle but stopped as a third nurse snapped a leather crop against the wall and then wagged it in his face.

They were quiet as they strapped him down, arms at his sides, the silence broken only by brief outbursts from nearby rooms. Once he was secure, the nurses rattled in an uneven cart filled with syringes, a large jar of hydration solution, and rows upon rows of tiny vials. A worn tube with a needle at one end was connected to a large metal box above Roykur's chair. He tried craning his neck to get a better view—it looked like a typewriter. The nurses fitted the hydration jar in a slot in the metal box and began doing the same to all the tiny vials.

"Teufel, is it?" Doctor Arakul stood in the doorway, checking the clipboard in his hand. The man was almost unrecognizable. His black hair was thick and slicked back, his glasses no longer on edge of his nose. The aging doctor looked like a young man just starting a career in medicine.

"Where is Adalia?" Roykur's voice cracked. His rage rekindled, though it was tempered by exhaustion.

"Empathy. That's a good sign, Teufel. She is getting settled in her room as we speak." He scribbled something down. "I am just going to ask you a few questions to get to understand you a bit more. Then we will determine a diagnosis and begin your treatments."

"You can't keep me here. I am not sick, and you can't just kidnap me off the streets like this."

Doctor Arakul clicked his tongue. "Young man, you have much to learn. You are not an adult. Your father has a legal say over what happens to you. Leondal admitted you to this asylum, which means you are a ward of the asylum until we deem you mentally fit to return to society. I have heard some disturbing news about your behavior recently. So yes, you are sick, very sick."

"Adalia is an adult. You can't keep her here."

"Very good, young man. She is an adult, if barely. However, it would be completely unethical to not perform a preliminary examination of her current health. In fact, it is our legal obligation to ensure the health and safety of the citizens of Ver'a'saile." Doctor Arakul smiled, looking over the top of his glasses as he continued to make annotations.

The nurses finished placing the vials into the contraption, then wiped a cloth soaked in alcohol over his forearm before inserting the needle. Roykur shivered as the cold rush of the liquid coursed into his veins.

"What do you think of this machine? I came up with the idea and had some engineers whip up this prototype. Each vial is a different elixir . . . elixirs I found to be useful for correcting mental deficiencies."

The nurses finished and stood calmly, waiting for instructions.

"Engineers like Myrmilla?" Roykur asked.

"Thank you, that will be all," said Arakul, without looking up from his notes.

The nurses left, and the door closed behind them. Arakul moved casually so he was directly in front of Roykur, and with a single finger pulled down Roykur's shirt, revealing the stab wound.

"Didn't quite hit your mark," said Roykur, and Arakul's confused expression flickered with annoyance. *That's all the proof I needed.*

"We will start out with a simple stress test to see how you react to stimuli and then move on to the treatments." Arakul started clicking dials and pushing buttons on the machine, and the tube to Roykur's arm filled with a pinkish tinge.

"So, you killed Roykur, and now you're going to kill me and Adalia? Where's your mask, you psycho? You should be the one in this chair."

Arakul face was twisted in a sneer, his eyes locked onto Roykur's, calculating. "Fine, no more pretense. Yes, I will kill you. Eventually. First, I want to know just one thing . . ."

"The black thing burned up. It's gone."

Arakul's voice snapped, hissing. "It was mine! You stole what was rightfully mine!"

"You stole it from Roykur." His heart fluttered. *Answers, finally. Just keep talking, crazy psychopath.*

"Roykur was a fool! He was given a gift from the Gods, and he had no idea! He only had the ultimate step—instead it was left dormant, untapped power for decades. Such a stupid and weak man does not deserve to be chosen for that gift." Arakul was shaking with rage, but he drew in a deep breath, forcing himself to calm down. "I sacrificed everything for this, and I've waited this long. I can wait a while longer, especially with this new elixir . . ."

Roykur had stopped listening, his heart pounding at this revelation. Was that what happened to him all those years ago? He'd stopped the ritual but still walked away with a part of it. *Oh Gods! What if I hadn't stopped it? What would the Kolkrabba have done with that gift? The Gods? The Gods have never been real, right?*

"What was the ultimate step?" said Roykur, so quietly he wasn't sure Arakul heard him through his ranting.

Arakul sneered and scoffed with disgust. "Dying, of course. The host must die. It's always about death, my boy."

"What is this gift? What does it do?" Roykur squinted against the lamplight, the room seeming brighter than before.

"I was hoping to find that out myself, but it looks like you robbed me of that opportunity. You see, I have another ritual site being constructed, but it will take some time. Months even. Until then, you are going to keep me occupied."

"What do you mean?"

"You don't think I brought you here just to silence you? You have touched the gift, and that makes you special. Your body must have changed, must behave differently than others. I finally have a subject for genuine discovery. I spend my days using treatments to fix people with disorders, but those are predictable and boring. With you, I can really test your limits. However, these treatments have never been tried on a healthy person. I have two theories. The first is that nothing happens. After all, they should only fix what is broken. My second theory, and by far more likely, is that the treatments will cause something to . . . snap. I am very excited about the outcome." Arakul's voice reverberated off the walls of the room, ringing in Roykur's ears.

"Drop dead, you fucking djavul." Roykur winced—his own voice was almost deafening.

"I see the elixir has made its way through your system. This one enhances the senses. Your eyes take in more light, your ears take in more sound, and your body is more receptive to pain." Arakul cinched down the straps on Roykur's chair, each one tight on his skin.

It was a slow thing at first, but the tightness grew from an uncomfortable pressure to a crushing pincer, squeezing harder and harder. Roykur blinked through tears from the pain and the brightness. He started breathing heavier, each lungful of air scraped like shards of glass.

The doctor pulled a strange-looking cylinder from the cart, with slits cut out of the sides, and wound the device, placing it over the lamp in front of Roykur. Arakul then doused the other lamps in the room, leaving the single source of light peering through the slits in the cylinder. He clicked a switch on the device, and it slowly spun around the lamp.

The device clicked rhythmically with its cyclical movement, and the strobes of the light washed over the room in waves. Roykur's eyes burned every time the light flashed by, and he closed them, but the light still shone bright behind his eyelids.

"The spinner will go for about an hour. The nurses will be by periodically to wind it through the night. We'll see how you're doing in the morning. I have another patient to attend to." With that, Arakul stepped out of the room, leaving Roykur to the flickering light and the metallic clicking.

Ӂ

GREAT TOWERING redwoods pressed against the eastern side of the city, like the natural world imposing its will on the manmade. The buildings nearest the forest had bridges extending to the giant trees and ramps spiraling down, which formed walkways for the people of the city. However, the ground was sacred to the Treemolkvar, and so they lived only on the surface, no treehouses or burrows. The bridges were the extent of the construction that was allowed by the city; the king, generations ago, had seen that the Treemolkvar forest was given special protections under the crown.

Treemolkvar settlements in places like Maw'licor were built over, and the people were forced to integrate into the city proper or flee, elixirs becoming almost nonexistent. In Ver'a'saile, when the threat of cultural destruction came, the Treemolkvar elders were quick to plant one of their own as a mistress in the king's bed, and so soften his heart to their people.

Wahrlich smiled fondly to herself at that thought. A couple hundred years ago, she had saved her people's entire way of life.

She sauntered along the forest floor, breathing in the fresh air she rarely got anymore living in the city. She passed beautiful homes inlaid into the hollowed-out bases of the trees, heading to the brewmaster's lodge. The lodge was carved directly into the side of a fallen tree, long and cylindrical. Wahrlich stepped out of the harsh underbrush of the forest, her bare feet sinking to her ankle in the soft, mulched dirt that surrounded the lodge. The artisans who brewed the elixirs almost never left their lodge, and they were afforded certain comforts. Hopefully when it was her turn at the kettles, her feet wouldn't go as soft as the city folk.

Wahrlich passed a flimsy shed near the lodge. It held hundreds of elixir jugs, but this batch was supposed to be gone already. That was the reason she was here, after all; production had slowed and so schedules had been thrown off, and in turn, people were in complete turmoil. They were not great with sudden change.

Her recent bout of nostalgia ended, and her agitation returned. Why did a diplomat, the speaker for her people, have to come down here for a straight answer? Her messengers had said, over a month ago, that production had slowed because of a distilling issue, whatever that meant. Then it had slowed yet again a couple of weeks ago; she had fired the messenger before the words "distilling issue" had come out of his mouth.

She flung the door open to the lodge and strode in. The brewmasters jumped at the sudden intrusion. Wahrlich enjoyed catching people off guard. She stepped carefully through the lodge, staring down each of them. All refused to meet her gaze, their bodies stiff with apprehension. The interior of the lodge was extremely hot and humid, steam drifting by from farther inside.

"Melitoss!" Wahrlich raised her voice, but her serene exterior remained intact. A lanky, hunched male stepped out from a collection of pipes, his eyes trained on the floor. The bark on his skin appeared bloated from the humid air, and the leaves on his cheeks and arms were brown and drooping.

"Speaker Wahrlich, we weren't expecting you and don't have anything prepared . . ." He gestured with his dark, charcoal-stained hands.

"I sent word two days ago I was arriving," Wahrlich said flatly. Melitoss opened his mouth to speak, but she cut him off with a wave. "First you claim that no brewmaster helped the king make his elixir, which I still find hard to believe, and now we can't even make our own? I want an explanation now, but if the words 'distilling issue' come out of your mouth, I swear to the Old God, I will hurt you."

"It's the source. It's, uh . . . umm . . ."

"Spit it out," Wahrlich demanded.

"Running out? Well, its potency has waned, and we draw more water than the essence. So . . . when we distill, we get less of the essence concentrated." Melitoss wilted as he spoke.

Wahrlich's jaw clenched. "Show it to me."

The men in the lodge rushed to the far end. Wahrlich followed behind, attempting to avoid the gouts of steam from random pipes along the way. At the end, where floorboards had been removed and pipes protruded from the hole, they all scurried down one by one. Embedded in the ground at the bottom was a roughly hewn stone well to which all the pipes connected. Wahrlich's eyes widened, her usual practiced, calm control breaking down into pure disbelief.

"Why isn't the water glowing?" she asked.

"It is still there, Speaker. Faint, but if it goes out . . ."

"The world will end."

CHAPTER 17

SWEET DREAMS

R oykur jolted awake from yet another of his watery nightmares, his hospital gown damp with sweat. They were getting worse. The hours of ramped-up sensitivity and bright lights had made for a dreadful night, but he'd spent worse. He knew with increasing dismay, however, that this was just the beginning. He flexed, instinctively testing the tight restraints that held him to the bed, heavy straps across his torso and forehead. Defeated, he stared at the ceiling of his room. His eyes watered, and he forced back tears, taking deep breaths, trying to prepare himself for fresh horrors.

For three days, the nurses had moved him constantly between different rooms. Each room had its own "treatment" for him to experience, and they had been varied. After the strobe lights, he had spent the rest of the next day hanging upside down by his feet. The following day was filled with alternating ice baths and warm needles inserted into his muscles. Yesterday, the treatment had been focused on purging. Several shallow cuts along his thighs had let the blood drain from him slowly. The nurses had not let it go on for long, but that afternoon was filled with ipecac and unrelenting regurgitations.

173

Each series of treatments was accompanied by an elixir, each one chosen carefully to undermine his resistance to whatever the day had in store. Today would be no exception.

Doctor Arakul was only present intermittently for the treatments, but he was always there at the end to see the results. He was a diligent notetaker. Roykur heard the tapping of feet approach his room, and his dread deepened. The door swung open, and a nurse entered, pushing in a wheelchair, followed closely by the doctor. The wheelchair had a tall pole attached at the back that supported the metal contraption.

The nurse undid the buckles that held Roykur to the bed. He attacked her immediately, throwing all his strength into a wild swing. Smoothly, the nurse caught his arm and hoisted him gracefully out of bed and into the wheelchair without a hint of recognition of the attempted assault.

"Good morning, Teufel—the bloodletting incisions are healing nicely," Arakul said as the wheelchair straps constricted Roykur once more. "We've gone through the preliminary sessions. I call them the cleansers. We have scrubbed clean your mind and body and removed anything that might have been lingering within."

"I want to see Adali—" Roykur was cut short as a spoon filled with porridge was jammed into his mouth. It was thick, bland, chalky, and altogether not very pleasant, but he was starving.

"You might see someone . . . or something today, but it won't be your friend. I have drafted a special concoction for you." With an attempt at showmanship, Arakul revealed a rack of three brightly colored vials he had been keeping behind his back. The elixirs were luminescent as usual, these ones vibrant pink, teal, and purple. "A mixture of three elixirs—the first enhances your memories. They will become vivid. The second expands the imagination—some people claim they have hallucinations, but that might depend on the individual. Last but not least, the final elixir dredges up the deep subconscious, everything you didn't even know you knew. Your desires and your dreams."

Roykur turned his head away from the spoon. "Wait, dreams?"

"Oh yes. I haven't had the opportunity to use it more than just the one time, so this will be quite exciting for me. I will get to listen to every dirty secret you've ever had, and you won't even realize you're telling me. It's absolutely brilliant!" The nurse hooked up the tube to his arm like every day, and the hydration fluid poured into his veins.

"I don't have dreams; I just fall asleep and wake up. Nothing in between," Roykur lied. Very convincing.

"Is that so? That's very rare indeed . . . we will keep it in the mix, regardless," said Arakul, narrowing his eyes behind his spectacles. Then the doctor started slotting the vials of elixir into the blocking metal mechanism above Roykur's head.

"No!" He panicked and flailed in his chair, rocking it back and forth. Arakul waved his hand, and the nurse grabbed the chair to steady it. Roykur twisted his hand around, grabbing her arm. His thick, untrimmed fingernails dug into the nurse's skin, and she yelped, more in surprise than pain. She pulled her arm free, and a barely perceptible tendril of smoke pulled free of Roykur's fingers, absorbed into the nurse's scratches.

His breath caught, and he froze, looking to see if Arakul or the nurse had noticed the smoke. Arakul cleared his throat, shooting a disapproving glance at the nurse and returning his intense focus to the dials of the box above Roykur, no doubt making sure the mixture was just right. The nurse rubbed at the scratches on her arm and mumbled under her breath, something about not having children. It seemed neither had seen it.

The cool chill of the hydration solution turned frigid. The tube had taken on a muddy brown look, like water after cleaning too many colors of paint off a brush.

"This environment will be enough for the elixirs to have an effect, but we want them to work at their full potential. We will see maximum results if I give you some more privacy."

"Privacy for what? Do I need to be naked for this elixir?" Roykur asked as the nurse wheeled his chair out of the room.

"My dear boy, privacy of the mind." Roykur watched a malicious grin spread across Arakul's face. He followed the doctor's gaze and saw three nurses standing at the end of the hall. The middle one held a sturdy brown jacket, with buckles and straps cascading down the sides and back. What made Roykur pale was the room that stood behind the nurses. It was thickly padded and without light.

The two large male nurses grabbed his arms, and the nurse pushing his chair started unbuckling him.

"Careful, this little djavul scratched me." The woman extended her arm to show her coworkers. The other nurses grimaced.

"Yikes!" said one.

"You should get that looked at. Might be infected," said the second.

"Yeah, I think you might be right." She finished with the buckles, and the nurses holding his arms yanked him hard from the seat, forcing the jacket onto him. He couldn't have struggled if he tried. *Damn, these nurses are strong. They whip me about like a godsdamn rag doll. I miss being heavier than a terloq's chew toy.*

The thought seemed odd to him. For most of his life, he had been aware of his size. It was true he had enjoyed the adoration of his strength, but being that large had interfered with everyday things. His clothes always had to be custom made. He hit his head on door-frames more than he would have liked to admit. Roykur had even broken a few chairs by sitting down too quickly, and many other inconveniences. Now he missed all of it.

With the last of the buckles done, the nurses pulled his arms across his chest and secured the sleeves behind his back. He was placed against the back wall of the room, and they retreated.

"Dinner is in eight hours. See you then," Arakul said with more giddiness than a child in a sweet shop. The door slammed shut, plunging the room into complete darkness.

The air was stale, and Roykur pushed himself against the wall, slithering up onto his feet. He moved forward but misjudged the four-by-four-foot room and knocked his face into the padded door. Without arms to help keep his balance, he teetered to one side and fell back onto the floor. Roykur scrambled up to his feet again, but this time panic stabbed at his chest. *Oh Idrok, lend me courage. Which way am I facing now? Did I fall completely to my left or . . .*

Roykur ran his shoulder along the wall, hoping for a door seam. There wasn't one. Every door had to have a seam, right? How was he going to get air? He started breathing faster—the stiff air was thin, and his chest tightened further. How long had he been in this room? Minutes? Hours?

A sliver of light appeared, blinding him as he tried to see past it. Roykur stood frozen, waiting, but the door didn't open any further. He crept to the door, and with his shoulder slowly pushed it open.

He stood in the asylum, the hallway empty, not a soul in sight. There was no sound either. The usual hum of wailing patients was gone.

"Hello?" Roykur's voice echoed, getting louder the further it went. A crashing noise made him spin around. His isolation room exploded with terrible force as a Kolkrabba burst through the wall behind it. The shockwave knocked Roykur off his feet, but the Kolkrabba's tentacles were around him before he could hit the ground. It just stared, its eight eyes fixed on Roykur's. The colors of its slimy skin pulsed waves of greens and blues. Then it dropped him.

Roykur didn't hit the ground—in fact, there was no ground. He fell, and fell, and fell. An endless portal to an unknown abyss.

When he hit the water, he sank deep into a bright expanse. This was more water than any Human had ever seen in one place, and it consumed him. The water glowed with light, but there was nothing to see until he realized he was already looking at it. Roykur floated, the focal point of light he had seen in his dreams. The source of his nightmares. The eye opened fully, and the whole cosmos was displayed for Roykur's unprepared psyche. His mind raged with fear at the awesome power he beheld. The eye was larger than any city, and faint glimpses of a body—tentacles, arms, and legs, all leagues away—shifted as he tried to see them. They morphed and changed; the size was inconceivable, yet somehow he knew they pressed against the ends of the world. It started moving. Roykur cried out, and his lungs flooded.

Darkness was all around him, and Roykur took in heavy, desperate breaths. He kicked around, feeling the padded walls around him.

"It wasn't real. It was just the elixirs," Roykur whispered to himself.

"Of course it was real." The voice came from the other side of the room. "Just as real as you are."

The voice was male, but it shimmered, a voice completely unlike a Human's.

"Who are you?" Roykur whispered to the walls.

"I am your compliment. Your other half. I am constantly trying to impress you and always waiting for you to catch up." The voice switched back and forth from male to female with each sentence. A body, cut in half, dangled in the middle of the room, a beam of daylight illuminating it from above. "You have called me Husk Slayer . . ."

A figure made entirely of translucent yellow crystal stepped up to the body, the crystals interlaced with thread, and it held a long knife in its hands. The crystals that made up the face twisted into what Roykur could only assume was a wide smile. The figure slapped the face of the dead body with the flat of the knife.

"This was the first step on our journey together. Remember how excited you were at the prospect of catching another serial killer?" The voice pitched high and low, the tenor of a child one moment, then a deep baritone.

"I was young and foolish. Eager to prove myself." Roykur shook himself. He knew this was not real, but he was drawn to this hallucination. His quarry was right here.

"Yes . . . your enthusiasm faded the more memories we made,

and we made so many memories." The crystalline creature gestured to the side and rays of lights flickered to life one by one, each revealing another victim of the Husk Slayer. It walked through the expanding museum of its work, and Roykur followed behind it.

"The elderly woman, Chabni, who was found in the south market square. You suspected she had blackmailed quite a few people. The thug, Gripnod, who was found near one of the central sewer pipes. You found out he abused children. The merchant . . ."

"Why are you bringing up these people's crimes? Are you trying to justify your actions?" Roykur scoffed, incredulous.

"Am I? Or are you? Why would you highlight those specific facts in your memory when you knew they were killed for being Husks?" The figure stopped in front of a wooden bathtub, the water dark red, limbs poking out of the surface and intestines hanging over the sides. Roykur shivered at the familiar sight. "What was different about this?"

He sighed. "It was completely outside your usual methods."

"But why?"

"I don't know! You tell me! You're the one who did this!" Roykur jabbed a finger at the crystalline figure, which made him realize he had the use of his hands again.

"I'm not real, Roykur. I can only guide your thoughts."

"Alright, fine, I'll play along. Let's see . . . It was a prosperous year. Record-high harvests, poverty, and unemployment were practically nonexistent. I had proposed just days before this happened. Besides these murders, the crime rate had never been lower."

"Let us continue." The figure moved forward, naming the bodies they passed, rehashing Roykur's old theory of how the Slayer discovered his victims had been Husks. It would not have been difficult. Those recovered from the war were listed in the papers when they returned. As they walked by, the glassy eyes of the dead followed them, full of accusations and judgment.

They stopped at another similarly gruesome scene. Roykur frown and squatted next to the body.

"Your second outburst. I wasn't even assigned to this case, but I knew it was you," said Roykur.

"You briefly assisted the other Conservator's investigation. You didn't make the call on this case, but you saw the scene, you saw everything you needed to here." Roykur walked around the scene, a perfect re-creation of his memory. The victim had been an herbalist, dismembered and buried into the soil of her gardens. The Husk Slayer's tools lay nearby, abandoned. Roykur knelt over the planter box, trying to pick out the tiniest of details. And there it was. The tiny letters *R U K S O*, the blood soaked into the side of the wooden planter box.

"I remember only half paying attention . . . I—I pointed these out to the lead Conservator and hurried back to my wife, she had just given birth to our son . . . Oskur." A deep dread settled into his gut, and he raced back to the wooden bathtub. He slid to his knees, craning his neck around the base of the tub. Just as he had seen all those years ago, very large, painted in blood letters, E N I A L I S. The woman in the tub was named Fetalis and Roykur had dismissed it as the Husk Slayer misspelling his victim's name—the blood was messy, and words smeared. He really looked hard this time.

Flipped, the letters spelled "Silaine," his wife. The first message was meant for him, after all.

"Show me the last one." The figure nodded, and the garage appeared to Roykur's right. Roykur looked around but was now surrounded by the piles of scrap metal. Adalia stood frozen, holding the lantern. The horrific sight lay before him, but Roykur ignored the carnage with a cold, clinical precision. The elixirs must have been sharpening his memory, because he could see the letters clear as day: R O Y K U R.

Roykur knelt down, his mind furiously working on this new connection. Had it always been about him? Was the Husk Slayer setting Roykur up to take credit for the murders all along? Or did he lash out anytime something significant happened in Roykur's life?

He'd never contacted Roykur directly. *I was just the Conservator that worked his murders. Had he become obsessed with me first?*

Roykur looked up, and the man with the torn-out lungs now hung directly over him. The metal scrap and the crystal figure had disappeared. Roykur's arms were bound once again in the jacket, and he fell down on his back, pushing himself away from the body with his legs. The lips didn't move, but a distant voice sounded from the body. "Why did I have to die? Why didn't you save me?"

Roykur stopped pushing away when his head touched the dangling hands of another victim. The voice was slightly different, but it uttered the same words. "Why did I have to die? Why didn't you save me?"

Everywhere he looked, the faces of the victims appeared, each lending a voice to the same damning question. The cacophony of voices roared in Roykur's ears, and he could feel the condemnation of every single one. Roykur clamped his eyes shut and tried to yell above the din. "I failed you! I'm sorry. I should have been better."

Roykur opened his eyes—the darkness of the padded room had returned. He sat in quiet reflection for a long while after the visions ended, but the voices of the dead still echoed in his mind. Light flooded the small room, and two nurses dragged him out. He was unceremoniously cleaned of his urine-soaked gown, fed, and secured in a bed for the night.

CHAPTER 18
HIDDEN WITHIN

The morning was much the same as the last, except for the lack of the doctor's presence. Nurses administered the elixirs and hurried Roykur through the morning routine. Then, like he had never left, he was back in that tiny, padded room.

The absolute worst part about not being able to use my hands is the damn itch on my nose. Roykur chuckled. Best to keep things light-hearted. He wished he knew when these hallucinations would hit. Roykur remembered hearing once that happy thoughts helped soothe issues with mind elixirs. He would do anything if it meant not going through the previous day's visions. *I mean, turloq kittens, fresh meat pies, warm spiced ale, those two dimples above a woman's buttocks . . .*

Roykur could feel his hands holding something. He opened his eyes to see them free of the straitjacket and cupped around the supple, pear-shaped butt of a woman. The naked woman turned to face him, her silver curls whipping across his face. A cheerful smile and loving eyes were fixed on Roykur. Tears welled in his own eyes, but he did his best to return her expression.

"Silaine, my love, oh how I have missed you," Roykur croaked out. Her smile broadened, and the lines at the corners of her eyes creased, a testament to her many years of infectious joy.

"It wasn't your fault." Silaine wrapped him in a tight embrace. Roykur let the tears flow, and they fell onto her bare skin.

Silaine started jerking, slowly at first, then much more violently, until she convulsed backward out of Roykur's grip and onto the ground.

"Not again, please, not again," Roykur mumbled helplessly, knowing he was about to relive his worst memory. Silaine arched her back, and her limbs contorted at agonizing angles. She held her breath, unable to scream, even when her blood vessels rose from her skin and bubbled. Silaine's eyes rolled back into her head, her mind lost to the pain.

Tears streamed from Roykur's face as he watched her struggle. A loud clunk made him jump, and Silaine's head rolled away from her body, ending her suffering.

"Silaine! No!" Roykur screamed, and felt something heavy in his hands, his battle axe dripping with the blood of his dead wife. "This isn't how it happened. She just died—I didn't have the strength to end it."

A stream of blood poured out from the shadows, flooding the ground. Silaine's body sank beneath the surface. Roykur looked up and saw a hill looming over him; no, it was not a hill, but a massive pile of bodies. He clambered up the hill to avoid drowning in the blood, and at the top, the disembodied voice of the Husk Slayer rumbled like crackling thunder.

"You damn me as a killer . . . a monster. Yet, in just a few years, your battle fervor snuffed out more men and women than any one person in recorded history. But they were Husks, right? You had no choice. Or did you? Did you ever try to save a Husk? No. You condemned them without a second thought. They were the monsters, not you, right? Like they have any choice to be the way they were, to have their minds enslaved."

The voice had grown disdainful, scornful. "The truth is, you chose to slaughter as many as you could, and you reveled in it. You made it into a game, and your company became the best murderers in the world. When you all came back from the war, you told yourselves lies, so you all could cope with your own atrocities. You briefly sacrificed your humanity for the safety of the kingdom. All draugker shit. You all loved the killing. That scared you. Not the trauma of the killing, but the pleasure of it. So tell me, Roykur, how are you any different from me?"

"You're wrong! I did what was necessary to save our city. I took no pleasure in it. I did it to ensure that future generations of the kingdom would be free from becoming Husks. Free of the Kolkrabba." Roykur stood and lifted his chin. "You killed former Husks, people who were no longer a threat. You targeted these people because you were scared, at first. Then you just needed an excuse to justify your sick impulses."

"Did that sound convincing to you? I didn't find it convincing, and you can't lie to yourself, Roykur. You could never establish my motive. You guessed, and that guess was good enough to satisfy everyone else, but not you. We both know you don't like to assume."

The metal door screeched loudly as it was jerked open. The light dissolved the bodies, leaving the small, padded room in their stead. Hands grabbed Roykur's jacket, and he was dragged from the room and into the hallway. A figure stood over Roykur, and he blinked through the blinding light, trying to see the shadowed face.

Arakul's voice and expression had gone rabid like the night in the warehouse. "Who is Silaine to you?"

"You heard me in that room?" The muffled banging of nearby patients started to swell in reaction to Arakul's shouting.

"Of course I could hear you in that room. Now answer the fucking question!"

"You're just a hallucination." A sharp stinging shot across Roykur's face, the slap muddling his vision.

"Still think so?" the doctor asked.

Roykur grew queasy. The room had started spinning. Behind Arakul's head, translucent images flickered in the lantern light, although nothing he could firmly pick out. "She was . . . my . . . girl-friend, a few months ago."

"Was she a good girlfriend?" Arakul's voice was pure venom. "Well, she must have been if you loved her. Though not all deserve our love. I knew an older Silaine, Silaine of House Heimvelt, a bit before your time. She was a huge bliest, cheated on her husband constantly."

"You djavul!" Roykur roared the words before he could stop himself. A twinkle flashed in Arakul's eye, and a wry grin slowly spread across his face. The anger was shifting to the crazed look he had seen in his eyes during the fight in the warehouse.

Shit. Did I really fall for that trick? That elixir must still be hitting me hard.

"This is more than I could ever have hoped for. And—" A harsh battle cry sounded from down the hallway, and both Arakul and Roykur looked up to see a nurse fly through one of the open patient doors. The woman hit the opposite wall with a crunch, her neck twisting at an awkward angle. She did not get up.

A puff of black smoke trickled from the cut on her arm. It drifted toward Roykur and vanished beneath his jacket. A strange surge of sensation traveled up and down his body, skin prickling. Briefly, he felt satiated, like after gorging himself on a feast day. Then the feeling subsided.

Adalia stepped out from the room, and upon seeing Arakul kneeling over Roykur, her face contorted with rage. Sprinting at full speed, Adalia charged the doctor. Arakul grasped desperately at a knife at his belt, but he fumbled with the strap. Giving up, he tried to dodge at the last moment. It didn't work. Adalia slammed into the doctor, and they both slid across the floor. She recovered first and straddled Arakul, smashing her fists into his face.

The blows sounded like thunderous drums in Roykur's ears. He rolled onto his side, the room still blurry and spinning. "Adalia, stop! We need him alive. He has the answers."

She continued to pummel the doctor, heedless of Roykur's pleas. Then a door slammed open, and men in glittering silver armor rushed in. They ripped Adalia off Arakul and pinned her to the wall, then forcefully bound her and Arakul's hands. More and more armored men charged their way into the hallway, forming barricades at each door. Several stood directly over Roykur, large halberds pointed at his chest despite the fact his arms were clearly bound tightly against his shrunken frame. These were not the armor and weapons of the Sentinels, but rather the Royal Guard.

If the royal guard was here, that could mean only one thing.

Right on cue, the king paraded past his armored escort to stand imposingly over everything. His red brocaded tunic was accented by the gold gauntlets and large gold pauldrons that widened his already impressive shoulders. Legast held his youthful face in deep scrutiny at the scene before him. It still surprised Roykur to see the black square beard chiseling the man's jawline. He had not worn one during the war, but it suited him. Legast had always been aware of the latest fashions, but beyond that, the beard lent an air of authority to his face, just as the king now stood commanding everyone's attention.

"Doctor Arakul, by my right as king, I arrest you on suspicion of murder and treason to the crown." Legast's jaw was clenched, a mixture of anger and grief clear on his face. He tore his baleful stare away from the doctor and waved to the royal guard. "Take him away."

Roykur watched Arakul led from the room, the insane doctor's face swelling. He stared at Roykur with a hint of a grin before he passed through the doorway, out of sight. Visari rushed in a moment later, tears streaming down her eyes. A man in doctor's browns trailed close behind her.

"Where is she? Where's my baby?" cried Visari.

"I'm right here, Mom," Adalia managed to croak out. Visari saw her daughter pinned to the wall and squeaked with shock.

"Release her, for the gods' sake. She is who we came to rescue," Legast ordered. The guards let go and stepped away, just in time for Visari to wrap herself tightly under Adalia's arms.

"Doctor Mythran, take some men and check every room; I want to see who else might be trapped in this house of horrors," Legast commanded.

"The boy is with me," said Adalia.

Legast nodded in understanding. "And get this boy out of his restraints. He's with Adalia."

Roykur was hoisted up and set on his unsteady feet. As the buckles were undone, his muscles spasmed, cramping from the days of tension. Despite all that, he smiled fondly as Adalia embraced her mother. They squeezed each other and talked softly, only to squeeze tighter still. Tears blossomed in Roykur's eyes, emotion overwhelming his faculties, and he let out a deep breath to steady himself. These elixirs were really messing with his ability to maintain control.

He watched as Adalia released Visari and gave Legast a brief hug. The king gave her a weak smile and a curt nod before he returned to issuing orders. Adalia paused for a moment, making eye contact with Roykur, tears in her own eyes. She looked unharmed, aside from the needle marks on her arm. Then she rushed over and scooped him up in a big hug. Roykur grunted as he was hoisted into the air and squeezed tight.

"Alright Adalia, I appreciate the hug, but I prefer not to dangle," Roykur squeaked out, the embrace taking longer than he expected. Adalia set him down and cleared her throat. Red tinged her cheeks, her features not quite returning to normal as she looked around the hallway full of people.

Two voices rang out from farther down the hall. The king and his procession moved to the first open door to see an emaciated woman staring lifelessly at the ceiling. Everyone in the hallway mumbled in sorrowful unison, "May the gods care for this poor soul."

They continued to the next open door with a guard, and there sat a girl rocking on her bed, wild eyes flicking in every direction. Visari pressed a hand to her mouth and squeezed Adalia's shoulder.

Several other rooms had patients who appeared to be lucid and responsive. They were escorted to another area by guards. The group then came across a larger room that Doctor Mythran's keys could not open, but after some encouragement from the guard's kicks, the door swung open to reveal dozens of rows of shelves, each lined with jars upon jars of organs floating in a thick, opaque fluid.

The organs looked well preserved aside from a few in jars near the front that had been knocked off the shelf, now smashed to pieces on the floor from the door having been kicked in. The stench from the broken jars was unbearable, but Roykur was intimately familiar with facing unpleasant scents. He studied the massive closet quickly through the press of bodies in front of him while they reeled from the aroma. These had to be from old victims. There was no way the asylum took in that many patients. Why would he have Husk Slayer murder victim organs in his asylum so close to where he worked? This didn't make sense.

The Royal Guard began pulling out the jars and placing them in wooden crates they had brought in. A familiar chest was the last thing removed from the closet, the same one that Roykur had briefly looked through. He moved to the man holding the chest.

"May I see that? I believe it has some valuable insight into this situation."

"No. All of this is evidence to be processed and stored at Sentinel Headquarters." The guard walked pointedly out of the hallway. He tried to follow, but his path was blocked by the crowd formed in this tight space.

Legast addressed the dazed doctor. "Doctor, you're in charge of this facility now. I want every patient reevaluated, and if they can be, I want them released. Get a team from the morgue to recover any bodies, and make sure they are properly dissolved; the dead shouldn't linger."

The doctor wiped his sweaty brow with a cloth and nodded absently. Visari plucked at the white sheet draped over Adalia as a hospital gown. "I think it's time we went home now, dear. We'll get you into some proper clothes."

"Teufel is coming with us," Adalia blurted. The idea that he was not automatically going back with his family had not struck Roykur until just now. Of course, he was still a stranger to them.

"The boy? Why? Who is he?" Visari took a moment to look Roykur up and down for the first time since entering the building. She gave an appraising look, most likely the same one Roykur had worn upon seeing Teufel. He could not imagine what he looked like after the past few days, but if his smell held any hint, it was repulsive.

"A friend. He helped Grandpa with his investigation and has been helping me." Adalia walked over and placed a hand on Roykur's shoulder. Roykur tried to give his best smile. *Please let me go back to my own home.*

"Oh alright, I won't let a kind act go unrewarded. He can stay the night as a guest, but only the one, mind you." Visari gave the "we are not a charity" look.

"Thank you," said Roykur, and saw Legast moving away. He pushed past his family to catch the king before he left. Roykur was stopped just short of the king by crisscrossing halberds. "Legast, I need to speak with you about Doctor Arakul."

Legast spoke without turning. "Most refer to me as Your Majesty, sire, or King Legast."

"My apologies, Your Majesty." Roykur understood his misstep, but the formality with his best friend still stung. "It's about the Sentinels—well, actually, it's about the warehouse—"

"Let me stop you there. I have many other crises that require my attention. However, since it appears you are a guest of House

Heimvelt, we will all have plenty of time to discuss events at the Autumn Festival Banquet."

"Pardon?" Adalia said, stepping up behind Roykur.

"Visari has graciously accepted my invitation on behalf of your House. I shall see you all at the palace tomorrow evening." Legast strode out of the asylum, his guard in tow.

CHAPTER 19

WARM AND COLD

The hearth's warmth radiated through Manor Heimvelt, through Roykur's body and into his bones. The perpetual chill he'd felt since his forced inhabitance of this child's form had finally relinquished its icy hold. He awoke in the morning under thick, soft blankets, delighted at being home. More than that, he delighted in the day's normalcy.

Adalia was up before dawn, milking the draugkers with the workers. Visari had hired a seamstress to make an outfit for Roykur, something suitable for a meal with the king. Of course, Visari insisted on putting her own skill in the craft on display by providing her unbidden assistance to the seamstress. The woman politely accepted the help, but Roykur could tell she was doing her best to hide her annoyance.

They took a break once the pungent scent of warmed cheese wafted through the manor. Breakfast was a medley of baked roots and vegetables covered in melted draugker cheese, and on the side was dried and peppered draugker jerky. Some of the finer place settings had been arranged at one of the beautifully carved tables in the banquet hall. Visari sat at the head of the table, Roykur's usual

191

spot, while Roykur and Adalia, now washed from her chores, sat on either side.

Roykur rolled up the baggy sleeves of the oversized shirt, a loan until his new clothes were finished. "This looks amazing. Do you always eat breakfast like this?"

He knew the answer was no. The family only ever ate dinner at the table, and the only time Roykur had seen the good place settings used was at the last party held for the Initiative. He looked around at the servants standing in the banquet hall and saw a few unfamiliar faces.

Visari smiled and dabbed at the corner of her mouth. "We are a noble house. We work hard to take care of a vital resource for the king and the city. As such, we receive rewards for our service."

Adalia rolled her eyes. "No, we didn't used to eat like this. Mother hired more staff for some reason."

"A-Adalia!" stammered Visari, breaking her practiced composure. Roykur saw the look in Adalia's eye. There was an argument coming.

"We don't need to be waited on all the time, Mother. Three-course meals every meal is ridiculous, and I don't need someone to help me get dressed either." Her words were sharp and accusing.

"This is what it means to be a proper noble house, and we are going to behave like proper nobles. Please show some decorum in front of our guest." Visari took a delicate bite of food as if to punctuate the end of the discussion.

Roykur barely tasted his food while he watched them fight, knowing he should say nothing.

"Grandpa didn't want this house to be like other noble houses. Grandpa—"

"Roykur was a cruel and selfish man!" shouted Visari. Roykur and Adalia shared a look of incredulity at her outburst. "It was always his way. Nothing was ever to that man's standards. Ever since I joined this family, I have been nothing better than a servant in his mind. I raised you, I managed the manor, and yet I am the villain for wanting to improve this house."

"Grandpa was a good man! He never treated you as a servant," said Adalia, her face tinted red.

"How would you know? Roykur doted on you constantly, always taking you away on adventures together, while I was the one who set the rules. He slowly turned you against me." Tears brimmed at the edges of Visari's eyes. "We were supposed to have that special bond. Just a mother and her daughter . . . but we never got that chance."

"I can't believe you are making this about you. Grandpa is dead, and you need this to be about you. I am done." Adalia jostled the table as she stood abruptly, dishes and silverware clashing together. She stomped away, leaving Visari and Roykur at the table, the silence punctuated by a slamming door.

Visari looked at him and flushed with embarrassment. "Excuse me."

With exaggerated intent, she moved from the table and out of the banquet hall. Roykur glanced at the servants, who shifted uncomfortably.

So it took Roykur dying for his daughter-in-law to finally speak her mind. *She really saw me as selfish? By giving my granddaughter a happy childhood? Overdramatic as usual.*

He shrugged and finished his meal.

THE BREAKFAST DRAMA SOON ABATED, and everyone resumed their daily chores. Roykur spent the day outside, soaking in the sun's rays and cherishing the fresh air. He volunteered his time repairing the feeding troughs and shoveling draugker dung. The physical labor was rewarding and reminded him of simpler times. However, it wasn't long before his mind turned from his pleasant reprieve back to the mysteries at hand. The elixir had induced its torments, but while painful and horrifying, they had also been clarifying. Now bathed and dressed in his freshly tailored suit, he watched the sun wane in the sky, consumed with deciphering his visions.

"A copper for your thoughts?" Adalia said, leaning against the porch railing next to Roykur. She was radiant in her styled hair and tight-fitted dress, similar to the one she wore to the last party they attended but with a bit more frill. A thick woolen coat was draped across her arm, which she quickly slipped on after the first touch of chill from the autumn evening breeze.

"You look lovely tonight," said Roykur, smiling proudly. *I always pushed her to be the best Sentinel, but I don't think I encouraged her enough to be comfortable with who she is already.*

"Thank you. You as well. I really like that outfit my mother had made for you."

"I appreciate it. I've never been fond of this style, though." Roykur opened his coat and pinched at the overlapping vests across his bare skin. The soft fabric was a mixture of deep blues and violets, complementing his dark skin. "This doesn't even look good on people with proper shoulders and arms."

"Well, I think it looks good. Big arms are overrated anyway." Adalia gave him a playful punch on the arm. "So, was that all you were thinking about?"

Roykur looked around, making sure no one was nearby. "The smoke, the black ooze or whatever it is. I can feel it growing."

"What do you mean by growing?" said Adalia, an eyebrow arched.

"When I attacked Wisiel, and the smoke left me, I immediately felt empty and hungry. Somehow, I knew that there was some remnant of it left. However, I didn't pay attention to that feeling until a few days later, in the asylum. I pushed the smoke into one of those nurses, the one you took out. I don't know how, but the smoke came back." Roykur shifted with nervous energy. He squeezed his fists, as if the smoke flowed just beneath the muscle. "But more. A lot more. I don't know what this smoke can do yet, but I know it can go much further now."

"Are you scared of it?"

"I'm not sure. On one hand, I want to have more of it. No, I *need* more of it. On the other hand, I'm terrified. The cost of power is never truly paid." Roykur's mood soured further. "Also, I've been thinking about how Arakul was the one who killed Roykur, and that he knows about the black ooze. Apparently, Roykur had the stuff in him for years and wasn't able to use it. He killed him specifically for it. After his . . . experiments, he knows—he knows I have it."

He also knows I am not Teufel. Hopefully, if he tries to tell anyone, it will just be the ramblings of a lunatic.

He was not the only one who could have knowledge about the ooze. Legast had been there, sixty-six years ago, when Roykur had first come in contact with it. However, he had been unconscious at the time. Roykur had not discussed that day with his friend since, both of them eager to forget. Regardless, Roykur had cleared Legast of the Husk Slayer murders years ago. But considering this additional motive, perhaps he let slip the other details of that day to Arakul, or Lord Wisiel even.

"He's in custody now. He can't go through with his plan," said Adalia, trying to be reassuring. "We will have justice now for my grandpa."

Roykur shook his head. "He told me he has people preparing the ritual again. It's more than just him. The Initiative is providing him support, I know it. I just don't have proof. They must believe he can get this remnant of the Kolkrabba for them. They don't know how much of a madman he is, or they just don't care."

"The Initiative? I thought they were covering up for the Husk Slayer? Why would they protect two monsters?" Adalia turned her back to the railing.

"Or they're protecting just the one monster." Roykur started digging his nails into the sides of his thumbs.

"You think Arakul is the Husk Slayer?"

"Could be. He's old enough, and he had a closet full of organs. I think that's fairly convincing proof." Roykur threw his hands up. "Not that being old means anything anymore with the elixir of life. Sentinels will have to figure out a new system to determine the age of any suspect from now on."

Adalia leaned in close to Roykur, and he could see the wheels turning behind her eyes. "Hear me out. We know that the Initiative was covering up a Husk Slayer murder by pinning it on my grandpa. Obviously, they are trying to achieve some political agenda, but it's possible they don't have a relationship with the Husk Slayer and are just taking advantage of the current situation. Separately, Arakul targeted grandpa for the smoke, ooze, whatever. The only connection we have that Arakul may be the Husk Slayer is the organs. It's lucky we stumbled on those, or the trail would have gone cold again."

"Yeah, lucky." Roykur grimaced at the recent memories of his stay in the asylum. Shaking himself away from those dark thoughts, he looked up at Adalia. "You know, you're going to make a great Conservator one day."

Adalia beamed. "Aww, thanks! I think you have a promising career path waiting for you, too."

Roykur sighed. "Thanks, but once we have the Husk Slayer tried and executed, I'm done."

"What? Teufel, you're as talented as my grandpa was, more so even, and you haven't even begun with the Sentinels. Imagine the good you'll do for the kingdom!"

"Maybe you're right . . . I guess I'm just tired."

"Yeah, it's been a long couple of weeks," agreed Adalia.

More like a long fifty years. Olacka, it's been a long life.

"Adalia! Teufel! Time to get going!" Visari shouted from a carriage as it pulled around from the side of the house. Two neatly groomed draugkers lumbered to a stop in front of them, and they climbed in.

Visari did her best to keep the ride to the palace occupied with light conversation. She discussed the intricacies of the needlework on Roykur's outfit. She asked him questions about his home life, which Roykur tried to answer as vaguely as possible. Then she recounted the tale about how Roykur became a lord and obtained Manor Heimvelt. He tried to stay politely interested, but he himself had told this story more times than he could count.

He stared out the window. Every shop and home on every level they passed by on the Crescent Road was decorated for the autumn festival, with each building trying to outdo their neighbors. Lanterns were covered with orange and red shades, lending a warm glow from the heart of the city. Large, colorful banners were stretched across platforms or draped from the bridges, and kites soared by the hundreds.

Their carriage drew close, and as the dark of night descended on the palace, it bloomed with pillars of fire built on pedestals to illuminate the perfectly arranged decorations littering the front of the palace. A mass of people had gathered, pressed to the gate and walls of the main entrance and spilling back along the road. The carriage slowed, falling in behind the line of carriages being inspected before entering. People ran along the side of the carriage, whooping in excitement or pushing to get closer to the gate.

The royal gardeners and event planner had outdone themselves, just like every year. Roykur had seen almost eighty of these festival decorations—well, sixty that he could remember—and each always seemed to one-up the previous, and this was no exception.

Long tapestries of flowers and leaves cascaded down the front of the palace. The color patterns created swirls that tricked the eye into seeing movement. The crowd around them burst into cheers. Looming, shaped bushes that had been placed up on the parapet were suddenly backlit by the exploding firelight bringing to focus the various fauna of Erden, from the fierce turloqs, strangleteeth, and carnids to the innocuous draugkers, nirvashi, and nagas.

Roykur tore his attention away to see that the conversation had stopped. Both women were as transfixed by the scene as he was. Adalia glanced over, her smile full of awe, before returning her gaze to the display. Roykur took a deep breath, suddenly anxious as the palace loomed closer. There were a lot of people out here, and there would be quite a few in there, as well. He fidgeted, digging his fingernail into the side of his thumb.

The pyrotechnics had ceased before they pulled into the palace courtyard, but the fires on the pedestals still burned bright, casting wide, flickering shadows across the courtyard. The wind rippled the flowers covering the face of the palace. Everything about the night seemed surreal to Roykur. A daze clouded his thoughts, like the ache that sets in days after intense exercise. The weight of his experiences sat heavily in his mind. Roykur was the last out of the carriage, easing himself down slowly. He paused at the strange looks from the guard and his family, who had stopped their progress toward the palace.

"You alright? Your legs hurt?" Adalia inquired, a single eyebrow raised.

They did not. Old habits. Roykur cleared his throat and hurried to catch up.

The procession weaved through curving white marble hallways opening to a richly furnished great hall. Two dark wood tables stretched across the middle of the room, one littered with steaming vegetables and meats, the other set with candles, crystal glassware, and expensive place settings. To the left of the twenty-foot tables, a massive fireplace roared with intensity, yet the expansive room and vaulted ceiling stole much of the heat away. There were leather couches and chairs tucked into every corner, with finely dressed people conversing and smoking pipes. Families of the noble houses, influential merchants, and some members of the council, if Roykur recognized everyone correctly.

He swallowed, trying to think how he would get the king alone for a chat. The party was filling quickly, servants and guests alike, jostling through with purpose. House Heimvelt, and its relatively small representation, found an unoccupied space to stand just on the edge of the chaos.

Roykur spotted Lady Ingrail of House Becoven in the far-right corner, speaking with Lord Utheril of House Chesture. She looked like she had lost weight. Eyes sunken, she fidgeted nervously, leaning in and appearing to whisper. *I guess her missing husband has caused some . . . distress. I'm not sure which would be worse though—him finally showing up, or staying gone.*

Legast entered the great hall from the wide staircase at the back, the one that led to the balcony Roykur had been on just weeks ago. The sharp clop of his hard-soled shoes pierced the low din of conversation. A hush slowly washed through the party guests. The king moved down the stairs, taking in the crowd as it gathered before him. He stopped on the last step, and the room fell silent. His flowing robes fell about him, intricately woven and thickly layered.

"My esteemed guests." Legast spoke evenly, but his voice carried through the room. "This feast, for the Autumn Festival, has brought us together to witness not only the changing of the seasons but the changing of a nation. This kingdom has experienced boundless peace and prosperity for many decades. It has allowed us to become the most advanced society in existence, and the most inclusive with our integration of the Vogel and the Treemolkvar peoples. No other nation has been so lucky as ours. So, to allow our nation to grow and take the next step in our journey, I have decided to dissolve Ver'a'-saile's monarchy and institute two ruling councils."

The last part was barely heard in the uproar. Legast merely raised his hands, and the crowd simmered to silence.

"Rumors of my decision have no doubt filtered through the city for many long months, but I did not come to this decision lightly. The concept of a king in our advanced society is outdated, and our way of life has to be put in the hands of the people. It is best to do this peacefully, before it is reached with bloodshed. The details of the new system of rule have been worked out with the new councils, and we have drafted guiding documents. I will remain in the palace until everything has completely transitioned over, and then I shall retire. I am sure you have many questions, which I shall do my best to answer, but first let us eat before the food gets cold."

Finally, a sentiment that Roykur agreed with, his stomach growling in assent.

He, Visari, and Adalia sat nearly on the opposite end of the table from Legast, which perturbed Roykur a bit, until he started eating. The moist meats dribbled down his chin as he devoured a leg of succulently spiced nirvashi. He got lost, savoring the seasoned, grilled vegetables, the tomatoes and squashes, each covered in melted cheeses. From his peripherals, he knew he was drawing stares, but in his ecstasy, he couldn't be bothered.

Roykur grabbed his mug of ale, foam dancing across the top, and gulped down the golden nectar. He spluttered at the horrid taste, the ale shooting up through his nose and down into his lungs. He coughed hard, trying to clear his breathing. Adalia pounded him hard on the back until his coughing subsided.

"This ale must be spoiled. It tastes like vomit and crushed spiders." Roykur burped, tasted the awful flavor again, and gagged.

"Let me try." Adalia took the mug from Roykur and sipped carefully. "Nope, tastes like regular golden ale to me. You must not like ale. Which is fine. Not everyone has to enjoy everything."

Roykur looked back at the mug, the feeling of loss hitting unexpectedly. He slumped back in his chair and cleared his throat. "I guess you learn something new about yourself every day . . ."

Kick a man while he's down—I can't even enjoy a cold ale anymore.

Adalia nudged him near the end of their meal. Everyone was standing to mingle and ask the king their questions. She leaned close and whispered, "Besides Lady Ingrail, I only see two other members of the Initiative here. Wahrlich and Magister Didris. But who knows how many people work for the standing members?"

"That's assuming they are all involved. But better to assume they're all involved and sort it out later, right?" Roykur whispered back.

"Exactly. Oh wait, isn't that Bode? And who is that with him?" Adalia asked, more to herself than him. Roykur craned his neck to see where Adalia was looking and gasped audibly at the petite feminine terror speaking with Bode. "What is it?"

"That woman would be Ilienie," said Roykur. He stared for a long moment at the image of Ilienie fifty years ago. Her dress left little to the imagination, and she laughed loudly at probably nothing in particular, but Bode appeared entranced. *By the gods, the damage that woman will do to the city and its less fortunate citizens . . . forever.*

Pulling himself to his senses, he noticed Wahrlich speaking amiably with the man next to her, but she was staring, not so subtly, at Roykur. Those gigantic eyes and sharp features sent a chill through Roykur. He felt them on him like they could see into his soul. Perhaps they saw more than they let on. Witches were made of more secrets than just their elixirs. *First Ilienie and now Wahrlich. Any other powerful women lurking in the shadows?*

Turning his attention back to Adalia, he said, "We need to speak with Legast when he isn't surrounded by people. Probably need to stick around for a while. After the guests start to leave, we will have a better chance."

"Hopefully he's sobered enough by then." Adalia nodded to Legast, who had just downed a large mug of ale and was waving for another.

Roykur looked down wistfully at his own ale mug, still mostly full. "I would need that much ale too if I was going to answer the same questions all night long. You know . . . if I liked the stuff."

Adalia sighed, oblivious to her grandpa's existential crisis, and glanced at the bubble that had formed around the king, along with the rest of the partygoers waiting patiently nearby. "Let's head up to the balcony. There's a terrace that overlooks the city, and we'll be able to keep track of when people leave."

Roykur pushed away from the table, patting his full belly. "Good idea. I could use some fresh air. It's getting stuffy in here."

Adalia grabbed his hand and dragged him up the stairs and

through the large doors to an open terrace with potted bushes and benches. She leaned on the stone railing and breathed deeply as she looked down into the city. The icy air was cut by the pillars of fire that raged beneath the balcony. The firelight was focused on either side, but the rippling rainbow of flowers reflected a dancing spectrum all around and into the balcony.

"It really looks like a whole different world from up here. There! You can see the parade!" Adalia hopped up and down, pointing somewhere off in the distance.

"I'll have to take your word on it," Roykur said sourly. Adalia glanced down at him, sputtered, and broke into hysterical laughter. Roykur stood on his tiptoes, eyes barely over the edge of the railing, trying to see more than just the tops of the towers. He grunted in frustration as his attempts ended in vain.

"Need some help?" Without waiting for his response, Adalia picked up one end of a bench along the wall and dragged it next to Roykur. He stepped on it and leaned on the railing, his height matching Adalia's.

"Thanks," Roykur muttered. His face was feverish, anger boiling in his chest, from the sheer annoyance of this kid's pathetic frame. He couldn't drink, and he didn't think he'd ever get used to being this small.

Soon, the drifting sounds of the festival soothed Roykur's temper, and he tried to soak in the relaxing atmosphere. After all the craziness of the last few weeks, and the weeks he knew were to come, it was nice to enjoy a moment of peace.

Warm breath brushed the nape of Roykur's neck. An unsettling shiver traveled down his spine, and he turned just in time to see Adalia's flush face, closed eyes, and puckered lips before they pressed into his. Utter shock hit Roykur, his stomach turning with revulsion and panic. He tried to jerk his head away, but her hands were suddenly around the back of his head, pulling him in. Eyes wide, he thrashed, pushing against her, and made muffled shrieks. Adalia's eyes opened with a confused look, which turned to horror as she realized the situation. She released Roykur, who, still pushing away, tumbled over the back of the bench, taking it with him. He landed flat on his back, grunting from the impact.

Roykur recovered, mind still reeling. "What the fuck was that?"

"I . . . I just thought we had a connection. I thought you liked me . . ." Adalia's face was a mixture of confusion and hurt.

"Oh Adalia . . ." Roykur sighed and stood.

"You know what? No. You don't get to blow this off, Teufel. You don't get to make me look like the crazy one here. I see the way you look at me. You were always there for me, even though you didn't have to be. This cannot have been a one-sided thing." Adalia's defensive tone quickly evolved into an offensive one, and she went on. "So, what's the deal? Am I too tall? Is it because I'm stronger than you? Or am I not your type? Do you even like girls?"

"Stop, please stop, and let me explain."

"I can't believe I thought this was a good idea. I don't even want to hear your reason. I'm going back to the party." Adalia dabbed at tears that had started to form.

"I am not Teufel!"

Adalia stopped and turned to face him, her face balanced on the brink of absolute fury and regret.

"Teufel never made it out of that warehouse. I had only met the boy once before, but he seemed like a nice kid. He must have liked you, because he ran in to save you, even after I told him to run for help. I don't know what happened in there, beyond what you've told me, but all I know is I woke up in Teufel's body."

Tears had broken through their precarious perch and were streaming down Adalia's face.

"I was there for you because I always have been there, ever since the day you were born. You saw me watching you because I was watching my little Dralm handle this madness like a true Conservator, and I was proud of you." Tears started welling in Roykur's eyes as well.

"Grandpa?" Adalia's voice quivered. She ran and embraced him, squeezing him tightly and lifting him off the ground. Then she set him down and stepped back. "You've been alive this whole time and you didn't tell me! Why didn't you tell me before now? And before I kissed you! Oh gods, I kissed my grandpa . . ."

Adalia paled at the realization. Roykur put what he hoped was a comforting hand on her arm. "Would you have believed me if I had told you right after the warehouse? Without any proof? That would have sounded crazy, right?"

Adalia slid her arm away from him, scooting back a bit. "Yeah, probably. It was a super freaky ritual. But I would have asked some simple questions that Teufel would never have been able to answer. Wouldn't that be proof enough? I believe you now, don't I?"

Roykur scratched his head. "Uh . . . right . . . that makes sense. I guess I should have said something earlier. Sorry about that."

Staring into the distance, Adalia blurted out, "Let's avoid physical contact for a little while. It's too weird right now."

Roykur cleared his throat. "Yes, of course. It's extremely weird."

"So what does this mean for Teufel? Is he really gone?" Adalia asked.

"I don't know for sure. Arakul told me in the asylum that death was the final step. I can't say why I emerged from the ritual and Teufel did not, but I doubt he is still around." Roykur lowered his gaze, guilt gripping him.

Adalia's eyes welled up again, and she move to the far end of the balcony. "I need a minute. I may have gotten my grandpa back, but lost a friend."

After more than a few minutes passed by, with Roykur standing awkwardly in the night air, his impatience got the better of him and he called out to her. "You alright?"

Roykur could see Adalia wiping her face and taking a couple of deep breaths before walking back over. "Sorry, I will be okay."

"I know it's a lot to adjust to so quickly, but we should try to speak with Legast before he gets too drunk," said Roykur, and they both hurried off the balcony.

A large majority of the guests had left the dining room as the night had progressed, and the king had only one woman still speaking with him. Naturally, it was Wahrlich. *That damn Witch.*

Legast sat slumped in a bronze leather chair, sipping another mug of ale. From his responses to Wahrlich, he was heavily intoxicated and clearly trying to give her the cold shoulder, which she did not seem in the least bit pleased with. Roykur kept a respectful distance. His presence would only hinder the situation, but he could still hear their conversation as Adalia approached.

"Please, Your Majesty, the Treemolkvar hold the creation of elixirs as sacred. We merely wish to know how this elixir is even possible. What ingredients are you using?"

"Share how you make your elixirs, and I will share mine with you." Legast's words came out a bit slurred.

"You know we can't share our elixir recipes; it is forbidden," said Wahrlich, sounding frustrated.

"Well, you heard my announcement earlier this evening. I am retiring, and this elixir will be my legacy. So, if I told you how to make it, then I wouldn't have a legacy, now would I?" Legast raised an eyebrow as if he had just won the argument with some profound insight.

Adalia spoke up before Wahrlich had time to continue their debate. "Sorry to intrude, Your Majesty, but there were some things we need to discuss with you. In private."

"Of course. Anything for you, my dear, and absolutely anything that will get the Witch to stop talking to me." He waved for Wahrlich to step back, and she did so with a respectful bow, but Roykur saw her clutching trembling hands behind her back. "So, what is it you wished to speak to me about?"

"It's about Doctor Arakul and the Husk Slayer."

"The Husk Slayer. Not a very imaginative name. Just sort of straight to the point."

Adalia spoke with the intentional care and patience necessary for the heavily imbibed. "Yes, yes, it is. I know Doctor Arakul is arrested, but there is a chance he is not the Husk Slayer; he could have worked directly with the Husk Slayer. We need to speak with him and figure out what he knows. Either way, he will be the key to confirming the murderer's identity once and for all."

"Didn't you hear? The Sentinels are in agreement. Arakul named Roykur as the killer, so they are shutting down the Husk Slayer investigation. There hasn't been a murder since your grandfather died, and with all the evidence at the asylum, that is the popular theory. For now, with Roykur dead, they're content to take Doctor Arakul to trial for his part in it."

"My grandpa was not the Husk Slayer," said Adalia, grinding her teeth. Their family's infamous temper was bubbling up.

"I agree, believe me. I knew that man better than most. He was good, honest, and true. He could never have been the Husk Slayer." Roykur smiled at his friend's devotion. "But unfortunately, there is nothing I can do that would make any difference. I could force the Conservators to keep the case open and make Commander Volmirk put everyone he has on it, but without any further murders . . ."

Roykur stepped up beside Adalia. "Let us continue looking into the murders. We just need to speak to Arakul before the trial. What do you have to lose from a few hours of talking?"

"You got some spirit, kid. I think Roykur would have liked you. Very well, here is what's going to happen. You will have free rein to speak with Arakul until the trial, supervised. I expect you to report anything you find to myself and Commander Volmirk, and I will make sure you have a voice during the proceedings to present your evidence. That is truly the best I can do." Legast barely managed not to slur his words as they came out.

"Thank you, Legs, this means a lot." Roykur extended his hand and Legast frowned at it for a moment before taking it.

"You still need to work on your etiquette, young man." However, the rebuke was diminished by the warm smile that bloomed on the king's face. "Roykur always called me Legs. Gods, I miss that man."

"Yes, thank you, Uncle." Adalia skipped the handshake, opting instead for a hug.

They were interrupted by a distance wail, followed by crashing sounds. Everyone turned at the commotion echoing through the hallways. The doors to the dining hall flew open, revealing a man stripped to the waist, glistening in sweat. Muscles stretched at skin, showing veins and sinew. A hard carapace protruded from where the hard edges of his bones touched the skin, all along his forearms, collarbones, and shoulder blades. Behind the man, through the open door, lay the bodies of unmoving guards.

"Where are those brats?" The voice was harsh and ragged, but unmistakably Lord Wisiel of House Becoven.

CHAPTER 20

THE THINGS YOU MAKE

Sound evaporated. Silence formed like a pocket of pressure, building and waiting for the breaking point. It broke with a roar from Lord Wisiel as he charged the far corner of the hall, where the lounge chairs, Roykur, Adalia, and Legast now stood.

A few supplicants, including Wahrlich, still stood off to the side, waiting for their moment to speak to the king. They screamed, dashing to the side, but then seemed to notice that they were not the focus of the monster's malice. They turned and sprinted for the door. Wahrlich's high-heeled shoes slipped on the marble floor in her haste, and she crashed down.

Legast bravely pushed Adalia and Roykur behind him and took a fighting stance. Roykur was confident in his friend's fighting ability, but less confident against a monster like that. Legast teetered off balance for a second, and a loud hiccup escaped him. *Oh boy.*

Three Royal Guards stepped from the sides of the hall and formed a shield wall in front of the king. Wisiel crashed into it with a metallic bang and a ferocious snarl. Over the tops of the shields, Roykur could see the lord's bloodshot eyes flitted around, a wild look, like an animal trying to take in everything at once. Halberds lunged at him from each of the guards, but Wisiel moved with inhuman reflexes, like he could see each attack coming at him in slow motion. He grabbed a halberd and pulled it out of the guard's hand.

Roykur tried to watch the fight as he and Adalia grabbed Legast and pushed him toward the kitchen door. The sound of bashing shields and straining grunts filled Roykur with a potency, an alertness, and blood pounded in his ears. A halberd skimmed past his head and impaled into Legast's back, square between his shoulder blades. A sheet of blood splashed across Roykur's face. Blinking through the red in his eyes, he saw the king topple to the ground.

"No!" The scream ripped from Roykur, as did his heart.

"Run . . . run!" Legast choked out with blood pooling on his lips. A yellow crust started forming around the point of the protruding halberd.

Fury boiled over every other emotion. Fear, anxiety, helplessness, they faded to a whisper next to the roar of rage that flooded his senses. Roykur turned, head dripping with blood, and faced the monster. His monster. Black fog trickled down his arms, tendrils of the thickened smoke arcing like lightning around him. Roykur forced his hands together, and a sphere of concentrated smoke materialized between them. Before he knew what he was doing, the sphere shot from his hands toward the men, still fighting with such force that the recoil knocked Roykur to the ground.

The sphere exploded in a cloud around the guards. There was a moment of quiet before the men broke into a unified scream. The cloud was sucked into each guard like the last remnants of a drink through a straw. In their shock, they dropped their shields and halberds, each clattering on the ground. *Oops.*

Wisiel shook himself from his confusion and, with the agility of a terloq, scooped up another halberd and dashed past the guards, straight at Roykur.

Roykur scrambled to his feet as the lord lunged with the halberd. Adalia leaped in from the side and kicked the weapon down into the floor, staggering Wisiel's charge. *I suppose those dress slits have a function after all.*

Adalia followed the kick with a quick palm strike to Wisiel's face. There was a snap, his nose now bent at a wrong angle. They bounced back and forth, feinting and dodging. Wisiel ducked a kick intended for the side of his head and spun, sweeping out the halberd in a wide circle. The blade swung much farther than Roykur expected, slicing across his side. A burning pain shot across Roykur's ribs, and he collapsed to his knees, holding back the blood that seeped through his fingers. The three guards grabbed Wisiel from behind, attempting to wrestle him to the ground.

Roykur's vision blurred, and he closed his eyes, trying not to faint as his adrenaline pumped his blood faster out of his body. Time seemed to slow. A distant voice spoke in his head. *"Let me help you."*

He opened his eyes to see Silaine. She knelt in front of him with her arms outstretched to his. Roykur placed his hands in hers, his hand numb and cold like icy points digging into his fingers. Her voice said, *"Pull."*

Roykur pulled. Instantly, Silaine was gone, and the three guards and Wisiel stopped struggling. They gasped as if cold water had been poured down their backs. The black smoke flowed out of their bodies, covering the floor in a heavy blanket. It drifted lazily toward Roykur. A desperate need ate at his stomach. He pulled harder, and the smoke rushed into him. He strained as it filled him to bursting, but the sensation lasted only for a moment.

Everything went quiet. Blinking and taking deep breaths, Roykur glanced around the room, taking in the destruction of the last few minutes. One of the dining table's legs had collapsed, and shattered plates and glasses covered the floor. Wahrlich was collecting herself on the far side of the room. Everyone else who remained in the hall was on the ground. The guards, Legast, and Wisiel lay unconscious, while Adalia sat holding her hip. Roykur pulled back the flaps of his sliced shirt and coat to look at his wound. Still fresh, it stung as the blood-soaked shirt peeled off. The cut no longer bled, however, and within the cut lay a pool of swirling black. Certainly useful.

Roykur checked on Legast next. The king was breathing steadily, and the yellow crystals from the elixir had stopped the bleeding around the halberd. "Thank the Gods. I think he's going to be okay."

The click of heels on the marble floor grew louder, and Roykur turned to see Wahrlich standing over him. "Please, come find me in the Treemolkvar enclave. I can tell you what this power is and why you have such bad dreams."

"You know about my dreams? But you are part of the Initiative—why help me?"

"I joined the Initiative to stop all this from happening, but it appears I have failed. The other members were suspicious of my objections. Now, I must seek the protection of my people. If you want answers, that is where you will find me." Without another word, she carefully stepped over the unconscious king and through the kitchen. The three guards stirred and groaned, but remained lying down.

Not a moment later, the thunder of boots sounded from the main entrance, and waves of the Royal Guard rushed into the dining area. No, not the Royal Guard, Sentinels, and among them Lady Ingrail, disheveled and perspiring. Roykur still hovered over the king and before he could address the Sentinels, Lady Ingrail started screaming.

"They're after the king! They have killed my husband and the king's guards! I told you there were assassins here tonight. I told you! It's that woman and her lover—they are the assassins!" Lady Ingrail's shrieks started sorrowful and afraid, but grew more wild and vengeful with every accusation. "Kill them! Kill them before they kill the king, don't let them get away!"

Adalia grabbed Roykur's arm and hoisted him to his feet. "The king can explain all this. I don't think we need to worry."

Roykur took Adalia's arm and began pulling her back toward the kitchens. "The king doesn't look like he's in any condition to explain anything, and Lady Ingrail doesn't appear to be in the 'letting us live' mood. This is the Sentinel jail all over again. If they take us, we'll be dead before Legs wakes."

Adalia hesitated just a second longer, but her charging Sentinel brethren, spears leveled, seemed to convince her. Roykur maneuvered the kitchens with dexterity, surprising himself as he ducked under a table and hopped over a full washtub, dishes abandoned. He glanced back to see Adalia limping along behind him. She knew she was lagging, and began pulling down food crates and barring every door they went through. The voices of Sentinels faded down the winding path of servant corridors until Roykur and Adalia heard the low rumbling of a large group just ahead.

Carefully, they pried opened the last door into the courtyard. In front of them was a mass of a hundred servants huddled together, chatting nervously while a few Sentinels guarded the group. Roykur gently closed the door and examined the room. Servant uniforms hung on hooks against the wall. He motioned to Adalia, and they began changing out of their bloody finery and into the plain black garb.

Adalia ripped her dress and used it to tie a wad of cloth to a long gash across her hip and buttocks. The cloth immediately soaked up the blood, darkening significantly. Roykur gave her a worried look, and Adalia returned a dismissive gesture. Her eyes widened, and she pointed at his cut as he removed his shirt. Roykur spread the sides of the wound, revealing the blackness underneath, and Adalia's jaw dropped. She extended a finger, but Roykur slapped it away and motioned for them to hurry changing.

The two of them stepped out into the courtyard at the back of the servant crowd. An elderly woman turned at the tiny noise, seeing the two of them emerge from the door.

"Oh, you poor dearies! You alright? I thought we got everyone out." The woman looked them up and down thoroughly. "Are you two new? I don't recall either of you being on staff."

"Just started last week, ma'am," Adalia said, ducking her head and giving a slight curtsy.

"My child, are you well?" Roykur looked from the servant woman's face to Adalia, and in the bright courtyard firelight, he could more clearly see her clammy, pale face. The woman's eyes flicked to Adalia's side and the wet patch.

"Deary, you have to learn to keep your uniform in proper order." The woman took a towel from a pocket and dabbed at Adalia's hip. The towel came back red. "Oh, eight gods! Child, you're bleeding."

"Bleeding?" said a man with a thin, pointed nose. "Who's bleeding?"

Roykur shifted nervously. Most of the servants were turning around to see what the commotion was about. One Sentinel tapped the other on the arm, and they began pushing their way through the crowd.

Roykur smiled. He had an idea—a chance to use a trick that he had been on the other end of so many times.

Roykur put on a face of panic and tried to pitch his voice high and scared, which was not much different from his normal voice. "She was stabbed! Madman right behind us, stabbing servants and nobles alike. He's headed this way!"

Adalia took the cue and raised her bloody hands to the crowd. It was the perfect ignition to Roykur's fuse, and the crowd exploded with mob frenzy. They surged through the courtyard, wailing and shoving.

The Sentinels held their ground, but just barely, and Roykur and Adalia slipped by them, hidden amid the stampede. The Sentinels tried to hold back the servants but to no avail, and their shouts for backup were lost in the cacophony. The crowd dispersed once through the courtyard walls, and most of the servants continued at a hurried pace down switchbacks, off of Crescent Road and into the city.

Roykur and Adalia fell in with the flow of servants. Two servants insisted they help with Adalia's limp, and they made it to the city before long. They found a bench in a park between rising towers and sat down. Roykur's mind buzzed with the implications of the night, but most important was what they were going to do next. His immediate concern was getting medical attention for Adalia's wound. She had lost a lot of blood, and her condition wasn't getting better. It was late, and almost everything on this section of the surface had closed its doors.

"Adalia, can you walk? I think I know of a bar a few blocks down that will have water and clean cloth for bandages."

"Maybe, but I'm really tired. My hip hurts a lot. I think I'll just rest here for a while." Adalia winced and blew out a long breath.

"Alright, I'll run there and get some water and bandages," said Roykur.

"See if they have any elixirs that might help. Like the—"

"Like the Quick Knit elixir, of course. I'll see if I can grab any of those. Keep that hip elevated." Roykur took off at a run through alleys and streets to the bar he mentioned. It was shut tight, with a sign that read:

Attending parade, open tomorrow night.

Roykur cursed loudly through his hard breaths. Scanning the streets, he spotted lights from a small shop on the next level up. Racing against death itself, he dashed up the ramps. His thighs screamed for him to stop, but he pushed through the burning ache.

Rounding the top of the platform, Roykur leaped up the steps and pushed the door open. A gruff-looking Vogel stood on a stepladder, organizing his wares.

"I need clean water and bandages. Quick Knit if you got any."

The Vogel's voice, like all Vogels', was mostly a series of clicks with raspy, harsh words thrown in between, their pincer mouths not made for Human speech. "First aid supplies in the back, water behind the counter."

The Vogel stopped organizing, got down from the ladder, and moved to the counter. Roykur went to the back of the tiny, ten-pace-long shop and found a single clean rag and an elixir bottle labeled *No Pain*. This would have to do.

Roykur flipped a coin onto the counter, grabbed the water from the shopkeeper, and made his way back to Adalia.

The way back took much longer, as running threatened to spill everything. The supplies, mostly the water, were hard to hold comfortably, and he ended up shifting the weight back and forth in his arms.

When he saw the empty, bloodstained bench in the park, Roykur stopped in his tracks and almost dropped all the items. He set the items down on the other side of the bench and moved to examine the area. A trail of light blood spatters led away from the bench, south, into the street. Roykur was just starting to follow the trail when a loud crunch came from under his foot. He pulled a crumpled note out of the dirt and examined the barely legible handwriting.

Grandpa, a Witch found me. Taking me to the enclave for help. Find me there.

Roykur breathed a small sigh of relief, but his chest tightened regardless. He had a powerful fear about the state he would find her in when he returned. This was proof she was still alive and likely getting better help than he could have provided, but he was supposed to protect her. He never trusted the Witches, though that was probably the safest place she could be.

Roykur shoved the bandages into one pocket in his servant's uniform and took a long swig from the water jug, preparing for his several-mile walk. Normally, he would try to hail a carriage, but at this hour and with the festival, it was unlikely. Roykur braced himself against the frosty night and trudged southward. The servant's uniform was everything he needed this night, black, thick, and bulky.

Roykur kept to alleys, weaving around towers to avoid major streets. A strong breeze picked up, and he went to the first lower level to avoid the harsh chill. The level was almost as rich as the surface, with fine shops and cozy cafes, but Roykur didn't even pick his head up to admire the expert craftsmanship of the buildings or the new clothing styles and inventions of modern life. Those things may have interested him on a normal night, but right now, only the puzzle, the mystery, the questions kept his thoughts occupied. Worry pierced his normally stoic thinking. His mind churned with the murders, the scheme of the Initiative, and the strange powers he now possessed, but he could not fit it all together. Worry coated with frustration plagued his rational intellect, and not long after he began his walk, he had a hand to his head, nursing a headache.

Lost in thought, it took Roykur several minutes to realize his shoes were no longer clicking on the cobble roads but crunching through leaves and soft dirt. He had wandered straight past the edge of the city and into the Treemolkvar enclave. Light had broken the horizon, beams shooting through the massive treetops, which swayed and groaned ominously as if they themselves were waking in the early morning.

"Let's go talk to some Witches, shall we?" Roykur mumbled to himself.

CHAPTER 21

DARK OMENS

It seemed like the whole enclave was awake before the light of the dawn reached them. Witches tended their gardens with unhurried efficiency. Roykur trudged onward, exhaustion settling on his body like the damp through a wool coat. Carts rolled past him, bound for the city markets, each loaded to the brim with vegetables or elixirs. He sneered briefly at the sight of the latter. Having been forced to consume so many had not improved his attitude toward them.

Roykur strained his neck, trying to peer at every face, hoping to catch a glimpse of his granddaughter. After a short while, he noticed the faces were staring back. The Treemolkvar he walked by would do a double take, stopping their work at the sight of him. *I must be a terrible mess.*

A female Witch approached him abruptly, startling him. She had a concerned, motherly look about her. "Son? Are you alright? Are you lost? You're covered in blood—you know that, right?"

"I am looking for Wahrlich. I was told to meet her here?" The woman paused, took a step back, mumbled under her breath, and gestured a sign across her body. Then she addressed Roykur again,

"The Gefahr, of course. She told us of your coming. Please, follow me."

"Have you seen a girl? Blond? Tall? She was brought here wounded."

She shook her head. "Sorry, I didn't. You said she was wounded? Our medicas might have her in the healing tents. Regardless, outsiders usually find their way to Wahrlich."

The woman led Roykur through the thriving forest society. The Witches lived rather simply compared to the hustle and bustle of the city. Most of their time and effort was poured into their gardening and hunting. He saw an enormous slab of salted meat being hoisted in the air to dry by a young child cranking a lever. Everyone wore very little clothing, despite the frigid weather, and almost all of their exposed skin was covered in intricate tattoos. The ink usually accentuated the pattern of their bark.

Tents extended the entryways cut into the giant trees, each left open, no flaps or doors, everyone's lives laid bare. After a few minutes of walking, they stopped thirty paces from a massive fallen tree. The trunk had pipes sticking out the top, billowing smoke, and hooded figures moved about the grounds, carrying jugs and heavy crates in and out.

"You will find Wahrlich in the lodge." Before Roykur could say his thanks, the Witch had turned and run back the way they had come.

Roykur started toward the lodge and then felt something, an icy clawing at his chest and a sensation to his left. He turned to face the strange feeling and saw yet another tent extended from the base of a tree. Roykur could not read the Treemolkvar sign on the tree, but it was obvious this was an infirmary. Witches under the tent milled about in uniform white wool smocks, tending the patients who lay on the canvas cots. One caught his eye—young woman, asleep, a tight bandage around her waist.

Roykur dug his heels in the dirt and ran to Adalia, relief washing over him in a tidal wave. Then a large body blocked his path, and Roykur skidded to a halt. Roykur had to crane his neck up to meet the man's stern gaze. The medica's accent was thick, and his Human was clearly not practiced. "Please, no entry. Patients rest."

Just as he finished speaking, a female Witch at the far end of the tent groaned and thrashed about. The medica and his colleagues rushed to her side, producing salves and needles swirling with colored liquid. Roykur, no longer the focus of anyone, stepped into the tent. He placed a hand on Adalia's forehead, then froze when her eyes snapped open.

"What are you doing?" Adalia asked, annoyance laced through her voice and features.

"I was just checking your temperature." Roykur dropped his hand.

Adalia closed her eyes again. "Ah, well, the Witch medicas said I don't have a fever and that I just need to eat and rest."

"That's great! I mean, you nearly died, so this is great news by comparison."

"I know what you meant."

Roykur took out the less-than-fresh bandages and elixir from his pockets and placed them on the table beside her. "I did actually get the things I said I would . . . you just weren't there when I got back."

"No offense, Grandpa, but I think these guys were a bit more capable than a middle shop's first aid supplies."

"Nonsense. I patched up plenty a battle wound in my day with far less." Roykur tried to feign offense but couldn't keep the smile from his face. "It's good to see you in one piece."

"Back at you. We should go. Wahrlich is waiting for us. I haven't checked in with her yet. I figured I would wait until you got here."

"Alright, I'll go see what she knows," Roykur said just as Adalia sat up sharply and sucked in air with a hiss. Holding her hip, she eased back down. "No, just me. You are going to rest here a while longer. These medicas will take care of you, and I can fill you in later."

"Fine. I'll stay here and try not to bleed over literally everything. I guess that's fair. I'll try not to leave you this time . . ." Adalia trailed off as exhaustion overtook her.

"Out! No entry, patient only!" the medica shouted. The thrashing patient had settled down, it seemed.

Roykur scurried from the tent and back toward the lodge. Relief at seeing his granddaughter alive lifted his spirits, even as he focused on the ever-present threats looming in his mind. Geyser water started falling through the openings in the tree canopy, wetting the soft mulch surrounding the lodge. Roykur hesitated at the door, unconsciously digging his fingernails into the sides of his thumbs. *What the hell am I afraid of?*

Steeling himself, he pushed through the door and into the lodge. Thick clouds of steam greeted Roykur as he stepped into the building. Pipes rattled along the entirety of the lodge, hissing as steam was released from irregularly spaced pressure valves. The place was filled with the pipes, an intricate network connected to hulking metal tanks that lined the building, leaving only a narrow walkway on the side. Witches in long robes clamored back and forth between stations along the line of tanks, tweaking small configurations. One fiddled with knobs releasing steam, while another two stood atop a ladder, stirring from the top of the tank and delicately dropping in measured amounts of colored powders.

The complexity of the system was dazzling. Roykur had been to factories and large breweries in the city, where new types of engineering had improved the productivity, but nothing like the scale he was seeing now. Everything was perfectly synchronized. No wonder there was always so much elixir.

"Hello?" Roykur shouted. There was no response. The workers continued their tasks as if the slightest interruption would spell disaster. Perhaps it would.

Roykur followed the walkway. The steam clouds thickened, and the building got hotter. Before he had even gone halfway, his clothes were damp—from the steam or his sweat, he couldn't quite tell. The lodge ended abruptly, the tangle of piping congregating at a large hole in the floor. Roykur looked around and spotted a lever. No one had expressly told him not to touch anything, so he did what he had always done—better to ask for forgiveness than permission. Roykur's fingers wrapped delicately around the lever handle, and he pulled. There was a loud click, and a rhythmic scraping of gears. A section of the wood flooring near the piping dropped onto a track and slowly retracted underneath its neighbors.

Without the insulation of the flooring, Roykur could hear the voices that now trailed up through the opening. They grew louder, and as they came closer, Roykur could make out a single sharp speaker.

"What dumb, stunted, wool-brained idiot opened the hatch I explicitly said *will not be opened under any circumstances?*" Wahrlich poked her head out of the opening, scanning around the room, trying to identify the target of her wrath. Her expression changed from annoyance to surprise once she noticed Roykur, who had taken up a casual posture leaning against a wall, and then it returned to annoyance.

"Come, come. We have little time for swagger you do not have." Wahrlich's head dipped, followed by three robed witches emerging from the opening. Each of the figures was similarly clothed, like the rest of the Witches in the lodge. They hurried down the walkway or under the metal tanks. Hesitantly, Roykur stepped up to the opening. Peering down, he could see a small ladder leading down to another floor that flickered with a warm candlelight glow. *Ladder to a dark hole? That's familiar . . . well, I guess I'll never learn.*

The room below was cramped and dark, save for the few candles scattered about. The tightly packed pipes continued down and broke the surface of the floor, their destination obscured. Wahrlich stood hunched over a table, making notations in a book. She continued to write as she spoke. "So, my little Gefahr, do you wish to know what you have become?"

"We can start at what Gefahr means. My Treemolkvar is a

little . . . never learned." Roykur shuffled closer, his whole body still weak from the events of the past day.

Wahrlich smiled weakly. "Quite literally 'the danger.' Although I prefer, as most of us do, a different interpretation. 'Herald of the end times.'"

"Good, I was afraid it meant something incredibly boring. It has been a while since I had a good story, so let's hear it." Roykur propped up a stool and took his time trying to get comfortable on the hard surface.

Wahrlich stopped for a minute before continuing to write. "Is your companion well? Does Adalia still travel with you?"

"She will be alright after a bit of rest. She doesn't need to be here for this."

The Witch chuckled. "Hiding things from her, are we?"

"No, nothing like that. I will fill her in on everything once she is feeling better. She had a rough night."

"Very well." She cleared her throat. "You know the mythology of your Human gods?"

Roykur rubbed his face, trying desperately to scrub away the fatigue. "Vaguely. Deities that ruled over creation . . . uh . . . eight gods, and each god created something different. Let's see, Idrok and Elska created Humans, Wutheril created the Wit . . . Treemolkvar, Edel created the Vogels, and—"

"And so on and so on. The thing is . . . those were no gods." Wahrlich flipped a page in her notebook and continued to write.

Roykur rolled his eyes. "Well, I am not a believer. I know there is no such thing as a god, no need to convince me."

Wahrlich raised a finger. "Ah, but you should believe."

"But you just said— "

"I said those were no gods, at least as you know them, but there is a god."

Roykur folded his arms, and his frown deepened. *Great, so another "yours aren't real but mine are" situation. Well, I'm a damn*

Conservator. I need proof, not stories! Let's see if there's any truth behind this myth.

"The center of this world, Erden, is water. We all know this, but floating in that water is the shriveled corpse of a god. The Old God."

A shiver ran down Roykur's spine. Flashes of memory raced through his brain, his dreams floating in a great expanse of water. "Well, if it's dead, then what's the fuss? Wait. Why is it dead?"

Wahrlich finally set her pen down and closed the notebook, continuing to lean on the desk. "Little has survived since my people were told the tale. However, there is one thing that has remained consistent. Gods don't die. This world is like a prison, keeping it trapped in a deathlike state."

Roykur straightened on the stool. "You're saying a lot about a thing and then immediately saying the opposite. Are you just trying to sound cryptic, or idiotic?"

"Just shut up and let me finish." Wahrlich gave an exasperated sigh and continued. "It is unknown how or why the Old God was imprisoned; this was eons ago, before any of our species existed. Regardless of how it happened, the Old God was foretold to eventually break free, so its essence was removed and divided into eight pieces."

"Oh, like the eight gods! So, Humans weren't wrong after all," said Roykur.

"Of course you Humans were wrong. Some Human heard a single number and created an entire pantheon of bizarre personalities and disgusting reproductive escapades just to explain how the world was made. Absolutely insane." Wahrlich took a sharp breath. "Don't interrupt me again."

"Sorry. So, this black smoke I have, that is one of these essences?" Roykur squeezed his eyes shut and rubbed his temples. *This Witch expects me to believe I have the essence of a god in me?*

"What I have told you so far is general knowledge for my people." Wahrlich cleared her throat and spoke a little softer. "This next part, we do not share outside of the Treemolkvar. However, you are a special case . . . considering your state. This world was created as the prison for this Old God. We are merely the parasites that grew on the moldy surface of its cage. If it awakens, it will break its cage, and our world along with it. That is why the Treemolkvar swore to do everything we can to prevent that from happening."

"And how do you know all this?" asked Roykur.

"My people pieced this knowledge together long ago through visions and dreams, which, no doubt, you have been having."

"Other people have had essence before me, and you say that through their extremely vague nightmares is how your people got all their information?"

Wahrlich turned and shot daggers at Roykur. "Yes. Almost all the essences have had a host at one point, as far as we know, but never yours or the last essence. The essences connect their host to the Old God somehow. When they dream, they become closer to the Old God for a time. Now listen closely. This is the important part."

Roykur scoffed. "Fantastic. Your previous revelation was a little dry."

"The essences build in energy once they are released from the nexuses, or pools as you call them. If the host dies, the essence is pulled back into the pool and its energies dispersed. If all essences were freed at the same time and enough energy was absorbed, I fear the Old God would wake." Wahrlich paused, sipping her drink.

"Can the essences be destroyed? That would stop it for good."

"We have spent centuries siphoning the residual energies from an essence. That's how we can make elixirs." Wahrlich pointed to the mass of piping jammed into the ground. "Unfortunately, the energies seem to just keep regenerating. Until recently."

Roykur stood up from the stool quickly. "Hold on, there's another essence right here? And that is how elixirs are made? Olacka!"

"The waning of this essence can mean only one thing. It is the last one to be summoned. Which is why we call you Gefahr, the harbinger of the end. You are second to last, the warning, the last opportunity to put things right. If this last essence were released, with all seven essences still out there, then the world would end."

"If the other essences have been summoned from other locations, what is stopping them from summoning this one from somewhere else as well?" asked Roykur.

"The fact that we draw in the energies from here keeps it isolated. The ritual would not work from another location as long as we keep tethered to this site. It seems to have forced the essences to be drawn out of order." Wahrlich turned to scratch a quick note down.

"If this is a ritual site, then where are the stone pillars? The creepy ancient temple aesthetics?"

"We have destroyed all of those components, and any ability for the summoning ritual to be used at this nexus," Wahrlich said, folding her arms.

"Unless you get Doctor Arakul in here to fix that," said Roykur.

Wahrlich eyes narrowed. "What? What does the doctor have to do with this?"

"He built a whole ritual nexus thing in a warehouse. Made it out of mechanical parts and pieces from a different ritual site. It worked. You should know all this; you're part of the Initiative. Part of their master plan." Roykur hopped off the stool and made a sarcastic gesture in the air.

"I was not aware of this at all!" Wahrlich's eyes flared to fury. "How do you know this?"

There was no way she would reveal any of this if she was part of the Initiative's plan. She has been very upfront about all the ritual details, and he desperately needed more allies. Time to come clean.

Roykur started circling the pipes in the ground, attempting to peer down between them. "Huh, I guess they have been keeping you out of the loop. Well, Arakul kidnapped Adalia. I went to save her, and Arakul ambushed me. I don't quite remember the details, but Adalia said I was strapped to the ceiling with a spinning metal apparatus around me. The essence was ripped from my body into a metal tub. Then I woke up with this tiny little body, and I hate it."

Wahrlich's mouth drooped further down as he spoke, the incredulity increasing. "You transferred into a new body? That's not possible. How did you get the essence in the first place? Who were you before this?"

"Wait, if you didn't know about the transfer, how did you think I got the essence?"

"From Leondal. He has been pestering myself and the lodge for years for information about our elixirs. Since you are his son—well, supposed to be his son, I figured that was the connection. Besides, Leondal was the only person I thought was likely to pay the cost."

"Ah, I guess that makes good sense." Roykur stood for a moment, digging at his fingers. The memories of the Kolkrabba ritual came unbidden, quick and clear. "The cost?"

"An unthinkable one. Which makes me really curious to know who you were and how you got that essence." Wahrlich's voice was ice cold, and she straightened, not so subtly holding something behind her back.

"I kind of like the mystery." Roykur gave her a smile, hoping to break the tension, but was met only with Wahrlich's impatiently raised brow. "Fine, fine. I am Roykur, and I got this essence when I stopped the Kolkrabba from finishing their ritual during the war."

Wahrlich relaxed, if only a little. "Roykur . . . hmm, well, the impatience, witless humor, and bitter remarks certainly match. But that is hardly unique to you Humans. I have seen much in my long life, but transferring to a new body is certainly new."

"Perhaps you have spent too much of that long life around us. It appears we're rubbing off on you." Roykur gave her a wink, but she had gone back to her usual calm composure. He sighed, abandoning his attempts at building rapport with this Witch. "You mentioned your people have had essences in the past. To have the dreams. So, they paid that unthinkable cost?"

"Yes. Many hundreds of years ago was the last occurrence. Those were much more savage times. I am ashamed to say it was only forbidden once we uncovered the danger rather than the barbarity of the ritual."

"And how is the ritual performed exactly?"

Wahrlich pulled the knife that she had kept sheathed behind her back and started casually cleaning out the dirt from under her fingernails. A long silence drew out before she spoke again. "We can talk about the details of the ritual later. It is extensive. The Kolkrabba were dark creatures, with no morality to speak of. They would try to conduct the ritual whenever they had the chance. We knew they had one essence during the war. I didn't realize they had tried to release another."

"They had one already? You mean this wasn't the first they had summoned? But we killed them all," Roykur said, confused.

"Oh yes. They're all dead, and the essence is returned. However, they had a different essence for a while and used it to create Husks. I realize now that Husks would have made summoning more essences much easier."

Roykur's stomach dropped, pieces of the puzzle finally fitting together. "Husks were created by an essence. Is that what I did to Lord Wisiel?"

Wahrlich sighed. "No, each essence does things differently. It appears your essence alters others, strengthens them, at least from what I have seen. Like I said, it has been a long time since these essences were drawn out. I don't know what power they will imbue."

"His body had changed, muscles bigger. He also had hard bones covering parts of him. I don't seem to have any of that strength myself." Roykur squeezed the damp sleeve that clung to his rail-thin arm.

"I don't have any idea what these essences are capable of. It also seems like you don't know what you are doing, either," said Wahrlich.

Roykur moved toward her. "That's part of the reason I came here. Can you explain more about this essence?"

"No. I couldn't help you with that, even if I wanted to. Like I said before, the Treemolkvar vowed to keep these essences locked away. I would kill you now and send the thing back if I didn't need your help." Roykur took a step back, glancing at the ladder behind him. "Relax, I said I need your help. Besides, some Treemolkvar interpret the Gefahr to be our savior. Perhaps you will be."

"What do you want from me? And why would I help you?"

Wahrlich pushed off from the table and walked over to Roykur, speaking as she went. "It is very simple. I have a very strong suspicion that one of the other essences is free in our beloved city. Unfortunately, I fear it is in the possession of someone far less . . . reasonable than yourself. It is the only explanation for what has created the elixir of life. An elixir far more potent than it ought to be, made from a unique essence, different from the one we use. Which also means that—"

"That the king is involved." A pain settled in Roykur's stomach, and his breath quickened. It was not possible for his friend to be responsible for all those deaths. There had to be another explanation.

Roykur was breathing too fast. His vision tunneled. He turned and scrambled up the ladder. As his head crested the opening, he popped, bile hitting the floor and running down the rungs of the ladder.

CHAPTER 22

UNRAVELING THE THREADS

Roykur paced in the cramped office area above the hidden room, his thoughts dark. The steam tumbling from the large tanks stifled the air, making it hard to breathe, much less think. The crushing dread had passed, but he still felt queasy. He glanced over at Wahrlich, who sat sipping hot tea at her desk, completely at ease with the moisture and heat.

The minutes stretched by, and Roykur tried to fit the pieces of his entire life together. Geyser fall pattered against the roof above, thudding against wood and pinging off pipes. The familiar sound was comforting, and he took a deep breath, trying to soothe his frantic mind.

"So," Wahrlich said, finally breaking the silence. "If it makes you feel better about the situation, personally, I don't think the king has the essence."

Roykur stopped and met Wahrlich's eyes. "How do you mean?"

"Well, I don't know for sure. But just because he's involved in the elixir's production doesn't mean that he has the essence. Didn't he mention, at the council meeting, a team of chemists he had working for him?"

"Yes, I remember that. But Legast said—" Roykur stopped himself. He had never verified Legast's claim about the chemists being moved under House Becoven. He never even verified that there were chemists at all. That possibility just hadn't occurred to him until now.

"But what?"

"Nothing." Roykur rubbed his face, his eyelids heavy. "I'm just tired of all these secrets. I'm tired of people dying. Mostly, I'm just tired."

"We have beds, a few trees over, if you need rest."

"That's not the kind of tired I was referring to. But now that you mention it . . ." The extreme exhaustion he had felt when entering the enclave had been pushed to the back of his mind while he focused on the fresh revelations. Now, Roykur's thoughts drifted to the soreness in his muscles and the slight nausea of sleep deprivation. "It feels strange to stay awake like this. It wasn't long ago that you got an hour past sundown, and gods themselves couldn't keep me up."

Roykur stretched and yawned loudly, his body soaked in the steam, and that soreness seemed to fade a bit as he released the stretch. Wahrlich set down her tea and motioned for him to follow. As they stepped out of the lodge, the piercing cold felt painful after finally adjusting to the extreme heat. Roykur quickly wrapped his damp servant's coat back around himself and hurried after Wahrlich.

Despite the early morning sun, the recent geyser fall had already frozen thinly over the soft mulch ground, adding a crunch to their steps. They hastened to a nearby tree, Wahrlich stopping at the entryway and beckoning Roykur inside. There were soft-looking beds arranged in a circle around a crackling fire, with thin wooden partitions between them providing the barest bit of privacy. Several male Treemolkvar were asleep on the beds.

"Who are they?" asked Roykur.

"The night patrol. Relax, you'll be fine sharing their barracks. If it makes you feel safer, take this." Wahrlich handed him the dagger.

"Please rest. We will discuss more once you have slept." She inclined her head and glided away, leaving Roykur alone in this hollowed tree.

He removed his coat and shirt, inspecting the slice across his chest. Blackness no longer shimmered under the gaping wound, the tiniest amount of skin already knitted together. The pain was not the blazing fire of a fresh slice, but the dull tenderness of a large bruise. Roykur lay back gently, and sleep seized him before his head hit the pillow.

HE JOLTED AWAKE, the nightmare once again assaulting him, destroying his respite. He stared into the darkness, nothing visible around him. A knock at the entryway startled him, and like smoke blown away by a strong wind, the darkness swirled around and into Roykur. The room now stood barely visible from the pale moonlight that spilled through the cracks in the door and the smoldering embers at the center of the room. His roommates stirred from the knock but seemed unaware that the room had been engulfed in smoke. Compared to his dreams, the inky black smoke did not frighten him. In fact, the essence was starting to seem familiar, like a favorite pair of shoes, worn in and comfortable.

A female Witch poked her head in. It was difficult to tell in this light, but she appeared to be the same one who had escorted him through the enclave. "Excuse me, but Wahrlich has need of you."

"What time is it?" Roykur yawned and rubbed at his crusty eyes. His head pulsed, several small headaches already forming.

"Nearly two hours until sunrise."

"Elska's embrace, I nearly slept a whole day." Roykur pulled his shirt and coat on and followed the Witch, who began weaving her way through the trees. Stepping outside the tree, Roykur was whipped with a frigid early wind that thrashed his unbuttoned coat about him. Holding the halves tightly to his chest, he felt his fingers and ears numb quickly. The coat did nothing against this biting cold.

The thick trees became dense, a shelter from the wind, with roots overlapping atop the ground like natural stairs up the small hill. Roykur could hear the faint, sweet singsong of music from somewhere ahead. At the top, trees had been cut away to make a clearing, and the amphitheater therein. Two massive stumps formed a stage where a dozen or so Treemolkvar twirled and pranced. Off to the side, another dozen played furiously into their woodwind instruments. Their coverings hung loosely around their bodies, defiant of the cold.

The mostly filled seats were arrayed out from the stage in random lines branching in various directions, as if following the roots beneath the ground. Roykur was led to a row of empty seats next to a female Treemolkvar with heavy furs draped across her bare shoulders. Fashion rather than function.

"Good morning Gefahr, just in time," Wahrlich said in her silky-smooth voice.

A fur-wrapped head poked up from the high-backed seat in front of Roykur and gave a little wave. Adalia's voice was muffled behind the thick furs. "Nice of you to join us, sleepyhead."

"Hey there. How are you feeling?" asked Roykur, smiling while his teeth chattered.

Wahrlich shushed. "Not now. Turn your attention to this part of the play."

The dancers rolled a basket onto center stage, followed by eight more performers dressed in dark clothing. They spun in circles around the basket, each with a bright blue symbol painted across their face. The music pitched, then went silent. A low chant rose from the performers, and the audience slowly joined in.

"These ritual sites are scattered all over Erden. The pool and the eight stones," said Wahrlich.

A line of dancers leaped across the stage, tossing red ribbons into the air before pretending to dive into the basket. The chanting grew louder.

"Hundreds of lives were required to activate the site," Wahrlich said, raising her voice.

A purple sheet rose from the basket with someone dancing beneath it, making it appear to ripple. The entire audience now joined the chant.

"The essence would present itself."

An individual stepped onto stage wearing a white robe and danced in the opposite direction of the stones, tapping each one on the head. The chanting quickened.

"Each stone needed to be touched in a specific order."

The performer in white snatched the purple sheet, making a show of it moving beneath their robe. The chanting had reached a fevered pitch.

"The essence then enters the host."

The white-robed performer produced a knife and plunged it in their armpit, falling behind the basket in dramatic fashion. The chanting stopped.

"The host must die . . ." The performer jumped up, white robe now exchanged for a purple one. "Before they are reborn," said Wahrlich, almost reverential.

The audience cheered, and the woodwind instruments played a jaunty tune. The performers gathered on stage and began bowing.

After some patient waiting, the audience trickled out of the amphitheater, and the three of them sat watching as the stage props were removed. Roykur cleared his throat. "That's more or less how the Kolkrabba did it."

"It's a crude representation, I know, but this is how my people pass down our history. Not all the Treemolkvar share the same views. Like I mentioned yesterday, to some of my people, you are their savior, and to others, you are their doom. Either way, be careful while you are here." Wahrlich stood, adjusting her furs. "I apologize for getting you up this early, but I thought you would find the play . . . educational. Unfortunately, this is all I had time for today. I have pressing engagements. Regardless, you look like you have more resting to do. We can speak more about this tomorrow. Enjoy the enclave."

Roykur watched her go with a trepidation. She had to be hiding something.

"Ew, Grandpa, stop staring at Wahrlich. She's old, even for you," Adalia said from over the back of her seat.

"I wasn't . . . oh, very funny." Roykur stuck out his tongue. A passing Treemolkvar gave him a strange look but kept on moving. Roykur cleared his throat again, and Adalia giggled at his discomfort. "I see you are feeling better."

"Much. We didn't have time to really talk after the palace. There was a lot going on. Like what did you do to Wisiel? I barely recognized him." Adalia said it so casually, it took Roykur a moment to process.

"The smoke did that, I guess. It seems I can make people stronger with it. Change them."

"It's not like he wasn't already a monster. You just made it so everyone else could see it plainly." Adalia winced as she shifted in her seat. "When you absorbed the smoke, did you get more than you had? Like before?"

"Way more. How do I put this?" Roykur stared up at the opening through the tops of the trees. "The best way I can describe it is being so full after a meal that you might burst, but then you let out an enormous burp, and you suddenly feel like you can eat a little more."

Adalia wrinkled her nose. "Ew. Can you not be so gross?"

"Fine. How about leaving a bucket outside to collect water? Instead of the bucket filling up all the way, you discover it gets deeper, holding more and more each geyser fall." Roykur held up his arm and pushed the sleeve down to his elbow. He closed his eyes for a moment, and when he opened them, trails of smoke poured off his fingertips, cascading down his arm and vanishing into his coat sleeve.

"You know, it's kind of pretty when we aren't in a life-threatening situation," said Adalia. The smoke stopped as soon as Roykur glanced toward his granddaughter, his concentration broken.

He sighed. "I think it's getting easier to control. It takes a lot of focus when it's not the heat of the moment. Almost like it's easier when my blood is pumping."

"You should play around with it more, while it's safe. That way, you'll have a little practice the next time we get attacked by the crazed monster you accidentally created." Adalia yawned, her fatigue reflecting his own, and he yawned in turn.

"Stop it. Okay, let's get some food and get back to bed," said Roykur, rising from his seat.

"You go ahead. I already ate, and the medicas are going to take me back to the tent. They want to keep a close eye on the wound, in case it gets infected. Come by and see me after you wake up."

Roykur was going to object, but the growl in his stomach had become insistent. "Alright, I'll come see you later this afternoon. Love you, my little Dralm."

"Love you too, Grandpa." Adalia gave a weak smile, and her eyes drooped low.

Roykur placed a hand on her shoulder and gave it a quick squeeze before he headed back down the hill. The sun peeking between the trees had quickly broken the morning chill. He wandered through the enclave, following the smell of cooking meat. It didn't take long for Roykur to stumble across a large carcass, slowly turning, roasting on a spit. The meat had a glistening sheen across the lightly browned skin. Drips of fat ran down and sizzled into the flames.

There were a few Witches already sitting around the fire, eagerly awaiting their turn. He wasn't sure what manner of beast they were cooking, but his mouth watered. Roykur stuffed his hands into his pockets, looking for coin, but only came up with bandages and lint.

The Witch, turning the spit, sliced off a limb at the joint and handed it to Roykur. "For the Gefahr. No charge."

Roykur noticed that the small circle of Witches were staring at him, some with fearful anticipation, others what looked like hope. "Thank you."

Roykur slipped away from the cook fire and made his way back to his bed, glancing over his shoulder between bites of meat. He discarded the bone before stepping quietly into the tree. The Witch soldiers still slept on the other beds. A thought occurred to Roykur just before he lay down—this might be the best opportunity for some practice.

Roykur concentrated, and the smoke spilled out from his hand, the wisps difficult to see in the dark room. He sensed, more than saw, the smoke enter the soldiers. Each of them rolled over, or made a move to scratch an itch, but all appeared undisturbed. Interesting.

Little pricks of awareness bloomed along Roykur's head, and he could sense the Witches. Their bodies materialized in his mind as the smoke moved through them. There was something else. An understanding. Knowledge that he could do something more. One of the soldiers stirred, and Roykur pulled, quickly calling the smoke out. Nothing came.

Ah, shit.

This was the first time he had used the smoke on a Witch. Perhaps it worked differently on them. What if he couldn't get it back out?

Roykur instead lay down and threw the covers over his head. The Witch soldier got up, and Roykur heard water being poured from a pitcher. Sounds drifted around the room, and he tried to focus on what the Witch might be doing, but the bed was soft and warm. His eyes blinked slower and slower, and soon he was asleep once more.

CHAPTER 23

TEA AND BATHS

A tapping on his shoulder jolted Roykur from his nap. The same female Witch stood over him.

"Olacka!" Roykur sat up, startled, breathing hard. "You're not exactly the face I wish to see every time I wake up."

"Wahrlich requests your presence," she said, devoid of emotion. Roykur noticed that the beds around the room were empty. The soldiers had departed sometime while he slept. He could still sense their general direction. *I guess Adalia and I will deal with this today.*

"Lead the way." Roykur followed the Witch out of the tree and into the early morning air.

After a short walk, the Witch stopped in front of the widest tree Roykur had ever seen. In the dim light, he wasn't sure how far around the tree went, but it easily doubled the size of the one he had slept in. This tree had no hole or tent—it appeared whole.

The Witch knocked on the side, and an imperceptible crack in the tree peaked open. When had hidden doors become the new craze?

Needing no invitation, Roykur darted in, the warmth of the room seeping into him. There were various colors of pelts overlapping across the floor. Fur-covered chairs surrounded a small, round table,

237

one of which resembled a throne, and perched upon it was Wahrlich, sipping from a teacup. The lavish room caught Roykur off guard for a moment. Witches were not typically known for their extravagance, but perhaps Wahrlich had adopted some Human habits in her time as ambassador.

To Roykur's relief, he spotted Adalia reclined in a cushioned seat to his left. Bundled in many thick coats, she looked stiff, but much of the color had returned to her smiling cheeks. Roykur took a couple of quick steps toward his granddaughter, then stopped at a loud throat clearing.

"Would you please have a seat? My guest has time-sensitive news." Roykur turned to see the door swinging closed, revealing Volmirk sitting on the opposite side of the table from Wahrlich, a delicate grasp on his own teacup. "I have caught the commander up on everything."

"Hello, little one," Volmirk said through an exhausted smile.

The smile froze on Roykur's face. "Everything?"

"Of course—everything we witnessed at the palace." Wahrlich winked at him over her teacup.

Humans had definitely been a bad influence on her.

"Don't worry, Fritch informed me of the Initiative's part in Roykur's murder after he dropped you off at the safe house. Apparently, he lost a lot of House Heimvelt's coin in acquiring that place, which turned out to be an enormous blunder. He lost you two as well as the gold. I was hoping to receive another update from him, but I've been busy. I started my own investigation into the organization, and I found some . . . things. Any luck, and they will be useful during the trial."

"I wouldn't hold your breath waiting on Fritch. He's . . . dead. Husk Slayer got him." Roykur glanced over at Adalia, who was craning her neck to listen in. He pulled out a chair and sat down at the table. Roykur proceeded to fill in Volmirk on their discovery in the scrap garage. Each gory detail was absorbed by the commander's worried stare. Wahrlich drifted over to her stove at the far end of the room, adding more fuel and preparing another round of tea.

"I see. That is certainly unfortunate." Volmirk rubbed his hands across his face as if trying to scrub the stress away. "I came to summon Wahrlich to trial, but truthfully, anyone who may have evidence against the leading members of the Initiative is being summoned. After the complete debacle with Doctor Arakul and Lord Wisiel, I presented my findings to the king, and it was decided that a trial be held to determine if the Initiative had become an insurrectionist group."

"You saw the king? How was he? His wounds?"

"Not a scratch on him. Someone must have gotten more of that new elixir to him just in the nick of time. Man, it sure does the trick."

"Amazing . . . so he's alright." Roykur sipped the tea and felt the warmth radiate through his chest.

Volmirk shook his head. "I wouldn't say he's alright. In fact, I'd say I haven't seen His Majesty this pissed in all my time as commander. After Roykur, and now this, he means to see someone pay."

"I don't blame him. I would do the same if I were in his shoes."

"Aye," Volmirk said with a solemn expression. He cleared his throat and straightened his back, and when he continued speaking, his voice was lighter. "Well, with my report and your presence at the asylum and palace, you were on the court's list of the most desired witnesses. It was a pleasant surprise to find out you were here; Sentinels scoured the city all yesterday for you."

"Adalia and I are to stand witness in this trial?"

"Aye, along with many others. I am afraid the king demands it. There's no reason to be afraid. I'll walk you through the entire process on the way there."

"I have no qualms with testifying, but Adalia may need some help getting to the trial," Roykur said.

"Of course. Adalia is a very important witness. She is a noble who was involved in every single event of the past few weeks. Her word carries a lot of weight. I will do everything in my power to make sure she gets to trial," assured Volmirk.

Adalia spoke up from her cushioned bed. "Relax, the medica said I'm fine to travel." Grasping her bandaged hip, she rolled to her uninjured side and pushed herself to her knee with a whine, and then with a louder groan got her to her feet. Roykur scooted out of his chair to help her up, but she waved him off, seeming adamant. "I can do this myself. See, good to go."

"Teufel, are you feeling alright?" asked Wahrlich, returning with more tea. "You seem a bit jumpy."

"Of course I'm jumpy. It's freezing and I keep getting woken up by your creepy assistant," said Roykur, brushing his servant's uniform straight. He took one last sip of the hot tea. "Do we need to get going? Now, I presume?"

Volmirk cleared his throat. "Yes, the trial is later today, and we need to get you into some less soiled clothing and cover the basics of court etiquette."

"Wahrlich, didn't you need my help with other *pressing* matters?"

"Apparently, this cannot wait. We will address that issue as soon as this is over." Wahrlich stood up and settled a long pelt on her shoulders, trying to hide her less-than-thrilled look. "Perhaps the boy needs more cleaning up than new clothes."

She strolled out of the room, giving him a sidelong glance. Roykur sniffed at his arm. Oh, that was strong.

He made sure Adalia followed behind Wahrlich, and they all stepped out into the chilly dark. Outside the door was a squad of Sentinels, armed, alert, and on edge from the early-morning frost. The four of them were escorted to a caravan of carriages waiting along the enclave's main road. The lumbering draugkers at the front of each carriage worked their jaws through the frozen dew, chewing on what scraps of grass lay beneath.

Roykur was shivering immediately, and it continued long after their slow trek from the forest began. It seemed like he was always shivering in this new body, even when he had that heavy coat. He breathed in his hands, staring absently out the carriage window as the majestic trees were eventually replaced by the chaotic, monolithic structures of the city. The wooden wheels snapped the leaves that were sprinkled across the dirt road, then clacked on the cobbled city streets. The darkness cloaked the morning bustle of people, each of them trudging, either finishing a long night or off to an early start.

Volmirk rattled off an endless tirade of protocol and etiquette for the court room. Roykur stared out the window and tuned him out. All of them were rules he had practiced for years. Adalia mimicked Roykur's pensive gaze, as well as his silence, for the entire trip.

"Here we are. Follow me." Volmirk stepped out. The carriage had stopped at an all-too-familiar sight. Sentinel Headquarters, usually a gleaming bastion of justice to Roykur, now loomed sinister in the crack of dawn.

Volmirk led Roykur and Adalia to the large washroom used by the bulk of the Sentinels; two of them flanked the door. "Get washed up. There are clothes on the bench that will probably fit. Take your time. Trial isn't for another hour. I'll be back to collect you then."

Roykur hefted a pitcher and filled it in the steaming basin of water. He nearly dropped the thing, trying to carry it to the wooden tub, arms straining to hold just the few gallons of water. He stripped and sat down, ladling the rapidly cooling liquid across his head and shoulders.

From behind a curtain, in her own tub, Adalia asked, "How many trials have you been to exactly?"

"One for every murderer I've put away, and many others besides. Don't remember the exact number. I'd say less than a hundred."

"Would you say you know how this will turn out?"

"I'm afraid this is anything but a normal trial for me. Or anyone, for that matter. I don't think I've ever seen an entire group of people tried for conspiracy against the crown and the city, with murder on top of it. The group I created, no less."

"At least they will finally be stopped." A bit of hope was creeping into Adalia's voice.

"We shall see." Hope was a luxury Roykur rarely indulged in.

"Olacka! My bandage tore off in the bath. I need to replace this." Adalia stepped out from behind her curtain. Without having dried off, she was soaking through her clothes, and held a mush of soggy cloth to her side.

"The medical supplies are just a few levels up. Give me a second and I'll go with you."

"Don't worry, I know where it is."

"That's not what I'm worried about. We are not safe. Even here."

"I'll be fine. This may take a little while, so save me a seat." Adalia rushed out.

"Wait!" Roykur scrambled out of his tub and slipped on the slick floor. The damp curtain ripped free of its hangings and stuck to him. He pulled the thing off his head and bunched it around his waist while chasing after Adalia. Around the corner, the rest of the wash-room was empty. *Godsdamnit girl.*

Roykur didn't fancy going around the headquarters in only a curtain, so he ran back to put on some clothes. After dressing in his new plain brown wools, he glanced in a mirror, into the face of someone else staring back. He was still not quite used to seeing that face and not sure if he ever would be. His black, frizzy hair, still damp, had gotten longer, nearly covering his ears. His dark, youthful skin seemed stretched thin from stress.

The washroom door creaked open, and Volmirk stepped in. "It is time."

CHAPTER 24

THE WRONG TRIAL

Volmirk barked and shoved angrily at the crowd of people plugging the tunnel to the courtroom. They crammed themselves forward, hoping for a chance to participate in this spectacle. Pulled through the herd, Roykur looked up at the overflowing room, the cacophony of voices filling the area.

The courtroom was a massive amphitheater that took up the first two lower levels of the Sentinel Headquarters. Seats filled the majority of the space, forming a narrow circle at the base around the witness box and pressing nearly against the vaulted ceiling at the top. The three magisters sat on a large dais to one side of the room, the slightest of gaps between them and the audience seats. In his experience, this courtroom was almost always full, an excitement the city could not pass by. Leeches were always ready for blood.

Opposite the magisters, in another similar alcove, sat the king, mantled in all his glory and surrounded by his gleaming armored guard. As he sat tall in the high-backed throne, it was impossible to tell that he had suffered a near-fatal wound mere days ago. The crown rested upon his head, and he peered down at the numerous accused. His glare held none of the gentleness Roykur had known his friend for. That seat was rarely filled by the king. Today was one of the few exceptions.

Doctor Arakul stood behind the accused bench near the magisters, manacled. The doctor, now calm and dressed in formal attire, looked dignified despite his position. The rest of the Initiative leaders attempted to squeeze themselves onto the bench, trying for the same steady resolve, though perhaps less successfully—all except the lord and lady of House Becoven. Wisiel had reverted from his feral state, yet his bulk and bone protrusions were still present, visible from underneath his finely tailored outfit. Those two had donned their noble guise once more, a smug look on their faces and an air of absolute control over their circumstances.

Roykur really hated them.

Volmirk led the way to a spot near the very bottom of the seating and motioned for a couple in their early twenties to give up their spots.

"Are you kidding me? We've been here for hours just to get these seats." The young man sounded absolutely incredulous.

"You what, didn't think we would have witnesses for a trial this big? Move your asses," Volmirk said, his patience long since worn out. "Now!"

The young couple stood for a moment, looking up at the packed seating. Then the woman pointed somewhere up above, and with copious pardons, they made their way out of sight.

Roykur and the commander settled on the stone seats and were soon joined by Wahrlich, who squeezed in next to them. Roykur peered over at the accused's bench and met Arakul's eyes. A twinkle of recognition flashed, followed by a wide, toothy grin that made the hair on his arms stand on end. Why did that man disturb him so? He had handled deranged killers before. They had stopped chilling his spine long ago. Yet here he was, making Roykur as nervous as he had been on his first case, the djavul.

With some difficulty, Roykur pulled his eyes away from the doctor and looked to see which magisters would preside over the trial. His jaw dropped. "Magister Didris is presiding! Volmirk, that man is part of the Initiative. What the godsdamn draugker shit is this?"

Volmirk wheeling around fast on Roykur. "Sit your ass down on that bench, boy. I haven't the patience for your antics today of all days." He breathed in deep before continuing, forcibly calmer. "Half the city are members of that godsdamn group . . . technically even me! You want me to clap some manacles on the magister, drag him to the bench, and then go stand over there myself, hmm? No. Not gonna happen. Now, I'd appreciate if you would keep your mouth shut until it's time for you to speak."

Roykur's blood boiled as he kept his old friend's stare, but he did as he was told. The loud buzz of thousands of conversations filled the courtroom. Everyone was preoccupied with their own gossip. Even the magisters seemed content to lean close, deep in their discussions. Roykur started humming an old tune he used to know. He dug his fingernails into the corners of his thumbs, his knees bouncing, his anxiousness and impatience mounting.

"Where is Adalia? She should be here by now," said Roykur.

Volmirk stood up. "I'll check with my Sentinels. Don't worry we'll find her."

"Check the medical supplies level."

After a few minutes, Volmirk returned. "They're looking."

Finally, the magister in the middle, Magister Firad, waved a frail hand to a pair standing near the ceiling. They both pushed back large sliders built into the stone. The sound of rushing air was quickly replaced by the jingling of a thousand chimes from underneath the seats in the stands. The cacophony from the crowd quieted to a dull hum and then eventually to silence. Roykur closed his eyes as he felt the surge of fresh air flood into the massive room. Opening them, he could see all the revitalized faces in the crowd. *Eight gods, we never realize what we are missing until we get it back.*

The shutters controlled the air flow into the underground courtroom—a brilliant feat of engineering. A network of vents funneled air from the shutters, dispersing it to underneath every bench seat in the vaulted amphitheater. Chimes installed at each of the vents rang out whenever the air flowed in, an effective way to let the crowd know when to shut up and to restore order. Now, those shutters slid closed once more. The room fell still, if not completely silent. Magister Firad's voice bellowed out, echoing through the chamber. "Let the accused rise and face the charges against them!"

The entire bench of Initiative leaders shuffled around the slightly raised circle at the base of their bench, clearly not made for so many. A few chuckles rippled through the audience as the accused began nudging each other off while trying to stand on the circle. They eventually settled, with a few of them standing just off to the side.

"The accused, for the crimes of attempting to overthrow the crown, attempted murder of His Majesty, the murder of the king's guard, the murder of the head of a noble house, and several other murders, have been charged with high treason. The punishment for these crimes is disintegration at the Cleansing Shallow."

The audience erupted into a rumble of murmurs, and the shutters slammed open. Chimes rang out loudly, hushing the space. The magister swept his gaze around, daring them to keep disrupting his courtroom.

"The court will proceed undisturbed, or I shall have the chamber cleared." After a long pause, he shuffled some papers on his podium. "The commander of the Sentinels himself will present evidence and witnesses to the crimes. The accused's request to be judged individually was approved, and they shall each receive one hour to present their defense and one hour to offer witnesses, should they have any. Based on the number of you, the court anticipates three days for the defense. Commander, please present your findings to the king, the magisters, and the people of this city."

Roykur watched as the entire amphitheater shifted its attention to where he and Volmirk sat. A familiar scene, the crowd perched on the edge of their seats, a collective breath held, not daring to miss a single word. The commander stood carefully, keenly aware of the scrutiny upon him. Following tradition exactly, he walked the open circle around the accused, then snapped his heels sharply together and gave a perfect salute to Legast. Volmirk executed an equally superb display for the magisters, and then a somewhat awkward one to the audience.

"My king, magisters, and the people of Ver'a'saile, I bring before you facts of the crimes discovered by the Sentinels and testimony of those who witnessed it. A promising engineer, a member of the Initiative named Myrmilla, was killed by elixir incompatibility. Then, three days later, Lord Roykur of House Heimvelt was murdered as well. Evidence at the scenes, as well as several witnesses, name Doctor Arakul as the murderer. Two nights ago, Lord Wisiel of House Becoven was seen by no less than sixty witnesses assaulting the palace, killing three guards, and attempting to kill His Majesty."

The audience seemed to stir at every break in the Volmirk's speech, hurriedly digesting the information before he began again.

"After being questioned in Sentinel custody, Lord Wisiel admitted to a plot and named all accused here as accomplices, to overthrow the kingdom."

The king was stiff, a stern look upon his face, but even Roykur from his seat could see there was more than just a rigid formality. Legast was on edge. Roykur didn't think he'd ever seen his friend so angry. Well, angry at all, really.

"The night Myrmilla died, my Sentinels, with the aid of Lord Roykur, discovered that the food and drink had been tampered with. An elixir was introduced, one that Myrmilla specifically had an incompatibility with. Some weeks later, Lord Roykur was killed most brutally beneath the new elixir factory after tracking down Myrmilla's killer; a contraption of her design was found underneath. Additionally, I have a witness that saw Doctor Arakul kill Lord Roykur for discovering his crime. Those same witnesses were kidnapped by Arakul and subjected to torture at Merit-Postle Asylum. After the doctor was arrested by the king himself, jars filled with Human organs were discovered in Arakul's possession.

"Three weeks later, separately, Lord Wisiel, under the influence of what we believe to be several potent elixirs, carved a swath of destruction into the palace, killing guards and servants alike. At the end of his path, he threw a spear and gave the king what should have been a mortal wound, just before the apparent end of his elixirs. He collapsed right after, unconscious. After Lord Wisiel was revived, he raved in a maddened state, claiming he would destroy all who opposed 'the Grand Plan.' We picked out a few details from his babbling that the Grand Plan was not his but the Initiative's, and got him to name his accomplices, those before you all today."

"Thank you, Commander. Now please, present your witnesses."

The first witness was none other than Roykur's daughter-in-law, who emerged, petite and unassuming, from the seat not even ten paces away. A bit of shock rippled through his steadily rising ire. How had he not noticed her practically right next to them this whole time?

Visari recounted that night at the manor. Some details Roykur had been absent for, but most of it he remembered vividly. It always intrigued him how every event was told differently, depending on the person. The things they focused on, that stayed with them for the retelling, how they felt in that moment, what they saw, what they heard or smelled. Everyone brought a piece to the larger puzzle. She finished her story with the Sentinels arriving in the manor. The audience buzzed, eating up every detail.

The second witness to speak was an evidence officer within the Sentinels, oafish and extremely monotone. There was a long stretch where he presented the matching elixirs at the manor, the warehouse, and the asylum. He explained the findings that the elixir of life had been on the recent Husk Slayer victims before it had been released to the public. Then a small wooden chest was produced and placed in the evidence officer's arms.

"Sentinel Brindol, what is the significance of the item you have there?" asked Volmirk.

"Sir. This is a chest recovered from the scene of one of the Husk

Slayer murders. It was lost and later found again at the asylum, along with jars filled with organs."

"Doctor Arakul was at the murder scene, wasn't he?"

"Yes, and he had full access to evidence, including this chest."

"What's in the chest?"

"Strange documents. They are instructions on how to create an altar of some sort."

"Like the one beneath the warehouse?"

"Yes, sir," said Brindol.

"I see. Now, take a look at this schematic we seized from Myrmilla the night she was murdered."

"That is the circular rail that was beneath the warehouse."

"Thank you. Next, I would like to call Ilienie." A skinny, youthful woman stepped to the center, draped in even more jewelry than she had been at the palace festival feast. "Now, is it true you saw Arakul at the warehouse with jars of organs?"

"Yes. Well, my son did. A whole wagon full. But I rented that space to Arakul myself."

Volmirk dismissed Ilienie and called up the warehouse guard and confirmed the various materials shipped in, as well as his encounter with Roykur. The commander then called up the three nurses from the asylum one at a time and asked them all the same questions.

"Is kidnapping part of your normal duties?" asked Volmirk.

Caught off guard, the nurse widened her eyes. "What? No. Absolutely not."

"How do you explain taking two people against their will to be tortured in your asylum?"

"We don't torture anyone. Doctor Arakul's methods are extreme, but they help people. We get house calls all the time. Though this one was a bit strange."

"Strange how?"

"Well, there were a few of those Jasper members about, and it looked like quite a bit of coin going around."

"Ah. There it is. Arakul had hired a criminal organization to assist in his schemes."

The shutters fluttered while the magisters tried to quiet the crowd.

Roykur became distracted, staring at the entryway. Adalia should have been here by now. His eyes drifted over to Volmirk, and he caught a furtive beckoning motion from the man. The stadium had gone still, the previous witness now gone from the center, all eyes patiently trained on Roykur.

This is it—keep it together, old man. Finish strong, for family, for friends.

Wahrlich gave Roykur a comforting look, which he returned. He moved to the center of the room, glancing to Legast for a similar comfort, only to find a contemptuous stare. The pathetic drunken phase of his grief had clearly ended, and the senseless blame and rage were well underway. It was silly to think his best friend would be angry at him, put any sort of blame on him for the murder of himself. Of course, Legast remained unaware, but it was still painful to see the hurt in his friend's eyes. As soon as this was over, Roykur would tell him. No sense anymore in letting him think he was dead.

Roykur stood, exposed to masses, more nervous now than in any case he had testified on—this was way too personal. He was not the one presenting evidence this time or breaking down facts, coldly building an indisputable wall of logic. He was just here to tell his story, tell it well, and trust that justice would be done.

Something dawned on him, then, and his mouth hung open. This story was not from his perspective. He had memorized Teufel's story well enough by now, but it still caught him off guard.

"Are you well, son?" Magister Didris leaned over the lip of his podium to examine Roykur better. "Teufel, was it?"

"Yes sir, and yes." Roykur forcibly relaxed himself and oriented his thoughts, then retold the story. He left the account of the warehouse vague, hoping Adalia would better fill in those details. He covered the asylum and the attack at the palace, going into specific detail about Conservator Fritch's murder and how he had seen Lord Wisiel try to cover it up. When Roykur finished, he was dismissed to his seat. While the magisters scribbled furiously, whispers rolled through the crowd, who were likely forming their own opinions on his testimony. The king appeared to be holding back a fresh wave of anguish at the retelling.

Volmirk boomed once again. "So, to summarize for the court. A murdered woman's designs were used to kill Lord Roykur on an altar beneath a warehouse that produced elixirs found in other murder victims. One of those other victims translated the instructions to create that altar. Doctor Arakul was at the manor, the warehouse, the murder scene, and the asylum. Then, Lord Wisiel made an attempt on the king's life. Clearly, Arakul and the Initiative's true intentions are to remove key figures who would oppose them and seize control of the kingdom."

CHAPTER 25

IRONCLAD DEFLECTION

The cavernous building remained stiflingly hot throughout the day. For every member of the audience who left, either bored or having to get to work, another quickly took their place. Witnesses continued to recount the slaughter at the palace and various other actions deemed seditious. There were accounts of Initiative members paying bribes and maneuvering their way onto council seats. In fact, there was a good deal more evidence presented than Roykur had been aware of. It was a genuine surprise that any investigating had been accomplished given the state of the Conservators. Most of the testimonies were about Lord Wisiel, which seemed quite unnecessary at this point. There had been ten witnesses describing him throw a spear through the king's chest. Wahrlich had gotten her chance to speak as well, though it was another reiteration of the events of the parties at the manor and palace.

Regardless, Roykur was worrying. His testimony had been the only real detail given about the warehouse. Adalia's testimony was vital, but she was still nowhere to be seen. Roykur had tried to sneak out earlier, but a Sentinel had escorted him the whole way to the bathroom. *Where on Erden is my granddaughter?*

Another round of the chimes beneath the seats signaled the end of the day's events and the end of the accusation's side. Tomorrow, the three days of the accused's defense would begin. The auditorium burst with movement and sound as the audience got up to leave and Sentinels directed the accused to their cells.

Roykur jumped out of his seat. "That can't be it! Adalia hasn't been called as a witness yet. Volmirk? Volmirk!"

"Stay here," the commander shouted over his shoulder. He was already ten feet away, disappearing into the rush of people.

Roykur shook his head and threw his hands up. Fury burned in his chest, and he ground his teeth. "She should have been here. Something is wrong."

"She would have said basically the same things you already said. Maybe she could have expanded a bit more about the warehouse, but I think the judges grasped the idea," said Wahrlich, standing up. She had a weak smile and appeared to be holding back concern. It wasn't difficult to see that she doubted her own words.

"It's not about the minutiae of events but the number of people who can confirm the story. By not allowing her to give her side of the story, they don't have a single person who can back up the events at the warehouse." Roykur was pacing in his seat and forcing out exaggerated breaths, a poor attempt at calming himself down.

He attempted to locate Visari through the outpouring of people from the courtroom. It would be nice to speak with again after all this time, see how she fared after the palace attack. Unfortunately, his daughter-in-law was nowhere to be seen.

Volmirk returned holding a room key. Roykur prepared to unleash his frustration out. "What is going on? Where is Adalia?"

"She is missing," the commander said solemnly.

"What do you mean missing?" asked Roykur, panic settling in his stomach.

"Exactly what I said. My Sentinels have looked everywhere, and they can't find her."

"By the gods! We need to find her immediately—she is in danger." Roykur voice rose high, frantic and pubescent.

Volmirk placed a firm hand on Roykur's shoulder. "None of that now. Just because she's missing doesn't mean she's in any danger. If she's still in the city, we will find her. I doubled the Sentinels searching for her." He sighed. "But you can't leave. The court requires witnesses to be present for the accused to question as part of their defense. We have rooms here at the headquarters you must stay in during the proceedings." Volmirk turned and stomped his way toward the exit. "Follow me."

The rooms were one level above the holding cells Roykur had stayed in not too long ago, and just as uncomfortable, with Sentinels posted outside to make sure he remained in his room. Food and sleep were meager for Roykur, as he remained worried sick over his granddaughter, eager for the trial to be done.

Ж

THE NEXT FEW days dragged on, taking what seemed like forever. Each accused individual pleaded their innocence. All of the Initiative leaders sounded more or less the same, bleeding together in Roykur's mind, almost as if they were saying the same things.

"Lord Wisiel asked me to pay some people for their continued support of the Initiative. It isn't a conspiracy," said Halot.

"My husband has gone quite mad. There was never a Grand Plan." Lady Ingrail claimed.

"We set out to help the people, not destroy the country," said Maulk. "Lord Wisiel has always had his own agenda."

"I have several witnesses who will disprove these petty crimes and display the full capacity of my character," said Reynaldon. "Lord Wisiel, on the other hand—a liar and a thief, that one."

"Myrmilla was one of our own," said Nicademo. "A very dear friend—none of us would ever wish to hurt her. Although Lord Wisiel never liked her."

"Just because we all joined the Initiative does not mean we are responsible for the actions of one member. Lord Wisiel acted completely on his own," Theodorick proclaimed.

Each of them turned on Wisiel as if he were the embodiment of evil and the orchestrator of all their sins. The leaders called the maximum number of witnesses, having them explain away the various crimes, each more obviously rehearsed than the last. It was smart. No reason for all of them to go down together when it was Wisiel and Arakul who had the majority of evidence stacked against them.

After the sixteenth alibi and denial of a Grand Plan, Doctor Arakul stepped up to center stage. Roykur felt the emptiness in the pit of his stomach, the dryness of his throat.

The doctor stood and confidently addressed the room. "Esteemed people of Ver'a'saile. I am but a humble servant of the crown and this city. I have dedicated my life to medical research and the restoration of the feebleminded. I was charged by our king to run His Majesty's sanitorium, Merit-Postle Asylum, where I worked diligently for decades. I was asked to provide my expertise by Lord Roykur himself, which I only did out of a desire to stop killers running free in our streets. After many years of retirement, I selflessly returned to my position after reacquiring my youth. I am not sure how many patients I took care of, but it was countless, many of them your friends, your family, your neighbors, and that boy right there."

Doctor Arakul turned to point a finger, all the heads in the room swiveled directly at Roykur. "Teufel, would you be so kind as to join me here?"

Roykur eyed the magisters, who motioned for him to proceed.

Arakul continued, "Thank you. Now I only need to clarify one point. In your recollection of events, you said the deranged person who killed Roykur wore a mask, yes?"

"Yes, you wore a mask," said Roykur flatly.

"Yes, you claim it was I who wore the mask, yet you hold no further proof. It could have been anyone behind that mask."

"No, it was clearly—"

"What does this mask look like?" interrupted Arakul.

"The mask looked like . . ." Roykur swallowed. It hadn't occurred to him to ask for a description of the mask. He ventured a guess. "It was a creepy mask, with designs on it."

"That describes every mask. You claim to have seen a mask but can't even describe it. I have no more questions for this witness."

"It was you! I know it was you," Roykur yelled, his voice carrying through the cavernous chamber.

The doctor spun on him in an instant. "How? How do you know this so-called fact?"

"You confessed it! You claimed the wounds upon my flesh. You had jars of organs in your closet. You let—"

"This mentally ill child claims I confessed murder to him." Arakul walked a circle around the room as he spoke. He chuckled, and the crowd laughed in reply. "And that my tending to his wounds is an admission of guilt as well. I hope you have more than that."

I tortured a man and suffused him with some unholy power to get my answers.

Roykur strained to think of some other way he could have known, but the hall took it as his choice to remain silent.

"Please return to your seat," said Magister Didris.

"This boy here was admitted to my sanitorium by his father. Not a kidnapping. I assessed his mental condition to be highly fragmented as well as delusional. I have no doubt he witnessed such a traumatic event as he described. However, the details cannot be trusted. It is my assessment that he had not recovered from the trauma of such a brutal murder, and the stress of being committed caused him to confuse the two events. It was much easier for him to make me the sole source of his pain than confront his own helplessness."

Roykur seethed in his seat.

"I would like to recall Lady Visari," said the doctor. The doors to the chamber opened, and Roykur's daughter-in-law stepped through, flanked on either side by Sentinels. Once she was settled at the center of the hall, Arakul continued. "If I am not mistaken, you are the principal reason for my arrest, yes?"

"I simply made a request to the king to save my daughter, whom you were holding captive!" A surprising display of fierceness from the meek woman, despite the puffy features and worn expression. It had been a harrowing time for them all.

"Indeed . . . we can all understand the actions of a concerned mother," Arakul said, looking at the audience as if for confirmation. "However, I am a doctor and so, based on the head trauma, the sickly conditions she was sleeping in, and the unstable company she kept, it was my obligation to make sure she was healthy before I could, in good conscience, release her. An obligation set by the king's own mandate. I swear on my life that your daughter was to be released that day."

He continued, "Unfortunately, because of the lady's impatience, I was taken into custody, and some of my patients, not ready to face the outside world, were released before they had the chance to finish their mental care."

Visari sniffed. "What about that dead patient? The jars of organs?"

"People do not come to the asylum if they are healthy and happy, and some arrive in worse condition than others. My staff and I do what we can, but some die. Instead of letting perfectly good organs to go to waste, we store them for medical testing. It is important for medical science to push the boundaries of what we know to better stop future patients from dying of the same maladies."

There was a murmur of agreement from the audience. A plausible explanation; however, it was the doctor's confident, calm demeanor that set the tone. The courtroom had the air of a lecture hall, with Arakul, the tolerant professor, guiding their minds to the logical conclusion.

The king sprang to his feet, causing a stir throughout the courtroom. "Roykur is dead! You killed him! You were seen at the warehouse by more than just this boy!"

"Your Majesty. Please let the accused make their case," Magister Didris chided.

"It's alright." Doctor Arakul turned smoothly to the king and bowed with a smile that was closer to a sneer. He spoke slowly, patronizing. "Your Majesty, please allow me to put aside your doubts. I recall Ilienie."

The woman stepped up again, looking far too pleased with the attention.

"Why did you say I rented that warehouse from you?"

"I recognize your voice. Very distinct."

"Ah. So you never actually saw who rented the space from you. Is it possible two people could have similar voices?"

"It's possible, I guess."

"And your son—did he mention me by name?" asked Arakul.

"No. But it was the same person."

"Where is he now? Can we ask him about these sightings, or are we to only take your word?"

"I am not sure where he is right now. Probably on the floor in some pleasure den too drunk to move."

"So not only is his word secondhand, but it is the word of a drunk. Convenient. Thank you, that is all," Arakul said. Ilienie's smile faltered a bit, but she returned to her seat with an elegant jiggle of metal and stones.

"Now, regarding the death of poor Myrmilla," Arakul continued, "I do, as noted, use elixirs to treat my patients. This is still experimental and new, but my staff and I have made more progress with troubled cases than ever before. This is not evidence of anything." Arakul spun around and pointed a finger at a random person in the stands. "What is your business, my good man?"

"Me? Uh . . . I'm a scraper. I mean, I scrape the railings; you know after a while they get a buildup of that gunky stuff."

"Very good, very good. Do you not see elixirs everywhere you go? How many do you see sitting in the windows of the local market shops? How many do you yourself use?" asked Arakul.

"I see them a lot. I only use one, just because I don't want hair on my back."

A chuckle swept through the crowd.

"Thank you. As you can see, elixirs are everywhere, and everyone has access to them. I was not the only one there that night with elixirs, and no witnesses claim to have seen the actual deed." Arakul raised a finger to the king, waylaying any impending objections. "I call Conservator Simune."

Roykur whipped his head around as the smug djavul strolled to the center. The conservator stood slouched, uniform askew, and stared daggers right at Roykur. The predatory intent was disturbing. He should have hit him harder.

"Simune, you are the lead conservator on the recent string of murders, are you not?"

"That's right."

"Well, that boy over there"—he pointed at Roykur—"claimed you took bribes from Lord Wisiel in order to frame Lord Roykur for one of those murders, is that correct?"

"Yes, it is. In fact, Wisiel paid me many times to do little favors for him."

"Were some of these favors in relation to the events of this trial?"

"Yes, Wisiel paid me to take that wooden chest from the murder scene and place it in your asylum. Also, he paid me to rent the warehouse from Ilienie, and drive shipments to the warehouse."

Confused murmurs rippled through the auditorium.

"Why would you come up here and admit to these crimes in front of all these people?" asked Arakul in a trite tone.

"Because, I was authorized to take those bribes from the Sentinel commander himself."

There was an eruption from the audience, and the magisters had the chimes ringing for minutes before the crowd was subdued. Roykur looked at the commander and shook his head. He knew what Simune was referring to—commanders did it all the time, but now it was going to backfire.

"Commander Volmirk, can you speak to this astonishing revelation?" asked Arakul.

Volmirk rubbed his face, deflated. The gruff man stood and trudged to the center platform. "Simune is referring to a policy I instituted that . . . allows for Conservators to take bribes as long as it is reported and used to convict a criminal. However, I was not aware of this particular—"

"Those bribes have now been reported and will be used in a conviction." Arakul began another lap around the circle, while the conservator and commander retreated to their seats. "So, good people of Ver'a'saile, let me summarize. No one saw anyone spike the food at Manor Heimvelt. No one can admit to seeing my face at the warehouse. My medical techniques can be unpleasant but have helped this city for generations. And finally, a Conservator admits that Lord Wisiel tried to frame Lord Roykur and myself."

Arakul returned to the accused's bench, clearly pleased with himself. Roykur had been feeling confident about the course of the trial until that moment. This had been an actual argument, compared to the incessant excuses the others had given. There was only one other member left to speak. Lord Wisiel.

With difficulty, the lord stood hunched, obscuring the various protruding bones. Even bent over, he was noticeably taller than he had been. Without moving, he spoke in a hoarse voice, "I have nothing to say to these accusations."

A low rumble rolled through the crowd. Magister Didris adjusted his spectacles. "Are you sure, Lord Wisiel? Nothing to say in your defense?"

"Nothing." His stony face didn't reveal anything more.

"As you say." Magister Firad raised his voice and bellowed, "The magisters will return henceforth with judgement of the accused."

CHAPTER 26

JUDGMENT

The doors to the hall closed tightly after everyone was excused. Only the magisters were left inside. Roykur was escorted back to the tiny closet of a room he had been sleeping in. He shut the door and jumped in surprise at the figure sitting on the bed. Adalia looked haggard, her hair a frizzy mess, bruises on her knuckles and a wild look in her eye.

"Hello, Grandpa," she said in a weary voice.

Roykur ran to her and checked her over. "Olacka, what happened to you? Are you alright?"

"Oh this? This is nothing, you should see the other Sentinels." Adalia gave a weak chuckle.

"Sentinels did this to you?" That ever-present rage began to bubble up in him.

"Conservator Binjek and a couple of other Sentinels found me while I was getting bandaged. They said they wanted me to identify some thugs they had in the cells." Adalia shook her head. "Well, when we got there, they pushed me in one of the cells and locked me up. They took turns watching me. After a couple days of yelling, one of them gave in and tried to gag me. Let's just say he might need help chewing his food."

"Those rotten djavuls." Roykur scoffed. "They were there to stop you from testifying. I guess that's why Binjek wasn't at the trial."

"How is the trial going?"

"Hard to say. The Initiative is working really hard to keep the attention on Wisiel. Your testimony would have helped a lot."

"I'm sorry."

"It's not your fault. Volmirk had the Sentinels looking for you." Roykur sighed. "Now I wonder if that was a lie."

Looking over at Adalia, Roykur could see her concern. He noticed the way she dug her fingernails into the sides of her thumb, just the way he had always done. Something about that made him smile, if only for a moment. It broke his tension, a brief reprieve.

A knock on the door came, and they stepped out into the hall. Then the doors to the courtroom were opened once more, and the audience jostled their way back to their seats.

The faces of the magisters were stoic as they passed various papers back and forth. Roykur got to his seat quickly, Adalia on the ground at his feet, and watched everyone resettling into the room. Several minutes went by, yet Volmirk and Wahrlich remained absent from their seats. Concern and suspicion flooded Roykur. Were they also part of this conspiracy? The overflowing crowd shuffled into their unclaimed spaces as the room filled up, unfamiliar faces pressing in against Roykur. Then the doors crashed shut, an echoing thunder that ended in silence. The room held another collective breath.

The magisters sat tall at their podium and in unison began calling the names of the accused. "Dittlemar!"

The pale little man stepped into the center, wringing his hands nervously. "This court finds you . . . innocent!"

The crowd erupted together in a deafening roar, the chimes barely cutting through their noise—contempt or adulation, it was impossible to tell. Roykur let out his breath, deflated. Roykur glanced at Legast, who mimicked the look of defeat, staring only at his feet. The magisters continued to speak in unison, carrying on despite the unruly crowd. "Bode! This court finds you . . . innocent!"

Like his chest was being struck with a hammer, Roykur felt it grow tighter with each judgment. The names came quickly now, the judgments expected. The proclamations of innocence rang out for each member in turn.

Finally, the doctor was called forth.

"Arakul, the court finds you . . . innocent!"

Roykur knew it was coming, yet it still sent an arc of white-hot fury, like a fever, down his temples and along his clenched jaw. The man couldn't be allowed to go free after all that he had done, and what he would continue to do.

Before stepping out of the center, Arakul nodded respectfully. Roykur jumped up on his seat, shaking, boring a hole in the doctor's back with his eyes, barely still listening to this mockery of a trial. "Lady Ingrail, the court finds you . . . Innocent! Lord Wisiel, the court finds you . . . guilty!"

Magister Didris stood at his podium with his hands outstretched, waiting patiently for the room to quiet down. "There was not sufficient evidence or witness testimony presented to prove anyone here had any significant connection to the crimes they were accused of, Lord Wisiel being the exception.

"The testimony of the witness Teufel, with respect to the murder of Lord Roykur, could not be corroborated by another witness. We do not hold to the idea of executing a citizen of this great city based purely on a single account.

"Finally, Wisiel's execution by disintegration will take place at the Cleansing Shallow at dawn." They nodded to the side, and two Sentinels escorted the deformed former lord out of the room. The Initiative leaders' shackles were removed, and they were all escorted out a moment later. Each was stoic, yet plainly relieved as they left the courtroom auditorium.

"This trial has concluded," the third magister intoned, and on cue, a last rattle of the chimes rang out and the simultaneous exodus of the crowd. Roykur remained where he was, the people flowing around him. He watched the backs of the Initiative leaders as they shrank down the long passageway.

Arakul stopped in the cramped exit, the crowd overtaking him. He turned slowly as the flood parted around him. He scanned the courtroom until he met Roykur's eye. Smiling, he slid a creepy mask onto his face, no one else appearing to notice. The doctor stayed for only a second more before disappearing into the mass of people.

"Fucking djavul!" screamed Adalia, sprinting forward before Roykur even registered that she must have seen the mask, too. He quickly darted after her but was forced to halt as the masses pressed tightly together, shambling forward at an excruciating pace. Roykur lost sight of Adalia, the crowd towering over him, pressing in from all sides, and he started getting shoved back and forth to the rhythm of the impatient advance. Panicked, partially from the claustrophobia, partially from the idea of losing track of the chase, Roykur used his small size to his advantage and slipped into the occasional opening. He made quicker progress than the general pace of the crowd, but he was also at the perfect height for the stray elbow, which caught him in the cheek, the temple, and nose before he made it near enough to the front that people spread out.

Pinching his nose, Roykur stopped at the edge of an intersection, and Adalia pulled up next to him. His mind raced as he spun around and around, trying to spot any sign of the madman. Up or down the ramp, or straight across the corridor to the west, or the next tower over; regardless, the expanding possibilities made it impossible to continue this pursuit.

"Wait, is that him there?" Roykur said as he spotted a figure standing in the distance, still staring.

"That little draugker shit is taunting us." Sure enough, the creepy ritual mask turned away from them again just around the tower on the other side of the ramp. Their shoes scraped on the dirty stone floor, followed by the clacking and pounding of hard footfalls.

Roykur was quick and nimble, but that couldn't compete with Adalia's long stride, and she pulled ahead. Curving around the tower, a low laughter echoed through the narrow stone walls and off the various side passageways. It grew louder and shriller the farther they went. *Almost there, you piece of shit.*

Adalia and Roykur had run almost completely around the tower before Arakul came into view, standing, arms outstretched, chest heaving, cackling all the while. Adalia grunted and slowed down, holding her hip. Speeding past her, Roykur felt his skin prickle as he focused on the smoke, trying to will it over to Arakul. Like the feeling of sweat gushing out of his pores, the smoke rolled out, lazily at first, then shooting to Arakul as if sucked through a narrow wind tunnel. The manic laughter cut off just before the smoke forced its way beneath the mask and Arakul began convulsing.

Awareness blossomed inside Roykur's head, a sense of familiarity, control, and understanding, which grew as the smoke spread through the body. He continued to barrel onward, letting out an anguished battle cry, full of rage and pain.

Roykur felt pulses, or more like emotions, from his connection, an eagerness for instruction.

He smashed into the stunned Arakul, tackling him to the ground.

The pain in the doctor registered in Roykur's mind, but only as another dot of information bombarding his psyche. All the knowledge and building possibilities were becoming clear. His anatomy was twistable by Roykur's very thoughts; this body's functions were his to command. The physicality was easy to manipulate, mold—he could dull the senses or enhance the pain, but right now just needed him to hold still.

Roykur jerked Wahrlich's short, jagged knife from his belt. "Die, you son of a bliest!" he cried, and rammed the blade into Arakul's neck, watching him twitch helplessly. He pulled it free and forced it back down, again and again.

His awareness of Arakul's body finished expanding, the knife jabs flaring in his mind, but something else was wrong. He could sense—

something about the body was strange, unexpected. Roykur concentrated on the connection.

This was not the body of a man.

He slid the knife out one last time, letting the blood stream out, pooling in the dirt and stone. The body went limp almost immediately. Fear gripped Roykur's throat as he reached a blood-soaked hand for the edge of the mask. He pulled it free, and found the vacant eyes of Visari staring up at the ceiling. That keen awareness in Roykur's mind vanished, and a slow trickle of black seeped out the edges of her mouth, eyes, and out of the ears. The heavy smoke drifted lazily back to Roykur and disappeared beneath his clothes.

"No, no, no no no!" Adalia screamed with sheer horror, standing above the corpse of her mother. That harsh, shrill cackle began again somewhere off in the distance, then slowly faded away.

Roykur dropped the mask. His heart wrenched awfully in his chest, but it sank further still as he noticed the sizeable crowd that stood watching the murder unfold.

CHAPTER 27
UNMASKED

A woman shrieked; a retching could be heard among the indistinct murmurs. The people's shock held for a mere moment before being replaced with indignation. Roykur's eyes flicked from the slowly forming mob to the blood that coated him. His granddaughter was paler than usual, staring down at her shaking hands. Roykur realized he still clutched the knife; a wave of bile rose in his throat, and he tossed it out of sight.

A sharp voice rang out from the group of witnesses. "Murderer! Monster!"

"That's the boy from the trial."

"Someone call for the Sentinels!"

"We got to stop him!"

"Break his legs so he can't run!"

Roykur would have to worry about facing the reality of what had just happened another time. This crowd was about to exact their own form of justice.

"Adalia, we need to get out of here now. Adalia!" Roykur said, firm but hushed. He inched backward, keeping his eyes on the crowd.

She flinched from her stupor. "Yes, we do. Can't stay here."

"Back the way we came, and head through the northern corridor—"

"He's trying to escape! Get 'em!" The hesitant mob bolted forward, bent on their quarry. The people jostled, bumped, and tripped over one another in their haste.

Roykur and Adalia sped back the way they came, both panting heavily, having had only a few moments to catch their breath. Adalia pivoted on the balls of her feet, sliding on the thin layer of dirt on the rock floor, and dashed down the northern corridor with Roykur right on her heels. Various passageways flew by as they ran, but most ended in private residences, dead ends or the like, certainly not their salvation. They glanced back as the furious horde rounded the corner not thirty feet behind, squeezed together with only enough room for four abreast.

He and Adalia had been running for too long. Roykur could tell they were both slowing down. Just ahead, large sacks of trash had been set along the sides of the corridor. As he passed, he ripped them into the air, scattering refuse like the wind whipping spring pollen.

"Adalia, on your left." Roykur took advantage of the momentary visual disturbance and threw himself down a side alley after her. Even as he scrambled into the darkest corner, he willed himself to be hidden. Smoke boiled out from him, filling the small space around them with absolute darkness. He held his breath, listening to the thunderous footfalls grow louder, interspersed with the cries for justice. They grew louder and harsher, then softer and quieter until he could barely hear them.

It had actually worked.

Roykur pulled the darkness back in, leaving the two of them in the dim lamplight spilling from the corridor. Adalia stayed sitting against the wall, blood-caked hands pressed to her sweaty face. Roykur stepped toward the corridor and peeked out the way the crowd had gone. Leaning against the wall was a well-dressed, brawny man with skin just as dark as Roykur's.

"Hello, son." Leondal smiled wickedly. "I have to say, you have made me quite a bit of money lately. I guess you were worth something after all."

Roykur turned and immediately hit a wall. No, not a wall, but close to it—the shabby, amorphous blob that was Marge, displaying her rotten teeth for him. He focused his energy, willing the smoke into both their bodies. That hope vanished with a thud as a crashing pain bloomed in his head, and then nothing.

Ж

Roykur awoke, head pounding, vision swimming. He tried to shake his head but succeeded only in flitting his eyes from side to side. Not just his head—he couldn't move any part of his body. Blinking through the darkness, he felt strange, numb, a chalky dryness on his tongue. A light spilled into wherever he was, just outside of his peripherals.

He was suspended in the air, staring down, and whoever had walked in was standing just out of sight. He heard some hushed voices as a bit of drool dripped from the corner of his mouth. What kind of rotten mishmash of elixirs had they given him this time?

"What do you mean, they just *appeared?*" A whiny, harsh voice. Doctor Arakul.

"Weren't followed. They just showed up." The deep, rumbling voice was Leondal's.

"Well, get rid of them. That what I am paying you for." There was a brief pause. "Go on then, we haven't got all day, and I can't be interrupted. Not again."

Footsteps pattered away, and the individual holding the torch turned and moved toward Roykur, the light revealing the clutter of things beneath him. They stopped in front of the barrier of objects, and Roykur craned his head with all his strength. It finally loosened, but only for him to find himself staring at Arakul's smiling face. "I'm not entirely sure if I need you awake for this, but I like to keep as many variables constant as I can. I already had to use a different concoction on you, but that was all I had available, I'm afraid."

The doctor stepped back, moving out of sight. Roykur heard the crackle of flame, and light bloomed to the right and then to the left. With Roykur's head propped up in a new position, he widened his eyes in disbelief.

He was in the ritual chamber of the Kolkrabba. The grooves in the floor, the pocketed in-lays of the walls, the stone pillars, and of course the calm water of the well at the center. The center lay directly below Roykur. He saw his reflection in the glassy surface, and uncertain recognition overloaded his thoughts. This must have been what he had seen that night in the warehouse.

The torchlight glinted off a familiar metal contraption affixed above and around the well. The device he remembered seeing before everything had faded in the warehouse. The design had been modified from the previous iteration, this time with two concentric rails that circled the base.

Next comes the pain. I think. Well, can I feel pain like this?

Roykur reached for the essence within, willing it to respond, to act. There was a prickling at his skin, gooseflesh, but nothing more, and he was left listening to the ratcheting, clinking, and whining of metal on metal while Arakul tinkered away.

"You know this is not my specialty. Myrmilla was always the mechanical genius, but her blueprints were not terribly difficult to decipher."

"Figures you would say that." It startled him to hear the words actually come out of his mouth. They were slurred, and his tongue was thick in his mouth. The numbness was fading, though. Beyond the circles, Roykur spotted a work bench strewn with tools. Arakul leaned against it, facing Roykur, and to his right was the handle of a lever. He strained hard, lifting his eyes to meet Arakul's. The doctor had his head tilted curiously.

"How do you mean?" He had stopped his adjustments for the moment. *Just keep him talking and away from that lever.*

"You always had to be the smartest in a room. All these years, you were constantly condescending, correcting people or spewing facts no one cared about. No one likes a know-it-all. That's why you had to join the Initiative, just to get invited to any sort of gathering." Roykur was sounding clearer, managing to put some fake sympathy in his voice.

Arakul stood and slowly walked toward him, eyes narrowed with scrutiny. "Is this mind game supposed to impress me? Congratulations, you deduced my lack of a social life."

"I didn't deduce anything, you badly brewed, dirt-breath idiot. I saw it firsthand. Now tell me where my granddaughter is, you sick fuck!" As he shouted, he found he could flail his limbs a bit.

Arakul's expression flashed with amusement. "Aha! I knew it! How long have you been in this body?"

"Since you killed me, djavul. Then I woke up, suddenly pubescent." Roykur felt a prickle at the back of his head.

"So, the energy was not all that transferred . . . this changes my earlier theory. I hypothesized the energy revived the boy from death, but after the asylum . . ." Arakul began pacing back and forth. "Does the previous consciousness always take over, or did it only do that because the new vessel was empty? Many more variables to consider."

"Hey, worst doctor ever. Where. Is. My. Granddaughter!"

"Haven't the slightest idea. Lord Leondal of House Jasperion, as he insists on being called, brought you. If I may be blunt, I care about one thing and one thing only: that energy inside you. The small army I hired will keep this session private, even from your precious granddaughter."

"I guess that justifies the murder of countless innocents."

"Two hundred and eighty-three—eighty-four, if you include

Myrmilla. Besides, from what research I could find, these energies were summoned many times long ago, each time paying the costly tribute, and if the holder died, another would make the tribute yet again. I have done what no one has done before. With this technology, I will ensure that price need never be paid again."

"How noble of you." The prickles on the back of Roykur's head drifted to where the entrance lay. Realization of what those sensations were came to him, and he concentrated on them. Awareness of dozens of smoke-filled bodies lingered somewhere above ground, almost a hundred feet away. Roykur closed his eyes, forcing a thought into reality.

Free me.

Like he'd triggered a rockslide, they moved.

"I can't take all the credit. I wouldn't have even known about these energies, this very chamber, if His Majesty hadn't brought me in on his work."

Roykur's thoughts shattered instantly, his focus gone.

"What does Legast have to do with this?"

A cruel smile crept onto Arakul's face. The doctor had found the right point to prick. "His Majesty? He showed me this place—he paid me to study this chamber, decipher its secrets. Took me nearly thirty years, but I laid bare the price the Kolkrabba had paid the day you extinguished them. Well, I had the help of an admittedly talented scroll worker. There wasn't much progress until he deciphered the Kolkrabba script. I thought that was it. Then, many years later, King Legast revealed to me he indeed had collected the tribute. For obvious reasons, he was hesitant to share, but pleasantly surprised at my lack of . . . moral grandstanding."

Arakul leaned against the circular rail, scoffing at the memories. "Let me tell you, seeing that wall of organs was a bit offputting, to say the least. Unfortunately, we were a bit stumped as to how to perform the ritual—that is, until a brilliant young Myrmilla was introduced to us. By you. It only took her a few months to evaluate this place and design a prototype for this wonderful device here. Too bad she couldn't keep her mouth shut. I regret taking Myrmilla's life. It was the only one I have regretted, but she left me with no choice. Legast, well, he was the one with the true talent for killing. I just cleaned up the loose ends. It wasn't just a means to an end with him —he truly enjoyed it."

The little points of awareness drifted downward as they continued their descent.

"In the end, Legast of course got to reap the reward of his years of . . . harvesting. However, this is where my genius really shined. I was the one who figured out his energy could be distilled into an elixir. I am the one who gave immortality to this city, not the king. He would have foolishly squandered it, unable to realize its potential. Just like you did. He still hides it like the coward he is."

Arakul moved back toward the lever. He gripped it tight, that wild hunger reappearing in his eyes. "I was the one who realized that Myrmilla's machines could do more than make the ritual work. I modified them to perform the ritual in reverse, as you are well aware. And I modified them again, this time combining both designs, accomplishing something that has never been done before. I have eliminated the need for a tribute, and I can keep the connection open indefinitely. It is me who is ushering in a new era of gods!"

Roykur's eyes widen with panic. "You can't! It won't work the way you think—"

Arakul whipped the ritual mask from beneath his coat and slipped it on. He slammed the lever forward, and the series of switches and gears clicked metallically. Then the innermost ring ground along its rail, deafening. The light in the well flared with the bright blue glow.

Shouts echoed throughout the chamber from the cavern beyond.

As the inner ring reached its peak speed, Roykur was jerked down against his chains, and he nearly retched at the tearing of his soul. Every fiber of his being was racked with pain, and he seized in pure torment. The smoke started drifting down, drawn by an unseen force.

Arakul threw down a second lever, and the second ring fired off in the opposite direction from the first. As its speed peaked, the pain eased into pulses, with brief respites from the agony. The ball of smoke froze, unable to be fully ripped from Roykur and unable to retreat into him.

He gazed into the glowing abyss, which now vibrated uncertainly. Blood trickled into the water from the wound on his ribs, the tension tearing it open anew. The waters swirled downward, the shallows suddenly endless. Roykur's consciousness fell through the vortex, traveling deeper and deeper until it came upon a darkness within the light. The dark mass jerked to life, and a planet of tendrils writhed, an awakening. What had been only a nightmare was now tearing its way into reality.

CHAPTER 28
OUT OF CONTROL

Screams and shouts reverberated through the chamber. Then dozens of individuals burst in through the doorway. Roykur blinked rapidly, his mind ripped back to his body. He tried to regain his bearings while taking in the surrounding chaos. From the very corner of his vision, he could see only feet scuffling into the chamber. Closing his eyes, he focused on the smoke in their bodies. Now he could discern the outlines of the people pressing their way toward Arakul, while some held the entrance with shields and swords. Roykur could hear the familiar sound of bolts whizzing through the air, some clattering off the cave walls or thudding into wooden shields.

Some people drew close to the spinning contraption, and Roykur could make out the bark-covered exterior of their flesh. He remembered the Treemolkvar soldiers he had shared a barracks with and the smoke that he had tested. Each held significantly more smoke now than they had before. Also, there had not been this many Witches, not nearly this many. The smoke must have spread. On its own.

A male and a female Treemolkvar looked to Roykur, and with a shared look of concern, or possibly confusion, they grabbed the side of the rail. Even as they squatted to pull at it, their fingers were sheared off where they curved over the edge, and they both tumbled backward beyond Roykur's vision, their screams joining the chaos.

Olacka! My bad. Roykur closed his eyes like before but was interrupted as another spasm of pain racked his body, blocking all thought. When it subsided, he snapped his eyes open. Tears spilled out into the vortex below, along with an unfathomable rage. He screamed wordlessly and projected his will again.

The levers! Pull the fucking levers!

He could sense the smoke react as all the Treemolkvar jerked violently at the command and moved toward them. Unfortunately, this included the ones blocking the entrance. Roykur flinched as a bolt flew through the unguarded entry way and skimmed just past his nose.

Several more cycles of pain pulsed into Roykur, and each time, he could feel a reaction from within the waters. Feel it reaching, stretching from its long slumber.

An awful screech came, and with a loud clanking of metal, the contraption Roykur was on lurched. Beneath him, the water crashed on itself before erupting and drenching his whole front half. He tried to shake it free from his face, but then he felt an arm around his torso, holding him as his limbs were released. The flood of relief was halted by the loud thud of a bolt sinking deep into flesh, which seemed to explain his savior dropping him into the water and immediately falling directly on top of him.

Panic gripped him tight, the crushing weight above him and the nightmarish depths below. The well was again shallow, and Roykur had to brace his back against the bottom and push with all his meager strength. The enormous form of the Treemolkvar barely even budged, and Roykur struggled for minutes, bit by bit, lungs burning, panic pitching, before finally wiggling out from underneath him.

Roykur sucked in air and tried to quickly clear his vision. The chamber had filled with roughly twenty of Leondal's thugs holding back on one side while the Treemolkvar did the same on the other. Furious shouts echoed unintelligibly across the space. The nine remaining Treemolkvar held shields out in front of them. They also held Arakul, a long blade placed urgently against his neck. The threat to their employer was apparently enough to keep the brutes at bay.

I guess they haven't been paid yet.

A gentle tickle pricked along Roykur's skin from under the water, and he felt energy surge into him from the fallen body next to him. He unleashed a torrent of smoke toward the thugs, and they jerked back in surprise. *Drop.*

A bolt whizzed by his head, and Roykur realized that only three of the men had followed his instructions. Cursing to himself, he instinctively reached for the greatest source of strength near him. The Treemolkvar stiffened while thick plumes of smoke tore from their bodies across the room and into the remaining thugs, both groups now frozen to his will.

Climbing ungracefully from the well, Roykur still panted heavily. "Alright . . . let's all gather round and have a friendly chat, shall we?"

The entire room melted from its extreme positions of violence to a calm campfire setting as both sides began sitting down around the heated metal that had been the complex contraption of Erden's would-be demise.

"You. Front and center." Following the gesture, Arakul moved across to face Roykur, a strange amalgamation of terror and curiosity plastered across his features.

Roykur plopped down, breathing hard, eyes barely open as the tangled mess of opposing figures arrayed themselves facing him on either side of Arakul. Roykur squeezed water from his shirt sleeves and looked up, jerking back a bit in surprise as he noticed for the first time the faces of the surrounding individuals. Despite their calm physical posture, their eyes whipped around the room, expressions twitching away briefly from a forced calmness to fear or anger, and then back. It was disturbing.

"Relax, a little." Like everyone had heard the most amazing news, they each sagged in relief, some miniscule level of control returned to them. The Treemolkvar and Jaspers alike worked their jaws and rolled their shoulders, but their hands and feet stayed pressed together like heavy iron manacles bound them.

"So, Doctor, what were you saying about new eras?" Arakul tilted his head to look at Roykur, but he kept his mouth shut. "Ah, lost your vigor, I see. Not too surprising now that your horrifyingly stupid plan fell apart. You spent so much of your vast genius on trying to make the impossible happen, you didn't even consider what actually lies beyond. Did you even stop and think about where these *energies* come from or why they exist?" Roykur shook his head. "What madman would, I guess? Regardless, I have lots of questions, and they will be on my terms, as will the answers."

A low, rolling chuckle spilled out from the last Jasper on Roykur's right. "Well, well, ain't this a neat trick? Did the doctor whip this up for you? Boy, I think you might actually be worth a damn. You let me and the men go, and we can have a talk about bringing you back into the Jaspers."

"I'll deal with you later, Leondal—for now, keep your mouth shut." Leondal's mouth snapped closed, the bulky man's muscles straining in stark contrast to his relaxed position.

Roykur took a deep breath, stoking the fury within, and turned his attention back to Arakul. "Was the king really responsible for all those murders?"

Soft drips of water and the creaking of cooling metal drifted through the cavern, but Arakul sat silent, defiant.

"I am cold, and I don't have time for this. Let's see how you like a bit of your own medicine." Roykur twisted and roiled the energy inside Arakul, forcing it to feel similar to what he assumed an elixir incompatibility might feel like. Veins bubbled along the man's exposed skin like they were boiling. The rest of his body sat unmoving, locked in place. Arakul's eyes rolled to the back of his head, and a throaty scream tried to escape from his tightly shut jaw. A tremor crawled down Roykur's spine, and he let the energy subside immediately. Images of Silaine and Myrmilla writhing on the floor bombarded him. His skin crawled at what he had just done. After a moment, Arakul regained his senses, still shaking a little, tears streaming from his eyes.

"What have you done with my granddaughter?" An eyebrow rose at that question, but his silence persisted. Ever so quietly, Roykur asked a question he had held for too long. "Did you kill my wife?"

A smirk joined the eyebrow for the briefest of margins, but Roykur caught it. "I guess it is fate that I am the only one willing to see justice done. Justice for what you have done to me, justice for the people of this city, and justice for my wife."

Roykur jumped to his feet. "Everyone up—we're going for a walk."

Rosy pink and orange splashed across the sky in ripples from the setting sun. The trees loomed, skeletal and menacing, leaves long caked into the ground. The icy wind stung at Roykur's face as his motley crew of bandits and Treemolkvar trekked a few miles west, to a point just south of the city in a grassy clearing surrounded by a forest. A terloq sat on a rock, stark against the bare landscape, its fur bristling as it watched the entourage go by. In the center of the clearing was a place Roykur had been to more times than he would have liked, but today he longed for it—the Cleansing Shallow.

He found himself wondering if Wisiel had actually been brought here to be executed or if that was a farce as well.

The green grass faded to rocky soil, then a brittle brown and yellow shale as they approached the subconscious place of foreboding. The Shallow bubbled with a steady regularity. As its name suggested, it spread wide across, but was only a few feet deep. This vibrant green geyser had never erupted, yet the heated, caustic waters sizzled with malice against the cool air.

With the group arrayed around Roykur as his makeshift tribunal, his thoughts forced Arakul to the edge of the Shallow. The wind whipped wildly about. A bubble from the Shallow popped near Arakul's feet, the wind blowing the water onto his shoes. The highly acidic water ate away hungrily from the tops of his toes, and Arakul let out a yelp in surprise.

"You haven't witnessed a disintegration before, have you? Or any dead body sent to be dissolved?" The strong winds forced Roykur to shout. "Funny how we use different phrasing for when a person is thrown in before they are dead and after. It's all the same in the end —takes only a minute or two. Your body will be gone in ten. Or . . . we could just start with a finger."

Arakul's hand moved toward the water. "Alright! Alright, eight gods, enough! What do you want to know?"

"Let's start with the easy ones. Why was Visari wearing your mask? How was she part of this?"

"She came to me months before your party, wanting to learn about elixirs and incompatibilities. She wasn't very clever about it. When I finally confronted her, she confessed to wanting to kill you. I couldn't have that, not before my plan could take place, so I played along, revealed confidential medical information about your incompatibility."

Roykur frowned. "I don't have one. But . . ."

"But Myrmilla did. I gave her the elixir, but Visari spiked the food. An easy way to eliminate a loose end. After that, she was mine, and all too eager to stay out of this pit. She had to put on that mask, or I would reveal her to be Myrmilla's killer."

"Why on Erden would Visari, of all people, want me dead?"

"I am genuinely surprised you don't know that." Arakul flashed a briefly puzzled look. "She despised you. According to her, you were always pushing her aside, the pitiful hanger-on after Oskur overdosed. Then you were Adalia's favorite, that you had stolen her away. Pushing your ideas, your paths on her. I guess Adalia joining the Sentinels was the last straw for her. Doesn't really matter. You killed her first."

Roykur scoffed and paced the perimeter of the geyser. His voice grew higher pitched as he vented his frustrations. "How could she possibly want me dead over that? I gave her a home, helped raise her daughter, my granddaughter!"

"That's all she told me. Like I said, she wasn't very clever."

"Fine. Whatever." He rubbed at a headache he was getting after trying to figure out that insane logic. "Where is Adalia?"

"I do not know where she is. We only found you this time." Arakul's hand moved closer to the water. A pop splashed droplets up, and a faint sizzling sound came from his fingertips. "I swear I don't know! Please, I don't!"

Roykur studied the doctor for a moment, gauging his truthfulness. If she escaped, she would go to the only person she thought she could trust—Legs.

He allowed Arakul to straighten up but kept his hand outstretched. A quick bend at the waist would be the end of his arm. The wintry winds gnawed through the overcoat he had thrown on and down to his wet clothes. He stepped closer to the edge of the Shallow. The heated air was faint, but the smell of burnt, rotten eggs was overpowering.

"So, you say the king, the most prominent person in the city, is also the most ruthless mass killer?" he asked, but in his heart, he knew the answer already. "I don't believe you."

"Believe what you want. He said it was necessary. The ritual would help him get something he always wanted."

Roykur's stomach twisted, and he felt like retching on the spot. "Why? He already had everything. Why massacre his own people for the rumor of something?"

"I am not King Legast. Ask him yourself." A trickle of sweat dripped down Arakul's forehead to the tip of his nose, where it dangled precariously.

"Oh, I will. Now, last question." Roykur stepped up beside Arakul and looked him in the eye. "Did you kill my wife?"

"No. I only met the woman a handful of times, but I remember her face. She had a pretty one." Arakul let out a long sigh. "But mishaps happen. They happen all the time. I suspect, like most mishaps, the elixir was badly labeled or some such. Ah, oh gods, my legs. Roykur, could you . . . could you please let me go. I'll do anything you want. What do you want?"

"Silaine . . ." Knowing the truth didn't make him feel any better. Roykur shivered, from the wind or the memories, it didn't matter.

The two men stared at each other for a while, neither recognizable from the people they should have been. Arakul a youthful version of his former self, and Roykur a youthful version of someone else entirely. A painful tightness grew in his chest—regret, fury, and sorrow fought for the leading role. The sun flashed through the trees, the blinding light breaking into the cloud of his gloom.

"I suppose it's about that time." Roykur nodded. "Let's get it over with."

Roykur blinked through the stinging wind and raised his voice as best he could without it cracking. "Doctor Arakul, may the deep take you, and be delivered to the very gods you hoped to summon."

Roykur watched him turn to face the boiling waters and lean farther over the edge. With a soundless jerk, Arakul's body convulsed as the smoke jettisoned out, vaguely Human shaped, before snaking quickly back to Roykur. Arakul slumped and slowly tipped, headfirst, into the seething pond. The splash lapped over the brim of the Shallow, wetting the hard, yellow-chalked ground.

Arakul, just like the many people Roykur had seen executed, struggled, but not for long. He flailed at the impact, and Roykur could see his skin tearing and blackening. With each successive thrash, more of the doctor visibly melted away. The minutes stretched out forever, but Roykur watched unblinkingly. No room for half measures, not when the entire world was at stake.

It took longer than he had expected for the bones to dissolve, and before long, the moons competed to outshine each other, bright on the cusp of night. Roykur began the hike back to the city, numb, considering his recent revelations. However, the night was anything but still. The surrounding forest teemed with wildlife. The creatures were restless under the full moons, screeching various mating calls or howling challenges for dominance. A particular sound caught Roykur's attention, a soft weeping from behind. He glanced discreetly over his shoulder as he ducked under a low branch and saw one of the Jasper bandits, a few paces back, crying softly, while another whispered consolation. A twinge of guilt struck at Roykur, but he brushed it off. They had tried to kill him, after all.

Roykur glanced over his other shoulder at the Treemolkvar and was surprised to see them smiling. They padded along behind like there was no place they would rather be. *Fucking Witches. Don't know whether that's more or less concerning than the crying. I hope it wasn't a mistake to let them keep their weapons.*

The path through the forest was dense and unforgiving. The cloaked underbrush snagged and tore at clothing and occasionally a foot, resulting in a loud crash and a slew of curses. A roar of a predator seizing on its kill echoed from nearby, far too close for Roykur's comfort. The makeshift group hiked long hours into the night before the tall towers loomed above the trees. The density of foliage broke into long, neat rows of orchards on the very edge of the city, and Roykur snatched the first apple he saw and devoured it. The bandits and the Treemolkvar did the same, with some unprovoked moaning, as if it were the best thing they had ever eaten.

Roykur addressed his entourage for the first time. "How long has it been since you all have had food?"

A Treemolkvar spoke between chews. "Just this morning . . . but I swear, I've never felt this hungry before."

The essence that filled the surrounding people, as well as his own, flared, swelling, stealing away what little hunger they had sated. They scoured the fruit from all the nearby trees for the next few minutes of furious craving.

"One more for the road." The collective party looked skeptical. Likely, each one of them had a different reason, but Roykur did not need to use the energies for them to pocket another apple. With a lurch, they all continued toward the city proper. Coming out of the apple orchard, they crossed a road, one that Roykur knew led to his manor. He stopped for a moment, wishing he could go there now and fall down in his bed and wake up to the smell of sizzling bacon. The moment passed. The only thing that mattered right now was protecting Adalia and stopping a killer.

They eventually crossed from dirt to cobbled road, and Roykur spotted a carriage letting out a pair of people. They stumbled, flush and giggling, evidently heading home after a late night. The couple was dressed in finery, well made yet tattered, as though several generations had worn those clothes before. Which was more than he could have claimed to own sixty years ago. They could have at least patched those tears.

Oh gods, has noble life really ruined me that much?

Roykur turned to his band of misfits. "This is where we part ways. I am going to take that carriage from here, and I don't see how we all fit."

One of the Treemolkvar soldier stepped in front of his brethren. He spoke in a thick accent, his voice raked and hoarse. "No, Gefahr, we stay with you. Your grand purpose is our grand purpose."

A zip out of the corner of his eye flashed past too quickly, a small glint of a knife as it flew by his head. The momentary distraction loosened his focus, and the Jaspers ran without another word. Roykur reasserted control over them before they took two steps, but Leondal was missing from the group. The man charged him, blade in hand. Shock and panic seized Roykur, and he couldn't stop the knife as it plunged toward his neck.

A hatchet flew, catching Leondal in the shoulder, the blade he held swinging wide of its intended target. Roykur turned to see the man scrambling to his feet, one hand on the handle of the hatchet, one on the knife. Many long slits ran down his arms and through his pant legs. No blood, just the black smoke filling the crevices, the wound in his shoulder similarly bloodless.

Leondal must have cut himself while everyone picked apples. The smoke seemed occupied with stopping the bleeding over taking Roykur's instructions.

"I know you ain't my son, but I should have killed you a long time ago." Leondal took a couple more staggering steps toward Roykur. The smoke resisted Roykur's attempts at stopping him. Two more hatchets sailed through the air—one planted its edge in Leondal's hip, and the other went through his collarbone. Leondal sagged to the ground, this time unable to pull himself up.

The smoke was connected with blood. He shared blood with this man, Teufel's father. Could that be the reason it resisted him now?

Roykur pushed through that resistance and seized the smoke within Leondal. He yanked it out, but it flowed slowly, like the sticky pour of honey. When it came free and nestled comfortably back into Roykur, all the cuts on Leondal flowed like heavy geyser water off a tall tower roof.

What an evil man. Roykur wondered if Teufel would have been thankful to be rid of him or furious that Roykur had taken his father. Had he forced the boy to commit patricide, or was there truly nothing left of him? Roykur set it aside. Questions for another time.

Roykur walked to the rest of the Jaspers, passing the Treemolkvar soldiers as they went to retrieve their weapons. "We will need some coin for the carriage."

"We ain't giving you our hard-earned coin, you freak." Mumbles of agreement went up between them. Coin was held in higher regard than their former employer. Regardless of their refusal, their rebellious hands dug into their pockets, holding out handfuls of coins, which Roykur collected one at a time. *These men have lived a whole life exploiting the weak. With the elixir of life, they can do it forever.*

"Consider your debt to society paid . . . to its fullest." A barely audible crunch came from all of Leondal's thugs, and they fell to their knees, gasping for air. Roykur winced. He'd meant for their ribs to go through their heart, not just the lungs; he had been trying to give them a swift death. A second crunch caused them all to go limp, the smoky black billowing out. Roykur turned and walked to the carriage, his new Treemolkvar guard in tow.

CHAPTER 29

LONG LIVE THE KING

The city was restless, still coasting off the feverish excitement of the festival and the trial. People hurried about with a strange urgency at such a late hour.

The courtyard of the palace could not have been more different. It was abandoned, the main gate left open, and the carriage pulled past the softly listing doors. Bathed in the moonlight, it gave off an eerie feeling of decay, kind of like that odd Maw'licor tradition Roykur had heard about. They referred to them as crypts. He pondered on the unusual customs and wastefulness of other cities while staring at the lightless royal residence in front of him. Letting his mind wander had been an attempt at a distraction from the nine large Treemolkvar bodies crammed into a carriage with him, as well as his feelings of utter betrayal.

The draugkers plodded away, pulling the carriage clacking along the stonework, leaving Roykur and his Treemolkvar to crunch their boots on through the sheets of ice to the palace doors. If only he had a warmer coat. His coats were never warm enough these days.

Roykur quickly strode into the palace, his new entourage ahead, pushing open doors and peering around corners. Every hallway and room they checked was empty. No servants, no guests; the torches were unlit, and the white marble sucked the very heat from their bodies.

The doors to the grand hall remained unrepaired. New doors lay against the walls on either side as they all quietly filed in, their boots echoing rebelliously. Near the far end, a fire flickered in one of the enormous fireplaces. However, its light was paled by a beam of moonlight from the upper balcony window. Two figures stood rigid in the moonlight, intent on the fire. The furniture had been cleared away from the grand hall, the emptiness increasing the solemn unease of the space.

Roykur dispensed with the ridiculous effort of trying to sneak around and strode confidently toward the end of the hall. The figure on the left turned, and Adalia's radiant smile greeted Roykur, flooding him with relief. She was unhurt. In fact, she looked cleaned up and more refreshed than when he had last seen her. He motioned for her to move away from the king, but she remained where she was, giving him a reassuring nod. The figure on the right remained facing forward, tall, back straight—the king himself.

Roykur stopped a dozen paces from the Legast. "Legs! Face me, you djavul!" There was a long pause before Roykur continued. "All these years and it's been you the whole time, hasn't it? Come on, Legs, I need to hear it from you. No more lies, no more hiding. Tell me the truth, all of it."

Legast turned his head by the smallest of margins to peer over his shoulder. Roykur could barely make out a tinge of struggle, whether grief or anger, it was hard to say. In a regal fashion, his voice was level. "My oldest and dearest friend is the only one who got to call me Legs. Now you barge into my palace, tarnishing that memory and making demands of your king?"

He turned, staring down into Roykur's eyes, where he once had to look up. "Arrest them. If they resist, kill them."

The sound of heavy sabatons clashed in unison from all sides as the entire Royal Guard arose from their cloaked positions along the walls. As they stepped forward, the fire and moonlight reflected off their polished armor and sharp halberds so brightly, even the shadows retreated a step. The Treemolkvar soldiers readied wooden shields and iron hatchets, making a semicircle behind Roykur, guarding his flank.

"Not this time. I am getting some fucking answers." His reserves had become substantial, and when he reached for the smoke, it flowed to his will naturally. Roykur commanded it to move, and like a limb, it did so almost without thought. This time, the smoke didn't lash out in small tendrils. It surged, falling off Roykur in waves, faster and faster, until all the visible floor was covered. It roiled up and reached out, clawing at each guard, squeezing between the joints in their armor. Some of them stumbled, trying to shake away the smoke. Their uniformed march faltered. Roykur's mouth twitched into a sneer, watching the guards flail about. Then, all at once, they snapped back to attention, frozen.

His triumph faltered when he returned his focus back to Legast. He had closed the distance, now only a few steps away. The smoke swirled hungerly around the king but was held back as if by an unseen barrier. Legast's stoicism had completely vanished, and in its place was a fierce excitement. He glanced about the swirling smoke around him, then back to Roykur. A sharp shriek of laughter burst out, unsettling and startling.

Adalia had not moved until now, and she took a few steps toward the both of them. Roykur waved her back. "Adalia, stay back. He's dangerous."

The king glanced over at Adalia just briefly before focusing again on Roykur. "It *is* you! I didn't dare to hope, but this power confirms it. My old friend, you are alive!"

Roykur was taken aback by the sudden switch in demeanor, but he kept the smoke swirling in between himself and Legast. "Yes . . . I thought it might take more convincing than that."

"No, I knew death couldn't stop you, stop us." Legast took a step forward, and the smoke parted around him. Roykur retreated, concerned, and his newly enthralled legion mimicked his movement.

"You have become very familiar with death, haven't you? You murdered all those people," he said. Despite his control over the armed warriors, Roykur was still keenly aware of Legast's belted sword and his own lack of arms.

"Of course—why wouldn't the secrets of the gods have a price? Just because someone else paid your bill doesn't mean there isn't blood on your hands." Legast took another step.

"I didn't choose this. You did. For what? Immortality? We aren't meant to live forever." Roykur stepped to the side, rotating their conversation, trying to maneuver his way toward Adalia.

"We are meant to live forever! I secured our future. The city's future." The smoke had encircled Legast, a black bubble that refused to make contact with the king.

"By wiping out the future of hundreds of lives? By wiping out mine?" Roykur found himself croaking. The buried emotion behind the betrayal rose swiftly.

"You weren't supposed to get hurt. The doctor promised he could unlock"—Legast gestured to the smokey tendrils spiraling around— "all this. To release the power of a god that lay dormant in your blood."

"He wasn't trying to unlock anything. He killed me and tried to take the power for himself. Somehow, I took over this poor kid's body instead." Roykur gestured to his compact frame, still wearing damp clothes and a thug's coat that was three times too big.

"I know that now. He will pay for his deceit." Anger flared white hot behind his eyes. "I'll kill him myself."

"Don't you think you've done enough killing?" Roykur pleaded. "Besides, he's been dealt with."

That overly excited expression returned. "Fantastic. That's one less problem to deal with. We can move on from that conniving djavul. How did you do it?"

"Have you lost your mind? This isn't a blissful reunion. Your actions have consequences, and we are not gods," Roykur shouted, his voice cracking.

Legast halted his steady advance and straightened. "I know what I have done. I sacrificed my soul for this. Just as you did against those Husks. We are both soulless men. We knew the Kolkrabba enthralled them, but you killed those people for the greater good, just as I have."

The king took a deep breath, and tears began rolling down his face. "I did this for more than the greater good. I did this for us. We missed our chance during our lifetime, but now we have a second opportunity! We have all the time in the world to be together, away from our responsibilities. I set up the council to take over so that I could step down and be with you."

"How dare you say this was for me? How did we miss our chance? I was always here for you when you needed me. I loved you like a brother, and now you are the cause of my greatest pain." His own tears spilled down his cheeks.

"I love you, but not like a brother. I may not have gotten to cherish you how Silaine did, but I still loved you. My biggest regret is not having confronted my feelings before it was too late," admitted Legast. He chuckled through a shuddering breath, relief at letting go a long-held secret.

"You did this for love?" Roykur's jaw was nearly to the floor. He blinked rapidly, his thoughts reeling from this revelation, but he had to calm his mind. "No. Your biggest regret should be the slaughter of hundreds of innocent people! You couldn't find someone else to love in eighty years? You're the godsdamn King. You could have had any man, woman, Witch, or Vogel in the city!"

Legast spoke bitterly through gritted teeth. "And yet, none of them were you. The only one that mattered was the one I couldn't have."

"You love me? You don't know what that is. This isn't love. This is obsession." Roykur's eyes narrowed with realization. "All those anomalies in the pattern, it makes sense now. The first murder, that was the day of my marriage. The second, when Oskur was born, and the third, when I died. You tore people apart because you couldn't handle your own feelings? That goes way beyond sacrificing for the greater good."

Legast waved his hand dismissively and forced a smile onto his face. "None of that matters now. Nothing stands between us. We can start a new beginning!"

"You can't force someone to love you the way you want. That's not a power either of us possess." Roykur took another step back from the king, sniffing and trying to wipe away his tears. He let the smoke around the man drift away, and it melted back into Roykur's body. "I'm sorry, but you cannot start a new beginning on a pile of corpses. That is not a foundation for anything except more death. It is clear to me that you have been a monster all along, one that I let myself be blinded to. I have failed this city, and you, and myself. I am afraid that it is up to me to make sure you won't hurt anyone ever again. Goodbye, my old friend."

The squelch of metal into flesh was far too familiar to Roykur, but it still made him jump as blood sprayed across the floor from Legast's neck. Roykur could hear Adalia scream from behind him. The Royal Guard's eyes looked horrified as he held the halberd, still frozen in the follow-through.

"Oh gods, what have I done?" the man cried out.

Legast's shocked face remained a moment longer before he smiled wide again, this time with a little more hurt in his eyes. The long, red gash across his neck had already crusted over with yellow crystals, which Legast brushed away, revealing completely unmarred skin.

"I know why you think you had to do that. I do. However, I cannot die. Not anymore. Now that that's out of the way, perhaps we can discuss more reasonable courses of action. Like say, dinner? Or is it almost time for breakfast?" Legast turned and patted the guard, still locked in post swing, the man's face a mask of confusion.

Roykur roared in frustration. "Dinner? Are you kidding me? Let's set aside the rampant murders and betrayal for a second. Do you have any idea what you and that crazy pet doctor of yours almost unleashed on this world? Have you seen the same nightmares that I have?"

The wide smile slipped. "I wasn't sure what to make of those dreams. I figured they were merely another small price to pay for this power. But they are just dreams."

Roykur shook his head. "No. The power we now have is just tiny slivers of that thing you dream of. We share a connection with it. I can't, won't, allow that thing to be free, to be fully awakened. It would destroy the entire world."

"*Almost* is surely the key takeaway here. As you say, if it had been released, we would all be dead, so now we just make sure that it stays sealed away. That can be our next marvelous adventure!" said Legast, his voice now pleading.

Adalia had stepped up beside Roykur, and he held a cautionary hand out. "Adalia and I will make sure that it stays sealed away. You know I can't let your evil go unpunished. We will put your invulnerability to the test, maybe try the Cleansing Shallow? If nothing can truly kill you, then you will be locked in your own prison. I will make sure you are put in a hole so deep that even if you live to the end of days, you won't get out."

Legast glanced to Adalia and back to Roykur. "Adalia, I had almost forgotten. I am so sorry for your loss. I was so very fond of her."

Roykur stepped in front of Adalia, shielding her from his former friend. "Oh yeah? You plan on murdering her, too? You won't lay a finger on her."

Roykur turned around to Adalia. "Back up, back up, you're too close."

"Roykur, who are you talking to? It's just us in this hall—well, and the guards."

Roykur gestured over his shoulder. "I'm speaking to my granddaughter. Has your mind really twisted so far you don't remember who she is?"

Legast grew very somber. "Adalia . . . died the night Wisiel attacked the palace. Her body was found on a park bench not far from here. She had bled out from her wound. It seems with the festival and trial, it was some time before she was found and properly identified."

"What?" The memory flashed in Roykur's mind, an empty bench with the note. Another flash, the note replaced with Adalia, eyes clouding over, her face so terribly pale. A trickle of blood from the bench pooling at her feet.

He turned slowly, knees weak and holding his breath. Adalia stood there smiling, a tender, consoling look. "I love you, Grandpa."

She leaned down and gently kissed the top of his head, then faded away like morning mist under the rays of the afternoon sun.

Roykur dropped, rasping, trying desperately to take a breath through the tearing in his chest. A strangled moan escaped as the air finally gave sound to his anguish. The guards and the Treemolkvar all collapsed to their knees, letting loose tormented howls, commanded by Roykur's sorrow. His entire world, everything he had strived for, everything he loved, gone in a single tragic moment. Roykur felt a hand press down on his shoulder. He recoiled from it, but it held firm. The cavernous hall echoed with haunted cries and screams. The wailing stretched on and on until Roykur's body ached with the effort.

All cries cut off as the remnants of the tall doors to the grand hall smashed apart. Roykur twisted around to see two blurry columns of Sentinels marching in. They broke off, filing into neat ranks on either side of the door, creating an opening for a collection of colorfully dressed individuals. Roykur cleared his vision with a sleeve and tried to choke down his blubbering. He reflexively moved the guards to a defensive position around himself and Legast.

There were nearly sixty newcomers, colorfully dressed, with their even larger Sentinel escort filling the room and moving closer, together, almost like they had practiced it. When they got close enough, that in the middle of this impromptu parade were members of the King's Council and leaders of the Initiative, along with other somewhat familiar faces. Some of them wore absurdly gaudy armor, almost certainly only decorative, while most stuck to their usual finery. They stopped several paces from the line of Royal Guards, forming their own.

Volmirk stepped out a pace from the crowd, his commander's uniform immaculate. He boomed with authority. "Legast of House Morfar, by the power vested in me as a sitting member of the Council of Ver'a'saile and as the Commander of the Sentinels, you are to be placed into custody for crimes against the city and its people. Teufel, for the murder of Lady Visari, the same. Both of you surrender now, and you will have a trial. Resist, and you will be presumed guilty."

CHAPTER 30

A NEW WORLD

The world was playing the cruelest joke. Roykur had been given the essence of a god, and yet he had nothing left that mattered. Silaine, Adalia, Visari, his best friend, the Initiative, his accomplishments—everything he had stood for, all gone. Now, those responsible stood arrayed against him and demanded he pay. Had he not paid enough? Roykur looked at the self-righteous smirks on the faces of the Initiative and councilmembers alike. He searched for any remorse, a hint of regret, but all he saw was a shared, smug victory.

His voice was shaky in his raw throat. "Your crimes took everything from me. Your schemes and machinations tore this city apart and left a bloody trail in its wake. Yet you are prepared to assume my guilt? You knew the king was a monster, and you kept it to yourselves! Was it all just greed? Or was there a little madness as well?" Roykur glanced at where Adalia had been standing just moments ago and sniffed back his runny nose. "I guess everyone is a little mad these days."

"Enough cheek. Last chance, boy, surrender or be executed here

297

and now." Volmirk drew his sword. The ringing of metal as swords were drawn gave no mystery as to which option the crowd preferred.

Legast had switched back to his air of commanding regality. "We all had a deal. If you try to kill either of us, you can say goodbye to living forever."

A worn and weary Lady Ingrail stepped out of the gathering and pointed an ornate dagger at Legast. "We're not going to kill you, just lock you away for the rest of eternity. You'll make us the elixir one way or another. Your little friend, however—"

"Still has a choice," interrupted Volmirk.

"Oh, I've made my choice." Roykur focused on the smoke as he stoked his fury. That concept of change he had sensed before was evident now, and he seized it with little effort. All the Royal Guard and the nine Treemolkvar soldiers arched their backs in pain. They all swelled, buckles and clasps breaking. Pieces of armor clattered to the marble floor, while other pieces shifted to make room for the enlarging muscles and protruding bones. The warriors' screams of pain deepened into snarls and growls, each of them standing taller and heavier than before, the smoke in them diminished, nearly consumed.

Smoke surged out once again from Roykur, enveloping his body and face, streaming off his skin like the curling smoke off of a burning log. An armor, a haunting visage, however useless for defense. Through the slits he left in the smoke, he saw Volmirk stumble backward and heard the collective gasp of the various groups. *This is all that's left. I am the Gefahr.*

He could hear a few quiet declarations of "monster" and "a trick" from the crowd. A few at the back turned and ran out through the door. The rest of them stood, taken aback by this change in circumstances, but resolute.

The nine Treemolkvar, who now marveled at their mutated forms, screamed out something foreign to Roykur's ears, and banged their hatchets on their shields. A battle cry. The only word he understood was "Gefahr." The smoke had faded enough that they were outside of Roykur's control. They charged past the line of Royal Guards, weapons raised.

"Oh, fuck!" Roykur whipped more smoke at them, but it was too little, too late. The line of Sentinels broke, and chaos erupted. The hulking Royal Guard and Treemolkvar soldiers attacked with savage strength. A shield strike caved in a breastplate, the owner collapsing. Several heads rolled free of necks as a halberd swung wide. Despite their fierce power, they were still vastly outnumbered, and Sentinels soon surrounded the brutes.

"Legast! Do something! Get your ass in there now!" screamed Roykur, but Legast just stood there with a blank look before toppling backward, hitting the ground hard. "What the f—"

A white flash tore away all of Roykur's senses. He blinked the light away before his eyes adjusted to his new surroundings.

He floated in familiar dark waters, haunting melodies from varied pitching whines drifting from everywhere and nowhere. He was moving up, but not just him. Hundreds of dark shapes swirled around him, singing their inhuman songs. He had a strange sense of purpose, all other thoughts pushed to the back of his mind.

A light trickled in from above the surface. He slowed, gently breaking the surface of a massive body of water. The hundreds of shapes broke the surface next to him—not shapes, Kolkrabba. Writhing tentacles, theirs and his, propelled this army forward, toward a torchlit shore. The kingdom of Saft'don, the city upon a geyser, drew closer. From behind, he heard the water splash about, the next hundred Kolkrabba surfacing.

Roykur's eyes blinked open, staring at the ceiling of the grand hall, the back of his head stinging with sharp pain. He rolled to his side and saw Legast coming to, panting, as if waking from a nightmare. Roykur tried to push himself up and found his own hands weak and shaking. The smoke no longer coated his body.

Is the world ending already? Has it begun?

Roykur whipped around at the pounding of boots and a howl to see a blade swinging down at him. He instinctually raised his hands at the same time he forced the smoke at his attacker, but not before the sword thudded into Roykur's forearm. He cried out, pain blocking all thought, the smoke faltering and fading back. Conservator Simune met his eye through the long slits of the Sentinel helm, grinned wickedly, and wrenched the blade free, leaving the arm dangling loosely by bits of muscle and sinew.

Roykur cradled his mutilated limb with his good arm and tried to scramble on his back, his legs desperately pushing away from his attacker. He still willed the smoke to stop Simune, but each movement radiated pain, cutting into his concentration. The smoke didn't respond to his commands. Simune swung his blade quickly, and Roykur rolled to the side, but not before it scored a shallow slice along his upper back. The smoke held back the blood that should have been gushing from his arm, but it was stretched too thin, and the cut along his back began bleeding heavily.

His energy drained away fast, and nausea slowed his crawling to a weak writhing on the floor. Simune stood over him and raised his sword high, then came down hard with a killing strike. Roykur closed his eyes against the dizziness and the inevitable. The sword squelched into soft flesh, scraped against bone as it passed through, and was punctuated by a pained grunt. Roykur opened his eyes to see Legast standing over him, a sword tip peeking through his shoulder blades.

Yellow crystals quickly formed around the wound, and Legast smashed his face into Simune's helm with another sickening crunch. The Conservator reeled back, and Legast followed suit, nose horribly broken. Legast clasped the sword handle and pulled it free with a desperate gasp, like his lungs could finally suck air in once more. Roykur propped himself up slowly, trying to get to his feet, but the nausea swept over him, and he slumped back down while Legast charged the disarmed man.

Smoke drifted back into Roykur from various directions. Following the source, he could see the Royal Guard falling, the Treemolkvar squad nearly dispatched. Pure strength mattered little when so greatly outnumbered. However, there were a great deal more dead on the other side of it. Bodies in armor or fine clothes now covered the floor. Roykur was reminded of the hallucinations at the asylum. This room quickly resembled those rivers of blood he so desperately wanted to pretend had been necessary. Just like these piles of corpses were also somehow necessary.

He now had enough smoke to stop the bleeding on his back, but it did nothing for the pain or nausea. Legast rammed the sword between Simune's plates of armor just above the knee and slid it out quickly, turning to face the horde of Sentinels cutting down his guards. The king roared a battle cry and jumped against the Sentinels with reckless disregard for his safety. It seemed he possessed even that luxury now. Despite the crippling blow, Simune was still alive, clutching his ravaged leg and cursing wildly. The Conservator gritted his teeth, and his attention snapped back to Roykur.

"Uh, Legs! You didn't finish this one!" Roykur yelled in a panic, but Legast was lost in a symphony of clashing steel.

A small hand axe, one of the Treemolkvar hatchets, pinged loudly off of a shield and skidded across the floor, coming to rest in between Roykur and Simune. They both glanced from the hatchet to each other, then dove for the weapon. Roykur's two good legs got him to the hatchet first, gripping the handle just as Simune's gauntleted fingers squeezed tight around Roykur's wrist. Simune flung him down onto his side, crushing his mangled arm underneath, then began slamming his armored fist repeatedly into Roykur's ribs and head.

Roykur's face was becoming a bloody pulp. His nose and cheekbones were broken. Pain was everything, and he wavered on the edge of consciousness with every blow.

By the luck of the gods, the strap on Simune's helmet snapped, and it slipped down over his eyes. The Conservator stopped hitting Roykur to take the helmet off, and Roykur felt the grip on his wrist slacken from the distraction. Ripping his arm free, he jabbed the hatchet blade directly between the knuckles of Simune's incoming punch.

The stitching between the leather tore through like a warm knife through butter. The metal backing bowed a bit, keeping the edge of the hatchet beneath it. Simune sucked a sharp breath in anticipation, the sensation not yet reaching his brain.

Roykur braced himself against the Conservator's bad leg and heaved. The hatchet wrenched loose, a wide, dark red wedge where it had been, and Roykur collapsed to the floor once more. Simune, half sitting, clutched his splayed hand, a scream finally escaping his lips. Roykur rolled, whipping the small weapon up, then down, using his momentum to cleave into the man's yawning mouth. The hatchet cut a thin grin down one side of his cheek and cracked the jawbone.

Roykur watched the last of his smoke trailing across the room as he slowly, painfully stumbled to his knees. What little smoke had returned was keeping him from bleeding out. Roykur's entire face throbbed. One of his eyes was swelling shut. He wiped some bloody drool on the back of his hand, still holding the hatchet, while the other arm dangled uselessly. Simune gurgled and coughed, choking on blood, the one working side of his jaw spasming.

Roykur stepped over him, adjusting his one good hand on the slick grip. The hatchet chopped into Simune's face, neck, and shoulders, over and over. Roykur let out a wild shriek while he hacked; only the ding of metal against the marble floor finally snapped him out of it.

He lifted his heavy head to gaze at the remnants of the triad: the Council, Sentinels, and Initiative warily surrounding Legast who, without a scratch, was falling back, flicked with the blood of his subjects and drenched in sweat. The hall was littered with bodies. All the Royal Guard and Treemolkvar were dead, with the triad suffering heavy losses as well. Roykur's brutes had done their jobs well, besides Simune slipping through. The carnage had been kept well away from him.

A combination of spears and shields pressed forward, harrying Legast's retreat and preventing any advance. The king was breathing hard, and he cursed when a set of weighted nets was pulled to the front. They could not kill him, but they could wear him out. A Sentinel lying still by Legast's feet jerked upright, panicked, brushing off the yellow crystals where a fatal wound had been. Legast jumped and cursed loudly, giving the phalanx an opening to pull the revived Sentinel behind their lines, while others of the fallen triad began to rise, their losses quickly disappearing.

Roykur glanced down and sighed in relief. The messy pulp he had made of Simune had not formed any yellow crystals. Regardless, the line of shields and spears was forming a circle around Roykur and Legast; this was going to end badly for both of them. His eyes flicked down to his ruined arm, where the smoke pooled like liquid.

"Legs, I hate to ask, but I don't see a lot of choices. Any chance I could get some of that miracle elixir? I could really use a hand." His voice was hoarse, barely above a whisper. He winced as he tried to emphasize his nearly dismembered appendage.

"I'm a bit busy. Can you . . ." Legast panted heavily and glanced over his shoulder.

The king turned and ran, spears scoring hits on his back. Blood briefly trailed him, replaced in an instant by yellow crystals. Unconcerned with the spear stabs, he sprinted with short, powerful strides, not slowing down as he got closer. Roykur tried to brace himself as he was scooped up, or more like tackled upward. Pain lanced up his arm. Legast slid to his knees on the marble floor just beside the fire, setting Roykur down gently, the light of the moons spotlighting the two of them. The heat from the fire prickled against Roykur's skin, and he shivered, realizing just how cold he was.

The Sentinel shield wall continued to encircle them slowly, in unison, unwilling to sacrifice their defensive formation to catch up. They knew the only escape now was through them.

"I was hoping to surprise you with this later . . ." Legast grabbed the skin at his elbow and pulled. Like removing a long glove, his skin slipped off smoothly, revealing a faintly luminescent crystalline arm and hand. The odd geometric crystals shifted and clicked, constantly reorganizing their alien patterns. Legast lifted Roykur's ruined arm and placed his unsheathed yellow hand down on it with meticulous intent.

The firm grip flared brightly, and a white-hot pain seared through Roykur as bone was replaced and skin knitted. The gash on his back, and all the recent cuts, formed thin lines of yellow crystals. All his physical aches, bruises, and pain washed away. Warmth spread through his body, the chill fading, the lethargic dullness of his thoughts and movement sharpening with each deep breath.

There was a brief hesitation before the shield wall resumed its slow push. The nets locked into the fully cranked launchers. Legast bellowed out, "Kolkrabba! The Kolkrabba are coming. In greater numbers than ever before. It's not a threat, it's a fact. You need us to . . . fight."

Legast mumbled the last bit and looked down at his hand, brows furrowed. Roykur followed Legast's eyes to see his free hand wrapped tightly around the king's crystal one, holding it in place. Roykur tried to pull his hand away, unsure why he had grabbed Legast's in the first place, but he couldn't release his own grip. It was then that the hunger hit Roykur. Not a starving hunger, but the hunger of someone who knows starvation. A craving to consume even after full, the desperate need to satisfy the lack and loss of the soul. Right at that moment, the crystals were all that and more. The perfect scratch to an unreachable itch. Roykur drew upon the energy inside.

With nothing left to heal, the smoke drank in the vibrant life force with gluttonous fervor. It swelled within Roykur to the point of bursting and beyond, outpacing his slowly increasing capacity. Uncontainable, the smoke spilled unbidden from his eyes, mouth, and ears, and then through the pores in his skin. Legast stared down at him wide eyed, with a mixture of discomfort and fascination.

The bang of iron hitting marble and the net dropping over them jolted Roykur from his rapture. Legast recoiled away, his hand less vibrant than it had been. The ropes were heavy, and there was barely enough room for both of them in the net. Legast, being taller, had most of the weight pressing down on him. He bowed forward, looking exhausted and completely spent.

Roykur managed to push himself to his knees, his muscles spasming and smoke uncontrollably spilling out in waves across his body like an overfilled jug rocking from side to side.

The shield wall formed a semicircle against the large fireplace, with spears held firm, inches from the captives at the center. The light of the moons was blocked from Roykur's vision. Only a faint radiance backlit the Sentinels, while the crackling firelight cast flickering shadows across their faces. Roykur heard muffled shouts, and two burly nurses stepped through the crowd of battle-adorned figures, holding hefty jackets with built-in restraints—a familiar yet unwelcome sight. The two thugs in nurse attire made it to the front and stood fast, sheer terror plastered on their faces. Someone from behind pushed one of them, and he let out a yelp before scrambling back.

Roykur must have looked like a dark creature from bedtime stories. He snorted as he glanced down at himself, a blood-spattered child, twitching involuntary and oozing black smoke. *Perhaps I am a creature. Perhaps that's all that's left of me.*

He released the tension throughout his body, and with it the torrent of smoke held at bay. It flew from him as if pushed by a forceful wind. The smoke kept flowing, blocking all visibility around the semicircle, the panicked screams and jostling of people growing louder. Within seconds, the entire grand hall was filled with smoke, all light smothered. The noise died down until utter silence dominated the room.

The smoke floated in the stillness for a few moments longer, then was pulled back, the room filling with moonlight once more as it retreated.

Release me, Roykur commanded.

The spears' holders took a step back, raising their weapons to attention. Five Sentinels rushed to the net, and there was a heavy bang as those iron weights around the edge were lifted off and tossed aside, piercing the quiet.

Roykur stood centered in the light while the last wisps of smoke melted into his skin. He looked over at the man who had once been his best friend, sitting next to the empty net a few feet away. Legast was blinking to adjust his eyes, looking in bewildered amazement at the scene. The swirling torrent of smoke inside Roykur paled compared to his rage and heartache. No room for anything else. He inhaled short, measured breaths, taking a moment to gather himself, needing to articulate rather than let out incoherent screams.

Roykur made the members of the triad space themselves out so he could see each and every one of them, and they could clearly see him. He swept his eyes across the room, making eye contact as he addressed them. "You djavuls are all idiotic, selfish wastes of water. Forget eternity. You don't even fucking deserve the lives you have. None of you can protect the kingdom. Not from the horrors I know are coming. The council has always been the king's worst idea. The Initiative was mine. It was a mistake to think a group of terrible people would make anything better."

The room, full of council and Initiative members, Sentinels, and Nobles, stood shrouded in varying degrees of darkness, their forced stillness a contradiction to their willful violence mere minutes ago. Roykur's attention landed on Volmirk, who stared back with disdain and contempt. Roykur shook his head in disappointment. "What this city needs is a king. Unfortunately, this one is no longer fit to lead, even if he still had any desire to. I don't want it, but there is no way I am letting any of you sacks of draugker shit lead this kingdom to ruin. I guess I have no choice."

Hail to the king.

They all dropped to one knee in perfect unity. Roykur could make out some faces closer to the light. Tears were streaking down some, while others held in defiance. He was not making them kneel out of vanity; it was merely protocol for a coronation. Roykur straightened his blood-stained coat and moved around the kneeling mob toward the stairs. "People won't come together to save themselves until it's too late. So, I'll do it for them. Bring the Husk Slayer. We aren't finished yet."

Several Sentinels stood and grabbed the former king roughly, forcing Legast to his feet. He didn't struggle, complying numbly, still dazed and exhausted. Weak but excited, he said, "We did it, Roykur! We—"

"I don't want to hear another word from you," he said coldly, and a Sentinel tore a piece of cloth off a uniform and shoved it in Legast's mouth.

When Roykur reached the top, he opened the glass doors to the balcony. He saw the overturned bench, and his stomach knotted with the memory. He got behind it and pushed the heavy thing upright, then stepped up on it and peered over the railing like he had a few nights earlier. Legast was leaning on the edge next to Roykur, the Sentinels still gripping him.

A flicker caught Roykur's eye, and he turned to see Adalia and Silaine casually sitting on the bench next to him, both smiling and glowing, as beautiful as he had ever seen them. Silaine spoke in her playful, soothing voice. "We will always be with you, my love."

He blinked and saw the bench empty once again. Hours stretched by, but Roykur did not move, not trusting his voice to speak without choking up. When the moons had gone, and the sun lit the morning sky, he cleared his throat and spoke. "I used to wish desperately to have all the answers. Now, I have all the answers, but it cost everything, and I just wish . . ."

He covered his mouth, trying to hold it together. He managed to grow calmer after a while. "I love Ver'a'saile. I love its mysteries. Every day was a fresh surprise, a new experience. In order to protect the city I love, I have to lose the thing I love about it. How very poetic." He stretched a hand out to Legast. "No more mysteries."

Legast's yellow crystal limb was wrestled forcefully onto the railing. The man struggled to free himself from the Sentinels, his protests muffled against the cloth, but he no longer had the strength left. Roykur placed his hand on the crystal one, feeling that same wash of energy and hunger. He drew in as much fuel from Legast as he could. The former king slumped into unconsciousness. Leaning on the railing, Roykur swayed, eyes closed, facing the rising sun.

His skin leaped with black wisps like a fire recently extinguished. When Roykur nudged his will forward, the smoke rolled off the balcony and down the side of the mountain like an avalanche. The darkness tumbled like weighted cotton from the palace grounds and into the city proper. Roykur could feel it filling every level, sinking down into the sub-levels and floating up onto the upper ones, into every street and building. It darkened the city; the sun was unable to pierce the miasma. The smoke cleared, and millions of pinpricks bloomed and danced across Roykur's mind. He was now aware, connected to everyone.

Roykur's focus snapped to the west end of the city, the Old Town district. "I guess there's one more surprise."

There was someone else he could not push smoke into. A lone figure, a void, out of his control. An anomaly, or an essence? Either way, it could wait a few hours. Roykur was beyond exhausted. He needed rest, a long one. He would face his tormented dreams once again. When he woke, he would investigate this oddity and prepare his new subjects for the reality his nightmares had become. Another war. Except this time, he had the power to turn every person in the city into something the Kolkrabba would fear. He would be their nightmare.

About the Author

Daniel grew up in Petaluma, California before joining the United States Air Force. He obtained a degree in Cyber Security and works as a Cyber Warfare Operator. He always felt a passion for storytelling and a love of books. Fantasy and mystery genres were always his favorite and so he wrote Murder on a God's Grave, combining both his beloved genres. Daniel shares his home with his loving wife, four rescue animals: two cats and two dogs, and a sassy horse.

www.murderonagodsgrave.com

facebook.com/OtherWorldly-Publishing

twitter.com/OtherWorldlyPub

instagram.com/otherworldlyllc

www.ingramcontent.com/pod-product-compliance
Lightning Source LLC
Chambersburg PA
CBHW021232310726

48971CB00006B/1780